The Esoteric Design

Written & illustrated by

A. R. Redington

Dovian's Journal: Gold Status Publishing

BOOKS BY A. R. REDINGTON

The Esoteric Design

The Esoteric Design: Disbanding Hope

The Esoteric Design: Civilization Lost

Predator: Eyes of the Demon, The Trophy

Masters of the Ellem

The Trouble with Mystery

Whispers from Beyond: 30 Miniature Tales

DEDICATION

This book is dedicated to Dad. If you hadn't always allowed me to stay up late and watch horror and action films as a child, I probably wouldn't have developed my twisted imagination. Though you didn't often read, I know you would've liked this story.

CONTENTS

"Civilization Lost"

ACKNOWLEDGMENTS

A special thanks to Cheryl, Robb, and Karen. Your feedback and editing advice have helped tremendously. Thank you to those who pushed, motivated, and cheered me on. Thank you to my fans on the internet. You inspired me to follow my dreams and create this. Thanks to Michelle, because you're awesome. And thank you to Marcus for listening endlessly to my ideas and readings. Also, thanks for the help with my weapon designs. They would have ended up looking like squirt guns.

Thank you to Jade Macalla for allowing me to use your amazing stock for reference. You're an immense help to those in the art community.

PROLOGUE

BAM!

The loading dock door to Bio-Tech Military Corporation: Weapons Division laboratory slammed harshly against the wall. Next came the hurried scuffling of black leather boots.

"What is this?" The head scientist, a middle-aged man with hair tinged in grey, turned his attention toward the noisy intrusion.

"The program is being shut down, Dr. Camery." General Jeron Feyette—a towering, chiseled man not much older than Camery—came forth, handing a digital form to the dazed scientist. Camery roughly tugged the item from the general's gloved fingers.

"What are you talking about? What is the meaning of all this?!" Dr. Camery shouted.

"Orders directly from the CEO. We are to terminate the project and all specimens immediately," Feyette said in a baritone voice.

"But, but what about the funding and all the donations given to the project? How is this possible?!" The scientist gasped, his heart pounding fiercely.

"All the donors have requested that we take a different approach to our research and defensive technology. What you are doing has been deemed unethical and dangerous. As much as Mr. Walten appreciates your hard work, he has decided to make some changes to your facility." Feyette signaled for his men to move. In a mad flurry, the soldiers scattered to all edges of the lab, shutting down the oxygen apparatuses supporting the countless specimens before removing them. "You will continue your work as scheduled for a more ethical solution to our problem." The militant's face held a condescending and toothy grin.

"What are you doing? Leave them alone! You can't move the bodies at these stages!" The general held back Dr. Camery. The haggard scientist could do nothing but watch the termination of his specimens.

"Sir, either you stand back, or we must detain you."

"But…what are you doing with them?!"

"Orders are to remove the clones from the facility and destroy them," General Feyette simply explained.

"Destroy?! This is my life's work! You can't! You just can't! These are living things!" Dr. Camery watched in horror as the unconscious clones were tugged from their placental containers, fluids spilling onto the tiled floor. Some bodies weren't fully developed, while others looked like ordinary sleeping humans. A shudder vibrated down the scientist's spine as a few pale-skinned specimens dropped onto the ground—their bodies twitching—and he nearly fainted.

"Exactly. That's the same conclusion the funding corporations have come to. It is unethical to create clones to fight in our wars. You produce them only to be destroyed." Feyette spoke to the doctor as if he were a child, ignoring the harsh glare sent his way.

"Much like you are doing now!" The two stared at each other, filtering their own hypocritical words.

Dr. Camery lowered his head, unsure of which action to take next. However, his thoughts halted as men wearing incombustible suits filed into the laboratory. Each member held a fire-spewing weapon, ironically the same design created by Dr. Camery himself.

"You're going to burn the clones? You can't do that!" The scientist rushed forward and was shoved again.

"Dr. Camery! These are our orders! Now, help us safely remove the specimens, or we can do this the hard way."

Dr. Camery thought long and hard before replying, "Just let me gather my personal things…."

"You have ten minutes." General Feyette narrowed his eyes, his voice dropping an octave.

The scientist quickly spun on his heels and nervously slipped into his private office, separate from the lab. He fussed with the heavy deadbolt on the door until the lock slid into place with a loud *thunk*. Rushing to the records case, he felt he couldn't move fast enough. To the side of the wooden casing was a plain device that appeared to be a thermostat. Camery flipped the cover and diligently entered a series of codes. After a second, the case slipped from the wall, revealing a cylindrical tank containing a beautiful little girl with dirty-blonde hair and skin pale as porcelain. Her face expressed a small, sweet smile. Anyone would think she was asleep if it weren't for her mangled lower half.

"You are my pride and joy. They've taken everything away from me, but they won't take you." Dr. Camery smiled with a tear in his eye. His hand ran over the thick glass, his eyes gazing upon the child's closed ones. He frantically pressed against a blinking red switch on the side panel of the giant tube. The container hummed, vibrating quietly against the exterior partition, and slid back into the wall before dropping down a chute.

Waiting on the lower floor of the Weapons Division lab was an automated armored truck that the specimen tank would drop in. The vehicle would conceal the top-secret possession and transport it to the doctor's private lab inside his 'vacation home'—that is, if nobody had discovered the truck yet.

Camery turned his tired gaze through the two-way mirror above his desk. The soldiers were having a heyday destroying his lab and creations as they confiscated his terminal's crystal drive and demolished the backup files. Thankfully, he noticed the soldiers burned only the hardcopy documents and underdeveloped clones. A loading van sat outside the facility where the clones were collected. They would most likely be disposed of at the garbage facility. The doctor gave a harsh sigh and turned away toward his office window.

"They'll never find you there," he whispered, watching the automated truck fade away into the distance.

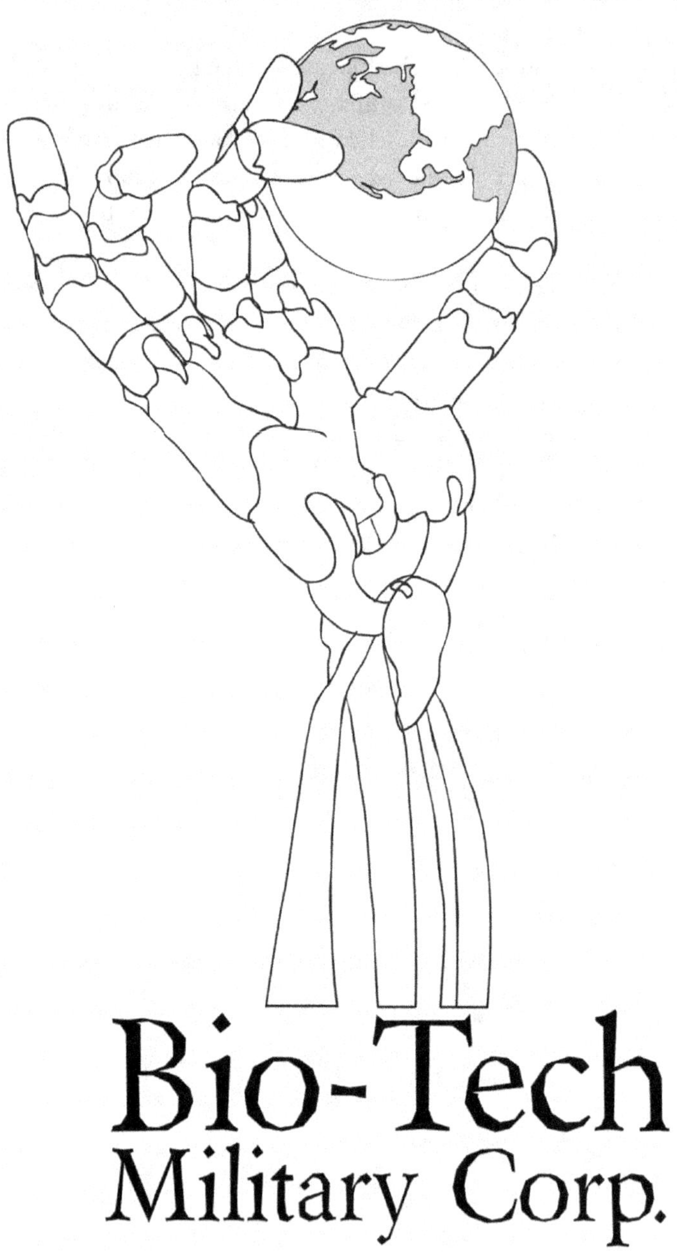

Bio-Tech
Military Corp.

CHAPTER 1

"OW! You freakin' did that on purpose!" Troy howled as he grabbed high on his inner thigh. He looked down at the small blotch of paint splashed over his pants. Too close for comfort. "Damn it, Aria."

"You're such a baby," Aria mumbled, rolling her eyes.

She turned her head around the corner of the metal barricade she hid behind and glimpsed Troy as he gawked down and watched the paint smear into the camouflage pattern of his uniform. "Dang, I missed," Aria sarcastically called out.

"You're lucky you missed!" Troy stood and raised his weapon, firing a blast directly at the woman's head. Aria quickly ducked, the paint spraying over the edge of the barrier. There was a moment of silence. Troy held his breath, his grin widening the longer the stillness continued.

"TROY!" the woman growled in anger. "You got it in my HAIR!"

Troy shared a small laugh. "Matches the blue streak!" He spun in a half-turn, hiding behind his wall, and listened intently to the shuffle of Aria's boots nearing his position. The man closed his eyes, waiting patiently. He continued his pause, counting the seconds, suddenly growing impatient.

Where is she?' A frown covered his features. Troy's eyes, olive in color, popped open; he tried to feel the area with his senses. *'Behind me.'* He gripped his gun, turned the corner, and fired one shot into thin air, the blast echoing in the silence of the warehouse.

"Wha—?" He felt his neck hairs stand on end.

Aria was sneaky due to her small, tight frame. She reminded Troy of a cat with black fur and bright green eyes—the type that was superstitiously the cause of bad luck.

The man crouched, moving his gun out to the side. He looked forward as he shifted his mock-up EM-M4 antique to the left and the right, checking his surroundings. A blue holographic screen projected the gun's camera images over his right eye. The camera allowed him a 360-degree view of his surroundings. He could simultaneously look forward and receive a peripheral view. Still, Aria was nowhere to be found. The man grunted.

Plop, plop, plop. The sound emitted from above him as paintballs slammed into his back. Troy spun, twisting and shooting into the air as Aria fell toward him fast. She had hidden atop the barrier he was using for cover.

'Just like a cat.' Troy guarded as the woman crashed against him. She slammed him mercilessly onto the ground, his helmet smacking the concrete. Without hesitation, the slinky woman jumped to her feet, lifted her rifle, continued to shoot the man in the torso four more times, and then raised the barrel ever so slightly to plant one paint splatter onto the front center of his helmet.

"Okay…I'm dead," Troy grumbled. He glared at the woman standing over him. In return, she smiled brightly, a pure expression of innocence covering her features. "I'm glad you smile only when you get to kill me." His words were sour.

"Oh, whatever, Troy." Carelessly, she stepped over the man and strolled toward the training center entrance. "I'm just trying to help you." Her voice rose in pitch as she waved an arm at him.

"By always kicking my ass? That doesn't help." He rolled to his feet, groaning as he did so.

"Well, it's not my fault you can't adapt to your surroundings and grow as a soldier." She looked over her shoulder and raised an eyebrow.

"You cheat," he said in protest, running a hand over his chest. The paint smeared beneath calloused fingertips.

"Using the facility's surroundings is not cheating. It's there for you to use. You can't just shoot and hide all the time. You have to strategize." The woman laid her gun on the table and handed her spare magazines to the clerk.

"I weigh at least twice as much as you do. I can't just silently scale a wall." The man's tone dripped with annoyance. Troy towered over Aria—the woman only standing up to his shoulder—and his build was nearly all muscle. Whereas he could handle most enemies with just his strength, Aria could easily beat Troy when it came to wits. When paired together, the two made the perfect team.

"I see you got shot this time." The clerk smiled at Aria.

The woman rolled her eyes upward and pointed at her head. The clerk nodded. "It's just splatter from the barricade. Troy still *missed*," Aria informed and quickly headed for the exit.

Troy raised his weapon and shot once, the pellet slamming against Aria's black leather-covered rear end. The woman gave a quick jump, followed by a yelp. She grabbed her right cheek, turned on her heel, and fed him a nasty glare.

"Looks like you'll have to take those to the dry cleaning." He shrugged. Aria opened her mouth and began to string together the most colorful slur of insults but was interrupted by a pink-haired, tan young woman sauntering quickly toward her partner. The young woman's small entourage of friends lingered behind, chatting and giggling.

"Nice helmet, Troy," she spoke to the man, patting him on the shoulder while giving a high-pitched giggle. Aria's nostrils wrinkled at the sound. It was disgusting.

"Well, when you're up against Satan herself, I suggest wearing a helmet." Troy smirked, pointing at the brown meshed bowl on his head.

"Oh…." The girl turned, her gaze following the man's hand to meet the glaring green eyes of Aria.

"She's rough," he growled.

"He's a baby," Aria added.

"You slammed my head into the floor! You'd crack my skull open!"

"It'd just match all the red paint." Aria shrugged, pointing out once again how badly the man had lost.

"I don't get why you two use those paintballs anyway. Don't they hurt?" the younger woman asked. Aria glared at the artificially-colored recruit.

"Well…" Troy began.

"No. Not compared to a real bullet," Aria butted in.

"Then why not just use the lasers? They don't hurt. Besides, the bracelet counts how many times you were hit and where you were hit." She raised her wrist to show Aria as if she hadn't seen one before. "Plus, it doesn't ruin your clothes."

The younger woman's statement brought Aria's attention to her attire. She wore tight pants with decorative pockets and a low-hanging top, and her friends wore a similar fashion.

"Because this doesn't train you for getting hit with a real bullet!" Aria shouted.

Troy could sense Aria's irritation rising. "She's right." He slid between the two women. "Getting shot by a paintball at least hurts enough to train the body for pain and quick reactions. It also teaches you to be aware of your position on the field compared to your enemy. A laser gun doesn't do any of that. You can get hit fifteen times and never even notice. Get hit once by a real bullet, and that can be your last. Lasers don't train you for real war; they train you for games."

"Speaking of games, when did this place start selling tickets to kids on the street?" Aria folded her arms, nudging her head toward the girl's companions. "This isn't laser tag."

"Oh, come on! It's just a game; it's not like we're actually shooting each other, like you said," the other woman protested.

"You're in a military facility! Get your friends out of here!" Aria ordered. "If you want to play games, go to the mall."

"Troy?!" The girl looked at him with her large, artificially teal eyes. She placed her manicured hand on the man's arm.

'Uh, oh….' Troy froze. He didn't need to turn around to see the glare Aria gave him. In fact, he could feel her eyes burning a hole in the back of his head.

Running a hand through his trimmed facial hair, he muttered, "Listen, uh…" he thought a second, "Amber. This is a training facility for military personnel. It is illegal to have your friends here. Why don't you guys go outside and play?" He nervously rubbed the back of his neck.

"But—"

"Now! Or I'll have you discharged immediately," Aria snarled.

They all stood still for a moment. Troy shuffled his feet awkwardly, and finally, the bubblegum-blonde turned after giving Troy a fierce look and left to get her group of friends.

"GOD!" Aria threw her arms into the air. "This is getting ridiculous." She hurriedly strolled down the hall.

"Mmm-hm." Troy nodded, struggling to keep up with the woman.

"I can't believe she would come waltzing in here with her friends! How'd she get them in here in the first place?!" Aria grumbled about the facility's security and continued about how the new virtual training taught the soldiers nothing. "Pain creates a real sensation, whereas laser guns are only as beneficial as a videogame for training." She went on about the weapons division, the President, and if he even knew what went on in the corporation, and then finally got to the subject of the color of the girl's hair and her fake skin tone. Throughout the rant, Troy nodded and offered a few grunts in acknowledgment. "And you're not even listening to me!" She stopped and spun about-face. He would have crashed into her if it weren't for her hand pushing against his chest. "I can't believe you slept with a bimbo like that."

"W-what?" Troy stuttered; his eyes enlarged with an expression of innocence.

"That ditz in there who thinks she's working for a theme park."

"I…uh…I didn't sleep with her." He nervously laughed.

"Troy, you sleep with every woman that talks to you."

"Not every woman! Only the hot ones. I haven't slept with you yet." He shrugged.

"Oh, my God," Aria groaned, tightly closing her eyes in irritation.

"Hey! I have an idea!" He grabbed the woman's shoulders. Aria limply moved with his swaying arms. She heaved a loud sigh. "Chester's?" He persuaded her.

She gave a small smile. If there was anything Aria liked, it was Chester's Bar and Grille down the street. They served her favorite drink and had the best chips and dip in the City of Fountains.

"I lost, so I'll buy." Troy fed her a boyish grin.

She snorted a laugh. "Yeah…I kicked your ass bad."

"Okay. Stop rubbing it in, or I'm not buying your drink." He roughed up her black hair, smearing the paint a little into her blue-dyed streak.

"Are you going to wear that?" The woman eyeballed his military uniform, ignoring what he'd done to her hair.

Troy shrugged. "Thought it'd catch the ladies' attention."

"At least get rid of the helmet…you look like an idiot." Aria smirked. The two continued down the bright white hall.

"Okay…Mom." He received a punch in the arm. "Ow."

Music droned in a low tone in the background of the bar. Aria's dainty fingers lifted a glass to her lips; the glowing blue concoction shimmered a similar hue against her face. Troy eyed her, watching the bouncing light dance across her smooth features and dark hair. He had always told her it was like drinking radiation, but it was her favorite drink. Neither wanted to know how or why the beverage looked like a child's glow stick.

"Cancer…." Troy pointed at Aria's glass. She glared at him, taking another sip.

"Likewise," she replied, flicking her finger against the tip of the man's cigarette. She thought it was disgusting, but, at the very least, he did smoke the real stuff. It contained no toxins, narcotics, or hallucinogens the other types had. Aria held her drink up next to the man's burning ash. "You think they are both made of the same stuff?"

Troy glanced down. Sure enough, the blue glow of her alcoholic beverage matched the blue embers of his cigarette. "Well, I assume that's the secondhand smoke eliminator." He grinned with the stick between his teeth. "What's yours for?"

"Just a pretty light to play with her pretty eyes," a male voice interrupted the couple's conversation. Aria felt an arm snake around her waist as lips pressed against her cheek. She rolled her eyes as the man dropped into the chair beside her. No matter how hard she tried, Aria couldn't hide the smile that crossed her face. "Or to match the pretty blue streak in her hair." He swiped a finger through her electric-blue tresses.

"Hi, Gavin." Aria swirled the liquid in her glass. He gave her a colossal grin, showing off his perfect pearly whites.

"Where the hell have you been? I haven't seen you in ages!" Troy handed his friend a cigarette.

"Ah, you know, been busy with the ladies. Was double-booked for a week!" The man chuckled, reaching across Aria to grab Troy's gift. The woman closed her eyes in annoyance. "But you know what? None of them were as cute as this gal here!" Gavin placed his arm around Aria's shoulder and shook her gently.

"And I'm so special that I'm never included on your schedule?" She raised an eyebrow.

"Oh, well, I—" Gavin stammered. He grimaced, running a hand through his shoulder-length brunette hair. The ends touched the leather collar of his pilot's jacket.

"It's okay, Gavin; I'm not your type." Aria lifted a finger, ordering another drink. She suddenly felt a bit sour.

"Uh-oh. Now you've done it; she's ordering another one." Troy snickered, winking at his friend.

Gavin grabbed Aria's waist again. He slowly moved his lips to her ear. "Aria, baby! My beauty! My—" her face twisted into a nasty scowl, "sassy cat." He yowled like an angry feline and quickly pecked her cheek to appease her.

"You two are the same," Aria murmured. She reached for a chip and dipped it in the creamy cheese sauce, suddenly wanting to be far away. The two men laughed to themselves. Aria only frowned, not finding it funny to be surrounded by lewd boys.

Gavin and Troy weren't only similar people but were best friends, much to Aria's dissatisfaction at times. The two men had first met years before in Special Ops training. They both were chasing after the same girl. At first, the macho men debated on fighting each other but then found that it was much easier to work together to get one girl and her friends together for a night of fun. Troy would say the two were cursed with excellent charm and good looks. Sadly, Aria had often been subject to the two's flirtations, especially Gavin's.

Being a pilot, Gavin was hardly around. He swooned over ladies across the continent, and the women fell for him, too. There's nothing like a man in uniform who can maneuver the fastest military fighter jet. Gavin was one of the elites, one of the top five pilots in the world who could fly one of the machines. The military said he was gifted with quick reactions, adaptive tactical skills, and a high IQ. Aria often debated the latter. She remembered reading a scientific study concluding that a man's IQ temporarily dropped when a gorgeous woman was in the room. She didn't doubt that at all. She also thought that since Gavin considered every woman a sex object, he was a complete idiot.

"Oi! What are yuh doin'?!" someone in the bar shouted, tearing Aria from her thoughts. The man's accent was so thick with its trilled 'r's and clipped word-endings, one could choke on it.

"I've had enough hearing you talk!" another man cried.

"Oh, great." Troy leaned back on his barstool.

Two men started to argue. Judging by his deep inflection, the man with the accent was a Scotty. Aria turned around once the punches started to fly, and people began hollering. The clash spread fast, as they typically did. It was complete ignorance, she thought.

"The guy should have just kept his mouth shut," Gavin murmured, shaking his head. "You can't be running your mouth with an accent like that 'round these parts."

"I'm wondering how he ended up in these parts to begin with," Troy added.

"There was a surveillance intelligence trade between MacMurray & Scott and our largest trader, Agricon. Perhaps he's one of the spokespeople," Aria suggested, grimacing as the foreign man blocked a punch and retaliated with a hard blow to the other man's jaw.

"An' I'm tired of lookin' at yer dark-skinned scadge of a lass!" the Scotty yelled, running a pale hand through his redder-than-considered "normal" hair. Everything about the foreign man was deemed reason enough to be killed for.

"Scadge! What the hell is a scadge?" Troy asked, sharing a quiet laugh with Gavin.

"Nobody can even understand what you're saying!" The local man held his chin, his girlfriend patting him on the back. "The damn freaks in the Underbelly wouldn't even want you!"

The Underbelly, a separate city beneath Fountains, was dirty, poor, and full of the strange and outdated in society. Anything that didn't meet the middle ground of the majority in civilization was often frowned upon. If the designer genes used during pregnancy didn't do the trick, a person was killed for their differences or moved to the lower city to take their chances at survival there.

"My skin isn't even all that dark! It's called Mocha Divine! I paid a lot of money for this color!" the dense woman rambled, waving a finger back and forth.

The Scotty looked repulsed. "Only a used up, numpty wench would pride 'erself in coverin' up 'er scabby, coital stains."

Troy gasped, enjoying the Scotty's language. "So much awesome wrapped up in that one sentence!"

"Are you taking notes?" Aria questioned, watching the fighting men with keen interest.

"That does it!" The local man growled, lunging forward to tackle the foreigner into a table, the girlfriend cheering for her significant other.

After a couple of mugs shattered against the floor, the bartender riled up, bellowing noisily for the men to stop.

"Should we do something?" Gavin finally asked once the Scotty broke the other man's nose.

"No." Aria shook her head. "Let the Lowers take care of it."

Lowers were the average cops, the lowest on the military totem pole. Lowers always got a hard-on for taking care of the petty jobs.

A couple of chairs turned over, a table smashed into pieces, and more blood spilled before a knife was pulled and thrown. It flew past Aria's head and landed only a few centimeters from the bartender.

"That's it!" Aria and Troy both grabbed their handguns at their waists. However, before they could do anything, sirens blared, and the front door violently wrenched open and snapped from the side of the wall. A dozen officers swarmed into the dark bar.

"Everybody on the floor!" A rookie cop drew his weapon. Everyone in the bar quickly dropped to the ground, save the three militants. Aria rolled her eyes. "I said on the floor!" The officer pointed his gun at the three by the bar. Gavin swiftly raised his hands. Aria frowned as she gripped her weapon.

"Easy, Nancy." Troy showed the man his badge. "Class A-4."

"And what would you have done if I shot you?" The cop slowly lowered his weapon.

"Shot you before your brainstem could fire its first synapses," Aria spat spitefully.

The police officer gave her a loathing look. "If you're so high and mighty, why didn't you break up this fight?"

"Figured you might need some help getting it up," she snarled.

"Just shut up and do your job." Troy pointed at the officer. "We were just about to break it up before you broke down the door. It's just a bar fight, not a murder."

Aria glanced at Troy. She wasn't so sure about that. The victim had an accent. With the world's hate, having an accent was worthy of being killed if you were in the wrong place at the wrong time.

"Had a guy murdered yesterday for having blue eyes," the officer said. Along with two others, he began cuffing those involved in the brawl while a few men questioned the bartender and patrons.

"Happens all the time," Troy stated with a shrug.

As the rookie led the aggressors into the streets, he added, "His eyes were brown. He was wearing blue optical enhancers."

"Damn," Gavin scoffed. "You'd think people would be tired of fighting with all the war."

"Hardly," Aria said, frowning. "These idiots can't stand people who are naturally different. Growing up in war, sometimes it's all people know how to do. It's like a part of nature now. Find a reason to hate and kill." The idea of it all depressed her.

Outside of the simple civilian lifestyle were people like Aria and Troy. They lost their parents at an early age and became the property of the military. Corporations like Bio-Tech received orphans as gifts and raised them as soldiers. The children grew up within the organization—military establishments owned by business CEOs who were the political leaders for the city-states. Corporations often fought with one another, not just over products and enterprise, but for land and ownership of small countries. Soon, the battles were no longer about political ideals but about buying and trading businesses and claiming each other's scientists and manufacturers. The elitists exchanged lives for goods, technology, and profiteering through consumerism. It was always about money, but Aria didn't care. She was okay as long as she had a home and something to do with her life. If it weren't for the military, she wouldn't be alive. But then again, if it weren't for the same entity, her parents would still be around.

Growing up surrounded by war and constant training had taught Aria and Troy how to watch their backs, and typically, they were never bothered, thanks to the high-class emblems on their weapons and jackets. If not for his military status, Troy could have been killed as a young adult for being so tall, even though he was 'normal' in every other way with his tan skin and brown hair. Long ago, Aria could have been left for dead in the streets because of her raven-black hair when someone had stabbed her. Troy lectured her for days, and that was when she decided to add a neon-blue streak to her hair to have an excuse to claim the color wasn't natural. It did help, but she still was given some crap now and then.

"Hey, you guys watching this?" The bartender's voice broke through the chaotic murmurs.

The small group turned their attention to the vidscreen above the bar. It flashed a 'breaking news' headline across the display. Static streaked the screen before revealing a reporter outside a destroyed military base.

"Turn it up," Aria ordered.

"This just in. We have reporter John Monroe. John? Can you hear me?" a female voice asked off-screen.

"Uh…Uh, yes. Yes, I can hear you…." The man on the screen looked ragged and trembled with fear. Grey dust and what appeared to be blood covered his clothing. "The 66th Intel Reconnaissance Base was attacked only twenty minutes ago. I…I was here earlier to report on the latest Missile Tracking and Defense System when we, uh, we were attacked. I, uh…oh, God!" Static rolled over the screen. "Not—uch time. They—"

"John?" the news anchor questioned.

"Oh, my God!" John screamed through the static. There was no visual.

The camera flashed back into the main studio of the newsroom, showing a wide-eyed female anchor. "We seem to be having technical difficulties. We're switching to audio-only."

"So fast. They were so fast. Susan!" John's voice called out.

"Yes, John?" The woman's voice broke. "Are you there?"

"AHHHH!" The man's shrill screams sounded distorted through the television. "They'll kill us all!" There came a dull vibrating noise followed by a low hum. All audio abruptly went to white noise.

"What's going on?!" Susan shouted before the whole station went blank. Aria lifted her head, looking from side to side as the lights flickered inside the bar.

"Freaky…." Gavin gaped at the screen, his cigarette barely clinging to his lower lip.

"Troy." Aria instinctively grabbed her weapon.

"EMP disturbance," he suggested.

All at once, all three of their DNAIS alarms went off.

"Time to go!" Aria swiped her wrist across the bar register's checkout screen. The laser light read the DNA Identification System—DNAIS—chip embedded into her skin, retrieving the proper credits for the bill before she headed for the exit. "Bring your sunscreen; it looks like we're headed for the desert!"

Troy and Gavin put out their cigarettes, swiped their wrists, and quickly followed behind the woman.

Heavy footsteps trailed through thick mud.

'*Where is she?*' he thought.

He looked at his surroundings, feeling detached from his body as if watching from the outside.

'*Don't look. Don't look.*'

He couldn't help it, seeing the bodies all around. He had to find her. She was somewhere in the pile of thousands. His eyes stung with tears, which he struggled to hold back. The freezing rain slowed him down, adding weight to his clothing and thickening his steps. Liquid crimson and armor surrounded him. Bodies covered the earth, some looking up at him with blank expressions. The smell of grime and rusty metal burned his nostrils. He tore his gaze away from one particular body, a child's. He had wanted to forget those precious eyes.

'You did this. It's your fault,' he accused.

Then he saw her and shivered as the chill air wrapped around his form. The gusting wind pulled him towards her gracefully resting dead body atop a small hill of soldiers. He dropped to his knees and grabbed her, hugging her tightly. He gaped into the woman's dead white eyes. Then, a smile crossed her face.

"It's the day you've been waiting for," her voice whispered in his mind. It haunted him.

There was an explosion. Bright blue light flooded high into the air and mushroomed out, covering the continent and swallowing him and the rest of the dead population whole. It ate everything—soaring, burning, annihilating, spreading over oceans, consuming all the lands, covering the planet, tugging the entire world into a bright light before disintegrating all of its existence into a cloud of dust that would forever soar through the vast, dark abyss of the universe. He screamed.

Flying up from his makeshift bed, the man choked on a gasp. He was soaked. A hole in the ceiling had ever so graciously poured rain all over his body while he was asleep. Thankful to have awoken despite the reason, he stared at the small puddle on the floor, his reflection glaring back with narrowed, glowing eyes.

"Is it that time already?" he whispered, holding a hand to his head. And then he sobbed, his shoulders shaking. "Will they be ready?" The quiet moans turned into a small laugh, mixing with the thunder far off in the distance.

"Troy's Portrait"

CHAPTER 2

"The attack occurred at approximately 1800 our time, 0330 their time. You need to deploy immediately. Gavin will take you by the Hawk 90. It'll be a three-hour flight, but it's the best we can do. We're not expecting many survivors, if any at all." The President, James Clarke, clicked on his digital keyboard. Aria noticed the military ring on his finger, a metallic eagle sitting upon an amber jewel. A patch hung over the right shoulder of his pristine charcoal-grey suit. Military pins decorated the black piece, presenting his elite status and accomplishments while on duty as a younger man.

A screen above the President's head flickered on, revealing an inverted image to Aria, Troy, and Gavin.

"Intel mission?" Aria suggested.

"Precisely." He flipped the screen around, the image twisting for the others to see. The display flashed, showing an inside view of an encampment. "This is a security camera for the facility. We've called all city-states; no one will fess up to it. Our country's military is online, and no one was near the site. But then again, that hasn't stopped our enemies before."

According to the camera, everything seemed to be running smoothly. The employees sat at their desks, working diligently. Aria stared at the man nearest the camera, an Average Joe just earning a paycheck. He sipped slowly from his coffee before rubbing his eyes and sighing long and low. People like this weren't usually top-notch battle-efficient. Intel processing was often the primary function of these bases, the brains behind operations. They had the largest supercomputer man had ever known—the highest encryption. Not a single person was ever known to crack the code. If someone needed something kept from any eyes, it was held there. A mini military equipped with top-grade weaponry guarded the facility. Fortified walls wrapped the building like a cocoon. The core crystal drive was hidden deep underground within a labyrinth of structures, shelling one over another with a barricade of weapons outside. The place was an armory inside an armory, all covered in chainmail and utterly top-secret, hidden from even the most advanced satellites. Those inside may not have been battle-ready, but the site was protected.

"Any flight patterns or disturbances?" Aria narrowed her eyes and watched a tremor that shook the entire structure.

"None whatsoever. We're looking into gathering seismology of the area." The President cleared his throat and pointed at the screen. Everything quaked. Poor Average Joe spilled his coffee on himself. His coworkers jumped with surprise, their heads turning side to side. A flash of light erupted, and everything cut out, static covering the feed.

"Seismology? Like an earthquake?" Troy questioned.

"We've got to look at everything. If nothing came in from the sky, then perhaps from underground. Also, there was a blast. We can determine what kind of weapon was used—nuclear, missile, mortar. Whatever it was, it was strong enough to break through every barrier around the facility and hit the core."

"Is this the only footage we have?" Aria folded her arms, putting her weight on one hip.

"There's another, right before everything went out, on the outside. This is what I really wanted to show you." Mr. Clarke opened a new file.

"So, we caught the ones who did it." Troy smirked. "Bet it was Russite."

"You always think it's Russite." Aria rolled her eyes.

"Well, they are always trying to screw things up, being our largest competitor," Gavin suggested.

The President cleared his throat, gathering the attention of the three.

"This is Sergeant…ly." The screen flickered while static momentarily interrupted a soldier's voice. "Attack began right at 0330. It started with a massive black hole on the horizon. We initially thought it was a platoon silhouette, but the landscape seemed to fizzle in and out." The sergeant caught his breath. Frantic screams, shouts, and gunshots echoed off-screen. The man held his earpiece tightly against his head. "I've never seen anything like it." He flipped his vidscreen toward the camera, giving the crowd a glimpse of what he saw.

"This is from a security camera near building 'D.' The disturbance occurred approximately 1,500 meters from the base." His computer screen revealed a quiet desert landscape. After a couple of seconds, a massive shadow broke on the horizon. The darkness grew taller and disappeared as quickly as it appeared. Immediately, the landscape began to distort and twist, streaking like static. Aria stepped closer to the President's desk.

"Was his feed just getting interrupted?" Troy asked.

"No." Aria pointed to the corner of the screen. "That's the edge of the fence. See how it's not getting disturbed?" Her finger trailed in a circle toward the center of the scene. "It's like a vortex, spiraling inward."

The security camera's image became fuzzier by the second.

"It's like an EMP disturbance." Troy gawked. "But…to the physical realm."

Suddenly, the picture blacked out, and the sergeant came back into view. "I don't know what to make of it. You should have seen it with your own eyes. It was just… unbelievable." The man's voice trembled. His words were quick and barely distinguishable. "Within seconds, our entire camp was ambushed! It was like a tidal wave! The static just came closer and closer at an impossible speed!"

Aria noticed the timer on the screen. Only five minutes would have passed if the attack had occurred at 0330. The video feed had distorted. Gunshots grew louder, as did the screams, but not all of the cries were human.

"What is that?" Gavin asked, wincing at the high-pitched shriek.

"You hear that?" the sergeant asked. "That's them," he whimpered. "I…uh, it appears that they are not from this world." The man shuddered as a horrific wail came from behind him, and a body flew through the background. The video began twitching and dragging snowy lines down in quick vibrations. A low hum sounded. The sergeant looked over his shoulder to where the battle took place. He jerked his head back to the recording device and cried, "Aliens!"

A blur leaped from the right-hand side onto the man, snow blocking a clear view of whatever it was. Monstrous shrieks and screeches distorted the sound through the speakers. The screen flickered wildly as the hum grew in volume; a flash ignited the monitor, followed by a low *Vooom*, and everything turned to static. Silence engulfed the room as the group stared at the flickering video, leaving an eerie calm.

"That's when we lost the feed," the President said. "The flash occurred at the same time as the other video I showed you."

"Looked and sounded like an EMP grenade. You think someone let one off?" Troy calibrated the watch on his DNAIS, setting different time zones.

"There is no EMP weaponry of any kind allowed in that camp. It would screw up every electronic device within the entire facility." Mr. Clarke leaned back in his chair, cupping his hands. "The enemy would have had to obtain our EMP technology to wipe out the systems like that."

"Did you happen to see the disturbance here?" Aria quickly asked.

"Aria, the blast occurred halfway around the world." The man leaned forward, raising his grey eyebrows to stare at her with chocolate-brown eyes. His peppered hairline twitched with his forehead.

"James, the lights flickered in the bar when we were watching the live video feed." Aria set her hands on the man's desk. Only she could get away with calling the President of Bio-Tech Military Corporation by his first name.

"She's right." Troy and Gavin bobbed their heads in unison.

"Well, then something had better show up on those Seismographs! Wait, you were at the bar at this time of day?" Mr. Clarke gave them a bewildered look.

"Helps us get through the day," Troy quickly added.

A man in a lab jacket rushed through the door. "Mr. Clarke!" he shouted.

"We are in a private meeting!" the President erupted.

"Important!" The scientist ignored the President's threatening stare and clumsily rushed to the large oak desk with a data-log in hand as his lab coat flailed behind him. He was from the communications division. "We have a satellite out."

"What?!" The leader nearly choked.

"We tried to get a view from space of the attacked encampment and…nothing." The man fought to catch his breath.

'Why is everyone freaking out?' Aria wondered.

"What do you mean, 'nothing'?" Mr. Clarke asked; his voice held a tone of annoyance.

"Nothing." The scientist shrugged. He scratched his scalp ponderously as he looked over the data-log. "It was as if everything just stopped working. The closest thing we can think of is electromagnetic pulse disturbance." The President glanced at Aria, who merely gave him an eyebrow raise.

"Okay, okay." Mr. Clarke's hands waved in the air. "Enough talk. Troy, Aria," the two militants mentioned stood at attention, "you are to infiltrate the 66th I.R.B.; gather as much evidence as possible. Grab the core crystal drive, and get the survivors out of there, if there are any. And if you catch one of these 'aliens,' kill it first and bring it here for examination. Gavin, you're their pilot; you know what to do."

"Yes, sir!" They all saluted with a click of their heels and excused themselves from the President's office.

"Oh, I have a terrible feeling about this," James sighed.

"Would you like me to get you a drink, sir?" the scientist asked.

"Got anything stronger than coffee?" the leader groaned.

"Of course we do! How do you think we get through our days?" The scientist smiled. He received a stern look from the President. "Uh, well…just kidding?"

"Just get it. I don't want to know the details of how my corporation actually runs." He placed his face in his hands as the scientist rushed out the door.

"If the employees require as much alcohol as I do to get through the day, then I believe Bio-Tech is in serious trouble," Mr. Clarke muttered as he reached inside his desk for a bottle of aspirin.

A pair of curious eyes locked onto Aria as she slept in her chair; her breaths slowly passed between her parted lips. She mumbled something and then giggled. Troy's eyes lit up as he watched the woman with interest. He had only heard her laugh like that in her sleep. It made him wonder what world her dreams took her to. The aircraft abruptly shook, bouncing Aria in her chair and jolting her from her slumber. The soft brow on her forehead furrowed as she groaned quietly.

"Gavin, your flying is going to make me sick," she moaned loudly.

Gavin looked over his shoulder at the woman. *"Did you get enough beauty sleep?"* he called through his mental chip. The sudden burst of noise was earsplitting after being in near silence for the past three hours. Aria turned in her seat and fed the pilot a fierce look. Waving a hand at her, he continued, *"Uh, guess not. Go back to sleep!"*

"Gavin," Aria sighed. She rubbed her eyes and looked over at her partner, Troy. He sat across from her in the small aircraft, finishing up cleaning his EM-M4 automatic rifle. He looked up at her, green eyes shining with anticipation for the upcoming mission. "Antique edition?" she asked.

"They have the best design." He nodded. Troy enjoyed his weapons having a classic look. Sure, the rifle appeared thousands of years old, but the gun had a more sophisticated usage than the newer models. He always replied that the gun kept him sharp when given weird stares or snide remarks. He was on his best game as long as he had something to do with his hands and eyes. Besides, it made him feel human, unlike the automated weaponry systems used by the other militants. Aria agreed with him. She eyeballed her EM-36C battle rifle. It had a handgrip with a Thermal Red Dot, an Incendiary Grenade Launcher with double-trigger action, and a grenade mag. She called it her classic on steroids.

"Which grenade mag are you using?" She stretched in her seat, her spine cracking as she stuck out her armored chest.

"Sabo." Troy smirked.

"Oh, you love to tear 'em up." She smiled. Troy grinned back at her, thinking the catnap put her in a lovely mood.

"Taking down speed," the pilot mentally called out.

The jet slowed drastically. The Gs pressed Aria into her seat as Troy leaned forward.

"Uhhh, hate this thing!" Aria groaned.

Flipping a few switches, Gavin alerted the other two. *"Going into 'copter mode, guys."*

The aircraft jerked, and the two passengers lifted slightly from their seats. The wings pulled upward, detached from the fuselage, and snapped and folded, reforming into four pieces connected to a rotary joint on the top of the craft. The new blades instantly spun, the Hawk stealthily approaching their destination.

Gavin further slowed the copter. It hovered just outside the 66th I.R.B. The low drone of the blades was almost silent upon their ears. Brilliant light blasted into the cabin from the new openings, along with a gusting wind, as the doors slid up. Troy stood, tightening his chest and joint armor straps, and glanced at Aria. She leaned out the side of the cabin, her hand tightly gripping the bar above the doorway. The orange glow of the rising sun radiated across her face, complimenting the bright green of her eyes and the electric-blue streak in her windblown hair. She noticed his gaze and returned a questioning look.

"You ready to go?" he sputtered, clipping the slick rope to his belt. The gust tore through his already messy mane.

"Waiting for you," she shouted back to him over the roar of the wind.

"Same here." He held out a hand. "Ladies first."

"You mean *leaders* first." She gave a cock-eyed smirk as she grabbed the rope and dropped out the helicopter's side, the textured grooves of the material rumbling against the leather of her fingerless gloves.

"Oh." Troy clenched his teeth together. "That's only because you cheated." He quickly followed her.

The two landed simultaneously, unclipping from the cord and raising their weapons. As the rope sensed no more weight, it coiled itself neatly inside the cabin. The couple darted toward the facility, keeping low and on high alert.

"Now, you guys know the signal if things get hairy. Get the hell out; your lives are a top priority on this," Gavin mentally called out.

"Tell that to the military," Troy replied darkly.

The two pressed against the first armory wall next to a doorway. Aria looked at the ground, inspecting the blast marks. A violent force had blown the door off its hinges. Whoever did this had some heavy artillery.

She waited, listened, and aimed her rifle at an angle, viewing the right side of the entrance and then the left through the optical camera at the gun's tip. The image processed a small holographic light over her left eye. Debris lined the floor, surrounded by lingering smoke, but she detected no visible movement or life signs, only dead bodies. Aria raised her hand and waved it, telling Troy to move forward. Together, the two rolled around the corner. Aria stayed low, walking along the right side of the hall, while Troy took the opposite.

'*Sounds quiet.*' Aria signed to Troy with her hands.

All of the soldiers at Bio-Tech learned sign language. Even though each military member wore a mental chip, a means of psychic communication, there were times when another form of silent speech was necessary. Some armies held technologically advanced devices that could detect any electrical reading—even something as minor as brain waves transmitting through the chips.

Troy responded with a hand motion of his own. '*Too quiet.*'

They glanced at each other, nodding. Something was still there; they both felt it. The two tensed up, walking slowly and quietly. Following the same motions, they rounded the next corner and entered another doorway. Like before, the entry was obliterated. Aria took notice of a man on the ground on the opposite side. Blood pooled beneath him. Troy checked both sides of the hall with his camera and waved to move on. A shiver ran down the woman's spine as she noticed deep lacerations on the man's back. She narrowed her eyes. It didn't look like shrapnel or bullets, perhaps lasers or blades.

"Shh," Troy hissed, gripping Aria's attention. He pointed at his eyes and then down the corridor.

There followed a skittering sound from around the corner at the end. A shadow moved. In an instant, the two rushed down the hall as stealthily as possible. They couldn't let whatever it was escape. The couple paused momentarily, reaching the third layer of the labyrinth. Aria checked one side while Troy checked the other. Together, they slid into the hall.

'*Left or right?*' Troy signed. He eyed a giant red splatter on the wall next to him. His gaze fell to the pieces of human remains on the floor. He frowned.

Aria listened for a moment. "Damn it."

A screech sounded to the left. Jointly, they moved, nearing the center of the facility that housed the core crystal drive. Glass crunched under their boots, and dust kicked up with each step—no use trying to be quiet when everything was underfoot. Aria cringed. It was like attempting to eat potato chips in a silent room full of people—everyone would hear. Then, a noisy, horrified scream seemed to shake the walls.

"Move!" Aria shouted in a whisper.

She and Troy dashed down the hall as the screams and shrieks continued. Aria scowled as she leaped over fallen soldiers and chunks of cement, passing by terrifying scratches and blood smears on the wall. All the while, there was a worry in her mind.

'*Where are these supposed aliens? Did we not even kill one?*'

Aria hurried around the corner and froze. Directly in front of her stood precisely what she was looking for—a monster, an alien, one could say. It was long, at least 2.5 meters tall. The arms looked broken as the joints appeared to have the ability to twist backward. The fingers were lengthy and molded into thick blades, which looked more like the nastiest claws Aria had ever seen upon further examination. And then there was the face. Some scarred tissue around its mouth raised its lips past where the nose should have been. The features mainly were gums and giant, pointed teeth. On the forehead, at the top of the squished skin, were two black slits, probably the eyes.

The thing scratched and clawed its victim. Sprays of red splattered the walls and dusty cement. Stringy drool dripped from the creature's mouth as it struck downward, quick as a viper, and viciously bit the man's neck. Aria felt each hair on the back of her neck stand on end as she reached for her gun and fired. *'Shoot first; ask questions later.'*

Troy had made a strange noise before he joined her, firing his weapon in an explosion of sound. The creature remained unfazed and turned its head as the bullets pierced its body. At least, that's what Troy and Aria thought before noticing the projectiles had disintegrated upon impact. The thing lifted its head and screamed something awful, a nightmarish sound like an old monorail putting on its emergency brakes. It didn't seem natural. Aria and Troy both grimaced at the noise. The thing flailed its arms as it appeared to flicker, much like the landscape in the video they had seen in President Clarke's office. Aria suddenly had an idea. Whatever it was, it seemed to have a vibration defense, much like the military had issued. She cleared the grenade magazine from her 36C, slipped it into a side pocket, pulled out a different one, slammed the cartridge into the slot, aimed, and fired a blast at the creature. The grenade knocked the being a couple of meters back, and an electric pulse of light shocked it and its protective shielding into submission. Aria stomped toward the creature and shot multiple times into its chest and face, one after the other, trying to block out the image of its bursting flesh and splattering hot blood.

"Whoa! Hey! Hey!" Troy grabbed the woman's shoulder. She pulled the trigger once more and glanced at the man behind her. "Overkill...." He sighed.

"They said to kill it. I was making sure it was dead."

"Yeah, well, I think it's dead!" Troy made a face of disgust. "It looks nastier now than it did before."

"Have you ever seen a horror film? If I had my way, I'd blast a couple more mags into it and then shoot it with some grenades." Aria glared at the beast beside her feet. She kicked it as hard as she could and aimed. Nothing. It didn't move.

"Aria!" Troy grabbed her shoulders and gently scooted her away from the alien. "It's dead." He kneeled beside the thing, looking at its face—at least what remained of it. "Fugly," he said, flaring a nostril.

Aria's eyes fell on the victim, who had previously been screaming. If she had hurried, she could have maybe saved his life. He looked like the rest of the soldiers—mangled. No lasers, shrapnel, or bullets caused this damage, just claws.

'Monstrous claws.'

She glanced at the man's clothing and ID badge and exhaled sharply. It was Average Joe from the security video.

"We better hurry in case there are more of them. Troy, gather that thing up. I'll grab the core crystal drive," Aria ordered. "Hopefully, it's not completely ruined."

Troy nodded in response, tugging at the pack buckled to the side of his belt and pant leg.

Aria slowly stepped over the downed human; a hand snatched at her boot. She turned and aimed her weapon, ready to shoot.

"No, no," the man gasped, choking on his blood. "Not…not aliens!" He scratched at her. "Get out."

"Watch out!" Troy stood, aiming.

"It's okay," Aria murmured to Troy, holding out a hand to stop him.

"We can't be too cautious! He could be turning into a zombie, for all we know!" Troy licked his lips, panting nervously.

"Troy…." Aria rolled her eyes. "Notice him from the video?"

"Oh, hey, it's that guy who spilled coffee on himself," he stupidly stated.

"They…it happened so fast," the man sputtered, blood seeping from the massive cuts to his throat and collarbone. "Take it! You must. Small satchel." His hand plopped to the floor over his head, pointing at a small black bag. "They don't…don't like it."

A shriek interrupted the panicked conversation, sounding from down the hall.

"Oh, shit!" Aria aimed her weapon at the doorway as she sidestepped toward a control panel. She entered a code, and an elevator retrieved the supercomputer beneath the surface. The woman pulled the core crystal drive from the central unit without hesitation. It glittered with a pulsating light, revealing tiny dots and lines decorating the inside. Downloading everything would take entirely way too long. "Troy! Put this in your bag!" She tossed the large item to the man.

"You're taking the whole thing?!" He opened his sack and shook his head. "No room, Aria!"

"No time, Troy! Make room!" Aria watched the shadows bouncing off the wall in the hall. She shot a grenade, and the electromagnetic pulse burst down the corridor, causing multiple screeches. It sounded like at least three more were nearing from that direction.

As Troy dumped valuable supplies and ammunition onto the ground, Aria listened to the scratching on the walls and ceiling. The things were everywhere.

"Troy," she called out nervously.

"I hear," he answered quickly, wrapping the dead creature in a black tarp. He clumsily strapped it closed and headed for the opposite doorway.

"Hold on; we'll get you out of…here." Aria looked down at Average Joe. He appeared dead with his pale skin, glossy eyes, and a puddle of blood around him.

"Aria!" Troy shouted. He dropped the makeshift body bag and spun, raising his weapon. "No way out!"

Aria looked all around; the creatures had them surrounded. They were in all the doorways. She felt the same chill from before, seeing at least a dozen lining the halls. They were massive. Tall and lanky, the creatures looked pure evil. Troy stared into the dark eyes of one that blocked his exit only a few meters away. It took one step forward, and Troy began shooting. It was like a gun firing at the start of a race. In a frenzy, the monsters leaped onto the tables. Some climbed the walls, their talons digging into the surface. They tore after Aria and Troy, pushing them toward the center. The militants pulled their triggers, firing clip after clip into the monsters. Aria was lucky. Firing the EMP grenade down the hall had left some monsters vulnerable.

"Duck!" she shouted. Troy crouched, reloading as Aria spun and blasted an EMPG into the pile of approaching monsters. She gasped as she noticed how many continued to roll in.

'*We're going to die.*' Her eyes widened. She turned again, shooting a wall of giants. The two militants stumbled, hitting their backs against each other.

"I need more ammo." Aria gasped.

"Me too." Troy felt her tremble against him. "Tossed it all to make room for the crystal drive."

"Damn it." She fired her last EMPG at the crowd. "Got your grenades?"

"Across the room, by the body bag," Troy whispered.

"Can you get me there?" she asked, watching the monsters as they slowly neared. Some crawled on all fours like animals, while others walked upright toward the woman as if they were human. Aria watched, frozen, as one creature raised a palm toward her face.

"Crouch, run as fast as you can. Go one o'clock, and it's to the left of the body," Troy advised. One monstrous finger lifted, grazing Aria's cheek. "Go!" he shouted.

The woman didn't hesitate. She ducked and turned, running right into the legs of another monster on the other side of Troy. She felt the man twirl with her, firing a SABO grenade. The familiar glide of the SABO blades sounded, and a few monstrous screams followed. Aria dodged the beings crowding around her. Her thumb slid over a side button on her weapon; the empty EMPG magazine dropped to the floor. Aria jumped, sliding across the ground to the body bag. Multiple blasts erupted from Troy's gun; blades spun across the room, slicing and cutting the creatures. The sound made the woman's hair stand on end. Aria reached down and snatched up Troy's grenade clip.

"Grenade!" She slammed the rounds into the front slot of her rifle, aimed at the ceiling, and fired once. The blast shook the entire room. Her ears rang as all the monsters shrieked in deafening vocals. Unexpectedly, something tugged Aria off the floor. She heaved her rifle beneath the creature's jaw and fired, *click*. The gun was empty.

"Whoa...." Troy tensed up. "You could've just blown off my head." He looked at her with caution. Aria stared into Troy's eyes; a look of surprise covered her features. She had never made such a rookie mistake in her life. Her stomach suddenly felt very sour.

Troy grabbed the body bag's strap and tugged it toward the center of the office under the massive new hole Aria had created. He lifted his weapon and shot a single flare into the sky, signaling for help as Aria fired the rest of the grenades into the room's corners, monsters shrieking and screaming. She ejected the grenade clip again and slammed in her incendiaries, her fingers not moving fast enough. Troy busied himself by strapping the woman to him, their hips banging together.

In seconds, the Hawk was over the top of them. The familiar black rope dropped beside their feet.

Aria's eyes fell to the satchel on the ground—the item Average Joe had told her to take. Her dirtied fingers lowered, and she grabbed it. Pocketing the thing, she shot another grenade. The hiss of the air-fuel filled the room. Troy hastily clipped the body bag to the rope, then worked on his and Aria's buckle as he gave the line a sharp tug, signaling for a pickup. They lifted into the air before he could finish, yanking away from the fiery hell. He watched as the flames flowed up and out toward their feet. Aria shot again, waited for a second, and fired once more. Despite the heat, goosebumps covered the soldiers' arms. They could hear the creatures scream, but it wasn't the screams that disturbed them; it was the fact that the monsters kept coming, crawling out onto the facility's roof. They were on fire but didn't even seem fazed by it.

"See…that didn't kill them," Aria murmured.

"You could've shot me." Troy looked down at the woman strapped to him.

She gazed up at him, a regretful look in her eyes. "I'm sorry. I didn't mean to."

"God! You could have *killed me*!" He stressed the last couple of words.

"Shut up, Troy!" Aria yelled. He chuckled at her. The vibration in his chest calmed the woman's nerves. "You're an ass."

"I'm not an ass. I didn't try to kill *you.*"

The rope tugged Aria and Troy back to the Hawk 90. The two quickly gathered the body bag, set it on the copter's opposite side, and returned to their seats. Troy aimed his weapon at the dead being. His eyes narrowed as he waited for the body to move. A loud racket shook them as the helicopter dropped, the blades breaking apart and gliding back into wings as the sides of the jet returned, the cabin doors safely enclosing the pair.

"What the hell was that?!" Gavin called out. He dashed out of the cockpit, his untied military boots thudding against the metal. He gaped at the mangled head of the captured creature in the plastic tarp and stopped dead in his tracks. "Whoa!"

"Gavin?!" Aria and Troy both shouted.

"Autopilot! I'll go back in a second!" He raised his hands defensively. "What the hell is that?"

"Freaking aliens!" Troy said as he squeezed the bridge of his nose. Aria rolled her eyes in response.

"No way!" Gavin's mouth dropped open.

"No," Aria sighed irritably.

"Aw, come on, Aria. You saw them. What the hell were they then?" Troy dropped his hand as he slumped tiredly in his chair.

"Let's not jump to conclusions." Aria fiddled with the black satchel in her hands. "If they were aliens, then where were their UFOs? Why didn't the satellites detect anything?"

"Cause they were fried from the blast!" Troy argued.

"That would have happened after they were on the planet." Aria glared.

"Maybe a blast occurred from space to put it out, and then those aliens teleported onto the planet," Gavin suggested.

"I dunno. I mean, that is a huge assumption. Why would aliens suddenly appear and destroy this base? How'd they know it was here and what it was?" She frowned.

"This place has all the info you can ever imagine! War strategies and history! Aria, if they can get all this information, they'd know everything about our military and how we fight." Troy patted the crystal drive.

"Can't they gather that from the satellites, too, since they have backup crystal drives?" Aria argued.

"Aliens!" Troy pointed a finger at the woman. "ALIENS!"

"God! You're such a child!" she fumed.

"She tried to kill me!" Troy moved his finger to point at himself. He stared gravely at Gavin. "She almost blew my head off."

"I'm not getting into the middle of one of your guys' fights." The pilot quickly stepped back.

"A new military creation?" Aria suggested, ignoring her partner's behavior.

"Russite!" Troy and Gavin glanced at one another.

"Possibly. You know about the biomechanical research. What if someone was cloning people and, I dunno, animals?" Aria shrugged.

"That'd explain the nasty claws." Troy nodded, wiggling his fingers.

"And the Faze Shields." Aria nodded with him. "Maybe someone's leaked some of our scientific research, and another military is trying to copy it or create something new."

"Oh, good!" Gavin slapped his hands together. "Fireproof animal clones!"

"Fireproof." Troy pointed. "Aliens," he paused, giving Aria a defiant look, "who stole our Faze Shields from the militants outside."

"Maybe Russite has an alliance with the aliens." Gavin pondered.

"Oh…and they'll take over the world with their alien, military, crossbreed technology." Troy shuddered.

"Oh, like in that one game where—"

"Or maybe they are something entirely different," Aria interrupted.

The two men looked down at the woman. She ran her hands over the item inside the satchel, feeling the grooves and ridges on the surface.

"What is it?" Troy asked, suddenly a bit more serious.

"He said to take it, that they were afraid of it." Aria raised the silver decorative crucifix for the two men to see. Along with the item, inside the bag was one of the oldest texts known to humankind—the Bible.

"The Brawler"

CHAPTER 3

"Well, what do you think, Dr. Camery?" Aria propped her body against one of the medical tables inside the laboratory. As the fidgeting scientist quickly sidestepped from his workstation toward the slab in the center of the room, she and Troy watched with interest.

The man was a wreck. It appeared Dr. Camery hadn't shaved in weeks. His overgrown hair was disheveled, matching the wrinkled look of his ill-fitting, outdated clothes and brown loafers, revealing the older man's actual age. However, despite his sloppy appearance, Camery's attitude was on the opposite end of the spectrum—superior and obsessed. He was a man of his work, not caring about physical appearances as much as intellect.

"Very interesting. I have only been able to do a few tests, but the results have been quite fascinating so far." The fanatical doctor rushed to the side, gathering his digital document viewer from the cart next to his gruesome-looking medical utensils. Aria averted her eyes, feeling her stomach turn a bit.

"Come, take a look." The doctor waved the two militants over to him.

Aria shook her head. "I'll pass."

Troy didn't hesitate. He looked at the creature, making a strange face.

Camery pulled back the flap of skin covering the creature's chest. Aria nearly vomited on the spot; the underside of the flesh was covered with mucus, making a sickening slurp as he pulled it apart. "Two sets of lungs." The doctor showed Troy. Aria raised a brow, now interested. "One set seems to operate much like ours, breathing oxygen. The other filters sulfurous gas."

"Sulfur?" Troy asked, covering his nose. "Is that why they smell like that?"

"Most likely. You see, it's also in their blood." Dr. Camery showed Troy a chart on his viewer. Aria finally decided to join the two men, not taking more than a glance at the monster.

"Sulfur in their bloodstream? How is that possible?" Troy handed the woman the digital screen, not being one who understood much science as opposed to science fiction. Show him the beast, and he'll be happy; explain how it works, and he'll shut off like a television or, rather, change channels.

"That's what I'm trying to figure out. Their bone structure is also very peculiar." Camery tapped on the large claws protruding from the fleshy hand. "The talons are made of metallic substances—mostly Beryllium and Cobalt."

"Is that why the claws look like blades?" Troy poked one of the phalanges.

"Precisely. They are nearly indestructible because of it. The bones, however, are made of iron and platinum. This creature's bone marrow is full of siderophile elements." Troy gave him a questioning look. "It means 'iron-loving.' Iridium and gold have bonded with the specimen's iron-based bones. The body is also full of siderophile bacteria. The lab work revealed that the creature has Siderophilia or hemochromatosis," Camery announced, his dark eyes glimmering with excitement.

"Okay, you've lost me." Troy sighed.

Aria spoke up, "Iron poisoning, Troy. But that probably doesn't faze them, does it, Camery?" She pulled a finger across the screen, scrolling to another page on the report.

"Not one bit. The tests indicate that it's not a disease to these creatures; it's something natural. It has the opposite effect. They need it to live and function."

"Bizarre," she muttered.

"Okay, so we basically have a metal-based organism." Troy thought long and hard. "Anything else?"

"Yes, you told me about how they seem fireproof." The doctor turned away, grabbing a small torch next to the table. He fired up the device, an orange flame flickering noisily, and held it over the monster's arm. Nothing happened.

"Yeah! What's up with that?" Troy exclaimed.

"It seems its skin is highly resistant to heat." Camery turned up the temperature, the flame glowing from orange to blue. After a moment, the skin started to burn; the sulfuric smell filled the air as blood dripped onto the floor. The creature jolted, the body shaking.

"Hey!" Troy and Aria both reached for their weapons. The scientist held up a hand, halting them as he removed the torch.

"Don't worry; it's just nerves. It has an overly sensitive nervous system, much like ours." The doctor walked around the head of the table, facing the two soldiers who had their weapons ready.

"How hot?" Aria asked, covering her nose.

"About 1,300 degrees…Celsius." The doctor turned off the torch. "Hotter than the upper mantle."

"So, basically, this thing had to come from Mars or Venus," Troy suggested.

"I would have to say no." Camery looked over his shoulder at the thing.

"No?"

"This could very easily live on our planet," the doctor informed. "Or rather, inside our planet…underneath Earth's crust."

Staring at the creature behind the doctor, Aria gasped, her eyes widening as she asked, "How about killing it?"

"What do you mean?" the doctor replied. "It's weaknesses?"

"Yeah, how can we kill it?" Troy repeated, aiming his weapon at the scientist. Aria followed his actions.

Camery raised both hands, wondering what exactly he had done to make the two so suddenly upset. "I-I'm not sure what's going on."

"Doctor, just get your ass down!" Aria ordered.

Behind Dr. Camery, the creature had sat upright and crawled to its feet. A low growl sounded from its wide, mangled mouth. It didn't seem too bothered by the fact that it had been through an autopsy, its internal organs revealed for all to see. Hearing the vibrating noise from the table behind him, the doctor immediately dropped. Bullets fired, exploding into the creature's insides. It screamed something terrible as Aria and Troy unloaded their weapons into its fragile organs. The rotting sulfur smell filled the room as the beast dropped heavily against the tabletop, hot blood plopping onto the floor in steaming piles. Gurgling, the creature twitched and hissed as its body dried out and turned dark grey. Only then did the barrage of ammunition cease. The room fell into dead silence as the three waited in anticipation.

"Look." Troy slowly approached the carcass. Aria didn't dare lower her weapon.

"What's it doing?" she asked.

Camery remained on the floor, covering his head. He trembled slightly at Aria's voice and opened his eyes. "I don't know; what is it doing?" he asked in an anxious tone.

The creature appeared scorched with its grey hue and cracked, dried-out body.

Aria replied, "Turning to ash."

"It *has* to be dead now." Troy gawked at the burnt creature.

"Turning to ash?!" Dr. Camery leaped to his feet in an instant. He swiped his finger across his digital viewer, writing against the screen. "Turning to ash once it dies. It's like combustion!"

"I don't like this thing," Aria murmured.

"This is what I was going to tell you. I honestly thought it was dead; the thing had no pulse! As I examined, the heart seemed to be made of pure iron, leaking liquid iron and taking sulfur from the secondary lung and placing it into the bloodstream. You see the steam?" He poked a small puddle of the creature's blood with his pen; it melted slowly into the pool. "These things have an amazingly high body temperature! The previous wounds had nearly cauterized instantaneously. See, its skin is much like ours—easy to penetrate—but its resistance to heat and high body temperature prevents bullets from burying too deep and bleeding out. It's a defense mechanism. Therefore, I believe it could live under the mantle beneath Earth's crust."

"Why have we never seen these things before? And how did they suddenly get onto our surface?" Aria asked.

"Who knows?" Dr. Camery shrugged. "We'd have to go back to where they first appeared and study the area."

"The I.R.B.?" Troy scoffed. "There's no way in hell I'm goin' back there."

"No, not the base." Aria pointed. "They first appeared about 1,500 meters from the base in the desert."

"You must take me there! I need to investigate further!" The doctor seemed overly excited about going to the I.R.B. despite Troy and Aria barely surviving the base's new inhabitants.

"It's too dangerous," the woman disagreed.

"But you must! We could learn so much!" the doctor pleaded with her as she headed for the door.

"We'll send you the video feed we have on file. Ask Mr. Clarke about investigating the Intelligence Base. You can go if you want; I'm not going out there again. At least, not without another military." Aria slid her wrist across the ID reader's laser light and pressed her thumb against the tiny blue screen next to the door's security device.

"Perhaps we can gather a live specimen," the doctor thought aloud.

"Live?" Troy stared at the man in disbelief. "If we hadn't been here when we were, you'd be dead. These things aren't simple animals. They're damned monsters!"

"Oh." Aria reached into the pocket of her military dress coat. "This was given to us by one of the personnel that worked there. He said that *they* were afraid of it." She handed over the Bible and silver crucifix from the tiny black bag.

"Interesting. I haven't seen one of these in years." Camery gave a condescending chuckle. "Funny how they always try to turn science into religion." He handed the items back to Aria.

"You think nothing of it?" she questioned. The door clicked; the security device timed out.

"We've already had our apocalypse. According to mythology, God has already sat on his throne. He had his rule and left us long ago, forsaken." The scientist smiled. "It's just paranoia and superstition. People, especially those trapped by fear or surrounded by death, tend to seek out a creator for answers. If it's something you've never seen before, it must be a sign from God or, the other solution, aliens." He eyeballed Troy. "It's more probable to have a simpler solution."

"Science?" Aria asked him, her tone a little bitter. She didn't quite appreciate him calling the text 'mythology' in such a dismissive tone.

"Precisely." He nodded. "Just another animal that has gone through adaptation or has somehow managed to stay out of sight until now." The man turned and headed back toward the creature. "Happens all the time."

"Yeah, it's every day you find a humanoid, molten-lava creature with the evil tendency to kill." Troy rolled his eyes. He noticed Aria's jaw remained clenched; he knew what she thought about the mythology. There was something about the ancient stories that interested her. Troy couldn't quite say the same about himself, but he at least respected her feelings on the subject. "Come on." He patted her on the shoulder, swiping his wrist and pressing his finger into the security slot.

"We'll get some security down here for you, Dr. Camery. Wouldn't want that thing to come back from the dead again," Aria sourly stated as Troy led her through the door. It quickly slid shut once they crossed the threshold. She suddenly didn't feel welcome in that lab.

"Well, for being a scientist, he's kind of close-minded." Troy frowned.

"He's a jerk," Aria grumbled.

The two walked quietly down the hall, taking the elevator up to housing on the 60th floor of the military corporation's 333-story building. Aria folded her arms, staring blankly at the lit-up keypad beside the elevator door. She moved her tired gaze to the window, looking out onto the dark streets of the buzzing city below. Giant skyscrapers crowded one another, most used for military purposes. Vehicles sped back and forth, stopping at extravagant hotels and bustling, noisy clubs. The woman's eyes dropped to the tiny bodies that quickly disappeared from view as the elevator rose higher and higher. The city only showed its beauty at night—electric-blues and reds mixing with the spiraling colors of traffic like millions of lightning bugs in a black meadow. It almost made her dizzy. Then, a grey haze fogged her view; low clouds ate away the scenery high on the landscape. She frowned, turning her gaze back to the door as the bell *dinged*, welcoming them to their homely floor. The whole level housed a few dozen people, but Troy and Aria's apartments alone took up over a fourth of the story, a gift from the President. The massive doors slid open, and Troy yawned, removing his black military trench coat.

"I'll see you tomorrow?" he asked.

"Sure." She fiddled with the pocket of her similar trench, feeling the grooves of the silver crucifix.

"Man, I'm crashing as soon as I get…back." He groaned after his sentence.

Aria looked down the hall. In front of Troy's living quarters was a slender young woman wearing her best nightwear of leather and lace. Her lavender hair swirled with shades of royal blue in a loose braid that hung between her bare shoulder blades.

"You have fun with that," Aria mumbled.

"I totally forgot about her," he whispered.

"Tell her you're beat, had a run-in with aliens. I'm sure she'd understand." Aria smirked, seeing the disapproving frown on the other woman's face. It seemed she had been waiting a long time for Troy to come home.

"Yeah, I bet," he growled. "If you hear me scream, will you come save me?" he asked as he trudged down the hall, clicking his wrist so the door would unlock for the woman.

"Come bursting in and announce that I think I'm pregnant?" Aria suggested as she clicked her wrist; the soft beep sounded from her door as it slowly slid open.

"Ha!" Troy stifled a laugh a few doors down. He looked at her from over his shoulder, grinning. "If you could get them to believe it."

"I'll just say I was drunk!" Aria shouted.

"And I'll say you tied me to the bed and forced me!" This comment earned him a nasty glower from the fake-tanned beauty, her skin shimmering in glitter and neon tattoos down her lower back. "Uh, jes an inside joke," he reassured the young woman.

Aria smiled as she heard the irritated "yeah, whatever" from the woman.

After watching the couple enter Troy's apartment, Aria slid into her own, quickly closing the door behind her. It was silent and dark. She waved her hand, turning on the lamp beside the sofa; the soft glow had a relaxing effect after a rough day. Undoing the long military coat, she draped it over a chair.

"Troy," she sighed and shook her head in disapproval as she slid between the coffee table and her oversized, cushy red couch. Aria slowly dropped onto the sofa, letting out a deep breath. "What a day," she moaned.

In the dead silence, the woman reflected on the day's events. Her morning was typical. As usual, she'd practiced with Troy and kicked his butt. There was the incident with the bimbo and her friends, and Aria thought she was peeved then. Things looked up after going to the bar, but then all hell broke loose. With the Intelligence Reconnaissance Base attack, they were immediately shipped out to the desert. The three-hour flight felt like twenty. Then, after expecting some foul play from another military, she and Troy found out the enemy was far more sinister.

They barely got themselves out of that place, and she would have killed Troy if it weren't for her running out of grenades. Aria closed her eyes, groaning.

'What a disaster.' She pushed the thought aside, not even wanting to think about what would have happened if she had killed her partner. *'What was I even thinking?'* She allowed the creatures to get the best of her and made a terrible rookie mistake. The gruesome image of a dead Troy on the ground flashed through her brain. *'God! Just stop it!'* she lectured herself—as if she hadn't seen enough violence for the day.

The worst part was the damn creature had been alive the whole time, only unconscious from the wounds, and could have killed Camery. But now, she didn't think that would have been such a bad thing. Dr. Camery wanted to go to the desert and get a live specimen, which seemed like a terrible idea.

"Only going to get more people killed," she muttered.

The tiny holographic clock on the wall flickered in blue light, humming in the quiet apartment. It was already long past two in the morning, which meant Troy's friend had been, "A booty call…ugh."

Aria rolled her eyes. She tried hard to keep out of Troy's personal life, but it seemed the drama always pulled her in—phone calls from Troy asking for her help, dating advice, and even the occasional glare from the girls on the training grounds. Troy got around, and he got around too much. It made her nervous. He was irresponsible, and she wondered how many of his illegitimate children were running around the base. And then there was the typical example of this evening.

"Who makes a date for a booty call?!" Aria wondered aloud. She tossed the thought aside, leaned forward on the couch, and rubbed her face. "I don't care. I don't care what Troy does…or who he does. Ugh." She dropped her arms. "Drink."

Rising from the couch, she bee-lined to the kitchen across her large parlor, snatched a glass bottle from the marble countertop, and poured a drink of golden-brown liquid. One then two ice cubes dropped in with a *plop*. Aria slowly sipped from the glass, staring at the massive painting hanging over her couch. She analyzed the art and nodded, affirming that it was an excellent decision to put it there. When asked, she told everyone it was a piece done by some hot, new trendsetter from the outer city. She'd listen to her guests' critiques and 'oohs and ahs' and tell some made-up story behind it. They didn't know that Aria had painted the blasted thing herself and was too embarrassed to admit it. The only person who gave their genuine opinion of the piece was Troy. He usually didn't like what she had painted, especially the refined stuff. It was the colors and squiggles. There wasn't much meaning behind the pieces as they were merely meditative creations—this color over that color, this line over that line. It was a soothing way to make a mess and not care. Art was Aria's small piece of disorganization in her otherwise organized world. She looked over the curlicues on the painting, loving the little blood-red details crossing over the tans of the background. The red traced over the canvas and seemed to fall off the picture. She imagined where the lines would continue and followed her gaze to the chair by the hall. Her military jacket hung from the back, and inside the pocket, she saw the silver crucifix pointing out the top.

Aria walked across the living room to the coat, picking up the cross and Bible inside the jacket. "Mythology, huh?" She ran her thumb over the textured cross. The thought of religion being only mythology bothered her. Why couldn't the creatures be more than animals living beneath Earth's crust?

Aria strode down the hall, waving a light on in her office. Momentarily glancing at two small burgundy urns on a shelf, she placed the artifacts on her desk. The woman then turned and wandered to the bookcase, which housed a collection of over one hundred books. While Troy watched TV, Aria read. She fingered through the stack, her lips silently moving as she read the titles. Finally, she plucked one from its place and hurried to her chair. The book was titled *Ancient Mythology and Prophecy: A Better Understanding of Religion.* The item was an antique and printed on actual paper. It also had been her father's. Being a bibliophile, he was skilled at finding rare books created before the end of the printing age five hundred years ago. Aria flipped through the worn pages, finding the section dedicated to the Bible. She skimmed the readings.

The Bible is a canonical collection of writings considered sacred to the Christian and Jewish religions containing the Old Testament (also known as the Hebrew Scriptures) and the New Testament (not followed in the Jewish faith). Being one of the oldest surviving texts, the book's origin and creation dates are unknown. Despite its age and decreased numbers due to the Great Biblioclasm of 17,100 S.F. (see Great Biblioclasm, pg. 207), *a small number of religious groups remain who follow the book's teachings on morality and sin and the story of the Son of God, Jesus Christ* (see Jesus Christ, pg. 316). *Few churches stand today. Private militaries, whose owners still follow the scripture, protect those that remain. There is no evidence of which version is accurate because of the diminishing number of books and their unknown origins.*

Over twenty thousand years ago, the world's economies and governments failed. Worldwide hardships such as environmental disasters, famine, and war destroyed nearly 75% of all life. This event was known to Christians as Tribulation. The following thousand years of history are only speculative as little evidence of the event exists. Christians believe it was the time of the Final Judgment, but the evidence is lacking as humanity's population fell to staggering numbers during this period. This event marks the date 0 S.F. (Second Fall). The first evidence of humanity existing around the time of 0 S.F. belongs in scripture from a secondary Bible found off the coast of Ives (see Ives, pg. 245), *written entirely in the ancient language known as Legacy. Inside the Bible were additional books not found in most early history versions called* Second Fall *and* Golden Prophecy. *Thought to be written by the early settled Sorcēarian, Elder Gaius* (see Sorcēarian, pg. 579), *this version of the Bible was met with both acceptance and contempt as some believed it to be a fake.*

According to the book titled Second Fall, *humanity received a second chance as the angels pleaded to God to spare those damned to Hell. Believing they could lead the souls of the damned, the angels sacrificed their place in Heaven to live on Earth with those reborn. The Sorcēarians' role was to rule over humanity, teaching scripture, but by being brought to Earth, they had become sinful like man and had succumbed to their own evils.*

The Golden Prophecy *leaves the Bible with no definitive answer to how humanity will supposedly end. Scholars believe this is because God left the world behind to only the Sorcēarian rule. A Sorcēarian, though divine, still is not a replacement for God and thus cannot give all the answers. In this instance, their actions and the judgment of a servant of God will decide humanity's fate. This servant is unclear, given no name but only labeled as the Arbitrator.'*

"Arbitrator…" Aria whispered. Her voice was loud in the eerie silence of her office. She shivered, looking over her shoulder in paranoia. Flipping the pages, she searched for the ancient race.

"Sorcēarian," she murmured; the word was familiar. *'There.'* Aria's finger ran over the title.

'Sorcēarians—or God's right-hand men—were a brilliant race. Besides providing counsel for humanity, a Sorcēarian's role consisted of preaching God's word and delegating powers for war. Being giants and having superhuman powers, Sorcēarians were thought to be aliens who used biblical references to relate to humanity. Others took a more fantastical approach. They believed these beings were sorcerers who practiced magic and kept to themselves on the Island of Ives (see Ives, pg. 245). As guardians, they protected humanity through their wars until a great battle broke out among the race. It is unclear how the conflict started or how it ended, but shortly afterward, the Sorcēarians were extinct. Whether they left the planet of their free will or died in battle remains a mystery.

Mythology and the ruins of Ives are all that remain of the ancient race. The world's governments enforce a worldwide ban on humans traveling to Ives. Violent ocean waters, endless typhoons, and beastly creatures prevent safe passage.'

"Beastly creatures…." Aria chewed on her lip. "What if these monsters came from Ives?" More pages flipped under her hand as she searched. "Ives," she let out a breath.

'Ives, the land of the blessed, home to the Sorcēarians—a magical race thought to be sorcerers— is said to be located on the southern side of the Indian Ocean. It is a restricted land, and travel is forbidden to all. Surrounded by severe weather, there is a belief the final wish of the sorcerers was to be at peace, alone, and segregated from the rest of the world. The last known entity seen on the large island, approximately ten thousand years ago, is known to be half-man, half-beast with magical powers, much like the Sorcēarians. It soars the skies with enormous wings, and many think it to be Ives' very own protector.

Inhabited by various endangered wildlife, Ives was a beautiful and sacred place. Only those who were divine could live there. But as humanity returned to sin, so did the Sorcēarians. Perhaps the half-man, half-beast is a monstrosity that depleted the Sorcēarian population. Maybe it is nothing more than a myth, told to keep people away from the island.'

"Hmm." Aria frowned. It wasn't as helpful as she had hoped, but she had possibly discovered the origin of the strange creatures that attacked the I.R.B.

'Sorcēarian,' she concentrated on the word, closing her eyes. It reminded her of a story her father told her when she was a child. He had said Sorcerers once lived on Earth, and someday, if she were brave enough, she would find one.

Aria's father had been a respected professor at a university. He had taught cultural and mythological beliefs. Above all other topics, the Sorcēarians were his favorite. Many nights as a child, Aria had dreamt of going to a land full of sorcerers and castles. She always had a taste for adventure and read countless fictional books as a little girl, filling her head with ridiculous ideas and romantic fantasies.

"One day, I will meet a sorcerer," she scoffed, remembering her childhood words. "How 'bout a monster?" Aria looked at the bottom of the page and saw the name 'Imp' written in bold letters. "Or a demon?" She shuddered at an old image of a woman sleeping on a bed with a tiny, dark creature sitting upon her breast. The woman's face held a troubling expression as if she had a nightmare. Aria put her glass to her lips and finished the rest of her watered-down drink. "Great, just what I needed to see before heading to bed."

Green eyes dropped to the sparkling cross on her tabletop. Superstitious or not, it wouldn't hurt to carry that thing around. She picked it up and slipped out of the room, waving off the light switch. She crossed the hall to the bathroom and grimaced at her reflection in the mirror as she passed through to her bedroom, the bedside lamp flickering on as it detected her presence. She was exhausted and dropped to the mattress, tugging off her knee-high military boots, fighting with the double laces before pulling at her tight, black, long-sleeved open jersey. After kicking off her camo pants, she removed the white halter and peeled off her sleek, black-and-white bodysuit. Getting undressed at the night's end was a chore, but as Troy often said, Aria was always the most fashionable woman out on the field. Aria couldn't help how her Optical Camo suit looked. Sure, there were others, but why choose the ugly designs when you could wear something more eye-pleasing? She admitted it was unnecessary, but she was human. And, as a human, she had vices like any other, and hers was having good style, though it had to be tasteful and somewhat logical.

Aria reached for a t-shirt on the bed and quickly tugged it over her head, her hair puffing from static. A low yawn erupted from her lips, and she flipped onto her stomach, her face burying into the pillow. She sighed, feeling the cold blankets with her bare legs and feet before clumsily reaching over the nightstand to wave off the lamp, eyeballing the crucifix on the table. Darkness swallowed the bedroom. Aria took a deep breath and let it out slowly, reminding herself to relax.

"ARIA!" A shout called out from the other side of the wall.

"Hrm?!" She raised her head, listening as she gripped the pillow.

Only one thin wall separated Troy's apartment bedroom from hers. Needless to say, some nights, she heard everything. A muffled scream sounded again, this time from a woman. Aria was on her feet in an instant. Before she could even process what was happening, she was out the door, dashing down the hall. As she approached Troy's apartment, the door slid open. The 'booty call' came rushing out with a mortified look on her face.

"That was fast…." Aria eyeballed the young woman.

"Ha! Whatever. It never even started! That asshole immediately fell asleep! I was gathering my things to leave when he suddenly woke up, screaming and throwing shit at me!" Her high-pitched voice was louder than necessary. Troy's shouts continued inside the apartment. "And he calls for you like you're his mother!"

"Whatever, whore," Aria retorted and went inside Troy's apartment.

"Damn it! Where is it?!" Troy stomped from his bedroom with his assault rifle in hand, wearing nothing but his boxer briefs.

"What in the *hell* is going on?!" Aria shouted.

"Ah!" Troy raised his firearm but immediately lowered it upon seeing Aria in his living room. "What are you doing? How'd you get in here? Never mind that!" He rushed to her side and ducked behind a chair, tugging her down. "Did you see it?"

Aria gave him an annoyed look. "See what?" she asked with impatience.

"It was in the bedroom! One of those…*things*!" He shivered.

Aria stifled a laugh. "You mean one of those whores?"

"What are you talking about?!" Troy gripped and shook her. "Why are you laughing?! I woke up, and one of those aliens was in my room!"

"Probably trying to anally probe you." Aria snorted.

"I cannot believe you are laughing!" He looked around the corner of the chair, aiming his weapon. "It was ugly, too! I started throwing stuff at it until I could get to my gun. It was screaming something awful! Gah! That sound will give me nightmares for a week."

Aria cackled with laughter.

"You do wish I were dead. You never laugh like this!" His wide-eyed stare made her laugh more, and his muscles twitched with every shout. "I think it's gone. I think I scared it away. Damn, it."

"What about your girlfriend that was here earlier?" Aria halted her laughs to a few quiet sniffs and breaths.

"Girlfriend?" He raised a brow and thought for a minute. "Oh, man!" He twisted, grabbing her shoulders again. "It took her!"

"God, Troy!" Aria slapped his hands away. "That alien in your room was that girl!"

Troy gasped loudly. "What?"

"I met her as she ran out into the hall. She was pissed, all right. She said that you passed out as soon as you got into the apartment, and when she was ready to leave, you woke up and started screaming and throwing things."

"No way!" Troy's face turned a bright shade of red.

"I don't think I ever heard you scream so loud." Aria laughed. "You even shouted my name. I rushed over here to see if you were all right! I thought maybe one of those things was attacking you until I saw her run out!"

"You're lying!" He lowered his weapon onto the cream-colored carpet.

"I am not!" she protested.

"Is everything all right?" a male voice came from behind them. Both jumped at the intruding sound. A tall, bulky security guard stood in the doorway. "Had a noise complaint."

"Oh…sorry." Aria glanced at Troy. "Just doing some training," she added.

The large man looked them up and down and shrugged. "Is that what they're callin' it today?"

"Uh…actually, she's the loud one. She couldn't keep her mouth shut." Troy stood, tugging Aria with him.

"Right. Well, I find that sometimes a pillow helps. Maybe try that next time. Stifle the sound." The guard chuckled as he turned and left the apartment, sliding the door shut behind him.

"Troy!" Aria shoved him.

"Hey! What was I supposed to say?!" A sideways grin crossed his face.

"How about, 'I'm sorry. I'm a damned pansy, and I thought the prostitute I rented for the night was an alien and screamed shitless for my comrade next door like a little boy?'" She mocked him, holding her small fists against her chest.

"Aria…." Troy stared at her, unfazed by her sad impression of him. "Are you in your underwear?"

The woman gasped, peering down. She wore a T-shirt, but it barely covered her black panties. "Oh, you are a pervert!" She tugged a blanket from his couch and hastily wrapped it around herself. "You're in your briefs, and it leaves nothing to the imagination." Her eyebrow rose.

"You like what you see. Admit it." He placed his hands on his hips pridefully.

"Okay, I'm leaving now." She trotted to the door.

"Aw, come on!" He laughed. "You're such a tight ass. You know I'm joking."

Aria didn't know which was worse—that he had just hit on her or was only joking about it.

"You know nothing of my ass and will never know anything about it," she quickly spat before opening the door, watching it slide into the wall. She stepped back and peeked at him, saying, "Oh, but maybe I should stay…in case the boogeyman comes?" before slipping into the hall.

"Eh, just get out of here!" He waved at her. "And I want that blanket back!"

He watched as Aria grabbed the sides of the blanket and ran it from side to side across her rear end.

"Ah, wash it first!" His words came fast as the door slid shut behind her.

Troy stood in his living room, looking around with a sheepish frown. Suddenly, it was uncomfortably quiet.

"Pansy," he mumbled as he headed for the bedroom.

"Aria's Portrait"

CHAPTER 4

Aria rolled over in bed, stretching as a high-pitched squeak slipped past her lips. The blankets had tangled around her legs. Black hair tousled about her slender face like a fluffy mane. One green eye popped open slowly, followed by another, and he stared at the alarm clock, wondering if she should get up now or fall back asleep and lock herself into another three hours of slumber. Too much sleep would most definitely put her in a sour mood for the rest of the day. The young woman groaned, closing her eyes again while yawning. If her old cat, Xena, were here, she would surely be awoken by an angry meow or two, telling her it was long past breakfast and that she had better plan on making some lunch soon. Aria whimpered, wishing the thought would shove through her skull and never again remind her of her long-lost beloved pet.

Beep. Aria's DNAIS chimed, announcing a new message. She fumbled with the node behind her ear, pressing softly against the small chip. A voice called out gently inside her mind.

"Hey gorgeous, how 'bout hittin' up Chester's tonight since our date got canceled last night?" It was from Gavin. *"How 'bout 1800?"*

Aria breathed a small laugh. Gavin considered any meeting with her a date. She rolled her eyes as she sat up in bed, kicking her feet to remove the constricting blankets, and growled a grumpy groan. The woman wouldn't reply to Gavin's message. She rarely ever did but knew he'd be there either way. If she didn't show, he'd be able to easily find a different and probably more enjoyable form of company.

The dark-haired woman tugged on a pair of plain black shorts and shuffled into her slippers. Sluggish, she made her way limply into the kitchen, readying a cup of coffee from a button on her refrigerator. She held her mug, yawning loudly as the hot, creamy, chocolaty brew poured. Her attention fled to the video screen inside her giant kitchen window, showing her a view of the bustling city cast by vibrant sunlight and the current forecast—bright and sunny with a cold front moving in later in the evening, followed by gusty winds. The screen fizzled as she sipped from her drink. Her bright eyes lifted as a message appeared. Gavin, maybe?

'Not so lucky.' She sighed.

'Attn: Aria

President Clarke requests a visitation with you at 12:00.

-Message Bureau. Please do not reply to this message.'

Aria narrowed her gaze. That gave her about an hour to be dressed and ready to present herself in front of the President. She would grab a sandwich from the cafeteria since grocery shopping had not occurred in over a month.

"Damn," she hissed under her breath, taking another gulp from her beverage before hurrying down the hall toward the bathroom.

The shower was quick since the hot water was conveniently turned off again for maintenance reasons. The woman grumbled as she threw on her clothes, shivering in the air-conditioned apartment, wishing she remembered the memo posted on her door two days before. It was nothing a quick cup of hot coffee wouldn't fix, but she saw she was finally out of the brew and received a mug full of watered-down sludge. Aria debated it momentarily, watching the muddy swirl among dirty water, and quickly tossed it into the sink, sighing. She searched for a clean bra for five minutes, fought with her knotted-up boot laces, and encountered multiple stops in the elevator down to the cafeteria, thanks to the lunch rush—only fifteen more minutes. The impatient woman folded her arms and glared at the elevator doors as they opened to reveal a bustling dining hall.

'For the love of God,' she inwardly cursed and rushed to the deli, her black coat flowing behind her. Aria tried to ignore the glares received for who knows what reason and the few odd stares that left her uncomfortable. She hated going to densely populated areas. People always stared, and it was one of her biggest pet peeves.

"May I help you?" a baggy-eyed clerk asked the woman as she gazed over the sandwiches.

"Do you have any more turkey?" Aria asked.

"Just sold out." The lady shook her head. "We have tuna salad."

Aria's shoulders slumped. She was sure her nose wrinkled upon hearing the news. Then, she noticed the lady's eyes dart to the side as she spoke. Aria turned and recognized the customer who had just taken the last sandwich she desperately needed. Her eyes glinted mischievously, and she abruptly strolled toward the man and snatched the sandwich from his hands as he lifted it to his mouth.

"H-hey!" he stammered as Aria took a big bite and smiled. "Aria!"

"Troy, you like tuna salad. I don't," she stated. Her eyes crinkled as her colleague stared at her in disbelief.

"You…whore," he accused. Aria didn't leave him any time to protest as she turned and walked away.

"I'll buy you lunch tomorrow; gotta run!" she shouted without glancing toward the man.

Troy hastily looked at the DNAIS on his wrist and let out a loud, exasperated sigh. That was the last of his credits until payday.

Aria fought to get onto the elevator. She would have taken the stairs but figured going up over two hundred flights didn't seem feasible. And since she had just showered and was to meet with the President, it was not in the cards to get sweaty.

"Excuse me! Important meeting!" she shouted, squeezing into the lift. A hand grabbed hers, quickly tugging her inside as the door slammed shut. "Oh, thank you," she said with a sigh.

"Looked like you had somewhere important to go in a hurry," a man with striking blue eyes, optical enhancers no doubt, and long raven-black hair, most likely dyed, spoke to her. Aria nodded with a shy smile on her face. "Which floor?"

"Uh…top." She pointed upwards.

"Oh? Meeting with the President? I'd say that's *very* important." He chuckled as he entered the buttons for the 333rd floor.

"*Very.*" Aria quickly bobbed her head. She cleared her throat as she felt all the eyes of the ten other people in the elevator staring at her. The man could sense she was uncomfortable and smiled at her.

"Not very often do you run into one of the higher-ups," he said, breaking the silence.

"We tend to stay away from highly populated areas," she stated, glancing at the other passengers. "People tend to give us weird looks or *stare.*"

"Well, I'm sure you're receiving stares for reasons other than your status symbol." He gave her a sideways smirk and a wink. Aria could feel her cheeks burning. She was not a practiced flirt outside of Gavin's constant teasing, but this guy obviously was and knew how to push her buttons. The elevator bell sounded much louder than usual, and the doors flew open. "Well, this is my floor. Maybe I'll see you around?" he asked as he stepped off the elevator to the training facility. All the others followed after him.

"Yeah," she breathed a laugh. "Maybe." Aria looked for his nametag and frowned when she saw none.

Quickly, the man's hand slapped the doors before they could close. He leaned in, and Aria realized how outrageously tall he was—a Goliath.

"Euclid." He held out a hand.

"Aria," she stated numbly, her hand shaking his. Tiny electric prickles surged through her body, causing her to shiver. Static electricity, maybe?

"Ah." He smiled and poked the side of his head as he leaned back. "Aria. I'll remember that." Putting on his charm, he stared into her eyes as the doors closed before him.

What was that all about?' She shyly smiled, her face scorching-red. Aria looked over her shoulders and sighed, relieved that the elevator was empty. Goosebumps covered the woman's arms as a sudden chill washed over her. In a flustered state, she hurriedly pushed the button to the elevator as if expecting it to go faster to the top floor. Glancing down, she noticed the sandwich still in her hand.

"Damn," she cursed, embarrassed that she had been holding onto it during the entire encounter with the dreamy man. She raised her wrist; the holo watch revealed she had less than five minutes to get to the President's office. She hastily shoved the sandwich into her mouth as the elevator ascended.

Seeing that James Clarke wasn't at his desk, Aria sighed in relief. Closing the heavy oak door, a luxury, she happily sat and nibbled on her lunch. Usually, James was early, and no matter what time she got there, she was always late. Only moments later, the door opened and closed behind her.

"I see you beat me," Mr. Clarke's voice erupted into the room. He rounded the desk and sat in his leather chair, twisting to face Aria. He saw her quickly swallow a bite of her sandwich. "Glad someone was able to get lunch. I had left mine at home and ventured to the cafeteria hoping to find a replacement, but alas, they only had tuna salad." He sighed and watched as Aria quickly popped the last bite of her sandwich into her mouth. She swallowed hard. "I see you got turkey."

"Sorry. Stole it from Troy." She ran her tongue over her teeth, hoping no food remnants existed.

Mr. Clarke softly laughed at her. "Your face is a little red, Aria."

"Oh?" She returned a nervous laugh. "Sunburn, I guess."

"Of course." He folded his hands, silence following for a second.

"You wanted to see me, right?" she asked nervously.

"I did. It's about the mission from yesterday," he began.

"Should Troy be here, too?"

"No, you can brief him later. He's got training today. And since he was late last week for Delta instruction, he's got recruit duty on the grass fields," the President explained. Aria smirked, relieved she was no longer required to do such tedious tasks. She felt for Troy. Training recruits was like scrubbing toilets. However, Aria was a regular backup and had covered Troy more than once due to his hangovers.

'Maybe I shouldn't buy him lunch tomorrow,' she thought.

James' voice interrupted the woman's thoughts. "Four more bases across the globe were attacked yesterday."

"Survivors?" Aria asked.

"Hardly any." He solemnly shook his head. "But what's strange is that nothing meaningful appears to be missing. Just some ammunition and a few weapons are absent from the bases, but as for intelligence, everything remains in location."

"That doesn't make sense."

"I can't make any sense of it either, and every attack involves these 'aliens.' Panic is spreading in some eastern city-states as reports were leaked to the public. We can't have the same happen here. The last thing we need is a worldwide panic involving aliens and world domination."

"Have you told the other bases to prepare the EMPs?"

"I have. Some have EMP arsenals prepared. Bio-Tech's EMP stocks have nearly tripled overnight. They've become an extremely valuable commodity. There hasn't been much of a use for those lately. However, some bases still refuse, lacking the proper static protection for their software. We've got teams of scientists working on new EMP arsenal recipes and military units on patrol to test them out if they run into any more of those things."

Aria's eyes narrowed, not liking the idea of sending more people to the dangerous bases, especially since she and Troy could have just been lucky. They still knew nothing about those creatures.

"I know that look, Aria." He pointed at her. She raised her gaze to meet his. "I have approved Dr. Camery's request."

"What?!" Aria nearly stood from her chair but halted as he held up a hand.

"I believe it is necessary to gather more information on those…*things*. Camery won't be at the base due to safety regulations, but his position is where the disturbance site initially began before the attack."

"You mean 1,500 meters off the camp? Where those things came from?"

"Yes."

"How many men did you send with him?"

"He has a small unit."

"How small?" Her questions were rather stern.

"Five."

"Damn it." Aria glanced to the side, her hand resting on her forehead.

"Aria, we do not have the workforce to send out for something like this. Most of our units are currently in Russite, keeping a close eye on Cherno."

"Bullshit," she hissed.

"He insisted on leaving immediately. We've already lost too many men at that base. We must think of keeping our base safe as well. We're already stretched thin."

"And now you'll lose one of the best scientists that Bio-Tech has."

"They have a tight timeframe. If anything unusual happens, they have to remove themselves ASAP. Camery is a top priority." Aria opened her mouth to protest. "Don't argue with me, Aria! I have sent small teams worldwide to investigate the current situation. We have a worldwide crisis here! The attacks all occurred within hours of one another. Tell me this—how is it possible that one army could move that fast?"

"They are not an army; they are monsters!" Aria shouted.

"Rubbish! "

Aria dramatically rolled her eyes.

"This is all rubbish! Monsters, aliens! We have a large-scale military operation that has created some mutagenic biotechnology, that's all. They have sent these animals out to attack our bases."

"Equipped with weaponry? When was the last time you saw a cat use a gun?" Aria sarcastically replied.

"I don't know! I don't know what to do about it, Aria! I was raised in this military the very same as you were! We must think logically and treat all threats the same way. We cannot simply run from these things. We can lose some men doing the research and eventually find a weakness to these bastards, or we can continue hiding from them, waiting for them to attack our cities and suffer massive losses. Which do you prefer?"

Aria did not meet his gaze. He was right, and she knew better than to argue with him. "You haven't seen these things. You had better take my word for it. You *will* need more men than that. If you're going to do this, then do it right. You had better hope Dr. Camery produces a solution…if he survives this mission." She stood from her chair. "I know you don't want to sacrifice any more than you have to, but putting small units like that out on the field without backup will only kill more in the long run."

He gave her a cool stare.

"Is that all?" she sharply exhaled.

"You're on-call," he stated, tearing his gaze away from her. Aria's eyes widened. "Troy and Gavin, too. You're to alert them of this. You are at my beck and call. If anything happens, I'll ship you out. If you want things done right, do them yourself, correct?"

Aria's expression tightened. A battle waged within her momentarily as she debated whether or not to contend, but instead, she saluted roughly. "Born a soldier, die as one." Her words were like poison. People like her, orphans created by war, were taken and raised as killers and strategists. She was a soldier for life. She had no freedom, had no choice. Aria's life belonged to the Corporation. She knew she'd die in the heat of battle one day, but she expected it to be against humans, not monsters. Aria fed the man a distasteful glare, turned about-face, and rushed from his office, slamming the door behind her.

The President sat in his chair with his fingers laced through one another, resting in front of his face. His eyes settled on a small image on his desk—a snapshot of him as a younger man in military dress posed with a little girl with black hair and green eyes. They stood in the deteriorated streets; a military helmet rested on the child's head as she grinned.

"Don't think that the orphans of Bio-Tech are not loved by their father," he softly spoke.

"This is just amazing!" Dr. Camery gawked at the free-floating boulder before him. He eagerly touched it, pulling as hard as he could. "Simply marvelous!"

"This is weird." One of the soldiers poked the stone with the barrel of his gun. It sat at shoulder height and was unmoving, floating midair.

"It won't budge!" The doctor pushed down on the rock. He glanced at the debris floating all around. Specks of sand and pebbles were suspended in the air, like the giant rock, with sharp edges glistening in the harsh desert sunlight. He shuffled to the side and laughed. The boulder was neatly bisected as if cut by a knife. Feeling the smooth texture, the scientist couldn't contain his excitement. The inside appeared nearly polished. "It seems like a disturbance in gravity."

"Have you ever seen anything like this?" a second soldier chimed in, warily watching the base from a distance.

"Never in my life! But I've read about things like this before, but it doesn't make sense. The stories read more like science fiction." The doctor stuck his arm across the boulder, reaching from one end to the other as if expecting his arm to disappear into thin air at a certain point.

"Science fiction?" the first soldier asked.

"Time travel. It was a scientific journal pertaining to portals and early hypotheses of the space-time continuum—objects moving from one location to another through time. They get disrupted visually and materially. It mentioned spaceships and satellites traveling through wormholes and returning as fused matter. In one story, all crew members had merged with the actual mass of the ship. Everyone died, of course. Gruesome, I'd imagine. In another case, a man claimed to have traveled through time and seen the apocalypse. He then returned to his present time to warn everyone, only to find out later that the events he had experienced had occurred thousands of years before. He died hours later. His insides somehow flipped around. Tragic, really."

"So…this rock went through some type of time travel?"

Camery chuckled. "Not necessarily. You see, the space-time continuum involves more than the three dimensions you know; it also deals with a fourth dimension, hypothetically—time. This is like a disturbance in frequencies. Perhaps these creatures are from another dimension in the same location, and they have somehow disrupted the frequencies to cross over to our plane. They can travel quickly over great distances through the fourth dimension, possibly like a wormhole. If I review the tapes and record the attack locations and times, perhaps I can run a few Euclidean tests. Or maybe—hmm, now that would be interesting." The doctor stared at the ground, an item catching his attention. He leaned down, his fingers trailing through the dirt, and picked up a small device. "Now…how would a Faze Shield get out here?"

"Those things had them equipped," the captain informed.

"That's right. Aria had mentioned something like that. Why would these creatures have one of my creations?"

The soldiers glanced nervously at one another.

"I don't know. Why would they have one of *your* devices?"

"Faze Shields…of course! They use frequencies! Perhaps they were using something like this to disrupt the frequencies between the dimensional fields!" The doctor glanced at the rock and set the device atop it. "Faze Shields use high frequencies to create vibrations. They demolish bullets, and certain types are strong enough to obliterate heavy arsenal warfare before the enemy hits his target. I assumed they stole them from the soldiers to protect themselves. But, to disturb the worldly frequencies, you would need something much greater to amplify the Faze Shield's vibrations." Snapping his fingers, the scientist exclaimed enthusiastically, "Of course! The beryllium skeletal structures of the creatures could amplify the vibrations. But would it be enough to disrupt the dimensional fields alone?"

A slight tremor shook the desert.

"Perhaps if I turn this on…." Camery activated the device. It didn't move or make any sound.

"Do you feel that?" one soldier whispered to another.

"Those vibrations?" the captain replied.

"Well, it's not vibrating yet. How about one of you take a shot at it and see if you can't kick it up," the scientist suggested, oblivious to the quaking soldiers around him.

One man obediently raised his weapon and aimed.

"Wait a minute. Are you trying to reactivate the portal through vibrations?" the captain questioned, bewildered by Camery's intentions.

"Precisely. Exciting, isn't it? I theorize that the high frequencies may have a particular effect on these boulders. It's worth a try, right?" Dr. Camery smiled, crow's feet marking the corners of his eyes.

"Not really. You open that portal, and what do you think will happen?"

"Guys, do you feel that?!" The soldier who had asked the same question before was now frantic, stumbling over his feet.

"What's going on?!" The captain turned his attention to his fellow soldier.

The militant screamed as the ground opened beneath him, rocks splintering and rising. He floated among the debris, shrieking in fear.

"What the hell?!" another soldier gasped.

They all watched in horror as the man's body distorted, bones breaking and twisting in all directions. A low humming commenced; the vibrations created a static effect in the area around the militant. A wave of snowy disturbance blurred the scene before them, and in an instant, three masses shot from the distorted mess, and the landscape immediately solidified. The man remained free-floating, much like the boulder a few meters away. He hung in a tangled bunch, with sharp rocks melded to his body. Some stones pierced his form, his clothing blending with the mineral like camouflage. Pebbles dotted his skin. One point near his shoulder was invisible, his arm protruding from the opposite side beside the other.

"What the—?" The captain of the squad gawked in disgust. The screams of his comrades followed his question.

Three terrifying beasts clawed and tore at the other soldiers. One creature clamped a clawed hand over a soldier's neck and clenched its fingers, nearly decapitating the man. Another secured its toothy jaws onto a comrade's face. The third soldier fought with one of the beasts, shooting and stabbing the monster.

"Damn it!" The captain moved. Firing a whole clip into the beast, he could do nothing but watch as it slowly tore his friend apart limb by limb. Soon, the three monsters, all saturated in red, turned their attention to the doctor.

"Run! Get out of here!" the captain ordered.

Dr. Camery was frozen in place, watching the horror scene unfold before his eyes. The captain stilled his actions as he saw the doctor wasn't paying any attention to the monsters around him but looked past him, wide-eyed. Static charged behind the officer, causing his hair to stand on end. The landscape swirled, disrupting the portal that held the broken soldier's suspended body.

"Impossible," the doctor whispered.

The creatures crawled slowly toward the men, hissing and drooling. Their talons scraped against the sand as they neared.

"S-sir?" the captain stuttered to the scientist. A quiet giggle came from the portal, reminding him of his daughter. He couldn't even utter a scream before he was torn to pieces and fell to the ground.

Camery felt ill, bile rising in his throat. The creatures stood centimeters from his face, smelling horribly like rotten meat. One opened its jaws, and drool dangled from its fleshy gums. Camery looked past them at the new intruder, absolutely flabbergasted about how any of it was possible. The innocent giggle sounded again, and tears dropped from the scientist's eyes.

Aria stumbled as she trudged through the door to Chester's Bar and Grille, the fluorescent lighting playing against her blameless features. She held a slight pout as she slowly regained her balance and composure.

"Oh, man!" Gavin laughed, watching the woman stomp to his table with a couple of books in her hands. She slammed the items roughly onto the tabletop with a loud *smack* and dropped gracefully into the seat opposite him. "Look what the cat dragged in." Gavin rested his chin in his hand. "I almost left, thinking you wouldn't show."

"It's only…1900," Aria murmured. "You won't be leavin' anytime swoon." She eyeballed him and caught herself. "Soon," she corrected.

"Have you been drinking, Miss Aria?" the man questioned her, the smirk on his face growing.

"Don't you…patronize me, Gavin." She pointed a finger accusingly.

"Whatcha got there?" He glanced at one of her larger books.

"Research," she mumbled and opened a page. "I'm going to go find me some mystical beast to help destroy those things out there."

"What are you talking about?" Gavin raised an eyebrow, enjoying every minute of the woman's uncharacteristic inebriation.

"Ives, Gavin." She rolled her eyes dramatically. "IVES!"

"No. Bad idea, Aria. Bad idea!" He sipped from his lager. "What the hell are you going to do in Ives?" The man leaned forward, listening carefully.

"I told you. Find some half-man, half-beast."

"No such thing."

"Yeah, well, no such thing as those things out there!" She pointed toward the door. "Right?"

Gavin smiled; his perfect pearly whites glimmered in the neon lights. "Right," he said with a low chuckle.

Aria stared, enthralled momentarily by the man's caramel-colored eyes. Resting a chin on her hand, she leaned on the corner of one book hanging over the side of the table. She quickly lost her balance, the item dropping onto the floor with a loud snap. Nearly falling off her chair, she cursed and leaned down to pick it up.

Gavin sipped, eyeballing the room.

"Um, what was I saying?" She quickly sat up, her hair mussed over her eyes.

"Ives," he stated with amusement.

"Oh. Well, logically, I think there may be a possibility that those things are coming from Ives."

"Half-man, half-beast?" Gavin thought aloud.

"Maybe, I mean, it's all considered mythology, but maybe, you know. Sheesh, it'd make more sense if I were making more sense," she fumbled over her words, frustrated.

"I get what you're saying. I've heard of this place before, actually."

"You have?" Aria asked. She didn't think Gavin would know a thing about the small continent.

"Of course." He chuckled. "My great-grandparents used to help operate one of the churches in the city. They passed down what they knew to my grandparents and then to my parents. It may be the watered-down version in my head, but I kinda got the gist of the whole thing," he explained.

"Wow, that's pretty cool. I haven't met too many people who know anything about the churches or *stories* about Ives," she sneered as she said 'stories.' "No offense, but you would have been the last person I would guess to know anything about it."

"Well, I don't know too much. Like I said, watered-down version." He swirled his beer, pondering momentarily. "You think Mr. Clarke would allow you to go there?"

Aria laughed. "I doubt it. Oh, by the way, we're on call!" She leaned forward and slapped the table, revealing the real reason for her drunken state. The bartender approached and slowly set an electric-blue drink next to the boisterous woman, knowing her order without her giving it. Her eyes lit up like candles, and she quickly snatched the cocktail.

"Whoa! Wait! What?!" Gavin asked, pulling the glass from her hands.

"What, what?" Aria looked up at him, her mouth open in confusion.

"On-call? We're on-call? You know this, and you're trashed right now?"

"Well, I'd rather be trashed than sober going out there to die."

"Out there? You mean he may send us back out to that base from yesterday? Does Troy know?" Gavin sighed loudly. Aria shook her head, the sudden barrage of questions a few too many to take in all at once.

"No. I haven't been able to reach him. He's been on training grounds all day."

"Damn." Gavin ran a hand through his long, dark strands. It reminded Aria of the man she saw in the elevator earlier. She thought about asking the pilot if he knew who the stranger was but then passed on the subject.

"Well, let's go find him!" Aria beamed. "I'll drive!" She began to stand, but he abruptly tugged her back down.

"How'd you get here?" he asked her, his tone slightly more severe.

"Hm…." The black-haired woman thought long and hard and then scoffed. "Shit, hell if I know. Aliens!" She shrugged.

"Aliens? Oh! Aliens! Tell me about last night!" Gavin laughed.

"Oh! You heard about that?!" she hooted loudly.

"Yeah, heard he thought the gal in his bed was one of those aliens!"

"Yup! He started screaming and shouting! ARIA! I was so scared! And I came running out into the hall in my underwear!" She slapped her forehead.

"Your underwear?!" Gavin looked her up and down. "Damn, Troy's a lucky bastard."

"Damn right, he is!" She giggled quietly.

Gavin stared at the woman. He was dumbfounded. Aria's personality had pulled a one-eighty. She was like an entirely different person. Too bad it was because she was drunk. His smile faltered, but he quickly shook the thought from his head. He didn't want Aria to know that he sometimes felt sorry for her because he felt sad for such a beautiful woman to have endured so much loss and pain. So much that the only time she smiled was when she wasn't herself. And Aria rarely drank so much, which meant something terrible happened, and he could only assume that it had to do with being on-call.

"So, I go in there, and he's out in his boxers with his gun, ready to shoot!" Aria rambled on about the story, leaving out no details. "But anyway, I just had a great idea!"

Gavin gave a curious look as the woman leaned forward and spat out a few enticing words.

"You, my dear, are a genius!" Gavin finished off his beer and jumped up, grabbing his brown leather jacket. With a couple of clicks on his wrist, he had their tab paid and rounded the table.

"Oh!" Aria snickered as he pulled her out of her chair. "Wa-w-wait!" She fumbled for her drink. "I'm taking this!" she shouted, but Gavin took it from her hands.

"You can't take it." He laughed at her.

"But—" She watched as he pressed a finger against his lips and secretly opened a flask from his jacket pocket. He took a big drink to empty the bottle and dumped the contents of Aria's glass into it. Sure, it was irresponsible of him, but how could he resist a smile from Aria? Besides that, he didn't want to feel the repercussions if he didn't let the woman finish her favorite drink.

"That burned." He gasped for air, feeling the heat from the whiskey. "There. Hold onto that for me." He handed the flask to the woman. She gave him a childlike grin, and together, the two darted out the door.

Troy walked with heavy footsteps across the outdoor training grounds. Cicadas and crickets chirped loudly underneath a navy blue sky, making his headache even more painful.

"What a shitty day," he sourly grumbled.

Training had been a complete nightmare. First of all, Troy was late for class again. The crew wouldn't listen to him all morning, and some newbie had shot himself in the foot within the first twenty minutes. The rest of the day was rocky at best, but at least no one died. Troy desperately wanted to call in and make Aria handle the recruits, but after last night, he figured she'd kill him. However, because of the little stunt she pulled earlier with his sandwich, he decided the next time he was assigned training duty, he would play hooky, and she would get called in. The thought made him smile. Being pissed off, Aria would yell at frightened recruits all day.

A small chime interrupted his thoughts. Troy looked down at his wrist and saw in his optical hologram that Aria had been trying to call him all day, and then he noticed a new message from her.

'Damn.' He pushed the inner monologue button behind his ear. Whatever the news was, it must have been important, but why didn't she come to look for him? His demeanor quickly changed as Aria's voice broke out through his consciousness.

"Troy?! Troy! Help! Oh, God! You have to help me!" The militant stopped dead in his tracks. Static faded in and out, distorting the woman's voice. There followed a slight growl, one that sounded animal. Aria's voice became scratchy, cracking as she spoke. *"Ah! Troy! They got me, Troy! Those…those aliens!"* A high-pitched sound had interfered with the message before everything went silent.

"A…Aria," Troy whispered, frozen and unsure what to do. Then, his body moved on its own accord. "Shit!" He sped off, running toward the military complex as fast as possible. He dropped his bags as he commanded his DNAIS to dial her. There was no ringtone, and the call went straight to voicemail. "SHIT!"

A wild, gusting wind swirled around him. Troy slowed, coming to a halt, and listened to the quiet hum emitted from the sky. Lifting his worried gaze upward, he saw nothing but a black void from a starless night. Small noises surrounded the area—clicks and drones followed by a terrible screeching and then a deep growl, the same growl from Aria's message.

"Shit, aliens. I was right, aliens."

The man lifted his weapon, spinning slowly in a circle. A horrifying shriek sounded from above, along with mechanical chatter. Troy raised his head as a spotlight popped overhead, blinding him. Fear paralyzed him as something soft and warm wrapped around his torso and tightened. Roughly, the rifle jerked from his hands as he began to fly skyward. And then he screamed.

"Ah, shit!!"

Chattering noises clicked in his ears as one of the things latched onto him. He felt the alien's hot breath on his neck, and then its tongue licked from his collarbone up to his ear. Troy fought with it, but its grip only tightened, and before he knew it, he was tugged inside an airship into darkness and dropped carelessly onto the cold metal floor. There was a clamor of noise, and before Troy could move, lights flashed inside the ship.

Laughing. He heard laughing. His eyes quickly adjusted to the brightness. Lifting his confused gaze, he found standing above him a hysterical Aria. She cackled as he'd never seen before. Her hands tugged on a rope clipped to her belt. As the wheels slowly turned in his mind, Troy finally grasped that Aria had fast-roped from the Hawk 90 and snatched him right off the ground. Still, the terrible alien noises ranted in the background.

"Oh, man! That was great!" Gavin's voice intruded, joining in Aria's laughing fit. The pilot came to the back and pulled a switch from the intercom system; the alien chatter shut off.

"WHAT THE HELL?! You bastards!" Troy sat upright, making a pained expression.

"Oh…my…God! You should have heard yourself!" Aria slapped her legs as she stumbled.

"You…you're wasted." Troy watched the woman in wonder, his anger temporarily fazed.

Gavin laughed as he responded to Aria, "Oh, he will. I filmed it all!" He held up a small recording device.

"Give it to me!" Troy reached toward the camera, but Gavin pulled away. The two men suddenly tussled before Gavin roughly shoved Troy away, laughing cruelly.

"That's not all…we have different angles! Gavin was filming up front. We have a camera on the side of the Hawk, and I," Aria held up her hand to show a tiny camera attached to her palm, "got a close and personal view."

"Why?" Troy whimpered, watching Aria as she smiled wickedly. "What did I ever do to you? And you stole my sandwich, too. You are just a bully."

Aria dismissively waved a hand at him as she sat in a chair.

"Her idea, Troy. All her idea." Gavin grinned. "We have got to get her trashed more often."

"I would if I could," Troy grumbled as he quickly wiped the side of his neck. His eyes widened as he realized Aria must've licked him on their way up to the aircraft. He gave her a questioning look, his eyes flickering with curiosity. "But she won't ever drink that much. How'd you do it?" He directed his attention to Gavin. The other man shrugged.

"She did it all herself." The pilot glanced at Aria, who held a rather sleepy expression.

"Uh, oh." Troy stood, stretching his back. Something had gone out of place after being dropped mercilessly onto the floor. "That means something bad must've happened."

"We're on-call," Gavin announced.

Troy twisted his head to meet his friend's stare. "What do you mean on call? We? All three of us? And you two have been drinking? Unbelievable."

"Don't blame me! She didn't tell me till later!"

"Aria!" Troy stomped his foot. The woman jumped in her chair, a little more alert. "We're on-call?"

"Desert," she sputtered. "The *President* said he'll ship us out whenever he needs us." Her words sounded rather bitter, but it all made sense to Troy. Aria was mad at the President. She never called him by his title but by his first name only. "Born a soldier, die a soldier," she muttered, her hand swaying back and forth as she spoke.

"Damn it…how can you be the most irresponsible, responsible person I know?" Troy asked, running his hands over his face. It was actually the first time Aria had ever done such a thing. He blamed stress. Didn't that do weird things to a woman's head if she had too much of it?

Three alarms abruptly went off. Aria, Troy, and Gavin all looked down at their wrists. They all three had messages to meet with the President ASAP.

"Shit," Aria grumbled, sounding a bit more sober.

"Come on; let's get our trusty leader some Hydrate or something," Gavin suggested.

Aria moaned, wishing she had gone back to sleep when she first awoke that morning.

"*Aria's Just A Bully*"

CHAPTER 5

The elevator ride to the President's office was more than excruciating. Everything seemed to move in slow motion as Aria swayed between the two men, each feeding her a Hydrate pill and a bottle of water. Her glazed eyes struggled to focus on the colorful lights from the streets below. Streaming vehicles played a light show between dark masses of skyscrapers and tiny, blinking traffic signals. A blur of digital advertisements lit up the building next to the corporations. One was about shampoo, the kind that smelled like flowers and candy all wrapped into one—a fragrance that relied on the imagination since something like an orchid no longer grew in the wild. The ad flickered brightly into a series of fast-paced cars racing down an urban highway, streaks of light spilling from the tires. The city was like a rave party at night. Traffic illumination and commercial billboards bled into a series of seizure-inducing dances, reflecting on the elevator's glass. Aria closed her eyes. Luckily, she didn't feel too bad, only full to the brim with liquid. She moaned as Gavin forced another bottle into her hand.

"You guys are treating me like a child," she growled.

"Grumpy, that's a good sign!" Troy gave a thumbs-up to Gavin.

"I will show you grumpy when I shove your ass through the elevator window!" Aria smacked the man's gesturing hand out of her face.

"You do not want to be drunk in front of the President. I am just trying to save your ass, Aria," he lectured her.

"I'm sorry, Troy; I should have made her behave herself." Gavin looked down at the woman, feeling guilty for her drunken spell.

"I'm fine! I've been worse off before!" The woman finished the water bottle and angrily threw the container at the pilot. "The one time I let loose, I get called into work! All because of stupid aliens!"

Gavin and Troy pointed at one another. "Aliens!"

"Shut up!" the woman roared.

The elevator gave a cheerful chime as the doors slid open. Aria moaned; she just wanted to go to bed already. The hallway leading to the President's office seemed never-ending. Gavin and Troy briskly took the lead, and Aria didn't mind. Right now, the last thing she wanted was to take point. Instead, she slowly strolled as depressing thoughts of her earlier discussion with the President plagued her. She was expendable. She knew her life wasn't any more valuable than the clones from Camery's lab. Troy knew it, too. Then why was she so miserable?

Looking over his shoulder, Gavin took notice of the woman's sad expression. Aria eyeballed him, and he quickly winked, giving a boyish, cock-eyed smile. Tiny butterflies fluttered in her stomach as she sighed. Now was not the time to blush at boys. After reporting to the commander-in-chief, she could deal with her self-pity and lack of a love life.

"Grayson!" Gavin cheered, holding up a hand to the rigid personal bodyguard for Mr. Clarke. The suited man, lacking enthusiasm, returned the high-five, allowing Gavin's palm to collide with his own. Gavin laughed, whereas Grayson remained stoic and expressionless, staring straight ahead through dark lenses.

Troy stood a moment at the door to President Clarke's office. Aria probed him with an ugly glare. He ignored the stare and took a slow breath before turning the knob and opening the heavy wooden door. A cloud of smoke fogged the middle layer of the room. Aria momentarily went on alert for the cause, but Troy and Gavin remained unfazed; they recognized the familiar scent of a cigar. Aria narrowed her gaze. James Clarke rarely smoked, meaning he had nothing but bad news for her team.

"Please, have a seat," Clarke welcomed the three, smothering the traditional stogie in its tray.

Aria gratefully took a seat next to the window furthest from the President. He watched her cautiously as the two men took their places before his desk. Grayson silently closed the door, remaining outside to stand guard.

"Sorry to bring you in at this late hour, but I have dire news about Dr. Camery and his team." The President cleared his throat, trying to ignore the green-eyed glare Aria gave him.

"Dr. Camery?" Troy asked.

"Were you not informed?" Mr. Clarke asked with interest. "I figured the news would have been relayed to you by now." His dark eyes shifted to Aria, who stared out the window in disinterest, watching the bright advertisements across the street—

Bio-Tech, a household name selling domestic products and assault rifles.

Troy noticed the tension between the President and his female comrade and sat up straighter. "Sorry, sir. I was in training all day and late into the evening. Once I was ready to turn in for the night, I noticed Aria had tried reaching me."

"Uh, I had left my phone on silent," Gavin quickly sputtered, pointing at his ear.

A small smile passed over Aria's lips. She appreciated the men covering for her, but Gavin was a terrible liar.

"It wasn't anything trivial," Mr. Clarke muttered lowly. "At least I didn't think it would be." Aria groaned at this statement. "I allowed Dr. Camery to take a small group of soldiers to the 66th Intel Reconnaissance Base insertion site."

"You what?" Troy asked with a little bit more volume than intended.

Mr. Clarke continued, "It was to gather information at the site where the enemy was first sighted."

"How many men did you send?" Troy's hands clenched the maroon leather arms of the chair.

"He had five men with him."

"Five? What, five hundred or just five?" he asked in amazement.

"I have a good reason for sending out so few."

"I don't think you can give me, nor Aria, a good enough reason for having sent out so few. You knew what we were up against! These things aren't your typical soldiers. They're monsters!" Troy argued.

"Enough! I've had enough of your and Aria's objections to my decisions! Any further disagreement will lead to contempt, you hear me?" Clarke folded his hands. His mouth twisted to the side disapprovingly.

'So, this is how it's going to be?' Aria glowered at the President.

"No more of your glares, young lady!" He pointed at her. "After all these years, you two are quick to show me such distaste."

The room fell silent. Gavin sat stiffly, feeling caught in a family quarrel. With Aria and Troy being orphans brought up within the military, President Clarke was the closest thing they had to a father. Gavin, however, chose to be in the military. He was one of the lucky ones, born in the city with a wealthy family who raised him well and funded his schooling all through college. It was much to their horror when Gavin decided he wanted to fly planes for the military rather than commercially. His father threatened to disown him for that decision, and that was something Gavin had always taken for granted. Having a father was a blessing, just as it was for a father to have a child, and that was what Mr. Clarke was. He was a father to all the orphans of war. Though it seemed like a parasitic relationship to the outsiders, Clarke genuinely cared for every one of his soldiers, especially Aria. It made sense why the situation seemed awkward, especially with the young woman in the room.

However, whether it was his father or not, the booming of James Clarke's voice made the strongest of men feel like a child scolded for sneaking one too many cookies before dinner.

"And after so long, I must learn to humble myself and admit I made a terrible mistake. I should not have granted Dr. Camery's request," Clarke continued.

"Any survivors?" Aria finally spoke.

"One…Dr. Camery."

"How?"

"He is one lucky man; I can tell you that. He fired a distress signal. A separate team in Jordania had responded to the call. Upon investigation, they found Dr. Camery incapacitated in the desert with minor injuries. The soldiers with him were all found dead at the scene." At this point, James Clarke had hesitated to continue. His solid gaze fell to the photograph on his desk. "The soldiers were all mangled beyond recognition. They were attacked by the creatures you spoke of."

"How'd he escape?" Troy rubbed his aching brow.

"That's what we'd like to know. The doctor barely had a scratch save for a wound on his head. It appears he was knocked unconscious. The doctor claims not to remember anything."

"May we speak with him?" Aria asked with piqued interest.

"That's what I had in mind. I would like you three to investigate this situation and another matter that occurred earlier in a training facility today."

"A training facility?" the three sounded in unison.

"On the 160th floor. It seems that Delta did not respond to their latest mission. No squad members have been seen since this morning's drills, nor could communication be made. Upon investigation, all team members were found dead within the training grounds."

"Dead?!" Troy gasped.

Aria nearly fell from her chair. "Troy, weren't you supposed to be assigned to that floor this morning?"

"Yeah," Troy gasped, feeling punched in the gut. "I was until I got reassigned to the recruit squad. And I thought I got the short end of the stick." After a second thought, he gasped again. "Team Phoenix?" he asked with trepidation. Aria showed a similar concern for her and Troy's original teammates.

"Team Phoenix was not on training grounds today. They are out of the country on another assignment," Clarke reassured them. Relief spread over the militants' faces as the President continued, "The cause of death for the Delta team has not been determined. We've checked the video feed, and an electromagnetic disturbance appeared beforehand, wiping out all our video systems in the area."

"How could this happen?" Aria stammered.

"We're looking into it the best we can. We think the attack is somehow related to the Intel Reconnaissance Base. The 160th floor is currently on lockdown until the mess is cleaned up."

'160th floor,' Aria thought. *Didn't that man, Euclid, I think his name was, get off on that floor?'*

"Have you watched the video feed on the elevator yet?" Aria asked.

"It's all destroyed. It seems to have encountered the same disturbance as the security cameras from the entire floor. What's strange is the EMP traveled each story as if it moved with the elevator. Everything below the 159th level was disrupted within twenty meters of the lift, except for the 160th, which was completely wiped out.

"That's impossible," muttered Troy.

"Not quite," Gavin spoke up. "If someone were carrying an EMP distributor like the one Dr. Camery developed, it'd be small enough to carry but big enough to knock out certain areas with its electromagnetic static., especially if someone had an amplifier."

"Sounds like we need to pay the doctor a little visit," Aria murmured. "Sir, I'd like a request for an Identity Scan."

"Identity Scan? You have an idea of who may be involved in this?"

"Just a hunch. I only have the first name, but it's odd enough; I doubt many share it." The woman stood from her chair. "Euclid."

"Euclid?" Mr. Clarke questioned. "Why do I feel I've heard that name already today?"

"The closest thing I can think of is Euclidean," Gavin mumbled aloud, rubbing his chin. The others stared at him in wonder. "My father works for Aerospace Technologies. I've had to grow up listening to him talk about things like that." It seemed that Gavin did have a brain, after all. "But don't ask me what it means. Plus, I think Dr. Camery mentioned it during his Faze Shield conferences."

"That's where I heard it." The President snapped his fingers.

"Also, I talked to my father last night and asked him about the satellite that went out. He gave me the usual answer." Gavin frowned.

"Which is?" The President lifted an inquiring eyebrow.

"Well, I asked if there were any UFO sightings or if anything weird occurred during the I.R.B. attack. He said it was all classified, but he could confirm that nothing was out of the norm. It appeared the satellite went out due to an EMP wave shot from Earth; the signal was strongest near the Jordanian area. He said it was similar to the Electrostatic Cannon's pulse wave Camery furthered development on."

"I don't like how these clues connect," Aria mumbled. "Where can we find

Camery?"

"Infirmary. Last I knew, he wasn't released yet." Mr. Clarke pressed on his DNAIS. "Courtney, get me an IDS on an individual named Euclid."

"Yes, sir," a female voice droned over the device. Clarke's DNAIS was connected to the computer network for Bio-Tech. His digital secretary, Courtney, had the highest clearance for the company and ran all of Clarke's searches and requests.

"Also, make sure Dr. Camery does not leave the premises. If seen outside the infirmary, have him detained for further questioning."

"Yes, sir," the system hummed again.

"Aria, you must report to me after meeting with the doctor. I want to speak with you about your next mission priorities."

The woman turned about-face and left the room with a nod, Gavin and Troy quickly following. Grayson gave a short bow to the three as they passed him.

"Am I the only one who finds all this completely confusing?" Troy hurried beside Aria.

"It's not that confusing, Troy. All signs point to Camery." The woman punched the elevator button.

"Yeah, but why?"

The three slid into the box. Aria hastily pressed against the numbers on the keypad for the infirmary's floor. The small cart seemed very stuffy. She rolled her shoulders, suddenly feeling a bit claustrophobic.

"I don't know. Mad scientist?" she retorted.

"Makes sense to me!" Gavin chimed in.

Troy scratched his head—a nervous habit. "Come on. Why defect now?"

"I don't know." Aria thought a moment. "Remember a few months ago? The termination contract?"

"When the clones were unplugged?" Troy's brow rose.

"Exactly. Is losing your life's work reason enough to want to destroy your employers?"

The doors slid open, and the three quickly filed into the pristine white hall, rushing toward the clinic.

"I suppose it makes for a good motive," Troy agreed.

The woman leaned toward the security door of the hospital, placing her thumb into the identity scanner. "Aria Ivanov," she said sternly to the clinic's database.

"Accepted," a small voice chimed from the speaker. The heavy glass doors slid open, allowing her access to the infirmary before quickly closing.

"Troy Moreau." The man rolled his eyes at the protocol.

"Accepted." The doors allowed the one man in and shut again.

"Gavin Sigo."

"Accepted."

Entering from the silent hall into the thunderous panic of the infirmary was unnerving. Nurses and doctors rushed from room to room with great haste to help the injured. In a world of countless wars, wounded soldiers were infinite. Doctors were always needed, even in a facility as large as Bio-Tech's. With the corporation housing more than 400,000 soldiers and 200,000 faculty workers, the infirmary was no match with 1,400 doctors and 6,000 nurses. Luckily, the main city hospital sat only a few blocks away but was continuously crammed with civilian patients wounded from street gangs or outside mini-militia warfare. Not to mention the other people that were naturally sick or dying.

"I've never seen so many wounded." Troy narrowed his gaze.

"There must be increased battles due to the base attacks worldwide. Panic always causes mass hysteria, which also means more trigger-happy soldiers." Aria turned her gaze toward the floor, avoiding the sight of the convulsing patient in a nearby room, the red alarm signaling for help.

"This is why I can't stand hospitals." Gavin winced while observing a man sitting on the floor beside a doorway. His arm was missing, but besides the blood covering his uniform and cheeks, he appeared bandaged and clean. The pilot shook his hands involuntarily, trying not to imagine what it would be like to lose a limb.

The screams and groans were more than uncomfortable. The environment had a way of making a person feel guilty for being alive and well. Aria hurried down the hall, dodging the countless doctors and nurses. She narrowly avoided running into a gurney as it twisted around a corner from an emergency elevator. After a few more turns, she made it to the private quarters of the hospital through a sliding glass door where the higher-ups were often treated. The area was nearly silent, and the sudden contrast burned the woman's ears.

"Are you looking for Dr. Camery?" a nurse asked behind the main desk.

"Yes. We have some questions for him," Aria confirmed.

The nurse stood from her chair and led the others toward the room housing Camery. Seeing that the woman had artificial legs, no doubt a casualty of war, Aria averted her gaze, not wanting to insult her with a stare. The woman tugged on her skirt, covering a red and black tattoo that decorated the thigh of one of her metallic limbs. Sure enough, the nurse was once a medical officer for the Marines.

"He says he doesn't remember much. He has a slight concussion, but I believe he'll be okay. Nothing more than a bump on the head." The nurse gave a slight roll of her eyes. "If he needs anything, let me know. I'll be out in the hall." She eyeballed Aria's shouldered weapon. "Those aren't allowed in here."

"Yeah…well, we're in code red right now." Aria opened the door.

"Since when?" The woman's eyes widened.

"Since now. If you see anything or anyone suspicious, report it to us immediately. Dr. Camery is to be detained until further notice." Aria swiped her wrist across the door scanner leading to the hospital room.

The nurse rushed to her desk and pressed against her mental chip and the intercom system.

"Ah! No. Top-secret." Troy waved at the woman. She gently pulled her finger away from the intercom and her ear and slumped nervously into her chair.

"Trying not to raise any panic?" Dr. Camery spoke up. He sat on the infirmary bed, holding a cooling pack against his forehead.

"We don't need a hospital full of injured soldiers to be in alert mode," Aria answered coldly.

"Of course."

"Dr. Camery, what happened out there?" Aria didn't waste any time questioning the man.

"I, uh, honestly cannot say." He shakily lowered the pack from his head.

"Really? You remember absolutely nothing?"

"Nothing," he stated in a defiant tone.

"I don't believe you."

"All I have is speculation," he answered.

"Funny, 'cause that's all I have, too." Aria leaned forward, firmly gripping her weapon.

The doctor lifted his chin. "Trying to intimidate me?"

"I can do more than that!" She removed the safety from her weapon.

Dr. Camery glared at the threatening woman. "And what, exactly, is *your* speculation?"

"That you have something to do with these attacks. It looks a bit funny when you are the only survivor, and the enemy is known to use Faze Shields and an Electrostatic Cannon—both your creations, by the way." Aria shared glares with the older man. After a minute of waiting, she continued, "And don't think for one moment we aren't taking the termination of your Biomechanical Android program into consideration as a motive."

The doctor swallowed thickly, knowing that the evidence had piled against him. He slumped, his hands shaking as he took a slow, deep breath.

"Upon examining the site outside the 66th Intel Reconnaissance Base, I determined that the beings use Faze Shields to disrupt frequencies but not as you use them. It is very well possible that these creatures are multi-dimensional entities capable of fluctuating between our plane and another. As noted in the autopsy reports, these creatures have an astonishing amount of beryllium in their skeletal structures. Beryllium alloy has a high-temperature melting point and exceptional flexural rigidity. This means the beings can conduct high vibration energies within their bodies. Notably, through the use of the Faze Shields, they can amplify this vibration, creating a heightened energy field within themselves, making them capable of somehow merging or fluctuating between dimensional planes. But that's only a theory right now. It could be something else entirely," he explained.

"Wow, that bump on your head must be going down. That was quite a bit of information you were withholding from us." Aria switched on the gun's safety. "Got anything else you'd like to share? Anything about the attack?"

"I…I was trying to activate a Faze Shield found at the site. There was a gravitational disturbance, and I wanted to test the area by setting off the vibrating device, except it wouldn't start. However, another portal had opened, and…those things returned and killed the soldiers. The last thing I remember is screaming…and laughing." The doctor trailed off, mindlessly staring at the square patches on the floor.

"Laughing?" Aria questioned.

"Huh?" Dr. Camery met her gaze again.

"You said you heard laughing," she repeated.

"Oh, did I? Well, mostly screaming and hissing. The animals made a lot of hissing sounds. I don't remember much else besides waking up in this hospital." The doctor shrugged.

Aria frowned. She couldn't help but feel the doctor still withheld information. She opened her mouth to press forward with the man, who suddenly seemed lost in his mental world, but an enormous blast interrupted her. The floors rumbled, causing tiles to drop from the ceiling.

"What was that?" Aria mumbled cautiously. Silence consumed the hospital. She readied her rifle; Troy followed her actions as they waited, listening.

Another loud boom sounded, and the floor jerked downward, throwing everyone onto the ground. Flames exploded outward from the elevator shafts, sending the doctors and patients into a maddening flurry.

"Everybody, get out!" Aria barked.

Outside the room, the nurse called a code red warning over the intercom, advising everyone to evacuate the building. Aria stumbled to her feet, tremors shaking violently throughout the structure. A loud groan sounded from above, and the quaking suddenly halted.

"What the hell was that?!" Troy cursed.

"Definitely a blast. I'm guessing explosive devices were placed earlier from this afternoon's attack." The woman turned to the side, hearing a splintering crack behind the wall.

"Do you hear that?" Gavin whispered.

"Sounds like scratching." Troy nodded. Suddenly, his eyes widened as he met Aria's frightened stare. The scratching seemed like talons rustling against concrete.

"We have to get out of here now!" Aria turned to grab Dr. Camery just as the wall behind her fractured open, blasting outward and sending their bodies crashing to the floor once again. A loud hum filled the room—a low buzzing oscillating in beats against the hiss of the spraying fire extinguishers in the ceiling. Aria struggled to her hands and knees, trying to get a clear view of her comrades and the doctor through the smoky air. Her ears tingled as she listened to the crackling flames and distant screams from the injured soldiers outside. A soft, choking sound came from beside her.

"Dr. Camery?" Aria called out, reaching toward the dark silhouette in front of her. Her hands gripped the body, and then she jerked back as a loud screech sounded, and a face—a disgusting face with giant teeth and fleshy gums—growled and snapped its sharp jaws toward her. It was one of the creatures from the I.R.B., alive and well and very angry. The thing leaped to the side and grabbed the frightened doctor, dragging his body back into the hole in the wall.

"Troy!" Aria screamed, rising. Gripping her EM-36C, she hopped into the hole after the monster without a second thought.

"Shit! Did you see that?!" Gavin shouted.

"Yeah, I did! Come on!" Troy followed.

Gavin stopped him. "You mean we're jumping through the hole, too?!"

"Do you have another way out?!" the soldier argued.

Gavin looked through the glass door. The hallway was engulfed in flame, blocking the men's path. The choices were to climb through the hole or burn to death in the tiny room.

"Lead the way, my man." Gavin held out a hand.

With Troy taking the lead, they dropped through the hole, following Aria and the beast. Troy reached for a thick support beam, lightly gripped the edges, and swiftly slid down the sides. He stared into the darkness, hoping Aria was okay and that an ambush wasn't waiting for him and Gavin when they reached the bottom.

"Double-time, Gavin!" Troy called out, the other man now a few meters behind.

"Hey! I'm a pilot, not a super-soldier!" Gavin whimpered, "I'm going to die. I'm going to die."

Like luminous ball lightning, electric bursts shot from the sides of the walls through tiny, black containers, each holding a pressure-sensitive maglev suspension system carefully hidden between each level of the superstructure. A low, foreboding rumble echoed above the two men as high-pitched alarms sounded the code red alert.

"Shit! Those are the safety lines!" Troy shouted.

"What do you mean, safety lines?!" Gavin cried.

"For the floors! The building is caving in on itself!" Troy exclaimed.

"Oh, my God! I'm going to die! I'm going to die!" the pilot continued his whimpering.

Another burst of electric current exploded near Troy's hands, sending the man sideways and free-falling down the shaft. Slamming from side to side, he reached out, gripping the edge of one of the I-beams, and came to an abrupt halt as the strap to his shouldered weapon snagged itself on the corner of the metal girder, nearly dislocating his shoulder in the process.

"Shit! Troy's going to die; we're both going to die!" Gavin sobbed, slowly inching his way down the central shaft.

"Gavin," Troy groaned, lifting his gaze upward to look at his friend, "shut the f—" Bright orange bursts of flame blasted down the floors, heading directly toward the men. Gavin slacked behind, still four levels above Troy. "Gavin!" he shouted.

"I know! I hear!" the pilot answered.

"No! We've got to drop!"

"What?!"

"We've got to drop! We've got to drop now!"

"Are you freaking nuts?!" Gavin strung together a few colorful choice words.

Additional explosions sounded as the flames erupted closer and closer. "Do it now, or you're dead!" Groaning and struggling to lift his arm, Troy unbuckled his weapon's strap, let go of the I-beam, and dropped. He aimed his rifle and slowly counted the floors in his head.

"Shit! I'm dead either way!" Gavin watched the level above him rupture. "Always preferred to fly," he moaned as he released the beam and fell after his friend into the darkness.

Troy loaded a fresh clip onto his rifle's side and carefully aimed to fire two shots down the hole. Vivid, green fluorescents flooded at high velocity toward the bottom, exploding at the base of the shaft into a glowing pillow of ooze. Troy tucked his knees and rolled to his backside, dropped into the sludge, and immediately halted on the bottom level of the Bio-Tech Military Corporation building. He pushed to the side, twisted to a crouch, and fired again, setting another safety net just as Gavin dropped from the ceiling through the hole. The pilot's screams were quickly muffled as the green light engulfed his form. He lay curled in a ball with his hands covering his eyes as the ooze dissipated.

"Gavin! Get to cover!" Troy shouted, rolling up and around to find Aria outdoors. He saw her military trench as she darted down the street, following the creature and the captive doctor. Troy followed in pursuit, mentally calling her, *"Right behind you."*

"It's got the doctor. It's heading into an alleyway," she replied.

"Gotcha."

Troy ran across the street, leaped over a downed soldier, and kept an eye on his partner. Goosebumps covered the man's flesh as he noticed the chaos consuming the city. Civilians and soldiers fired their weapons as the frightening creatures flooded the streets. Screams filled the air like raid sirens while dust and charcoal-black smoke mixed with the brilliant orange flame climbing the superstructures. Everything was going down—Bio-Tech, the surrounding corporations, and the apartment complexes. And it all happened without warning. Troy's boots slammed against the pavement, crunching against broken glass and water that flooded from the emergency hydrants. He rounded the corner, slowly catching up with Aria, but something knocked him sideways. Reflexively rolling to the side, he slammed harshly into a nearby brick wall, causing him to see white. He shook his head as his vision slowly cleared to reveal the sight of one of the beasts leaping from the shadows beside a dumpster. It clamped its clawed hands over Troy's shoulders, hissing and spitting as it snapped toward his throat but met the metal of his rifle instead as the man braced for the impact. Fighting the monster, Troy eyeballed Aria a few meters away. She halted and turned, a look of concern covering her suddenly pale features.

"Troy!"

"Get to Camery! I'll catch up later!" he responded.

He saw her hesitate before she turned and entered the dark alleyway. Troy's worry for her dissipated, allowing him to focus on his current objective. The last thing he wanted was for the woman to watch a monster chew him to death.

Aria narrowed her eyes as she entered the darkness, her optical camera switching to night vision. Dr. Camery's shouts echoed from a few meters away. She hurried past a group of garbage cans, sights locked onto her target as it aggressively scaled an apartment building wall, dragging the scientist behind it. Aria fired her weapon, releasing an EMP grenade. It smacked the creature's backside, sending it into convulsions, and it carelessly dropped Dr. Camery two meters into a crumpled heap on the wet cement. Aria then opened fire, but the creature fluctuated, disappearing. The woman continued her careful aim, twirling in a circle as she neared the downed scientist.

"Dr. Camery, are you okay?" she asked.

He groaned in response.

"Good, still alive." She turned left and then right, looking down the side alleyways.

"Well, we wouldn't have carried him out here if we wanted to kill him," a low, male voice sounded behind the woman.

Quickly, Aria spun on her heel, aiming her rifle at a man leaning against a nearby wall. He stared at her with piercing blue eyes, eyes that matched the blue embers of his cigarette. Long raven hair covered the right side of his face, falling across his shoulder.

"You…you're Euclid." The woman tightened her grip on her weapon. A deep, hollow laugh answered her. It sent chills down her spine.

"I'm honored to have you remember me, Aria." Her name rolled off his tongue, sounding much more foreign than she was used to.

A low vibration shook the ground, causing the woman to fall to her side as a deafening blast erupted. From above the rooftops, Aria could see Bio-Tech going down in flames. The floors quickly smothered one another as the superstructure folded in on itself. The building tilted, craning closer and closer toward the area Aria was in, giving an unnatural groan as it destructively shattered into pieces. Massive amounts of glass and metal tumbled across the surrounding buildings in a tremendous crash. An enormous amount of debris broke from one building, plummeting down the sides of the apartments toward the military woman. Aria watched in fear as the heap fell closer to smash her unrecognizably into the concrete. But, before it could hit, and much to the woman's shocking relief, the rubble abruptly stopped. She stared in disbelief at her reflection in the shattered glass only a few meters above her.

"Can't let you die yet," Euclid chuckled beside the woman. He held his palm in the air as if holding the weighted mass above the woman.

"Who, who are you?" Aria gaped at the stranger, her face sickly in color.

"I believe you already know my name." The dark man smirked.

"Are you the one responsible for all of this?"

He laughed again, waiting a moment before answering, "Not entirely."

"And what the hell is that supposed to mean?" Her voice shook along with her hands as she tried to grip her weapon. She could shoot the man and ask questions later. Yet, fifty tons of debris hovered above her at his command, sparkling in the orange, iridescent firelight.

"Aria!" Troy's voice sounded from the edge of the alleyway. He quickly neared the two, his rifle aimed at Euclid. "Who the hell are you?"

Euclid smiled at the helpless woman before him, ignoring the intruding soldier. "You'll find your answers somewhere else."

"Where?" Aria asked, despite feeling she already knew the answer.

Her jade-green eyes locked onto the inhuman cerulean of Euclid's. "Ives," he plainly stated.

A low hum sounded as his raised hand folded into a fist. He frowned, and the debris over Aria shook and rattled, bursting into nothing more than a thick cloud of dust. She curled into a ball, protecting herself, listening to the soft rumble of the man's laughter in her ears until everything fell into silence.

"Are you all right?" Troy rushed to the woman's side, wiping the thick dust from her hair and clothes.

Aria rubbed her face, opening her eyes slowly. Euclid was gone.

"Who was that?" Troy breathed heavily. His shoulders were gashed up pretty badly, blood soaking his uniform. He winced as he sat down and lifted his arm to rest on the woman's shoulder. Sweat mixed with the black soot on his face, dripping to his chin.

"Euclid. I saw him this morning on the elevator," Aria replied.

"Is he behind all this?"

"I don't know, but he's a key player, judging by his unnatural abilities." The woman rose to her feet and helped Troy to his. She balanced against the injured man. "Dr. Camery!" She turned and sighed aloud. The doctor was safe, pressed against the building wall as he stared upward at the burning conglomerate that once housed his life's work.

"What the hell's going on?" Troy asked.

"Not sure, but I feel like I'm in the middle of someone's game." Aria narrowed her gaze.

She didn't know whose game she was involved in nor why. All she knew was that she had more questions than answers, and she needed answers. Euclid, however, had confirmed her assumptions, which meant she and Troy had to go to Ives.

"Gavin's Portrait"

CHAPTER 6

Bio-Tech Military Corporation, covered in black smoke and twinkling from broken panes of glass, was left virtually destroyed. Everything from the 70th floor and above had been flattened or split off, the safety lines finally capturing the weight and stabilizing the building's structure below. An eerie red glow haunted the building as the emergency lights spiraled in alert, reflecting through the windows and cracks. Sirens blared in a haunting song as the air filled with the frightening screams of civilians wounded in the streets. Water rained from the sky, actually from the extinguisher systems of the nearby destroyed buildings and street hydrants. Thundering bellows moaned from the tittering Bio-Tech Military Corporation's upper floors that had crashed into the side of a neighboring conglomerate. The sight was devastating.

Aria stared at the top floor of the building, now seemingly smashed into oblivion. Water droplets lined her cheeks, mixing into the grey ash. She spoke with the President on the top floor only an hour ago. Had she and the others waited any longer, would they have made it out alive? Her thoughts trailed to James Clarke.

"I'm sure he made it out all right," Troy reassured the woman as if reading her thoughts. He, too, stared at the destruction in awe. It was like a nightmare. The feeling hadn't entirely set in yet. He never imagined something like this would happen to Bio-Tech, one of the wealthiest, most influential corporations globally, and so quickly.

"I'm surprised the safety lines held up so well," Dr. Camery said. His snobbish tone had returned.

"So well?" Gavin glared at the doctor. "Do you not see this? All of this?!" He waved his hands toward the destruction. "This is not well! This is a total disaster!"

"It could be worse. There could be nothing left. At least the safety lines kept part of the building intact," Camery retorted.

"Easy for you to say. The laboratories are on the lower floors." Aria fed the man a nasty glower.

"All that Bio-Tech is. We're lucky to have the laboratories still," Camery replied.

"All that Bio-Tech is?" This time, Troy had to have his say. "And what about the soldiers, huh? What about the hospital? All those that were on training grounds? What about them?! I say that today, Bio-Tech has gone down in flames! Screw your laboratory! It's nothing without the rest of the military!"

The soft rumble of a helicopter sounded in the distance, noisily cutting off the group's intense argument. Floodlights flashed overhead, illuminating the four. Slowly, the vehicle descended toward them, the landing skid crunching against concrete and shards of glass.

"James," Aria murmured before rushing to the cabin door, hair and jacket moving violently in the aircraft's breeze.

"Aria! Get inside!" James Clarke opened the entry for the woman. "I was so worried." He pulled her in with shaking hands. His hair was chaotic, the peppered grey matching his soot-covered suit, and his chocolate-brown eyes were wide with worry. His hand patted the seat beside him for her to sit. Troy and the other two men followed in after her.

"I was hoping you would have enough time to make it to the roof," Aria responded, her worry-wrinkled expression finally relaxing as she noticed the pilot, Grayson. Of course, Grayson was able to get the President to safety. He was the best at his job and never failed to watch James. She gave a small smile to the somber man as he looked over his shoulder at the occupants.

"I had more than enough time to watch my tower fall." Clarke stared numbly through the small cabin window; firelight played against his irises. "I suppose not all is lost. It will take months to rebuild completely. The labs are still intact, but we've lost too many lives. I can't even imagine the numbers…." He held the bridge of his nose. "I don't even want to think about it."

The compartment remained silent save for the running propellers. After a moment, the President regained composure, making eye contact with the doctor. Camery also had a worn and weathered look to his features.

"I see you were able to find Camery before the explosion." Clarke's tone sounded flat.

"Yes, indeed. I probably wouldn't be alive if it weren't for them." Camery swallowed thickly, glancing in Aria's direction. "I owe her my life, I suppose."

Aria scoffed. "I want to know why you were kidnapped, Dr. Camery."

"Kidnapped?" the President questioned.

"We were interrogating him when the first explosion took place. The wall in the infirmary opened, and one of those monsters we found at the I.R.B. grabbed Camery. They dragged him into the skeleton of the Corporation. We followed in pursuit, which led us outside. They took him to an alleyway and suddenly released him. Then I encountered the man who goes by the name Euclid."

"Is this the man you hoped to find in the ID Scan?"

"Yes. It was the same man I saw on the elevator this morning right before the attacks took place on the 160th floor." Aria narrowed her eyes at the doctor. "I believe Dr. Camery is involved with these creatures and this man, Euclid. Whether directly or indirectly is still unknown, but I would like your permission to investigate further."

"By all means, investigate away. Where do you plan on starting?" Clarke asked.

"I had my suspicions about a location, and it was confirmed after my little chat with Euclid." She hesitated. "Sir, I would like to explore Ives."

"Ives?" He looked at her incredulously. Camery followed with an amused chuckle. "Aria, what can possibly be in Ives?" the President asked.

"Perhaps the source of these creatures," Aria's voice softened. The President gave her a stern look, making the woman feel like a child. "I know it sounds silly, but the mythology does state that there once was a half-man, half-beast that inhabited the island. It only makes sense to check it out. Euclid even said that I can find my answers there."

"Preposterous! It's called mythology for a reason!" Dr. Camery laughed.

Everyone in the cabin gave the doctor equal glares.

"If this man told you to go to the island, I could only assume it would be a trap, Aria," Mr. Clarke protested. "What if we're attacked again while you are gone? What if I lose my best agents?"

Aria folded her arms. "Sir, with all due respect, you were willing to throw our lives away earlier today. Now is the time to send us out. You know that Troy and I are your best bet at figuring out where these things came from."

"And how do you plan on getting there? The typhoons won't allow passage by boat or plane."

"Hello? Top of aviation? Best pilot in the world?" Gavin pointed at himself. "Sir, my Hawk eats typhoons for breakfast."

Pulling up his DNAIS, Gavin searched for the weather patterns surrounding Ives. "If I can get the baby up to 15,000 meters, I think I can fly over one of the developing cells before it turns into a full-fledged storm. Then Aria and Troy can go for a HALO onto Ives." He paused. "However, once they're on the ground, they're on their own. There's no telling how big the storms will get or how long they will last."

"One-way trip?" Clarke retorted.

"Uh…I'll have to work on the extraction point. If all looks green, then I can maybe land inside, but guessing by all the electromagnetic static that Ives is said to emit, I could lose all gadgets," Gavin said nervously.

"Wait, what? It has a force field around it? What's with this place?" Troy let out an exasperated sigh. "Is there some dungeon we need to find on a mountain somewhere to retrieve some magic key that will let us inside?"

Gavin laughed. The President gave the young man a strange look while Aria and Camery rolled their eyes.

"Why can't you take anything seriously?" Aria mumbled.

"Aw, come on! Admit it! This is ridiculous! Monsters; forbidden islands; half-man, half-beasts!" Troy rambled. "It sounds a bit farfetched, right?"

"Glad someone else is seeing it the same as I do," Dr. Camery chimed in.

"I'm not agreeing with you on anything," Troy muttered sourly.

"Farfetched or not, Euclid mentioned it, so we must check it out. If there's nothing there, then we'll come back home." The woman sighed irritably. She reeled her gaze to the President, who merely shrugged in return.

"It's our best guess. Why the hell not? I suppose it makes sense in some way. It would be the perfect location to set up a secret base. It almost makes me wish I had thought of it before." James nodded. "Very well. Tomorrow, you three will set off for Ives. For now," he glanced out the window as the helicopter parked atop a rich-labeled hotel, "get some rest."

Dr. Camery slowly lifted a small diamond-cut glass of water to his dry lips with shaking hands. The liquid was cold but did nothing to quench the doctor's parched throat. The stench of smoke stuck to his clothing and hair, causing his nostrils to flare. Dark circles lined his eyes. Camery's mind sorted through his memories of the day's events with a weary look on his face. His blackened eyes gazed at the floor-to-wall window of his hotel room. He looked out, past the tinted glass, deep into the blank stare of his reflection. Feeling numb, the scientist seemed uninterested in the destroyed scenery of black night illuminated with the radiant orange and yellow of the dying flames that slowly consumed the buildings in the city's center. No other lights were visible due to the suffocating blanket of smoke. A slight movement caught his eye, drawing his attention to the short reflection behind him, almost appearing ghost-white and levitating above the landscape before him. The doctor turned slowly, matching eyes with the child standing patiently behind him.

"I wondered if you would show up," Camery stuttered. He returned his glass to his lips, trembling under the child's grey stare. "Well, I assume you had something to do with this."

A smile crossed the pale child's lips. "I'm glad you made it out safely," her sweet voice replied. The girl, no more than eight years old, strolled to the window. She gazed indifferently at her pallid self—pale skin wrapped in a white lace dress with white shoes to match. Even her lengthy hair, platinum in color, was ghostly against her ashen eyes. The flickering orange in the distance caught her dead stare, and a tiny crease formed on her lips.

"I-I almost didn't," Camery fumbled his words. "One of those things almost dragged me away. If it weren't for Aria, I'd probably be dead."

"If it weren't for the creature taking you, you would be." Her harsh stare lifted to meet his frightened expression.

"Then, you sent them?" he asked harshly.

"Of course I did. You've yet to finish your end of the bargain." Despite the high pitch, the child's voice sounded mature. She turned away from the window and walked to the man's bed with tiny steps, hopping onto the mattress with a slight bounce. She gave him her sweetest smile, eyes glittering in the light of the nightstand lamp. "Were you able to find your documents?"

"Y-yes. I managed to grab a couple before they forced me into the infirmary." Camery nodded. He reached into his lab coat's pocket with quivering hands. The handwritten pieces of paper, the only thing not monitored through Bio-Tech's computer systems, rustled between his fingertips as he organized things. He cleared his throat. "Um, yes. The Faze Shields are simple to make and, as you have found out, are quite easy to come by and maintain. But its radius of vibration is quite narrow."

"I need you to make a bigger one. Much bigger." She leaned forward.

"H-how big are you thinking?" Camery swallowed thickly.

"Very big. Perhaps one that can disrupt energy fields by fifty meters." The child swayed her feet back and forth, quietly humming as she did so.

"Fifty meters? That's a hefty piece of machinery. Whatever would you need it for?"

A small, innocent giggle slipped past the girl's soft lips. "I have lots of friends who want to play."

Piercing blue eyes stared from a lightless void. The glow flickered; the pupils were nearly nonexistent. Aria stared, feeling stripped down to her core. She couldn't move her body, frozen and strapped into place as the electric gaze watched her. She felt naked beneath the stare, shaken, turned upside down for her insides to be displayed for all to see. How eyes like that could make her feel so vulnerable was beyond her. The woman struggled, trying to call out, but her voice was no longer there. Her mouth widened as she gasped for air. She felt like she was suffocating. Heartbeats drummed loudly in her ears, quickening with her rising fear. A soft rumble shuddered in the distance, rapidly climbing in volume, nearing her very spot in the empty void. A soft breath sounded, and smoke, like a cigarette's, filled her sight, the smell of cinnamon entering her subconscious. Aria twisted her wrists, trying to free herself as the rumble consumed her, shaking her and vibrating within her mind. It knocked, becoming more form in sound, pounding louder and louder. Then, she was released and fell into the black pit.

Aria spun, falling over the side of the bed, and collided with the maroon carpet of her hotel room floor. Her eyes opened wide as she gasped. Another loud knock sounded. Lifting her head, her hair a wild mess, she gaped open-mouthed at the door.

"Aria?" Troy's muffled voice came from the other side.

She groaned, slowly climbed to her feet, and fussed with the tangled sheet around her ankles. Why was it so hot? Her hand wiped at her forehead, clearing the sheen of sweat. With aggravation, she swiped her DNAIS across the door, the panel sliding into the wall. Troy nearly fell into her room. He appeared to have been listening through the door.

"Jeez, sleepyhead! I was wondering when you were going to get up! Sleep well?" he asked, giving her an eye up and down.

"Hrm…not really," she replied.

"Yeah, I can tell," the man grumbled.

"What's that supposed to mean?" She spun and returned to bed, picking up her pillow and comforter. She needed a shower.

"Nothing." He cleared his throat. He watched the woman circle her bed, glance in the closet, and peer into the dresser drawers. A wry smirk returned to the man's face as the woman met his hazel stare. "Dry cleaning." He flipped his wrist over his shoulder, pulling a transparent bag from behind his back. Aria snagged the sack from his hand.

"Did you forget?" he asked with amusement.

Ignoring the man, she entered the bathroom and huffily kicked her boots out of the way. Troy entered her room, not caring that she gave him an ugly glare, and then plopped onto her mattress.

"We were supposed to leave an hour ago."

"What time is it?" she called out over the sound of the running water from the shower. Steam flowed back into the area where Troy sat. He curiously eyeballed the over-turned alarm clock.

"Nine," he grumbled.

Silence ensued. Troy sat in the room, staring at nothing in particular, listening to the woman as she bathed. The sweet scent of honey and flowers filled his senses. He stayed like that for a few minutes, spacing out as he thought about Aria's recent behavior. She had been stressed or bothered by something. He could tell she had nightmares all night. If the wrinkles that covered her forehead when she opened the door weren't any indication, her crumpled bedding gave it away.

Aria strode into the room, a towel firmly wrapped around her. She eyed the distant Troy. "Are *you* awake?" she asked him firmly as she tugged a brush through her tangled hair.

"Huh?" Troy shook his head.

"What are you waiting for? A show?" Aria grumbled as she lifted her dry cleaning and emptied the contents onto the bed.

"Does it involve removing your towel?" he asked.

"Get out!" She pointed her hairbrush at the door.

Troy quickly stood, a broad grin on his face. "I'll be in the lobby." Then he left.

The woman sighed loudly and then quickly began dressing in the eerie silence of her room. Tugging on the white halter, she paused and glanced over her shoulder. Her neck hair stood on end as she felt the familiar stare of piercing blue eyes gazing upon her, undoubtedly caused by the strange dream. Shrugging, she continued dressing, unable to see the invading glowing orbs that watched her and the invisible smile biting down on a cigarette.

A high-pitched beep sounded in the room, causing the woman to jump. Aria glanced at her wrist; Gavin sent a message saying he was leaving without her. Another alarm chimed, followed by a second message stating how angry he was that she showered in front of Troy, not him.

"Children," Aria griped through gritted teeth.

Grabbing her knapsack, the woman quickly left the hotel room, trotting toward the lobby area.

"Ah, there she is!" Gavin hollered with a smile. He waved at Aria as she descended the carpeted stairs and returned his smile. "I thought you said she was in a bad mood." He peered toward Troy.

Aria narrowed her eyes at the other man, slugging his arm quickly before heading for the elevator.

"Ow!" Troy growled, rubbing the sore appendage, which had been nearly gnawed off by a creature the night before. Aria smiled at his pain.

The three rode the elevator to the hotel's top floor in silence. They rounded the corner and took the emergency exit to the roof where the Hawk 90 waited.

"Got everything we need?" Aria asked, slipping on sunglasses as she entered the bright sunlight.

"Enough to equip a small army." Gavin opened the cabin doors to the helicopter.

"Good…I hope it's enough." Aria stepped inside and immediately began loading and organizing her arsenal into her rucksack.

"Enough?" Troy laughed, overlooking the cabin stuffed with assault rifles, massive containers of ammo, and every type of explosive Bio-Tech had ever manufactured. The man grabbed multiple handfuls of the SABO and EMP grenades. He glanced at the air fuels and hesitated before snatching some to add to his pack. "It may not kill 'em but can at least slow 'em down."

"Hopefully, we can do more than slow them down," the woman muttered. Her fingers trailed over the side of her rifle. "We'll need more than this," she said dejectedly.

"How is this not enough? If we can't keep ourselves safe with this, then we're screwed." Troy gave her a look of disbelief.

The loud whine of the starting propellers droned overhead.

"No, I mean, we'll need to engineer something more." She pressed against her wrist, and a holographic keyboard came into view. Her fingers typed against the pale blue lights. "I'm requesting Dr. Camery and his team to develop a kind of ammunition that will give the same effect as an EMP. Upon contact, they may send shockwaves that eat away at the Faze Shield's energy."

"That's a good idea, Aria. You should be a scientist." Troy smirked.

She gave him an amused stare. "I can come up with ideas, but don't ask me how to make them work." Her smile faded, and she glared at him instead. "Besides, I need to be here to keep your butt in line. Where would you be without me?"

"Probably not much worse off, seeing you almost blew my head off the other day."

"Stop bringing that up!" Aria smacked the man on the arm again before taking her seat. Troy gaped at her, grabbing his arm with a pained expression. She was particularly moody today.

The Hawk 90 jolted, lifting into the air. "We now have liftoff," Gavin's voice called over the intercom. "Thank you for flying with Hawk 90; I am your pilot, Gavin. I ask that you remain seated and buckled through the duration of our flight. At this time, please be sure your seatback is returned to its upright position and your tray table is stowed. As a reminder, all carry-on items must now be stored under the seat in front of you or in an overhead compartment. Please notice the emergency exits to the left and the right. Parachutes are located on either side of the cabin. In the case of a water landing, you can use Aria's chest as a floatation device."

Troy laughed as Aria rolled her eyes, unconsciously crossing her arms over her chest.

"Children…" she grumbled in irritation.

Rain pelted softly against the marble windowsill as Dovian stared absently at the nothingness surrounding the tall superstructure. It was a wasteland out there, nothing more than a garbage dump, ground zero. This was once a great city—a bustling, musical, beautiful city.

'A waste of civilization.' The man deeply exhaled. He closed his eyes, listening to the soft slaps the droplets created.

Harshly, the wind whistled through the torn metropolis. It mixed with the sound of low thunder and clattering raindrops. Dovian heard the voices, the whispers of conversation not far away. He could hear the laughter of flirting lovers, the chattering of young students, and the high-pitched twinkle of bells and flutes playing melodiously within the chambers. The footsteps echoed on the cobblestone pathways, and the shuffle of robes swished across the grass.

"Dovian?" The all-too-familiar whisper haunted him for most of his lifetime.

Dovian spun, glancing over his shoulder. "Lanthe," The name stumbled from the man's cracked lips. "I'-I'Lanthe…." His eyes lowered to the floor, staring at his path on the soot-covered marble. He was the only one who visited the room for years. There had been no one else in there before, and still, no one else made a presence.

The howl of the wind screeched from the streets below. Dovian turned his icy gaze back to the outside world. It was hard to tell where the cries came from anymore. Too much debris and rubble littered the land. Sometimes, Dovian would find himself standing next to the destroyed buildings, listening to the wind wailing between thin pieces of metal. It reminded him of voices, and sometimes, it reminded him of the screams that still haunted his dreams. Shrieks were the last thing he had heard—the death of his people, family, friends, and the woman he loved, all because of a nonsensical war.

"I'Lanthe," Dovian murmured. Even now, the name sounded foreign. "Do you haunt me?" He strolled away from the window and out into the darkness of the cathedral.

Like a freight train crashing into him, a murderous pain overtook Dovian. It nearly killed him every day but never pushed him over the edge, to the brink of death, something he often prayed for. As much as Dovian wished he could join the rest of his family, he knew he deserved to suffer in this world and suffer in it alone. There was no forgiveness for his actions. He wondered if even I'Lanthe was capable of such mercy.

Dovian wafted toward the broken pillars in the center of the Gothic core. He grimaced in pain, gripping his chest. Carelessly, he dropped hard to his knees, folding across a crumbling stone chunk on the floor. Water fell generously from a hole in the ceiling thirty meters above the man. It pounded heavily against his aching body, doing nothing to soothe the fire within him.

It was the pain he deserved, the punishment for his sins, the sins that God himself could never forgive.

"Forsaken," Dovian hissed, his hands gripping the stone notches. "Forsaken by my people…forsaken by my God…."

Thunder growled back in reply, reminding Dovian of *His* boundless presence. Dovian could feel the smolder of thousands of eyes upon him. He knew they were watching from the heavens—the great, beautiful, promised land—where Dovian would never step. He resided in a never-ending purgatory. A thin line lay between this world and Hell; Dovian could feel it looming. The heat of all sin rose, coming closer to the surface.

"It's too soon…." Dovian coughed. He knew that was a lie. He didn't spend his time wisely. The prophecy said it would come soon and that, in the end, Dovian would have to face fate. He would have to come out of the darkness to fight it. He would have to make the hardest decision of his life. He would have to decide the fate of the planet.

"Why me?!" the priest shouted at the heavens, the water washing away the dust on his cheeks. "Haven't I done enough?! Haven't I suffered enough?! Why me?! Why must I choose?! Why must I be the one to bear the weight and shame?! Why must I be the one to suffer? Why should I be punished when I was the one who cleaned up *Your* mess?! Why have You forsaken me after all I've done for You?!

What do You want me to do?! What do You expect me to do?!" Dovian continued his ravings, lowering his head to the filthy floor. Muddy water soaked his robes. His ceremonial dress was once a sign of high honor. Now, they were nothing more than drapes that covered his body. He had no status; he had no class, and he had no honor.

Something moved within the shadows.

"No," Dovian chuckled lowly. "Not quite alone." He turned his frosty eyes toward the source of the noise. "Nope! You left me with the magnificent presence of the LIZARDS!" the man cursed, glaring at his lanky friend, who scuttled toward him. The giant lizard, who was as long as the man was tall, hissed happily, its tongue reaching out to smell the humid air. "Leave me be, my friend. I am not well at this moment." Dovian waved at the creature. Sadly, the lizards didn't speak any known language, and the beast only skittered closer, its front legs standing on the stone pillar Dovian lay across.

"Hrm, I don't have any food," Dovian muttered, waving the creature away again. It crawled onto the man's shoulder, hissing. The reptile moved, and its swollen belly dragged across the man's shoulder blades. Dovian chuckled like a madman. "You're better fed than me anyway."

Why…why must my only companion be this sad creature?' Dovian felt the sting of tears in his eyes. *'He'll only die like all the others. How often must I grow attached to something and watch it die?'*

The reptile rubbed its nose in Dovian's ear, snorting. Dovian stifled a laugh, the hot breath tickling him. The laughter only made tears fall from his eyes.

"Please, Hector, my friend…you're only making things worse right now. Go look in the library." Dovian pointed a long finger toward the room in the far corner of the dark hall. "There may be some dried meat left in the bottom drawer."

The lizard, Hector, hissed and turned his gaze toward the pointed finger. His golden eyes followed the invisible trail leading to the library. With a snort, the creature hopped, making a soft plop as he hit the slippery marble floor and scampered down the hall into the library. Dovian waited momentarily to hear the crashing music of various objects falling over in the lizard's frenzy to find the hidden snack.

"Fat bastard." Dovian shook his head.

His body shivered, suddenly frozen by the rain. His fit of rage and pain had subsided for the time being. The priest stayed, however, letting the precipitation shower against his form.

'You're going to make yourself sick,' his mind lectured. Instead of listening to the warning, Dovian raised his palm into the air, letting the rain droplets splatter

against his bare skin. It felt like pins and needles, reminding him that he was indeed still alive and capable of feeling physical pain. Thunder growled in the distance, but this time from the opposite side of the kingdom. The storm had passed over and fallen away toward the distant, empty lands.

"Does it still rain where there is no soul?" Dovian whispered. "Is there still thunder?" He sat up, his hood falling from his head. "I wonder."

The tall man slowly stood. His soaked robes added twice the weight to his body. He stared at the doors enclosing him within the cathedral. It had been a while since he had gone out. And Dovian knew it wasn't healthy to stay indoors all the time. Cabin fever was such a pain. Deep in his thoughts, he waited for another second or two, debating whether he should go out. Then he decided, and in a flash, the man was out the door, following the rainstorm to see how far it would go before it disappeared.

Hector scratched at the wrapper around the dried meat. Agitated, he took the entire package into his mouth and swallowed. Sure, Dovian had often punished him for eating the wax paper covering, but Hector was hungry and didn't care. Besides, the meat was so tasty that the future tummy ache would be worth it. Hector licked the remaining crumbs off the dusty ground with a lizardly smile. He lifted his head and poked his tongue out. Sure enough, the air pressure had changed. As fast as the plump lizard could move, Hector dashed back into the cathedral's center, where he had last left his master.

Not there. The creature shifted his head from side to side, waddling toward the destroyed pillar on the floor. He crawled onto the stone seat and plopped into a sitting position. Cold air rushed in from the open entrance to the church; the weighted stone doors banged against the wall. Dovian was gone. With a huff and expansion of his neck flaps, the lizard laid down his head, waiting for his friend to return. He wondered how long it'd be this time. Hector suddenly cursed himself for eating his last treat in one gluttonous bite.

"I Have Lots of Friends"

CHAPTER 7

"All right, you two…this is it," Gavin's smooth voice called noisily over the intercom, jolting the two soldiers from their daydreaming slumber.

Aria leaned forward as the Hawk 90 jerked to a slower speed. Looking out the small window by her side, she gasped quietly at seeing the swirling clouds directly beneath the Hawk. The aircraft trembled with turbulence. A low roaring sounded as violent winds crashed against the sides of the vehicle.

"Seems a storm has just passed through," Gavin's voice scratched through the speakers overhead. "My radar shows everything is clear, but it seems another thunder cluster-fuck is headin' our way."

"How long we got?" Aria called through her mental chip, pressing a finger against the small bump behind her ear. Her breaths were heavy from the oxygen mask covering her face's lower half.

"Looks like fifteen, twenty minutes. Once that storm hits, I don't know if I can keep in contact with you. I'll have to set her down somewhere or pull her away from the island at a safe distance. Judging by the size of this thing, it looks like you guys could be down there for a while." The pilot tapped on the compass on his instrument panel. The red pin spun wildly from side to side. "Looks like an electrical storm, too. You guys may want to make a mad dash for it. I don't know how bad this thing is, but if it's already messin' with my gauges, I don't want to be in the air when it hits."

"Okay, Gavin. Try to keep in contact the best you can. I'll try setting my GPS. If you don't hear from us for a while, I want you to try to get an overhead view of our situation once the storm passes." Aria gripped the parachute, tugging the straps around her shoulders and

middle section over the top of her pressure suit.

"Don't worry. I won't leave you two stranded. If all else fails, I'll bring the cavalry." Gavin looked over his shoulder and smirked, giving Aria a wink from his seat in the cockpit.

Her eyes crinkled from her hidden smile. *"You get us out of this mess safe and sound, and maybe you'll get that date you always wanted."*

Troy tugged on his safety pack, switching gazes between the other two.

"Hot damn. That, missy, is a promise," Gavin hooted.

"Are you two done flirting?" Troy grumbled through his mental chip, kicking the cabin door open. *"I'd say ladies first, but I don't see any."* He made himself cross-eyed as he taunted Aria and quickly tugged on his goggles.

"You're the only lady here, Troy," Aria snarled and lunged forward, shoving the man from the cabin. *"Keep a close eye on us, Gavin."* She waved a small salute to the pilot, slipped her goggles over her eyes, and dropped weightlessly backward into the air.

Aria's limbs spread in all directions, pressed against the force of gravity. She felt heavy against the wind yet light as a feather as she fluttered toward the earth. It was a giant blue marble curving against space. A pale-white glow emanated on the horizon, filled with voluminous grey billows. Flickers of light danced across the charcoal clouds, filled with electrical storms humming and buzzing around the militants as they free-fell toward the lush land thousands of meters below. Large gulps of O2 filled Aria's lungs; the crisp air made her nose tingle. Her vibrant eyes watched the man below her. Troy slowly spun in circles, a gloved hand grazing the sides of the nearby black cumulonimbus clouds. Aria lifted her hand to the right, her fingers trailing through the vapor. A slight tingle ran across her fingertips, vibrating through the glove. It was an intense electrical storm.

A small bump jerked the woman back into an alert state. Troy had slowed up, running into her side. Aria glared at the man, but he only responded with an eye crease as he smiled at her. A violent flash lit up the area; a bolt several meters away dashed from one cloud to another, surging toward the earth. A deafening blast of sound erupted a second later, sending tremors through the couples' bodies. They met each other's wide-eyed stare.

"Uh," Aria mumbled before fading into a laugh, the sound muffled through her oxygen mask. Troy joined her, chuckling as the flashes of light danced around them. "Whoo-hoo!" Aria cheered loudly as another blast of thunder erupted angrily from the bolts.

Glancing at the altimeter on her DNAIS, she patted Troy on the shoulder and signaled for his parachute. They pulled the chords, their bodies jolting as the giant chutes fluttered open, high and wide, slowly bringing them safely toward the ground. They spiraled on the skyline and descended one after the other, Troy not so gracefully, onto the plush grass. Aria landed with her legs straight out, sliding back onto her feet. Troy dropped, boot heels chunking out the soil as he plunged onto his rear end. The woman detached herself from the parachute and unzipped her suit. She looked upward, removing her goggles and oxygen mask. The dark sky swirled like a typhoon around itself. The previously cerulean atmosphere was now a muddy mess of grey, browns, and even an ugly yellow as the storm grew broader and deeper. Aria felt as if the clouds would be close enough to touch in a matter of minutes. Violent streams of electric current spiraled from the dark masses; far off in the distance, a couple of funnels twisted and flickered violently. It starkly contrasted the vibrant green plant life where Troy and she currently stood.

"Damn…" Troy's voice interrupted the woman's serenity. He tugged off his thick goggles, gaping in awe at the landscape. His gaze drifted over the electric shocks flickering amongst the clouds, down toward the silver lakes occupying the bottom of a deep valley. The peaceful bodies of water rippled in the wind. Something caught his eye; a dark shadow passed over the scenery, reflecting against the slapping waves. "Hey." He pointed a gloved finger toward the sky. "You see that?"

Aria narrowed her gaze onto the shadow, then lifted her head. With a wide wingspan, flapping effortlessly through the storm, a black silhouette flew across the horizon down into the valley toward what appeared to be a desolate city.

"Yeah." She glanced at Troy. "Half-man, half-beast?" she inquired.

"Or some giant, great albatross," he suggested. Aria snorted. Troy had a thing for albatross. She didn't think it was because it was an extinct bird with a supposedly massive wingspan; he liked it because he thought it was a funny-sounding name. Troy loudly cawed as he trudged forward, waving his arms like an idiot with his parachute trailing behind him. The woman sighed, following him.

The rotunda seemed overly stuffy, slightly humid, with a stale stench. Dark-colored business suits packed the room, most of which dressed the bodies of the big-name CEOs owning most of the militaries and prime real estate of the city-states. James Clarke twirled his fingers around his wine glass, swirling the blood-red liquid; the color matched the floor-to-ceiling drapes of the vaulted room. The dry taste of the drink didn't help his already parched throat. He could sense the tension in the room. A few stares and murmurs directed his way from the suits.

"I just don't want to lose any more money than I already have!"

"Oh, please! What do household cleaners have to do with this disaster? I have three buildings that need rebuilding!"

"Well, I don't know about you, but my stock has risen substantially due to this disaster."

"Only because you are in the weapons business!"

"What can I say? War pays." A greasy smile spread over the bigwig's face. A couple of chuckles echoed across the room.

"My hospital is paying, that's for sure! I'm way understaffed as it is. I'll have to bring in doctors from the neighboring city-states! And that ain't cheap!"

"Did you hear about Jordania? Apparently, they were all wiped out last night."

"What do you mean wiped out?"

"Gone, off the grid. My sister-in-law's cousin owned a lot of the military up there. He lived in the city. I guess there isn't much left of the mess."

"What caused it? Those things?"

"I'm sure it's just some rogue military branch. Russite hasn't had much to say about the whole ordeal. I'm sure they're involved."

"It could be anyone's military, don't blame the Russites!" a burly man protested.

The arguing and complaining created a humming in the room. It was mindnumbing, hypnotizing in the waving sea of grey overpriced double-breasted suits—a contrast to the scarlet curtains, golden ceilings, and chandeliers that danced sparkling glints of light across the area against the glasses in every man's jeweled hands.

"And what do you plan to do about all of this?" Mr. Walten, a clean-cut young man with a good fashion sense, tapped on the honey-colored table centimeters away from James' hands. His caramel eyes matched the older man's. Walten, though the youngest, was the wealthiest man in the room. He had his fingers in nearly everybody's pie—home products, medicine, agriculture, natural resources, weapons and defense, and biotechnology. He was the CEO and owner of Bio-Tech Military Corporation and fifty other industries. He was also James Clarke's boss, the one who pulled the strings and made all the final decisions with the company.

"Well, it's currently under investigation." James shuddered beneath the dozens of eyes upon him. "I've got a unit deployed investigating a received tip."

"A tip?" Walten smirked, sipping from his glass of brandy. Slowly, he ran a hand through his slick, chestnut-colored hair.

"We're still unsure who the person is or whether he is a friend or foe, but it merits investigation. I've also deployed multiple units to designated locations worldwide, areas where we can only speculate future encounters may occur. As of now, nothing is conclusive." Mr. Clarke coolly drank his tart wine.

"Of course not. Nothing is conclusive when you're talking about monsters, right?" Walten laughed. Many others throughout the room mimicked the hollow sound.

"We're unsure as to whom or what attacked us. That is also under investigation. Dr. Camery, our top scientist, is currently analyzing all collected data." James narrowed his gaze, not much liking Walten's amused look.

"I'm very interested, President Clarke, as to what, exactly, this tip is."

"It was the name of a location," he answered quietly.

"Oh, come on. We're all shareholders of the company. I'm sure everyone here would like to know how their contributions are used." A few murmurs of confirmation rallied in the room, leaving the President in a tough position.

"The location currently under investigation is Ives," James finally muttered through gritted teeth.

Laughter filled the rotunda. "Ives!" Mr. Walten giggled as he raised the glass to his lips, his expensive ring clinking against the diamond-cut crystal. "Investigating fairytales?"

"Do some research. You'll find the connections. There's a real possibility there could be private militaries set up there. A whole new civilization could have been born there over the past thousands of years. As asinine as it sounds, it certainly deserves its theories." Clarke's tone rose slightly as the laughter ensued. "I've got my best down there. If anything is there, they will find it."

Walten slammed his glass onto the table. Quickly gaining his composure, he straightened his crimson tie. "Mr. Clarke, I trust your intuition just as my father did. I wouldn't have allowed you to take your current position if I didn't. As such, I am extremely interested in hearing your results. However, let me remind you, we don't fund ghost hunts."

The roaring laughter continued. CEO Walten gave the President a slight wink and finished off his brandy. He clapped his hands together and politely dismissed himself, giving out numerous handshakes and pats on the back as he and the other elitists slowly exited the room, leaving the ruffled caretaker of Bio-Tech to himself. James gave a small salute with his glass and emptied its contents.

"This is the place?" Aria muttered under her breath. She eyeballed the man next to her.

"Seems so." Troy looked over his shoulder at the hilltop where he and Aria had earlier landed from their HALO jump.

The two stood before an ancient structure destroyed thousands of years ago. It was a Gothic style with towering steeples that decorated the rooftops with sharp angles and intricate designs. The flying buttresses gave the illusion the fortress had wings. Parts of the arrangement were decayed, falling to pieces into the grey waters below. At one time, it seemed the walls were white but now stained with the ash and blood of war. The bridge before the two militants, who stood gaping at the scene, stretched above the lake, connecting about four hundred meters away to the entrance of the building. Bulbous clouds of white and grey threatened the chance of rain upon their heads, partially hiding the joyful light of the sun. The kingdom wasn't near what it used to be. Its elegant beauty was now that of a corpse whose memory had also faded into oblivion.

"Well, shall we?" Troy held out an arm for the woman.

"We shall." She cocked her head to the side, still scrutinizing the ancient ruins.

Together, they walked across the thin bridge, cautious of the missing support beams and spots with holes. Both thought quietly about how the trip had better been worth it. They had to drop from the Hawk 90, passing storm clouds only the suicidal would think of going through, and traveled for kilometers across rough terrain, avoiding creatures that modern text systems lacked a definition. Not to mention, Ives was an abandoned continent. No souls were ever granted access to Ives under any circumstances except theirs, of course. And it was all for the sake of ending up at some ancient ruins with the possibility of never being able to return home. Especially if Gavin couldn't find an entry point for his copter, let alone figure out the militants' location, as their GPS systems weren't working due to the electrical storms.

They approached the monstrous door made of stone with wooden designs beaten into it, all precious gems and gold removed after the empire's fall. The door was heavy and slow to move, but nothing a hard shove from Troy could solve. The woman contently watched as he struggled to squeeze through the tiny gap.

"Look at this place," Aria whispered as she slid close behind Troy.

It was dark and damp inside the structure, with trickling water echoing through the massive hall. A soft roar came from the distance—that of a gushing waterfall. Aria grinned with excitement. It was like something from a dream, and she couldn't wait to explore the place. Light flooded the center of the room from a small hole in the roof. Ghostlike dust particles floated through the beam like a fog. She took several steps forward, staring at the arched ceiling at least thirty meters from the ground. Undecipherable writings and frescos were imprinted on the walls. Squinting, Aria leaned forward but stopped mid-step as Troy tugged her back.

"W-what?" she asked, confused.

Troy had one hand on her shoulder, holding her still. The other hand pressed a pointed finger to his lips, telling her to stay quiet. His gaze wandered to a dark corner behind a marble pillar. Her eyes followed his, and they widened once she heard the voice.

"Trēאt, μērçℓϕϋλ יהוה." A tall, dark figure materialized from the black shadows. The voice vibrated with a deep, rich tone, speaking in an unrecognizable tongue. "€ הϋμæλē μ'ßēλϕ æēϕörē 'öϋ." The words were foreign indeed, but the way they sent chills down Aria's spine made her realize it was a language no longer used by anyone—a forgotten, ancient dialect.

The figure walked toward the light with his hands supine and lifting. He wore a robe, dark in color like ash. A scarlet coat sat atop the clothing with a large hood that hid the man's features, the long sleeves and drapes hiding the rest of him. Thick strands of the material crossed over his torso, wrapping around the abdomen beneath an armored waistband, dangling toward his feet. The dirty fabric of his matching red cape dragged slowly behind him, creating a cloud of dust as he moved.

Was he a priest watching over this ancient cathedral?

Troy and Aria remained silent, not knowing whether it was a good idea or not to interrupt the man. Ives was supposed to be abandoned; no man could live there. They watched a moment longer, and Troy held his breath once the figure froze. There came no more speaking, no sound at all. The mysterious man stood momentarily, staring at the light from the ceiling. Slowly, his head dropped, and he turned to look over his shoulder.

"Ŝℓњϕϋλ ͭⁿℓēвēß," the man mumbled a couple of words as he turned. Darkness shrouded him. Only one feature was noticeable—he had the palest of blue eyes. They seemed to glow the way the moon did on a cloudless night. He tilted his head, observing the two intruders. That was when Aria noticed he was monstrous in height.

"Um…hi," Troy managed to speak. He gestured a small wave toward the stranger. Aria elbowed her partner in the ribcage, rewarding her with a short, dissatisfied grunt.

"€δℓöt," the mysterious man muttered some more.

"You live here?" Aria asked quietly. She doubted he could understand a thing she said. The man hadn't seen civilization in a long time.

The tall stranger stared at his wrist, the robed sleeves sliding down his forearm to reveal a metallic armband with intricate designs and glowing lights. He poked at it a moment. A small chime sounded, echoing down the massive hall.

"Of course," the man replied. His voice sounded low like a hum when he spoke their vernacular. He had a regal-sounding accent and was a pro at the dialect. "Legacy isn't the only language I know."

"Legacy?" Troy and Aria glanced at each other.

"That's what you were speaking just then?" Troy asked the tall man. He appeared at least two head lengths taller than Troy, and Troy wasn't short.

The foreign man did not speak. Instead, he turned away and strolled back toward the light. Staring upwards, he allowed the beam to cross his face.

"What brings you here?" he finally asked. "I'm afraid there is no treasure left. It was all pillaged thousands of years ago. Probably all decayed themselves by now."

'How old is this guy?' Aria and Troy shared the same thought.

"We came for some information," Aria spoke up.

"Of what? The texts here are all in Legacy. You won't be able to understand a word of it. There are few translation books in your language, but I doubt they are what you seek." The man soaked up the light as if drinking water.

"We were told to come here. That we could find some answers," Aria offered.

"And what answers are you seeking? Perhaps I can be of assistance?" he muttered dryly. He didn't seem interested in them at all.

"Well, it's kind of hard to explain, you see," Aria sputtered about incoherent words. The man sighed irritably.

"We came to gather information on the enemy." Troy stepped forward. The stranger glanced to the side, acknowledging that he was listening. "Aria and I are at war. We—"

"War with what?" He closed his eyes.

"These beasts, we have no idea where they came from." Troy talked with his hands. He struggled to explain what kind of creatures they had faced at the I.R.B.

"What type of beasts?" Icy-blue eyes glared.

"…Demons." Aria joined Troy's side. Her partner gave her a bewildered look.

"Demons?" The dark man chuckled.

"I guess you could say we're on a full-out war with Hell," Troy scoffed, giving up on trying to sound logical.

"Hell…." The man stayed silent for a moment, deep in thought. "Then, that means the veil's been torn?"

"Veil?" Troy and Aria questioned.

"But it can't be. It's too early. Or is it already that time?" he mumbled, forgetting the other two were in the room. "That would prove the prophecy correct, however…."

He glanced at the two, anger in his eyes. Aria took a step back.

"You damn Homo sapiens. What have you done now?" The foreigner clenched his jaw, squeezing the bridge of his nose in irritation. "Haven't you had enough war for this lifetime?"

"Whoa, wait a minute," Aria laughed nervously, "you just called us Homo sapiens."

"That's correct," he stated casually, as if the others were idiots.

"What the hell does that make you then?" Troy folded his arms. He thought the man standing before them was a little nuts.

"I," the stranger held his arms out into the light, "am a Sorcēarian."

"Sorcēarian." Aria raised an eyebrow. "As in the ancient race from thousands of years ago?"

The man nodded in response.

"Ridiculous." Troy snorted. "I can't believe we came all this way for a crazy man."

"A useful, crazy man." The supposed Sorcēarian nodded. For how intimidating the Sorcēarian was, he sure did have a strange sense of humor.

"There are no more Sorcēarians. They were all killed in the war a *long* time ago." Aria gave him a look of disbelief. "Who are you, really?"

"My name is Dovian, son of Gaius III, civilian of Ives, warrior of the Sorcēarian Empire, Scarlet status." He bowed his head slightly.

"And how old are you supposed to be?" Aria decided to play along.

"Too many years have gone by." Dovian thought a moment. "What year is it?"

Giving in to the question, Aria answered, "Mille 19."

"Mille 19. You mean nineteen millennia? What's the *exact* date?" Dovian asked.

"Um, 19,999 S.F." She shrugged.

"S.F." Dovian smirked. "Then I suppose I am a little over seventeen millennia," he replied dryly.

"Right…." Troy rolled his eyes. "Well, if you don't mind, we'll be leaving now." He grabbed Aria's arm and tugged her toward the door.

"What are you doing?" she asked through gritted teeth.

"We're leaving. This man's a nut," he replied aloud.

"Not a nut," Dovian retorted, "a sorcerer."

Troy and Aria stopped.

"Then prove it, nut job." Troy spun around quickly, his shouldered weapon thumping against his back.

"If you wish." The man named Dovian gave Troy a stern look. He extended his arm, palm out. A loud scraping sounded from the corner of the room. In a flash, a large rod grated across the stone floor and landed smoothly in his hands.

"Nice trick." Troy nodded, still skeptical.

"Troy," Aria growled, nudging him again in the ribs. She saw a smile cross Dovian's face as he turned toward the light. He shouted something in Legacy and pointed his staff at Troy's chest. A crystalline ball sat between two tall, golden wings at the tip of the silver pole. The orb brilliantly flashed for a split second, like lightning.

BAM!

Troy flew back ten meters against the heavy door of the fortress, the impact slamming it closed. He hit the ground hard, his arms and body limp.

"Troy!" Aria shouted. She reached for the rifle slung over her shoulder.

"Nah-ah." At her side instantly, Dovian brought the rod's tip down hard on her hand. Aria cursed, rubbing the backside of her already bruising appendage. She looked fearfully at her companion, who struggled to push to his feet.

"Very…nice…trick." Troy wheezed. "Damn, Sorcēarian."

Dovian stood before the two, light cascading behind him, giving him an ethereal glow. His eyes hinted at amusement, saying, *"I told you so."*

"But I thought you all were extinct." Aria frowned.

"We are," the man replied in a low tone. "I am the lucky sole survivor of my race." He set his staff onto the ground and released his hand. The weapon stood upright by itself, waiting for its master.

"That's terrible." Aria placed an arm around Troy to help give him support.

"Could be worse," Dovian muttered as he looked cautiously about the room. He appeared paranoid that someone was listening. "I could have died as well, and then there would be no one to help you defeat the enemy," he almost whispered.

"Then, that means you'll help us?" Troy asked. He hissed in pain when Aria assisted him, leaning against one of the nearby pillars. Not only was his pride damaged, but so was his tailbone.

"Not quite." Dovian stared into nothingness. "You see, I can't choose sides."

"Why is that?" Aria asked, disappointed. He did not reply. He only stared into her eyes; the look froze the woman in her place. After a moment, he nodded slowly.

Dovian took a step back into the light he had been enjoying earlier. He lowered his head. His hands clenched as he held onto his chest and breathed in slowly. Aria and Troy watched curiously. The Sorcēarian chanted in his ancient language once again. His fingers squeezed tighter and tighter, tugging at the cloth around his torso. His voice resonated with a low growl as he spoke. A sickening snap, like bones breaking, echoed within the chamber. His veins violently bulged as he hummed. The couple warily eyed each other.

"Λℓгⁿt," a guttural sound emitted from the man's throat.

There came a whooshing resonance followed by a nasty split. The man curved forward; the robe he wore moved about his back. Up and down, the cloth traveled, and out sprouted a wing—one like an angel's. Feathers of white and silver coated the wing and glittered in the sunlight. He had only one flapping appendage. Where was the other?

"Do…most sorcerers have wings?" Troy swallowed hard.

"This is light," Dovian murmured. "But there is more." He stepped to the side, splitting his body in half by the beam of light and the dark shadow of the cathedral. He fell forward again, and a similar chant commenced. Aria and Troy watched again in interest until silence followed. Dovian's hand fell to the ground, nails digging into the stone.

"∆ℵrk," a frightening voice deeper than anything Aria or Troy had ever heard called out.

Another crack followed, and a second wing popped from the other side of the man's back. It was the polar opposite of the first—pitch-black. Instead of feathers, shiny black scales covered the surface. A thick ivory horn protruded from the tip of the wing. Aria and Troy gaped at the flapping set, and a soft chuckle rumbled from the sorcerer, giving the woman goosebumps. Dovian's eyes glittered in the darkness like diamonds.

"This is why I can't choose sides," Dovian's voice echoed in his chest. "I *am* both sides."

The two were speechless. The man just sprouted wings out of his back. He was half-demon, half-angel.

'*Half-man, half-beast,*' Aria thought, her mouth open. Was this man in an all-out war with himself?

"Proof enough of my heritage?" He turned his menacing gaze toward Troy.

"Proof enough." The young man pushed away from the pillar to stand upright.

"I heard that there was a Sorcēarian once…who could manipulate both light and dark." Aria thought of a fairytale she had read as a child. "But that was just a story, was it not?"

"Many had the powers to manipulate both, but almost all found themselves slaves to the power once transformed." Dovian lowered his gaze. "I, for one, have difficulties."

"Did something bad happen?" Aria asked. Troy watched the woman. Why did she pity this man? Dovian didn't get hit halfway across the fortress.

"You could say that." His eyes lifted. He held his hands out to his side. He looked left and then right, taking in his surroundings. "My home."

"You did this?" the woman gasped. "How could you? You destroyed your people?"

"It's one of the many things that come with being a Sorcēarian. You're left with too many choices and too many desires. Perhaps we were a race meant for extinction, but I will not fall until I've redeemed myself." The man sighed, tugging his arms inward. He glanced through the hole in the ceiling as the light faded behind the dark clouds overhead. "Once consumed by either light or dark, I can lose control. What I do is not always my decision." The light dissipated, his angel wing turning dark grey. Rapidly decaying, the white, fluffy feathers charred and fell to the floor one after another. "I change depending on my mood…or whatever the weather decides. For now, it says darkness." His eyes closed as the final feathers evaporated, and his angel wing began to fester and blacken.

"W-what do we do if you change into a dark angel?" Aria slowly raised her weapon, worried about his new transformation.

"I would suggest getting away from me by at least a twenty-five-kilometer radius." Dovian smirked, revealing a white fang out of the corner of his mouth. His hands clenched, and he grunted as the wings projected back into his dorsal side. "No worries. I can control the urges much better than when I was a mere…child." They all stood silently, Dovian taking steady breaths to end his theatrics. He remained where the daylight had previously been. As there was no light to see, he waved a hand over his staff. A burst of flame erupted inside the crystal ball.

"You did this when you were a child?" Aria glanced at the fallen pillars and crushed statues covering the marble floor. Dovian only looked about innocently.

"Oh, this? That was nothing." He cocked his head to the side. "Sorcēarians have unique strengths. A child of your kind vastly differs from a child of mine. And a child to us isn't perceived the same as a child to you."

Aria only wondered what his potential was now that he was over seventeen thousand years old.

A skittering sound echoed in the corner. Aria lifted her head, her thoughts extinguished. Dovian followed her actions. His brow furrowed.

"What did you bring in here with you?" Dovian glared accusingly at the scampering shadow running across the ceiling of his gothic temple.

"You sure we brought it in? This place looks like it could have had things like this living in here already." Troy slowly lifted his weapon.

"We haven't killed one of those yet." Aria followed her partner's actions.

The creature screeched something awful at the group down below. Crawling into the light, it hissed angrily. The beast hunched forward on all fours, its humanistic qualities contorted with joints pointed and bent backward. The mouth opened wide, allowing thick, stringy saliva to drop from piranha-like teeth to the floor. In the distance, there was an array of sounds. The sound of roars, screeches, tapping, and scratching slowly approached the team. Aria didn't know what was more frightening—these creatures or what Dovian would do to them for luring the enemy into his home.

"Whose genius idea was it to come to this damned place?" Troy muttered through closed teeth.

'*You Can't Be…*'

CHAPTER 8

The hissing and screeching rose in volume, surrounding the three in the cathedral's center. Dark shadows danced along the walls, moving across the pillars and banisters lining the upper balconies. There was no escape. Light from the holes in the ceiling cast across one of the creatures' backs, revealing sinewy muscle beneath lavish, dark-olive scales. It starkly contrasted the fiery-red mane running along the back of its scalp. Long pearly nails clicked against the marble stone, creating a panicked soundtrack for the approaching swarm.

"Well, any ideas?" Aria asked.

"Are you asking me?" Dovian grumbled, calling for his staff to return to his hand.

"You're the one with all the experience, right?" Troy circled to the side, watching a lingering beast as it leaped from one wall to another.

"Age doesn't always signify experience. Remember that," the Sorcēarian spoke lowly. "But, yes, I am probably more knowledgeable about these demons than you are."

"Are you sure they're demons? I mean, can't they be some weird mutants? Or aliens?" The male soldier fumbled nervously around the rubble on the ground.

"If it were any of those other things, would it make a difference?" Icy eyes glared at the young man.

"No. Suppose not."

"We can discuss the origins of these creatures later," Aria spat. She fired an EMP grenade at a soaring monster, its elongated hands reaching out for the woman, mouth open, baring razor teeth and dripping saliva.

The grenade hit the creature square in the chest. It flopped onto the ground, convulsing as the electromagnetic static shocked its system. This signaled the start of the battle. An onslaught of beasts jumped from the ceiling and walls, all shrieking and snapping in ferocity. Troy and Aria continued firing, alternating between EMPs and live rounds, the blasts slapping against the enemies' small, muscular chests. With their incredibly lengthened arms, the creatures' anatomy differed slightly from those at the I.R.B., but the weaknesses were the same.

"I see you two have figured out much on your own already," Dovian said in an interested tone. He lifted his staff to the side and smacked his hands together, sandwiching the item. A thunderous boom echoed, and a pale blue wave of light gushed outward across the church, causing violent tremors within the monsters' bodies.

"We did some homework before coming here," Aria replied. She reached back into her knapsack and loaded another massive clip onto the front of her rifle. Troy spun to her side and fired with her, releasing impact grenades. The blasts annihilated at least five separate beings, sending sickening, fleshy debris to the corners of the room.

"Not the most glamorous of tactics." Dovian frowned. He spun his rod, smacking one of the creatures atop the head. It disintegrated into ash. Following up with a couple more blows, he quickly dismissed a dozen foes in the same manner.

"Whatever works, right?" Troy shouted, sending another two blasts to opposite sides of the room. Explosive booms drowned out the constant hisses and screeches as the two soldiers destroyed the creatures with regular grenades.

"Indeed. Even barbaric traits come in handy, especially when outnumbered." The sorcerer twisted in a circle, mentally calculating the rising number nearing him. Aria watched from the corner of her eye. There were too many. Dovian was surrounded, and more entered the center.

Troy grabbed a SABO from his pack and hurled it toward the mass surrounding Dovian. The blades ejected around the center of the grenade's core, spinning wildly. It twirled like a boomerang around the crowd that reached for the ancient man, slicing off the creatures' upper limbs. It slowed a few of them down, but others steadily approached. Dovian gave an amused glance toward the other man.

"Interesting weapon of choice, dismembering the enemy." He smiled. "I think I'll give it a try."

Dovian slammed his palms together again, surrounding the center of the silver rod. Another pale wave gushed around him, rendering the enemy momentarily defenseless. The sound was deafening, much more violent than the last. Then, the Sorcēarian moved. Dancing with speed and grace, the giant man spun, a master with his weapon. He twirled the staff over his head; with all their pointed edges, the forged golden wings atop it were used as blades, slicing horizontally across the first round of foes' upper skulls. He twisted at his waist, curving his arms around to cut on the opposite side to make a complete circle. The sorcerer was powerful and seamless in motion as he twisted, pushed, and pulled his body and staff from side to side, expertly annihilating the creatures surrounding him. The waves of demons quickly diminished; some backed away, returning to their places high upon the domed ceiling. Aria watched in awe as Dovian continued tirelessly. He was like a machine, instantly calculating and predicting the monsters' following movements.

A blast close by made the woman jump. Troy pinned one of the beasts against the wall beside her, the blade of a SABO cutting its throat. He joined her side, gaping at the sight ahead of them. Most of the monsters had strayed away from the two humans, more concerned with the current threat—the millenniums-old Sorcēarian in the room.

Dovian lunged forward, his rod cutting through the torso of one fiend, impaling it. He pulled out to the side, cutting through it and into another. Chopping and slicing, the man was brutal. As Dovian concerned himself with the final five monsters before him, one lingered in the shadows unnoticed, crawling on all fours, waiting for an opening to attack. Another flash from the orb of Dovian's staff sent a wave, heaving back the last few, burning their bodies to the ground. The lingering beast from the shadows took a chance, running forward and pouncing. Dovian spun, his hood finally falling. His arms lifted, rounding the staff overhead, and he brought it crashing down. The symbolic demon wings' razor-sharp edges crushed against the reaching, leaping beast's skull, pushing it down chin-first into the marble floor in a violent crunch, hot blood pooling beneath.

The sorcerer stood still, the sunlight flooding across his face, reflecting against his surreal silvery-gold hair. His sapphire eyes glowed brilliantly with excitement. Yes, Dovian was very barbaric, indeed. He was a dangerous asset that Troy and Aria desperately needed. And he fought off so many, so effortlessly, without a single twitch of one of his wings. One could only fathom the amount of damage Dovian was capable of when consumed by his powers.

"I assume that when one asks for help, they partake in the endeavor themselves." Dovian quickly tugged the weapon from the monster's skull and straightened his posture. His eyes were a cerulean wildfire, his hair a glittering mess that seemed to emit its own light. "Not simply watch."

"They seemed to think you were more of a threat." Aria cleared her throat nervously.

"And you handled them so easily." Troy gawked. If he had any doubts about Dovian before, they were all quickly dismissed.

"Yes, but there are still many more lingering about. In fact, we best leave." The sorcerer narrowed his gaze toward the front door.

Aria and Troy quickly turned to exit the front, but Dovian shouted, "No! Quickly! This way!" The two others slid to a halt just as the door burst open, countless more clambering in.

"Shit!" Troy shouted.

The two spun on their heels and darted after Dovian, following his billowing robes closely. Shrieking and scratching echoed all around. Aria's neck hairs stood on end as she felt the evil presence approach nearer and nearer.

"We can't run forever!" she hollered.

"Just follow closely! I know a way we can escape," Dovian called over his shoulder.

As they sprinted down the corridors, monsters jumped from all sides, already above the three. The echoing of the stone chambers made it hard to detect the creatures' locations. Marble debris and statues littered the floor, creating obstacles along the way. The cathedral was massive, beautiful, and dark. Aria couldn't help but think how amazing it would be to have the time to sit and analyze every tiny detail, see the faces of each sculpture, and try to read the stunning language written along the walls. Ives was once a magnificent paradise of white stone and brilliantly colored robes. Now, it was a haunting tomb packed with hellish monsters.

Aria stumbled over a fallen pillar, slightly losing balance. A clawed hand gripped her boot heel, and she gasped out loud. Dovian glanced over his shoulder and fired a single burst of energy down the hall, slowing the creatures down.

"Quickly, in here." The Sorcēarian turned into a side room. Troy and Aria hastily filed in before Dovian swiftly shoved the door closed and bolted it. He mumbled something in Legacy; the words on the door sparkled momentarily, then faded to dull scratches. "Damn…."

The room they were in was small, like a private chamber. An old fireplace, ornate with engraved designs, occupied one side of the room. A desk sat beside it with what appeared to be strange, tall lamps for reading. On the opposite wall was a bookshelf, a small library packed with foreign texts. Next to it sat a long chaise with blankets draped over the sides. The objects all belonged in a museum. It was astounding that everything remained in good condition. Sorcēarians sure knew how to make their things last.

"Well, what do we do? Jump?" Troy asked sarcastically. He stood near a ledge by a broken balcony on the far side of the room opposite the entrance. The chamber opened to the outdoors with a magnificent view of Ives. He looked over the edge at the gushing grey waves hundreds of meters below. If they jumped, there was no way he and Aria would survive the impact, even if they hit the water instead of the massive boulders set against the edge of the immense architecture.

"It's been a while since I've dealt with humans," Dovian muttered.

"What? You forgot that we can't fly?" Troy asked incredulously.

A high-pitched hiss sounded from beneath the chaise.

"What is that?" Aria aimed her 36C.

A rather giant, plump lizard scuttled out from beneath the furniture. It watched Aria and Troy from its peripheral and neared Dovian. Its neck flaps expanded as its tongue poked the air.

"Wait, don't shoot." Dovian held up a hand. "It is only Hector."

"What is…a Hector?" Troy grumbled.

"Hector is a frilled monitor," Dovian said with pride. He gently patted the large lizard, Hector, on the head. "They are quite common on this island. My people engineered them long ago. They make for interesting pets."

"Dandy," Troy grumbled.

A loud pound on the door startled the bunch. Hector quickly skittered to the corner of the room near a hole in the wall.

"Go, Hector. It is not safe here anymore. Find the others. You must tell them what has happened today." Dovian spoke curtly to the lizard. Hector merely blinked his beady eyes.

"He is talking to a lizard, "Troy whispered to his partner.

Aria shrugged, watching the Sorcēarian as he spoke to the reptile.

"We are at war. Yes…*war*," Dovian slowly spoke as he said 'war.' Hector merely stared at the man. "No! You can feed yourself. You have plenty of fat to live off of." Dovian was a little crazy, but he was at least valuable. "Go! Now!" The lizard hissed loudly in return and finally scuttled into the hole.

The pounding continued, splintering against the solid wood. Even though it was enchanted to keep enemies out, the door was thousands of years old. It wasn't going to last long. Dovian rushed to the opening of the room. He placed his large hands around the railing and looked out, deep in thought.

"Aria?!" Gavin's voice called abruptly inside her mind.

"Oh, thank God!" Aria sighed with relief. *"Gavin! We're at the cathedral! Can you see us?!"* she mentally called out to the pilot.

"Yes! At least, I think I do. I've got a lot of life readings on my scanner. I assume you are one of those dots?"

"Yes! We are! But, all those other dots, those are bad dots! We've got enemies on our tail!"

"Holy! Aria, you and Troy need to get out of there! I'm rounding the corner of some old church."

"That's us! We're up high by the balcony! And Gavin, prepare for three to board."

Troy rushed to Dovian's side and wildly waved his arms, shouting, "Over here!"

"Three? You found someone?" Gavin questioned.

"Wait 'til you see him," Aria added.

Over the violent pounding on the door, hundreds of blows a second, the rumble of propellers echoed in the distance. Zooming around the corner of the cathedral, the Hawk 90 neared. Gavin pulled it close to the building, the side panels opening into the cabin.

"Okay! Better take a running jump!" Gavin called over the loudspeaker.

Dovian, Aria, and Troy all backed up against the far wall. The door crunched loudly; a hole cracked along one side; an arm snatched at Aria. The three took off, sprinting for the ledge with Troy in the lead and Dovian close behind. Aria, waving away the grasping hands, moved forward. Another loud bang occurred, and the door was off its hinges, flying behind the woman's heels. One after another, they jumped. Troy staggered into the cabin, spinning to ensure Dovian didn't need assistance. His eyes then fell on Aria. She had only a few more steps to take, but the door crashed, and dozens of monsters filed into the room. One chased after her on all fours, running wild like an animal. Aria jumped. The creature did the same. Something, however, caught Dovian's eye. Someone stood in the doorway, a dark silhouette with piercing eyes. Fear stilled the Sorcēarian.

"Catch her!" Troy shouted.

Aria reached, her right foot barely hitting the inside of the cabin as the left dangled in the air, snatched up by the beast's massive talons that tore at her flesh. She cried out in pain as she was pulled by the creature's weight, causing her to drop onto the floor. Dovian reached for her, gripping her fingertips, but the talons only tightened around her ankle. The monster swung violently on her legs, shrieking and chomping. It was cumbersome and wrenched with all its weight, and in an instant, Aria was torn from Dovian's hands, falling toward the raging waters below. Her shocked scream resonated down the valley.

"Aria!" Troy moved forward, but Dovian held him back.

"Hold this." He handed over his rod and swiftly dove out of the helicopter.

"The man's insane!" Gavin shouted, looking over the side of the Hawk.

"No kidding," Troy murmured.

Aria was free-falling. The creature no longer held her leg, but she heard it shrieking behind her. She reached toward the copter and saw Troy's worried look and the scarlet blur of Dovian falling headfirst after her. Two massive white wings burst from the man's back. Feathers trailed behind him as he picked up speed. Dovian's long fingers gripped Aria's wrists and tugged her upward into his chest. He carried her, zooming down toward the water. The woman screamed as they neared the surface, and the Sorcēarian pulled up, flying in a swoop back into the air away from the raging riptides and the drowning monster. Slowly, she let out a deep breath and relaxed, realizing her death grip on the man's neck. He looked away at the Hawk, his untamed hair blowing in the wind as he flew gracefully back inside the cabin. Dovian gave her a sideways glance with a slightly nervous look in his eye and gently set her on her feet.

"Ah!" Aria cried out. She fell to the side, and Dovian caught her and quickly set her into one of the seats.

"She's severely wounded," he murmured, looking at the nasty gash on her leg and ankle.

"Damn! Aria," Troy whispered.

It was bad, terrible. The cut was far too deep; blood seeped across the metal floor, dripping over the open side of the aircraft. Deep muscle tissue was torn and ragged, and a hint of something white poked through—bone, maybe? Troy covered his mouth, looking away. There's no way it would heal. She would lose her leg if she lived through the wound at all.

"Stay with me," Dovian spoke softly to the woman, cupping her face. Aria's glazed eyes struggled to focus on his—they were pale blue, light emanating from the pupils, vibrant against the crimson-red tattoos lining his eyelids. She swallowed thickly, feeling faint, and momentarily wondered if tattoos like that were painful. "This might feel strange, but it shouldn't hurt once I begin," Dovian said reassuringly. He turned his head to look at her ankle, revealing another vibrant tattoo lining his left cheekbone; it dipped toward his chin, the top pointing toward a small dot on his temple.

His large hands wrapped around her ankle, and Aria cried.

"Hold her," Dovian ordered.

Troy rushed to the woman's side, holding her arms down. Gavin joined the team, the copter flying at high speed to the opposite side of the island.

"What are you doing?" Troy asked, watching the sorcerer.

"Quiet…" Dovian murmured, closing his eyes. He mumbled in Legacy, something that sounded like a prayer. He raised his hand, drawing light from the orb of his staff into his palm, and he brushed it along Aria's leg. Quickly, her clenched jaw loosened, and her groaning stopped altogether. "Good," Dovian whispered. He pulled more light from the orb and repeated the actions several times, running his hands over the wounds.

"Holy shit." Gavin's mouth dropped open.

Aria's leg healed before their very eyes. Slowly, new muscle and skin formed over her wounds. Her fingernails no longer dug into the sides of the chair, and her previously fading eyes now held a vibrant hue. She gasped loudly, watching Dovian's hands rub against her calf.

"Shouldn't you be flying?" Dovian looked over his shoulder at the pilot.

"D'uhh…autopilot." Gavin gestured toward the cockpit.

"And the enemy could easily find a way to create further problems for us. That is if a raging storm doesn't hit first." The Sorcēarian gave Gavin a look most grave.

"Yeah. Right." The pilot nodded and quickly returned to his post, but not without giving Aria a winning grin and a thumbs-up.

"How does it feel?" Dovian gently asked the woman.

"Fine." She exhaled a laugh. Her eyes widened as she slowly bent her ankle and flexed her knee. "Even better than before!" She giggled again.

Dovian gave her a small smile and patted her knee. "Good. I was worried I may be a tad bit rusty." He met Troy's glare, and his face fell. "I assume everyone else is okay?"

"Fine." Troy sat in his chair beside Aria. He loudly let out a sigh, rubbing his brow.

Aria leaned forward and touched her ankle. She fed Troy a lovely grin. It seemed that Dovian's magic was also good at curing bad moods. Aria looked like a kid in a candy store.

"Feeling better?" Troy asked.

She bobbed her head, still smiling. Then she met Dovian's amused stare, and a pink tinge came to her cheeks. Was she seriously blushing? Troy rolled his eyes.

'You've got to be kidding me,' he thought.

The doors to the cabin slid closed, creating a silent vacuum as the Hawk 90 took the form of a jet. All remained quiet in the vehicle. Dovian's look hardened as he thought of the dark silhouette he had seen in the doorway. It had distracted him to the point where he could have lost Aria. The memory plagued him. Someone malevolent pulled the strings of this war, and that idea left a sour taste in his mouth.

"Where are we going?" Aria asked. Her little high finally faded.

"It seems we may not be going far," Gavin called out.

"What do you mean?"

"Storms," Dovian interrupted. "It is almost nightfall. You won't be leaving the island tonight."

"Then, where are we supposed to stay?" Troy asked in irritation. "Those things could be everywhere! How are we supposed to last the night with them running around?"

"There are some small ruins up north. We can hide out there. I trust this thing moves fast. We could possibly get there without the enemy following, but we'll have to leave early to avoid detection. I fear the worst is yet to come." Dovian narrowed his eyes, watching through the small, round window.

"I think I saw those ruins when I found an opening in the storm. It's pretty much out in the middle of nowhere, right?" Gavin asked.

"Correct," Dovian affirmed.

"Okay. We'll be there in five minutes!"

Dovian's eyes widened a little. "Your aircraft is much quicker these days."

"Bio-Tech has all the best toys." Troy nodded.

"Bio-Tech? That's where you are from?"

"Bio-Tech Military Corporation," Aria said.

"I'm assuming you've been experimenting with genetics again." Dovian frowned.

"You could say that. What do you mean *again*?" She watched the sorcerer with interest.

"You humans got in trouble for that once before. It creates unbalance."

"When? We've been messing with genetics for generations now." Aria smirked. "It's nothing new."

"I'm talking about a very long time ago." He paused, returning his gaze out the window. "Many times. Long before I was born even."

Aria wasn't sure what he was talking about, but Dovian's words and tone were slightly unsettling.

The Hawk jolted, the doors tearing open again to break into rotary blades. High-speed winds surged inside, startling the silent passengers. The helicopter slowly descended, nestling its rails onto the lush pasture. The whipping propellers sent a gusting breeze that flattened the surrounding vegetation, the blades of grass rippling like the waves in the ocean, flickering in hues of orange and purple.

"I'm gonna leave it in copter mode, guys, so we can make a quick getaway if needed," Gavin called out as the engine wound down.

Everyone descended from the Hawk, taking leery steps toward the small ruins a few meters away. The setting sun, casting a pinkish-orange light, quickly faded behind the black storm clouds. Dovian looked sadly upon the small hut, unmoving in the pasture. Aria took notice and stopped to look back. He shook his head and matched her look with a smirk as he held out a hand, telling her to continue.

"So, what exactly is this place?" Gavin curiously asked as he walked through the open doorway of the remains. He set his bags on the floor and hopped onto the stone countertop for what may have been a kitchen at one time.

"It was…a vacation home," Dovian stated quietly, looking about the room with tired eyes. "It belonged to a friend."

Judging by the look of the place, it seemed Dovian hadn't ventured to this part of the island in a long time. There was barely a roof left, and it appeared that not much more than a few lizards had traveled through, judging by the thick dust lining some of the broken shelves and ruined furniture.

"Well, I'm hitting the hay." Troy chuckled, patting his hand on a pile of overgrown grass in the center of the room. He plopped carelessly onto the heap, yawning loudly.

"We can leave at sunrise," Dovian assured. "The storms should lighten up by then."

The angry crackle of thunder and lightning responded to him. Like popping a balloon, gushing rainfall pounded against the tiny home, sending a drenching fall of water onto Troy and his grass pile.

"Son of a—" the man groaned.

Aria stifled a laugh. Gavin did not try much to hold his in, guffawing aloud and even pointing at his friend. Dovian merely watched the man as he pulled out an old chair to sit on. He rolled his eyes, muttering, "€δℓöŧ."

"What does that mean? *Hyd'ot?*" Troy asked, trying to articulate the word, giving a couple of awkward breaths and clicking at the end.

"It means much like it sounds—idiot." Dovian sat back in the seat. His weight instantly crushed the old item, and he ungracefully fell onto the floor. Troy, this time, joined in on Gavin's hooting.

"Hyd'ot!" the two men hollered, pointing at the Sorcēarian.

Dovian remained on the ground, staring at the cracked ceiling. A crooked smile crept over his lips.

"Hrm…" a slight groan sounded from the far side of the cottage.

"Holy shit, what was that?!" Gavin jumped off the granite countertop.

Dovian sat up, alert, as Aria and Troy slowly stood from the ground, grabbing their firearms. Another groan followed, and Dovian jumped to his feet, rushing to the front of the group. They took the small hall to the back of the home where a bedroom once was. Thunder boomed, and heavy rain poured in through the many holes in the structure, wetting down the Sorcēarian's hair. He held up a hand, telling the others behind him to wait, and he entered the small room, cautiously looking in every corner. Lightning flashed, illuminating the entire area; there was no longer a roof on this part of the house. The ancient man's eyes flickered as lightning flashed again, revealing a slender, nude body lying on the center of the floor.

"Oh, my God…is she dead?" Aria asked.

"She's so pale," Gavin whispered.

Dovian rushed to the woman's side, quickly removing his belt and scarlet ceremonial coat. He laid the item over the woman's body, lifted her into his lap, and wrapped it around her. She had alabaster skin. Her body was long and slender with tight musculature, soft-looking but hard. Long blonde curls framed her symmetrical face, curving around her collarbone. Pressing two fingers against her wrist, Dovian felt for a pulse. A frown wrinkled his chiseled features.

"How'd she get here?" Troy asked.

Dovian shook his head and reached for her neck, pressing slightly against the porcelain woman's throat. Nothing drummed beneath his fingertips. He eyeballed a chain around her neck, connecting to a small military dog tag. It only read 'Ivory.' It was a fitting name.

"Who is she?" Aria joined in.

"Her name is Ivory," Dovian's voice croaked.

At the mention of the woman's name, her eyes popped open—baby-blue orbs set behind long black lashes. Her slender hand lifted and painfully gripped Dovian's wrist. Frightened eyes met the man's, and her pale pink lips slowly parted.

"D-Do—" She gasped loudly, her eyes rolling back in her head as she passed out. Her bony fingers stayed wrapped around the sorcerer's wrist.

Dovian stared at the white beauty, flabbergasted. He was sure she was dead, but now, she breathed normally. Slowly wetting his dry lips, he stared at the woman's face. The curls flowed just right; her voice was small. How did someone like her end up here? And what was she trying to say? It almost sounded like his name. But that would be preposterous. No one would ever know his name, let alone some military woman. Still, there was something strange about the look in her eyes, the desperation in her voice. It left the man feeling a bit lost.

"We should get her out of the rain," Aria suggested. "I'll help dress her better." She bent down, grabbing Dovian's armored belt. Her bitter glare flew toward Troy and Gavin's direction. "Out!"

"What?" The two men shrugged.

Aria only hardened her scowl, and the two sighed and finally left the room.

"Are you okay?" Aria asked.

"Yes. Just a little confused, that's all." Dovian sat the woman in his lap carefully. They pulled the coat sleeves over the young woman's arms and cinched the article tightly around her waist, securing it with Dovian's armored waistband. He slowly stood, carrying the pale girl in his arms. Aria stared at the dog tag nestled securely between her breasts.

'Perfect eye candy for the other two men.' She sarcastically thought.

"Do you know her?" she questioned.

"No." Dovian removed his stare from the mysterious woman's ashen face. "I have no idea who she is."

"Dovian The Barbaric"

CHAPTER 9

The fire in the center of the living room area gave off generous heat. Flickering flame filled the small home with yellow light, causing contrasting shadows of black to dance across the walls. Soft snores merged with the sounds of the calm crackles as Troy and Gavin slumbered in nearby locations under the safety of areas where a roof still existed. Rain pelted softly against the stone floor as the storm slowly passed overhead, occasional thunder rumbling in the distance. Aria stared at the flame, sighing quietly. Despite feeling exhausted, she found it impossible to sleep. She unconsciously ran a hand gently through the blonde woman's hair in a silent daze.

"Can't sleep?" Dovian's voice quietly called out.

"Hm. You neither?" Aria shook her head, tearing her eyes away to look over at the robed individual sitting in the nearby shadows.

"I've had plenty of time to sleep." His blue eyes glowed in the dark hut. "With all the excitement lately, I imagine it will be hard for me to sleep in the coming days." Humor laced his voice.

The tall man rose from his position and made his way to sit beside the woman. He gazed wordlessly at the fire; the warm light bounced against the silver of his hair, creating an aura about his head. His icy eyes darted to the side as he looked at Aria, and that was when she realized she was staring.

"I noticed your tattoos." she pointed. Dovian remained silent, turning his gaze back to the flame. "Did they hurt?"

"No. It was quick and painless." He blinked, his long lashes momentarily covering the bottom lid's tattoo. "Our technology was always more advanced than yours."

"I can't imagine that. Even now?"

"I'm not sure. I'll have to study how advanced your world has become. But, judging by your weapons, I'd say your people are far behind, though you are more advanced than you used to be…before the Second Fall."

"Second Fall?" Aria murmured. "You mean as in Mille 0 S.F.?"

"Is that not what it means to you?" Dovian faced her.

"No one is really sure what it means anymore. I've heard of Second Fall; some dubbed it Final Sin, Sudden Failure," she scoffed, "and then something like Sine Fatum. Not sure what that means."

"Without fate," he spoke softly. His expression was one of pity as he gazed at the woman.

Aria sat silently for a moment. "You think humans are disgusting, don't you?"

"Not entirely, but most are. You all have more ego than humility. It's quite a curse," he spoke casually. Aria couldn't help but feel a bit irritated by his response.

"And your people weren't the same?" she gruffly asked.

Dovian's eyes narrowed. "My people were far more than you can comprehend."

"So, you think we're idiots, too?"

"Only uneducated," he paused momentarily, "clearly."

Aria glared at him in return. "It's been a long time since your kind has been around. Maybe things have changed."

"Not for the better," his voice lowered. "I can tell that already. If your *kind* were in good moral standing, you wouldn't be in the predicament you're in now."

Even though she wanted to argue, Aria decided to keep her mouth shut for a change. Besides, she knew the Sorcēarian was right. Humanity disgusted her. What kind of people kill themselves simply because of minor differences in eye color and dialect? The thought brought her attention back down to the woman resting beside her. Aria removed her hand from Ivory's golden locks, but not before Dovian noticed the gesture.

"How is she?" he asked, thankfully changing the subject.

"She seems to be doing all right. She moved earlier, so I guess that's a good sign." Aria's voice remained soft. "I can't imagine how she got here, and I don't want to know why." Her thoughts drifted to the woman's previous appearance—naked and cold, lying in the middle of some ruins out in the middle of nowhere on an unfamiliar island.

"In her condition, I cannot imagine one such as she would willingly come to a place like this in the nude," Dovian added, clearly matching Aria's thoughts.

"Bastards," she growled quietly. Dovian's eyebrow lifted in question. "She was probably raped and thrown out here, left to die."

The room suddenly became quiet, the air slightly stuffy.

"Your people do this type of thing regularly?" he asked.

"You could say that. I mean, she's lucky to be alive looking the way she does."

"What do you mean?"

"Well, she has very pale skin. Her hair is blonde unless she's dyed it, but I haven't seen a color like that in a while. I also noticed that she is tall." Aria listed things about the woman that Dovian thought were ordinary.

"And she has blue eyes. What's wrong with these traits?" he asked.

"Oh! Blue eyes, too," Aria chuckled. "In my city, people are killed thoughtlessly for naturally having any of those characteristics."

"Blonde hair and blue eyes are a bad thing?" Dovian asked incredulously.

"If a person is too tall or short, has any color of hair other than a brownish tone, eyes that are blue or anything other than brown-green, skin that's too light or dark, or—heaven forbid—an accent or dialect other than our own, then they are in danger of being harmed or killed." The military woman spoke simply of the matter. Dovian's expression, however, was one of horror. "Oh, and if you're disabled, have any genetic diseases, or anything like that…you're worse off."

"You humans are at an all-time low," Dovian whispered. "I can't fathom the ignorance of your society. In my time, a woman like her would be fought over." He added, "In a good way."

Aria glared at him. "What do you mean? She could be just as fake as the others. She could have dyed her hair and could be wearing optic enhancers. Hell, there are even dyes for your skin! If you're feeling extra daring, you can lighten and darken your skin to any shade desired. It's stupid, though, making yourself an easy target." She bitterly looked at the sleeping woman next to her. Aria couldn't help but feel a bit jealous of her. Was it all real? Could Ivory be so naturally beautiful?

"You speak ill of this woman. What would be the difference? She looks as she looks." Dovian stared at the sleeping Ivory. "And she looks beautiful. There's no doubt about it. Hate crime or not, she's a target for any predator."

It was true. Despite whatever color her skin or eyes were, Ivory was still attractive. Stories of unsavory happenings in Fountains and the Underbelly were a daily occurrence, so much so that society was nearly numb to it, as it was with everything else violent and cruel.

"And it's a bit hypocritical to say those things in such a venomous tone when you color your hair." He poked at Aria. "Unless you have evolved to have blue hair naturally." She gave the man a heated stare. When she began to speak, ready to let the Sorcēarian have it, a quiet whimper interrupted her.

"She's awake." Dovian's attention diverted.

Large blue eyes slowly opened with fluttering eyelashes as Ivory moaned. Slender fingers gripped Aria's pant leg as the mysterious woman warily lifted her head. She stared at the fire and lifted her gaze, taking in her surroundings. After a moment, she finally brought her attention to Aria. Ivory's eyes dropped to her hand, which gripped the other woman's clothing, and she quickly let go, pushing away onto her backside. Her frightened eyes met Dovian's, and she yelped, trying to scramble swiftly away. Aria took notice of her reaction. Dovian remained incredibly still.

"It's okay." Aria lifted a hand. "We're not going to hurt you."

"W-w-where?" a frightened, youthful voice erupted from the woman.

"You are in a small home on the island of Ives," Aria said slowly. "Do you know how you got here?"

"I-Ives?" She nervously looked over her shoulder. "I don't know. How did I get here? Who are you?"

Aria glanced at Dovian. He sighed, lowering his gaze to the stone floor.

"My name is Aria. I work for Bio-Tech Military Corporation. I'm a class A-5 operative. Everything will be okay. You are safe with us. I promise," she tried to reassure the young woman.

"And who are you?" Her blue orbs drifted to Dovian. A shuddering breath passed her lips as she felt scrutinized beneath the Sorcēarian's cold stare.

"I am Dovian," he introduced himself, rising from his seated position.

Ivory's eyes only widened when she saw how tall the man was. She gasped and cried, pulling her arms up to shield herself. "Stay over there!" She scooted away.

Dovian quickly melted to his seated position beside the alarmed Aria. He had forgotten how menacing his first impression could be to unknowing persons. The young woman continued to back up, colliding with the body sleeping behind her. A low groan sounded from Gavin. Ivory screamed, fully waking the pilot. Gavin's chocolate eyes popped open, and he shouted in fright at the proximity of her next to him. The cries then alerted Troy, who awoke with a start. He had his weapon in hand and aimed at the frightened woman within a second. How quickly everything turned into a disaster.

"Whoa! Wait!" Aria pushed to her feet. "Ivory, calm down!" She motioned for the woman to calm herself. "I need you to calm down."

"W-What?" Ivory stammered.

"What, what?" Aria asked with equal confusion.

"What did you say?" she asked timidly, looking around at the two baffled men on either side. Troy quickly shouldered his weapon, but he remained alert.

"I told you to calm down," Aria repeated. What was wrong with this woman?

"No, you called me Ivory. Is that my name?" The blonde trembled.

The room fell silent for a moment, excluding the heavy breathing coming from its occupants.

"You don't know your name?" Aria finally asked.

"I—" Ivory paused. Her face fell, and she looked lost, her confusion and innocence equal to a child's. "I can't...I can't remember anything!" Warm tears gathered at the corners of her eyes. "Who, who am I?"

She lifted a sleeve to her eyes, trying to dry the tears. Pulling back, she stared at the strange golden-seamed scarlet jacket decorated with shiny threaded designs. Patting down her torso, she trailed her fingers over the metallic woven belt. Seeing Dovian's concerned stare, her face contorted, and she sobbed. "And where are my clothes?!"

Ivory was pitiful—a tiny-framed thing with a head of messy curls and now rosy cheeks covered with giant, falling tears. Shuddering breaths shook her body violently as she cried into her hands. Troy and Gavin exchanged worried looks. Together, they pointed and gestured at one another until Troy sighed and apprehensively reached for the woman. His hand on her shoulder jolted her. She bounced to the side, gaping at him miserably as he slowly kneeled beside her. He didn't say anything, but his face looked concerned. After several sniffs, Ivory sobbed again as she wrapped her arms around the man's neck and cried into his chest. Troy hesitantly embraced the woman. He looked at Gavin with a wide-eyed stare; his friend smiled and gave an enthusiastic double thumbs-up. Troy's cockeyed grin quickly faded when he felt the searing glare from the other woman in the room—Aria.

After a few awkward minutes, the blonde finally detached from the male soldier. She took a couple of slow, steady breaths and spoke, "I'm sorry. I think I'm okay now."

"I was beginning to wonder," Aria muttered.

Ignoring the rude comment, Troy spoke quietly to Ivory. "Are you all right, physically? I mean, are you aware of any injuries?"

"No. At least, I think I'm okay." Ivory shook her head. Her small, shaking hands tugged on the corner of Dovian's coat. "I can't remember."

"Do you have any idea how you ended up out here?" Troy asked.

She shook her head again. "No. Like I said...I don't remember anything. I don't know where I am, where I came from, how I got here, or who I am." Another small whimper sounded from her, but she quickly composed herself. "I don't even know what Ives is!"

"Ives is my home," Dovian spoke up. Ivory gaped at him anxiously.

"Y-you live here?" her tiny voice cracked. She looked about the room in curious wonder.

"Not here in this house, but I live on this small continent. It's supposed to be restricted from any humans entering. The terrain and weather conditions alone are nearly impassable...." Dovian glanced at his new comrades. "Until now, that is."

"Humans?" Ivory looked at Troy, Gavin, and then Aria. "You mean you're not a human?”

"No. I am not a human," he answered.

Ivory's stare enlarged. "If you're not a human, what are you?" her voice squeaked. She hid behind her sleeves, looking up at the sorcerer.

Aria watched Dovian. He gave her a sideways glance and a small, crooked smile. Was he trying to scare this poor girl?

He watched the frightened Ivory from over the fire. "I am a Sorcēarian."

"…What's a Sorcēarian?" Ivory asked timidly. Dovian's amused expression quickly fell, and Aria snorted a laugh.

"He's a magician!" Gavin chimed in.

"A magician?" the woman's vocal tone perked up slightly.

"Yeah, he can use magic and stuff. Come on, Dovian! Show her a magic trick." The pilot grinned.

Dovian huffed, "I'm a sorcerer, not a magician."

"Aw, what's the difference?" Gavin feigned ignorance, trying to irritate the older man.

"I don't pull rabbits out of my hood," Dovian answered dryly.

"…But you could?" Gavin pointed.

Dovian ignored the man, turning his attention back to the flames.

"I-I like magic," Ivory spoke up. "I mean, I don't know if I've ever seen it before, but it sounds lovely."

Aria smirked. "Come on, Dovian. The lady wants you to show her a magic trick."

Dovian's glare slowly faded as he met Ivory's hopeful gaze. The woman had an innocence that Dovian hadn't seen for most of his life. He sighed, realizing he could only gain Ivory's trust by appearing kind and not frightening her. He patted his hand on the stone floor beside him. "Come over here."

Ivory froze, unsure if she should leave Troy's side. She gazed at the soldier beside her.

"Go on; he's not going to bite." Troy gave her his charming smile, which Ivory quickly met with one of her own.

Carefully, the woman stood and crept warily over to Dovian's side, bare feet patting against the stone. Her hands nervously gripped the silver dog tag around her neck. Dovian's brilliant, electric eyes dimmed slightly, and he slapped the floor again. Ivory quickly plopped next to the Sorcēarian. She stared at him, chewing on her lower lip.

"Let's see," Dovian groaned as he reached behind to grab his silver and gold-plated staff. He rolled it between his hands, showing Ivory the golden wings and orb on one end. She admired the craftsmanship, smiling eagerly. "Do you like butterflies?" he asked.

"Butterflies?" Ivory thought a moment.

"You've never seen one?" His face fell.

"They've been extinct for a while now. We only get to see old images of them in schools and museums," Aria replied.

"They have a funny name," Ivory added.

"Okay." Dovian smirked. "How about I show you a butterfly?"

"That would be lovely! You can do that?" Ivory leaned forward.

The other three humans also tilted forward, all interested in what Dovian had planned.

"Hold out your hand," he spoke softly to the woman. Ivory complied without much hesitation. Pulling the staff to the side, he held the ball and mumbled something in Legacy. Ivory's mouth hung open as the man spoke the strange language. Soft blue lights flickered inside the orb, rotating around each other like tiny atoms. After speeding around with a whirring noise, the particles burst into a wave of light, forming a flapping butterfly.

"Whoa!" Gavin laughed, slapping his hands together.

"It's wonderful!" Ivory giggled. She eagerly leaned across Dovian, looking into the glass ball. The blue butterfly danced wildly inside.

"Hand." Dovian lifted the woman's hand and turned it palm up. He tapped the ball against her fingers, and the butterfly bounced through it in a burst of light, landing in her palm.

"Look at it," she whispered. "It's the most beautiful thing I've ever seen." Its wings flapped madly, casting bright blue lights across the woman's face. Quickly, it lifted and fluttered over the fire. "You can create life?"

Dovian's face hardened momentarily before answering, "No. I can only imitate it."

The butterfly fluttered in a full circle before annihilating itself into the flames of the small fire before them. Ivory gasped. She quickly looked at Dovian with sadness in her eyes. "But sometimes imitations can be just as good as the original, right?"

The Sorcēarian watched the flames. "No," he replied in a low tone, "imitations are never as good as the original."

"Aw, come on! Don't be such a downer. You just pulled a butterfly out of your ass! That's pretty awesome if you ask me!" Gavin cheered, trying to lift the mood.

"I pulled a butterfly out of my ass?" Dovian inquired. "Your expressions are quite odd."

"And you talk like an old man," the pilot jeered.

Ivory giggled.

"Do you find me amusing?" Dovian eyeballed the blonde beside him.

"Well, you are a little strange," she chimed.

"You're all weird. I'm the only normal one here," Aria scoffed.

"Oh, please! You're far from normal!" Troy pointed accusingly at the woman. "Ivory, this woman here…she's got the biggest stick up her ass you'll ever see!"

"What?" Aria snarled.

"Aw, that's what makes her so great!" Gavin scooted against Aria, putting his arm around her shoulder. "She's full of sass!" He shook her gently and leaned forward, his lips pressing against her ear. "And we've got a date when we get out of here, right?" His warm breath sent shivers down Aria's spine.

"Gavin!" She tried to push the man away, her face beet-red.

Ivory gawked at the two.

"Trust me! She's as sassy in all departments of life if you catch my drift!" The pilot winked.

"Gavin!" Aria shouted again, shoving the man.

"Ew! No! Aria, you didn't!" Troy gasped mockingly at the military leader.

"Why do you two insist on making my life a living hell?" Aria covered her face in embarrassment.

"Oh, my." Ivory giggled, holding a slender hand to her lips.

"What's so funny?" Aria looked over her hands at the blushing blonde.

"Are you two dating?" Ivory pointed at Aria and then Gavin.

"Why, yes, we are!" Gavin hooted as Aria shouted, "No, we're not!"

"Well, I think you two would make a cute couple," the skinny blonde beamed happily.

"Hear that, sassy cat?" Gavin nudged the black-haired woman beside him. "We're cute together."

Aria ignored him, looking to the side to stare at the darkness.

"Well, are *you* seeing anyone?" Troy asked Ivory.

"Me?" She pointed at herself. "I, uh, not that I can remember." A small, nervous giggle passed her lips.

"Good! Cause I think you and I would make a cute couple." Troy jumped to sit beside Ivory and slung his arm over her shoulders.

"Oh." The woman fell silent and blushed.

"Why do I feel as if my IQ has dropped fifty percent in the last two minutes?" Dovian grumbled.

"Don't worry, Dovian. We'll find a hot female filled monitor to hook you up with." Troy waved dismissively at the Sorcēarian.

Once the joking and laughing subsided for the night, the crew slowly drifted to sleep. Morning came far too quickly; the thick, humid air left a sticky feel to everything. Pale morning sunlight eased through the holes in the ceiling and broken windows. Quiet cicadas and birds chirped in song. The soft howl of a breeze echoed in the tiny home, rustling the leaves and dust. Aria shifted and rolled over. Blinking, she rubbed the sleep from her eyes and yawned quietly. Everyone appeared to be asleep, and nothing seemed out of order. The sight helped her relax. Another breeze rolled through, and all of nature's song abruptly stopped. Aria froze, listening to the silence surrounding her. Nothing moved. Nothing chirped. She quickly reached for the sleeping Dovian beside her, tugging on the black sleeves of his robe. Her eyes fell on his face, and he looked back up at her, finger pressed to his lips and staff in one hand.

A loud shriek filled the air as the door to the small home flew open. Coming from the outside, the creatures from Dovian's cathedral darted through the front door, windows, and holes in the ceiling. Aria immediately opened fire with her 36C; the bursting of Troy's M4 joined her. She sighed with relief, knowing her partner was as perceptive as she was and ready for battle. Dovian thrust a shockwave toward the front of the room, sending multiple targets backward.

Alerted from his lazy slumber, Gavin quickly rolled to Aria's side. He reached into his knapsack and pulled out a small handgun—a new military-issued item. It shot liquid acid rounds, auto-aiming for the pilot. The military had gotten lazy over the years; all their new weapons had auto-aim capabilities and various ammunitions. The guns had pluses and minuses but allowed inexperienced soldiers like Gavin to defend themselves.

"Get behind me." Aria tugged Gavin behind her legs. He crouched beside her, shooting at the beings in the back of the home.

One of the creatures snatched Ivory, and she gave a shrill cry. Clawed hands gripped the collar of the red coat and dragged the frightened woman down the hallway. Dovian chased the beast, slamming a shockwave into the room and hindering all the others. Reaching the back bedroom, he aimed the staff toward the snarling monster as it climbed the wall, yanking Ivory. Dovian shouted, sent a lightning bolt of energy toward the beast, and hit it in the chest. The thing fell backward over the wall, dropping Ivory in the process.

"Are you all right?" Dovian rushed to the young woman. She gripped his arms and nodded as he lifted her to her feet. "Stay close. We need to get out of here."

Falling back into the main living area where the soldiers continued firing, Dovian had to ward off leaping attacks from the roof. The room was too confined to fight as he wanted. Spinning, he held the woman close to his chest as he slammed the end of the rod onto one creature's head. It fell to the floor in ashes. He followed up with a twist, tugging Ivory, and contacted another who attacked from behind. Darting to the living area's center, Dovian smacked his hands against the staff, and another burst gushed out, incapacitating the beasts.

"We need to leave now!" his voice boomed.

Luckily, the others had gathered their things and hurried toward the open door. Dovian continued blasting from his staff, sending wave after wave against the creatures, knocking them back. Gavin took the lead, leaping into the Hawk 90. He had it revved up with propellers moving in seconds. Aria and Troy backed toward the copter, firing relentlessly at the hoard as Dovian swiftly lifted Ivory into the cabin.

"Sit. Buckle up," he ordered. Ivory quickly complied. "Get this thing in the air!" he shouted.

Troy and Aria climbed inside and continued firing as the Hawk quickly lifted. A dozen beasts crawled out of the ruins like an infestation. Slowly, they faded away like tiny ants in the distance as Gavin flew the team toward the sea.

"Oh! What a way to wake up!" Aria sighed aloud as she limply dropped into the seat.

Troy followed her actions. "That was the worst alarm clock ever!" he groaned.

"What were those things?" Ivory whispered.

"I dunno. They just started attacking not even a week ago. We've never seen these things before, and they seem hell-bent on trying to take our military out," Troy said.

"You haven't seen them before?" she asked. Troy shook his head. "Have you?" She looked up at Dovian.

"Not for a long time," he answered slowly, sitting beside her.

"So, you do know what they are, right?" Troy asked; his face held a weary expression.

"I've already told you."

"Demons?" he scoffed. "Come on, really?"

"After all you've seen. You still don't believe?" The Sorcēarian gave the man a look of incredulity. "No wonder your world seems so upside-down."

"And you can honestly say that your world is any better?" a strange, deep male voice echoed within the cabin.

Dovian froze, eyes wide, as he registered the vocals. With hands gripping the chair, he struggled to catch his breath. "Euclid," Dovian's voice shook nearly above a whisper.

The mysterious man materialized from the shadows in the back of the Hawk. He wore cobalt robes similar to Dovian's. His long raven hair flowed over the right side of his face, cascading over his shoulders, and a sharp light flickered in his eyes, matching the blue tattoos lining his eyelids and left cheekbone.

"What the hell are you doing here?" Troy tried to aim his rifle, but Euclid beat him to the punch, swatting the item from the man's hands as he tugged him from his seat. He wrapped an arm around the soldier's torso and placed his long fingers around his throat, digging his jewel and gold-encrusted claw rings into Troy's flesh.

"Troy!" Aria stood with her rifle aimed at Euclid. Dovian had risen by this time and pointed his staff at the assailant. "Don't even think about hurting him," Aria growled, pulling back the charging handle of her 36C.

"My, my…somebody woke up on the wrong side of the bed this morning." Euclid smirked.

"I assume you're involved, somehow, with these attacks?" Dovian's voice lowered in tone.

"You seem surprised!" Euclid laughed; his pale blue eyes glimmered with amusement.

In an instant, Dovian lunged and tugged Troy from the man's grasp, clamping a large hand around Euclid's throat. "Do you mind telling me how that's possible?!" He viciously snarled. Their noses almost touched as Dovian pushed against the man, but Euclid stood much taller. Laughter fell from the raven-haired man's lips, only angering Dovian more.

"All things are possible if you make the right kind of deal," Euclid replied. Dovian's face paled. With his laughter rising in volume, Euclid shouted, "What's wrong, Dovian? You act like you've seen a ghost!"

Giving a violent shove, Euclid sent Dovian sailing toward the front of the cabin. Aria opened fire. The rounds disintegrated before ever hitting the man's body. He turned his cold gaze toward the woman. "It will take much more than that to stop me, love."

Dovian sprung back toward Euclid, but the man sidestepped, grasping Ivory's wrists as he unbuckled her. She cried out in fear as the cruel man held her to the side, dangling her outside the helicopter.

"No!" Dovian froze with his hand reaching out.

"Oh?" Euclid smiled. "You want her, Dovian?" He shook her, causing her to yelp.

"Your quarrel is with me, not her," the Sorcēarian's voice wavered.

"Is it?" Euclid tilted his head and released the young woman without hesitation.

"Bastard!" Dovian cursed and dove out the helicopter's side, charging after Ivory. Everyone fell silent as Euclid turned his eager gaze toward the two militants.

"Since that minor problem is taken care of…let's do something about you." Euclid brushed his hands against his robes.

"You son-of-a-bitch," Troy cursed, gripping his weapon.

"What are you going to do? Shoot me?" Euclid taunted, laughing at the two soldiers and their guns.

"Somethin' like that," a voice said from behind the wicked man.

Euclid turned to find Gavin holding a grenade launcher. With the trigger's pull, one massive explosion erupted against the giant. The violent force sent the enemy over the side of the cabin. Gavin promptly dropped the weapon and stared at it with unease.

"All right!" Troy cheered as he patted the stunned pilot on the back. Gavin swallowed thickly. He had never shot a man before.

The celebration ended, however, as the Hawk jerked violently.

"Shit! What was that?" Gavin rushed to the cockpit.

"Don't ask us that! You're the one who knows how to fly this thing." Troy followed his friend to the front, looking at the countless gauges with a face of confusion.

"What's going on, Gavin?" Aria asked.

"I, I dunno. She was fine yesterday." Another jerk occurred, and the two soldiers shuffled for balance. "Oh, damn!" An alarm rang out as tiny red lights blinked in alert across the panel.

"What?!" Troy gripped the metal frame beside him.

"The rotary blades! The wiring snapped on one side! Those damned things must've sabotaged the Hawk before they attacked!" Gavin flipped and pressed a multitude of switches and buttons. "We're using only two blades! We have to land now!" Another jerk sent everyone struggling to the side as an explosion boomed overhead. "Guys, get your chutes! We need to bail!"

"We're bailing?!" Aria shouted.

"I can't save her! Either you get out now, or we're all dead!" Gavin pushed the two into the back of the cabin toward the parachutes. He handed one to Aria and then another to Troy.

"Gavin," Aria fiddled with her pack, "there's only two."

"You guys put them on! Get out now!"

"But what about you?!" Troy shouted.

"Don't worry about me! I got my ejection seat!" Gavin rushed to the front, buckling himself in. The Hawk dropped, this time not lifting. "Get out!" He tugged on the aircraft's throttle, trying to gain a bit more air.

"I'll help," Euclid's voice suddenly rang out.

As Euclid's large hands flung her over the edge, Aria quickly buckled her pack to her body. A kick sent Troy spiraling out of the aircraft, his parachute flying from his hands. Euclid watched momentarily before turning to the pilot, revealing his torn-open torso damaged from the grenade blast.

"Later!" Gavin waved, activating his ejection seat. He soared up and out of the cockpit, the chair releasing a chute.

"Think you can get away that easily, do you?" Euclid leaped from the side of the Hawk, eyes on the pilot. Giant, dark wings burst from his dorsal side. He was by

Gavin's side with a flap, vibrant eyes glaring.

"Oh, shit! You can fly, too?" Gavin shouted.

Euclid collided with the pilot, sending Gavin's parachute in disarray. Strapped to the seat, the man began to tumble through the air. He reached inside his pocket for his military knife.

"You made a dire mistake, boy," Euclid hissed.

He gripped Gavin's hand firmly, slowly forcing the pilot to cut his parachute straps. Gavin, using his free hand, tugged Euclid's hair. Releasing his safety buckles, he slid from his pilot's chair and wrapped his legs around Euclid's middle. The two struggled in the air, and Euclid tried to fly away, his wings flapping erratically. Gavin pulled back and inserted the knife in between the large man's shoulder blades. Euclid cried out, trying to detach from the pilot.

"Always," Gavin strained with the other man, "preferred to fly." He tilted his head back, hair blowing in the wind, and watched the nearing earth.

Aria landed roughly on the hard desert ground. Dust swirled around her as she rolled to her feet. She quickly unstrapped the pack on her back and immediately looked to the sky. Troy fell slowly a few meters away. His arms were wrapped clumsily around the parachute's cords, never having the time to strap the item onto his back. He landed hard but was capable of standing.

"Troy!" Aria shouted, rushing to her partner.

"Where is he?" Troy gasped for air, looking toward the sky for Gavin.

A whooshing sounded beside the two; Dovian had neared with Ivory in his arms, both thankfully unharmed. He landed next to Aria and Troy with a couple of flaps, pulling his white wings back into his body.

"There!" Aria called out, pointing at the dots in the sky. Her heart skipped a beat once she processed the sight before her. "Oh, God!"

"This mission is fubar!" Gavin called out through his mental chip.

"Gavin! What happened?!" Aria mentally screamed at the man. Silence followed for a second.

"Aria, baby. Sorry, I didn't get to take you on that date as promised." Gavin's voice sounded dark, the tone like Aria had never heard before.

"No," she whimpered aloud. *"No! Gavin!"*

While listening in on the conversation, Troy stared upward, ignoring the tumbling parachuted seat but watching the two large dots—Gavin and presumably Euclid.

"I'm taking this bastard out with me." Gavin's voice began to cut out. The Hawk 90 shattered against the desert floor, a giant explosion following.

"Gavin! No! There's got to be some other way!" Aria held a hand over her mouth with a finger pressed behind her ear, tears welling in her eyes. She watched in horror as

the two dots neared the horizon.

"Troy." Gavin's solemn voice echoed in their minds. *"Take care of her for—"* Everything fell silent as the two silhouettes impacted the dry earth. Far away, a dust cloud kicked upwards from the collision.

"Gavin!" Aria howled a horrified scream.

"Fuck!" Troy chased after Aria as she sprinted toward the wreckage.

"No!" Dovian chased them. "No!" The Sorcēarian grabbed Aria; she kicked wildly, shouting obscenities alternating with Gavin's name. "You cannot go!" Dovian said through closed teeth, his mouth next to Aria's ear.

"Aria, don't," Troy warned the woman. "Please, don't."

"Let me go!" She flailed.

Ivory watched wide-eyed at the scene before her. Everything had turned into a nightmare.

"You cannot go!" Dovian shoved the hostile woman onto the ground.

She clawed at the rocky earth, squeezing the sand as she continued her rant. Dovian quickly motioned to run toward the wreckage. Troy followed closely after. "Don't!" The Sorcēarian turned toward the man.

"I am going with you!" Troy argued.

Dovian approached the militant, moving his face centimeters close to Troy's. "You do not want to see what's out there. You do not want to see your friend. You know very well at the height and speed he was falling," Dovian glanced at Aria and lowered the volume of his voice, "there isn't going to be much left of the man."

"You can't say things like that!" Troy shouted. His eyes were bloodshot, his face dirty from sweat and dust.

"You can heal him. You can heal him like you did for me." Aria stumbled to her feet and rushed to Dovian's side, clutching his arm.

Dovian pulled something similar to an optical camera from the inside of his robe. He placed the item over his ear, and a holographic screen covered his right eye as he searched for life signs. His frown only deepened, confirming what he already knew. Hard eyes looked down at the desperate woman.

"You can't heal what's already dead. Trust me, I've tried," he spoke softly.

Aria stared at Dovian. Her face held a look of shock, her eyes large as tears streamed down her face. Her mouth flopped agape, twitching as she gasped for words.

"Stay with her. I will check out the scene and deal with…everything else." The Sorcēarian gave a quick pat on Troy's arm and quickly made his way toward the wreckage nearly eight hundred meters away.

"No," Aria murmured in a whisper. She slowly walked after Dovian.

"Aria." Troy grabbed her shoulders.

"No!" she screamed, trying to pull away.

"Aria!" He tugged the woman into an embrace as she fell to her knees, crying. Troy sat on his backside, pulling her against his chest, and rested his chin atop her head. "I'm sorry, Aria. Damn it! I'm sorry!"

Ivory stood back, observing the chaos. She sniffled, tears falling down her cheeks as well. She may not have known Gavin well, but these people were all she knew. She awoke to a world caught in an unknown war and remembered nothing else. Slowly, she approached the two, kneeling beside them. Troy lifted an arm, letting the pale woman cry beside Aria.

The three waited roughly twenty minutes before Dovian returned. The look on his face was more than dreadful. It was downright murderous. He stood before the hunkered group, eyes blazing, and Troy lifted his head. It seemed Dovian mentally fought with himself. One second, his expression appeared enraged, and the next, calm. He spun momentarily, hands on his hips as he looked at the wreckage before facing the group again.

"Mind telling me why the *hell* you didn't mention Euclid?!" Dovian bellowed, making the two women jump.

"What?" Troy pushed to his feet. "Excuse me?!"

"Euclid! The man who killed your friend! Why was I not told he was involved in all of this?!" Dovian stomped toward Troy.

"How the hell was I supposed to know you had connections with that sick bastard?!"

"All you mentioned were monsters. You said nothing of a man named Euclid, nothing of a man who strangely resembles a Sorcēarian!"

"What?" Aria lifted her head. "Euclid's a Sorcēarian?"

"How? I thought you said you were the only one that survived." Troy glared at the taller man.

"Yes, I was. I am the sole survivor!" Dovian shouted.

"Then tell me what the hell that was! We have two corpses out there, and one wasn't supposed to exist in the first place!" Troy pointed toward the dark smoke on the horizon.

"No," Dovian growled.

"No?" Troy lifted his eyebrows.

"Euclid was not at the wreckage. All I found was—" Dovian glanced at Aria. Seeing the dreadful expression on the woman's face, the Sorcēarian briefly softened his tone. "—your friend."

Aria howled quietly, covering her face. Ivory softly patted her back.

"What do you mean? Gavin had that bastard! I saw it with my own eyes!" Troy hollered.

"Euclid has the ability to teleport. That's how he was able to appear out of nowhere. He's not there. I checked everywhere, and there was no sign of him. The only possible solution is he had gathered enough strength to teleport, probably through the use of your vibration shields that every one of those demons seems to be equipped with!" The two men fumed at each other, toe-to-toe.

"Okay. So, one of your so-called Sorcēarians just killed my best friend, and now he is nowhere to be seen. You said you're the only survivor, so what the hell is that?" Troy shoved Dovian out of his face.

"I have no idea how it's possible. Euclid should be dead. He is dead. There's no way he is alive," Dovian spoke slowly, trying to keep himself under control.

"Well, obviously, you are wrong."

"No, I killed him myself."

"Aren't Sorcēarians immortal or something?" Troy asked sarcastically.

"We live endlessly but are nearly as frail as you. Our abilities allow us to heal quickly, but sudden deaths come just as easily as Euclid's."

"Then you screwed up, didn't do it right, and now he's out to kill all of us!"

"I didn't screw up," Dovian growled.

"The hell you didn't!"

"I decapitated the son-of-a-bitch!" He stepped forward again, vibrant eyes narrowing to slits as he spoke slowly and with a lethal tone. "The day I killed my entire race, I unhesitatingly cut that man's head clean off. One swipe was all it took. There was barely a speck of blood, and I watched it roll away from his body. *That,* one does not heal from. We do *not* regenerate appendages."

"Okay," Troy stepped away from the irate sorcerer, "so something else is going on."

"Something very *bad* is happening," Dovian confirmed.

Silence consumed the group, leaving them all to their private thoughts. What more needed to be said? Only hours ago, they joked and laughed together. Now, everything had taken a turn for the worse. Aria and Troy had lost comrades before, but nothing quite like this. The first and only loved ones Aria lost were her parents when she was only nine. Troy could say the same; his father had died when he was eleven, and his mother passed while he was still a baby. Losing comrades in battle was expected, but losing a best friend or loved one was never easy. With Gavin gone, the war, for Aria and Troy, had suddenly become incredibly personal.

"How could you fail?!" Sapphire shouted in her shrill voice.

"I had her in my hands one second, and I should have escaped when I had the chance. I'm sorry." Euclid bowed before the child, his fingers pressing against the deep laceration between his shoulder blades.

"You decided to play games and failed. You do not play games with me, Euclid! I am not playing games!" The petite blonde rose from her makeshift seat of boulders within the dark cavern.

"If I had known that old bastard, Dovian, would be there, I would have been better prepared," Euclid groaned, struggling to heal the wound on his back. "Besides, I don't know how he's survived for this long. I figured he would have killed himself long ago."

"It was because of Dovian you lost at your game. If you had done exactly as you were told, we would have her by now." Sapphire gave a seething stare at the man crouched before her. Even when kneeling, Euclid towered over the child. He shifted his eyes to meet her chilly gaze. "I am not happy with you, Euclid."

"I also wasn't expecting that bastard of a pilot to blast me away like that," Euclid growled, pressing against his abdomen, trying to heal his wounds simultaneously. "He got what he deserved."

"Excuses!" Sapphire shrieked. Sapphire's multitude of hideous pets hissed within the dark shadows surrounding them.

"If your disgusting animals were more efficient at their job, they would have easily disposed of those militants!" Euclid snarled.

"I've heard enough." The girl's voice lowered in tone.

Euclid froze, his right arm pulling to the side of its own accord. He gasped and looked upon his stiffening appendage with frightened eyes.

"Wha-what are you doing?" he choked as his arm bent slowly. "S-stop it," he ground out through gritted teeth.

"This is your punishment for disobeying."

Euclid's arm twisted backward with an unseeable force, snapping at the elbow. He screamed, reaching for the broken arm with his other hand. Gasping for air, he dazedly fed the tiny girl a nasty glower. "You little bitch! You broke my arm!"

"Disobey me again, and I'll sever it," Sapphire said sweetly before returning to her seat.

The dark man moaned as he began to heal another wound, pressing his fingers against the broken joint.

"No matter about this slight misfortune. We'll have plenty of other chances to get what we want. And about Dovian, he may be quite useful to us." The child smiled, swaying her feet back and forth.

"Always Preferred to Fly"

CHAPTER 10

Standing in the center of the cemetery and listening to Gavin's mother's soft wails was probably the most miserable experience Aria and Troy had ever encountered. The pale tombstone was a dull contrast to the beautiful, lush green grass and the vibrant oranges and reds of the surrounding trees. Aria shivered in the cold breeze, her hair twisting about her neck. She stood with folded arms across from Gavin's weeping family. Troy shuddered beside her. Dark glasses covered the man's eyes but did nothing to hide his silent desolation. Aria stifled a sniff, hoping the autumn air would dry her eyes. The rustling leaves melded with the murmuring of the preacher's speech and the haunting cries and moans of those surrounding the black pit from which the young pilot's casket lay suspended.

The charcoal coffin was sleek in design, surrounded by thick bands of platinum. A stark flag lay draped over the top in bold colors of red, white, and blue. A symbol of an eagle wearing a maple leaf collar, snake in its clutches, sat wingspread over the thick stripes. Strange how the melancholy scene before the young woman was probably the most beautiful thing she had ever seen. Cemeteries were a place of death, yet the most decorated and well-kept locations in all the cities. Despite all the hatred and war, civilization seemed to have respect for the dead. Too bad there wasn't enough for the living.

"I knew he shouldn't have been a military pilot," Gavin's mother cried into a white handkerchief. "I just wanted him to be happy!" Her last word heightened in pitch as she wailed into the cloth, her shoulders shaking.

Aria had to look away. It was hard enough to attend the funeral without feeling the guilt that perhaps there was something more she could have done to prevent

Gavin's untimely demise. Another chilly wind wrapped around the woman, carrying the scent of cigarette smoke her way. Her gaze lifted, catching sight of blue embers and striking eyes of matching hue a few meters away. The woman froze, locked in the stare of the dark-haired Sorcēarian, Euclid. He gave her a crooked smile with a cigarette squeezed between his teeth. A hand gripped the woman's shoulder, breaking her from her trance.

"You all right?" Troy's warm tone sounded.

Aria met the man's gaze momentarily before returning to find Euclid's. He was gone. The trees swayed gently in the wind, colorful leaves trailing toward the ground.

"Yeah," she droned quietly.

"Salute!"

Militants in dress uniforms lifted their weapons toward the sky. Shots rang out, echoing in the mournful silence of the increasingly depressing cemetery. Aria jolted at the sound, staring at the casket before her. Another shot rang out, reminding her of the painful explosion of the Hawk 90 disintegrating into the earth in a fiery ball. The third shot left her heart sinking as she remembered the black silhouette of Gavin's body impacting the ground, followed by a brown dust cloud. Ultimately, he still apologized to her for not taking her on that final date even though she had promised him one. Two giant tears finally fell from her eyes. He had invited her to go out countless times, and she carelessly blew him off. She would take all those moments back and live like an ordinary person in that instant. His caramel-colored eyes, his radiant smile, how he dragged his hand nervously through his hair, and even the constant annoyances and flirting were all gone. Aria would never have that again. Troy wrapped his arm around her shoulders. She looked up at him and realized she was crying.

A quiet trumpet melody rang out in the distance as a sorrowful song played in Gavin's honor. One after another, the family members and friends dropped their flowers onto the casket as it slowly lowered into the ground. It was a traditional ceremony reserved only for the military and elite. Most funerals involved fake flowers, and the bodies were always cremated due to a lack of cemetery space. Services were often held in private inside a family member's home.

Aria slowly approached the casket, thoughtfully twisting the white rose in her fingertips. Gavin always liked white roses. He had given her one long ago when they first met. It probably cost him a small fortune as roses were painfully rare. Gavin constantly and desperately tried to get her to date him, which she complied with for a short time. Eventually, fear overtook her, and she refused to proceed with their relationship. Aria's smile faded as quickly as it came while she placed the flower on the flag.

"Goodbye, Gavin," she whispered.

"I'll be checking in with you, buddy," Troy murmured as he placed his rose.

The trumpet song faded to completion as the funeral procession ended, and everyone slowly made their way to their vehicles.

"Excuse me," a female voice called after the two. Aria and Troy both looked over their shoulders. "I'm sorry, but I just had to ask." It was Gavin's mother. She had eyes the same color as her son's. Her hair was also dark like the pilot's but decorated with honey-blonde strands. She placed a small hand on Aria's shoulder. "You're Aria, aren't you?" she asked.

"Yes," Aria spoke slowly, not sure what to expect.

"Oh! I knew it was you! I could tell by the blue in your hair." For the first time that afternoon, Gavin's mother smiled. "Gavin talked about you all the time!"

"He, he did?" Aria gaped nervously at the woman before her.

"Of course he did! I cannot tell you how happy we were to find out he had a girlfriend. We were so worried! He never talked about girls!" She smiled so brightly, it was alarming. Gavin's father leaned forward and shook Aria's hand. He fed her a lopsided grin, a distinct trait the pilot had inherited. "But I don't want to keep you. He always talked about how busy you were with work and everything, but I just had to meet you." Her smile faltered. "I just wish it were under better circumstances."

"I…I'm sorry, Mrs. Sigo," Aria stuttered, her eyes downcast.

"No, it's all right. Gavin wouldn't want you to be sorry." Mrs. Sigo reached into her coat pocket and pulled out a small black box. She sniffled before handing the item to Aria. "He…he would want me to give this to you. He said he would give it to you for your birthday."

Surely, it was some mistake. She and Gavin weren't dating. In fact, it had been ages since she indulged in his bold requests. The gift most certainly had to be for another woman. Mrs. Sigo looked at the military woman eagerly, and Aria hesitantly opened the box. A silver necklace with a small cat charm sat inside. It had green jewels for eyes, and Aria felt her heart sink. There was no mistake about it. It was meant for her.

"He said you had a thing for cats." Mrs. Sigo smirked thoughtfully.

Everything fell silent between the four. Aria fingered the item and quickly looked up at the couple. "Thank you," she managed to say.

"No, thank you for making our boy happy." Mrs. Sigo finally burst into tears. It was like pouring salt into a wound. Instead, Aria stared at the necklace, struggling to fight back her emotions. Mrs. Sigo glanced at Troy.

"Ma'am." Troy nodded.

"Troy," she stated shortly before quickly walking away with her husband, who followed closely behind. As the man passed, he gave Troy a sad look and a shoulder pat.

Aria eyed her partner suspiciously. He hesitated before stating, "I…uh, was considered a bad influence on Gavin. I kind of talked him into becoming a military pilot." Troy swallowed hard. Aria was stunned. She was sure he felt just as much, if not more, to blame for their friend's death. However, the soldier shook off his pain and examined the item in her hands. "Birthday present, huh?" He chuckled softly.

"Yeah," Aria mumbled. Then, she suddenly felt sick. Glancing at her wrist, she stared at the date. As if things weren't twisted enough, it was her birthday. She stood silently for a minute before walking toward the vehicle. "Can we go now?"

Troy didn't answer but opened the door for the woman before taking his place in the driver's seat. They sat in silence for most of the ride, taking the standard highway toward the City of Fountains rather than using the overhead speedy monorails—an extensive network of tracks that magnetically locked vehicles on a rail and allowed travel at high speeds into the metropolis. Today, Troy wanted to take things slow, and he knew Aria appreciated the more scenic route into the city. To her, everything looked artificial. Though it was beautiful with its holograms and vibrant lights, the constant flow of traffic, advertisements, and dank lower streets lined with garbage bins didn't help a nostalgic mind.

The cemetery stretched for kilometers before converging into dry fields and cracked desert land. A place that once, long ago, held heaps of vegetation and supposedly fed the world with its grains and corn was now a place of death. Nothing survived outside the cities. Instead, heavily monitored lab facilities housed the agriculture fields. There were farming districts within the city limits where each floor of the giant skyscrapers held a different form of cultivation. But, despite the dreary browns of the flat surrounding landscape, the outside world remained striking with its expanse of blue sky and bulbous white clouds.

With her head against the glass, Aria looked upward at the large, wispy vapors. No wonder Gavin loved to fly. Up there, high above the filth of the world, was a place full of beauty and awe. Soaring in the endless blue and white could quickly settle a person's mind. Even with the billions of pixels, the projection screens at home had nothing on the natural splendor of an open sky.

The car jerked as Troy took the exit ramp that suspended far above the ground to the monorail. They entered Fountains, and the monorail was easier on the eyes than the pedestrian and waste-laden streets below. As it climbed into the air, the vehicle moved toward the city, which rested on a platform 500 meters above the desert floor on metal beams. Above the platform, buildings touched the sky with the clean-cut architecture of silver and black, the cityscape adorned with its busy lights of vibrant hues. The upper metropolitan looked beautiful outside of the ground level. Hardly anyone lived on the lower floors of the city for aesthetic reasons. However, beneath the plate was an entirely different story.

On the underside of the metropolis, dubbed the Underbelly, was an upside-down industrial slum. Buildings below the plate were reserved for the mining, mechanical, and laborious districts. It also housed the civilians who were too poor to live on the upper side. Those individuals lived in small shanties and single-room apartments, nearly nine square meters, reserved for the 'wealthier' of the inferior class. The population below the plate was less than the upper side and contained the flawed individuals the elitists had nothing to do with. Often, those considered different moved to the bottom plate for protection. The Underbelly was cruel and ugly, but the people understood and respected each other better. They stuck together like a support group and held complete and utter disgust for those who lived on the upper side.

Underneath it all, drillers dug holes deep into the earth as the Underbelly mined for natural resources and aquifers. Supposedly, a whole faction of deformed and genetically diverse people lived underground, away from Fountains' filth and judgmental citizens. Whether they all moved there of their own free will or because of banishment was debatable.

The initial reason for the city's obscure design was to utilize natural airflow, not to divide its citizens. The area between the ground and the platform created a vacuum. Air moved directly beneath the city, pulling in the cold underground temperatures from the massive mining caverns. Because of this, the underside often had violent wind gusts, which was the reason behind the metallic architecture. However, the winds chilled the inner plate that housed the nuclear reactors that powered the entire megalopolis. Though the city had smog, it was considered one of the cleanest in the world despite the hundreds of millions it housed.

Due to the desert lands consuming the planet, only a handful of cities existed per continent. Hardly anyone lived on the outside other than those staying on military bases. The dusty land stretched for thousands of kilometers between each city-state. Because of this, people tended to remain in the city where they were born all their lives.

A sudden vibration shook the vehicle as it locked into place on the metal beams. The dashboard lit up, assuming autopilot, as the car nearly tripled in speed toward the skyscrapers. Aria's expression remained flat as the white clouds quickly turned to a dull greenish-grey, growing into smog that devoured the vibrant blue. In seconds, the skyline of beautiful clouds was replaced by an urban view, the open air full of smoke and flashing lights. Giant buildings lined the sides of the speeding vehicles. In a flash, vendors and tiny shops fluttered past in a colorful blur. The higher the monorail traveled, the cleaner and brighter the view became. Above the thin saturation of haze on the plate level was a brilliant and fresh landscape.

The car moved to the side, turning past a hovering playground full of schoolchildren. White panels floated, suspended by silver walkways connected to the skyscrapers' sides. In the center of the platforms were colorful patches of green grass and trees, small parks with picnic tables with locations for citizens to set up their personal comps, and fountains of all shapes and sizes lined with stunning bronze statues from ancient and modern times. As they neared the center of Fountains, advertisements blinked and screamed with loud chimes and music. Aria rolled her eyes toward one.

'Walten Industries: where you can get all your household and military needs in one location. If it doesn't say Bio-Tech, it's not the best.'

"Please state your destination." Troy's GPS, which he affectionately named Amelia, droned through the radio speakers.

"Home," Troy replied.

"Going home."

Troy removed his sunglasses, leaning back in his seat. He ran his hands over his face, sighing loudly. Tilting his head to the side, he looked at the quiet woman beside him. Aria didn't acknowledge more than a sideways glance. His olive eyes dropped to the black box, and she tightly clutched the item.

"You know he cared about you…a lot," Troy's deep voice, though quiet, was loud in the silent vehicle.

"I don't want to talk about it," Aria grumbled.

"Well, I'm just saying. So you know. Cuz I know you cared a lot, too…though you won't admit it. But I think he knew that, too."

"Stop," she whispered as tears wetted her eyes.

The car remained silent for the rest of the journey. Within a minute, the vehicle tugged into the parking garage's twentieth floor; the structure itself was half the height of Bio-Tech. The car jolted from the monorail system, slowing nearly to a stop as Troy assumed control of the wheel, taking the endless paths to his reserved parking spot near the elevating system.

"So, how do you think Dovian's handling things?" he asked finally.

Aria scoffed. "I'm sure he's having fun. He volunteered to be held captive for a few days."

"That guy has got a weird sense of humor. When they approached him, guns aimed and ready to fire, I nearly expected him to send them all to ashes. But no! He just raised his hands and smiled! 'Sure! Take me prisoner and poke and prod me all day with needles and endless ignorant questions!' He must be very lonely," Troy chuckled. Aria smiled at the thought.

After escaping Ives, Aria and the others landed on a nearby island. Even amidst chaos, Gavin directed them all safely to land. They had flagged the area, and with it being far enough away from the black hole named Ives, Bio-Tech's security systems promptly detected the SOS signal. A team arrived at the island within a few hours—the most prolonged hours of Aria's life. Upon landing in their zone, five soldiers rushed from their Hawk with weapons pointed. They had no idea what the SOS was for, and once they laid eyes on the giant Sorcēarian, the militants were on high alert for him being a threat. Troy and Aria repeatedly shouted to reassure the team that Dovian was an ally and that Ivory needed protective custody. But not before the general, Jeron Feyette, ordered the group to bind the taller man and take him in for questioning.

Dovian put up no resistance. In fact, he seemed delighted with the opportunity to meet with the general and be taken into custody. Aria protested, but Dovian only reassured her that there wasn't anything the men could do to cause any harm to him and that if anyone should be worried, it should be them. After the argument had settled, everyone safely boarded and traveled back to the mainland to return to the city. A cleanup crew promptly went out to deal with the remains of the wreckage. Aria and the others had been back in Fountains for three days and were not allowed to see the Sorcēarian.

Troy placed his car into park, shutting down the engine. He quickly left his side of the vehicle and ran around the back to open the door for Aria. She gave him a smug smile. Troy tried hard to impress the ladies, and sometimes, he treated Aria like one. Closing the door behind the female, he quickly opened the back door and retrieved a small, colorful sack. Aria eyeballed him suspiciously as they approached the elevator. She pushed the button for the housing level while Troy pushed for a different floor.

"You're not going to your apartment?" she asked solemnly.

"No." He rocked back and forth on his heels, his dress shoes clacking against the cement. "I'm gonna check up on Dovian and see if I can get him out of there today. Besides, Mr. Clarke wanted to see me and told me to meet him in the detaining facility."

"Should I go with you?"

"Naw." Troy gave her a reassuring smile as he loosened his tie. "He said to let you get some rest for a change."

The elevators swung open simultaneously. Aria began to enter, but Troy stopped her.

"But I'll stop by later tonight, all right?" He gave her his boyish grin as he handed her the colorful sack. "To have a little celebration?"

Aria fought back a smile and reluctantly took the package from his hands. "Am I the only one that forgot today was my birthday?" She looked inside and pulled out a large bottle with a homemade label titled 'Majestic.' It was her favorite neon-blue drink, which she always ordered at the bar and grille.

"Well…I was reminded of it constantly the past few weeks," Troy faltered. "But don't drink all of it before I get there!"

"How did you find this?" She gave him a curious look. The bottle didn't look professionally wrapped or designed.

"Uh, I pulled a few strings with the bartender at Chester's. He mixed me up a whole bottle himself for you." Troy nervously scratched the hairs on his chin.

Aria looked at the blue liquid and ran her fingers over the homemade label and cork. No doubt Troy decorated it. She giggled quietly. It was one of the most unique gifts she had ever received.

"If I can get Dovian out of there, I'll bring him by, too."

"Thank you, Troy." Aria lifted her eyes to his.

The man stared back at her with the corner of his mouth quirked. "Erm, no problem. Happy birthday. I'll see you later." He quickly moved into his elevator and gave a small wave as the doors slid shut.

Aria watched his lift as it sank back into the chute and glided horizontally toward Bio-Tech. She boarded hers and rode it to the side and upwards to the 60th floor. The woman stared blankly out the glass windows, passing by the cranes and construction beams placed in preparation for reconstructing the building's upper floors. The safety nets had been somewhat successful and kept most of the building intact. It only took a day to regain the power and secure the structure enough to allow people back into the building. Unfortunately, no one was allowed past the 60th floor due to the recovery and removal of bodies and debris. The place was depressing, but once the elevator opened to housing, Aria sighed with relief. She was home. Making her way to her apartment door, she swiped her wrist and entered the cozy residence. The smell of coffee invaded her senses, and she felt her nerves calm a bit as she removed her military trench and slipped off her tall black heels.

"I still think that is a lovely little black dress and suits you very well," Ivory called from the hallway.

Aria didn't respond but gave the other woman a small smile. She wasn't used to being around women, let alone having one live with her, but Ivory was different than most she had dealt with. The young blonde was kind, sweet, and non-threatening, a first for Aria. The dark-haired woman took a seat at the bar before the kitchen. Ivory walked quickly, nearly on her bare tiptoes, into the room. She wore Aria's shorts, which appeared extremely short on the female's long, pale legs, and a baby-blue t-shirt. It was also the first time Aria ever had to share clothes with another person. She decided that after things had calmed down, she would take Ivory shopping for better-fitting garments.

"Aren't you cold?" Aria asked.

"No." Ivory shook her head. "I'm fine. Coffee?" she cheerfully asked as she handed Aria a mug of the chocolaty brew.

"Thanks." She tasted it and raised a brow. "How'd you know I like it this way?"

"Well, I was looking at the settings on the refrigerator and noticed your grocery order. It seemed you restocked with that kind every month, so I assumed it was safe to say that was your favorite." Ivory beamed.

Ivory seemed to have excellent deduction skills, especially since one would need to enter a passcode to look at Aria's grocery order.

"Oh, look! What a pretty sack!" Ivory pointed at the bag sitting on the bar beside Aria.

Aria scoffed. "Oh, yeah. It's got some gifts inside." She pulled out the blue bottle of liquor and the tiny black box.

"Oh, wow! Look at that color! Is that a drink?" Ivory leaned in close. The glow of the liquid reflected in the woman's blue eyes.

"Yes, one of my favorites. We will have some later with Troy if you'd like."

"Troy will be visiting? How lovely! What's the occasion?" The woman swayed back and forth, resting her elbows on the countertop.

"Um," Aria hesitated, watching Ivory pick up the black box, "I guess it's my birthday today."

"It's your birthday?! You didn't tell me that!" The slender woman placed her hands on her hips. "Gosh! I need to make you a cake, don't I? How exciting!"

Aria sighed. The woman had far too much energy. Ivory had cleaned the entire apartment while she was away. Maybe Ivory was worth keeping. It made the older woman feel bad for making her stay inside the apartment all day, but it was for her own safety. Even though they lived in a military complex, Ivory was still subject to being harassed by others due to her appearance. And though Aria barely knew the woman, she already felt a bit protective of her, like she was Ivory's older sister. The thought appealed to her. Aria never had a sibling but always wanted one when she was younger.

"Oh, look! It's a kitty cat! How cute!" Ivory's cheerful voice drew Aria's attention. "And its tail moves!" She giggled like a child as her finger flicked the cat charm's tail back and forth. "Did Troy get this for you?"

"Um, no," Aria mumbled cautiously. "Gavin did. Well, his mother did. She said he bought it for me. I guess he was going to give it to me today."

"Oh." Ivory lowered her head and set the necklace on the countertop. Her pink-lipped smile quickly turned upside-down. "That's sad."

"It's Okay," Aria said quickly, closing the black box.

"Don't do that!" Ivory grabbed the case and opened it again, removing the piece of jewelry. "You should wear it! It's terribly cute! Besides, its green eyes match yours!" The blonde walked behind her, placed the silver item around her neck, and clasped it.

Aria looked down, running her finger over the happy fat cat resting against her collarbone.

"See? It looks good on you!" Ivory clapped her hands. She then decided to change the subject. "Oh, I love this! Here, let's make it a joyful day!"

Ivory made her way to the large floor-to-ceiling window inside the kitchen. She placed her hand against the glass and pulled up the weather map. The forecast read sunny with a chance of rain—fabricated rain—later in the night. After a couple of clicks and pokes, Ivory made the whole expanse of the kitchen wall fade into a bright green pasture surrounded by blue skies and puffy white clouds, much like how the outside world was supposed to look.

"Beautiful, right?" The younger woman grinned as she filled her mug with more coffee.

Aria nodded slowly and sipped from her own. It would be a long day, especially if Ivory had one more pot of the caffeine-enhanced brew. She would have to remember to tell the ditzy woman the hazards of having too much of the stuff.

"How's he been?" Troy asked James. The room was dark besides the dull light beams bordering the giant, horizontal one-way mirror.

"Well, he's been surprisingly cooperative…until this morning."

Troy approached the bulletproof window of the detaining room where the brilliant white walls reflected light from the glass-tiled backlit floor and ceiling. A metal table and chair occupied the center of the room, where Dovian sat with his hands cuffed behind him. His hair looked messy, and his eyes narrowed with an agitated glare, burning with an electric spark.

"You have him handcuffed?" Troy asked. "But you said he's been cooperative."

"He was until he threatened a guard this morning and nearly shoved him through the glass." Mr. Clarke pointed to the edge of the mirror on the left side. Cracks splintered the surface.

Troy sighed. "What happened?"

"Well, the past few days, we've been asking questions about who he is and where he came from. He's been good at giving answers but leaving out the whole story. Though he's good at revealing it condescendingly with a smile, he likes to shroud himself in mystery and seems to hold quite the revulsion for all of us." James smirked.

"Yeah, well, that's Dovian for you."

"Some of the police have been riled up. Many seem to think he's the one responsible for this whole mess. They've been blaming and trying all the reverse psychology they can on him, but Dovian only proves his greater intelligence each time by throwing the hypocrisies back in their faces. He's good at making one feel like quite the *sinner*." Clarke shook his head and said with amusement, "Even I felt I needed to confess when talking to him. But some are taking offense to his antics. This morning, one of the guards kept prying for answers. Dovian responded shortly but got angry when the man started mocking his religion. The idiot was trying to measure up and said some uncouth things about Dovian's beliefs, and that's when the Sorcēarian moved from his seat and smashed the guard against the window. All within a blink of an eye, mind you." The President laughed. "It was quite the show. It took five men to pull Dovian away. But, once he calmed down, he gladly accepted the handcuffs."

"I'm glad mocking him is entertaining, sir," Troy muttered.

"The behavior of my men does not amuse me. I agree it was uncalled for. The officer was promptly demoted and is on probation for his verbal taunts." James straightened his posture.

"Not to sound like he's a pet of some kind, but can I keep him?" Troy asked, watching the Sorcēarian through the glass. Dovian seemed to stare back, a smile spreading across his face.

"I'm working on that. Mr. Walten has requested all evidence of this interrogation. He's also ordered General Feyette to observe everything." James nudged toward the opposite side of the room where Feyette waited on guard, arms crossed. The man stood tall and proud, wearing his military suit, his many adornments covering his sleeve. His hat lay slightly tilted on his head, covering his dark hair and chocolate eyes, casting a shadow over his stiff, frowning face. Coupled with his black military dress and abnormally dark skin, Feyette adopted the nickname of Walten's shadow, his cold visage fitting the role of his nickname.

"What does Walten want with all of this? Isn't this kind of a top-secret matter?" Troy eyeballed the statuesque Feyette. "And you know how I feel about that guy."

"Walten believes he has the right to know everything that goes on with his company. Feyette's his lapdog and does everything Walten commands. He also keeps no secrets." James spoke quietly near Troy's ear. "I'm not sure what's going on, but I feel like those two are hiding something or know more than they are letting on about this situation. Rumor has it that some coded files went missing from Dr. Camery's lab the other day. I'm not sure which ones exactly, but now they are magically secure and back in place."

"I do not like the sound of this." Troy eyed Dovian. The white-haired man moved his cuffed hand from side to side, waving hello to the soldier.

"It's like he knows you're here." James gave a curious look.

"He probably does." Troy shrugged carelessly.

"Strange…." Mr. Clarke watched Dovian through the glass for an extra moment before returning his attention to Troy. "Anyway, I believe you should keep your friend close. He's been asking us about our progress on this investigation, and we have to keep lying to him, though I think he sees through all of it."

"And how are we doing?" Troy asked.

"Not good. We can't seem to sniff them out. Increased attacks occur each day around the world, and they are all random. There's no way to tell where they are coming from." Clarke frowned. "Dovian seems concerned and eager to leave now. I'll let him out if I can keep the doctors away from him."

"What have they been doing to him?"

"Taking blood samples, doing physicals, measuring brainwave activity, stuff like that."

"No drugs, right?"

"No. But they have been making him fast."

"Fasting? Why?!" Troy squeezed the bridge of his nose.

"Not sure. Probably to keep track of the effects of dehydration and lack of nourishment."

"When was the last time he ate or drank anything?" Troy asked with anger.

"Once since he's been here. They gave him a small meal with a glass of water, took a blood sample, and returned daily to see the effects. Strangely, he'll show signs of hunger and thirst by the night's end, but when he awakes the next day, everything seems replenished and back in good standing!"

"That's not surprising," Troy scoffed. "Why are they running such stupid tests? He's not a lab rat!"

"Don't ask me. Walten's orders." Clarke shrugged his shoulders.

"Please get him out," the soldier requested with irritation. "It's Aria's birthday today, and I don't want to give her any more bad news. Can I take him home?" he asked quietly, feeling Feyette's burning gaze upon him.

"I'll let you take him. I'll deal with Walten, but I suggest you guys keep on the down-low. Try to get out of here as soon as you can. I'll say you're leading the investigation. I think he's gotten wind that Aria's got that girl."

"What's going on here?" Troy whispered.

"I don't know, but I fear for your friend's safety. Walten's got a whole other investigation going on behind my back, and there's nothing I can do about it. Usually, I'd abide by all the rules, but with you and Aria involved, I worry things may get out of hand."

"I hear ya." Troy nodded.

"I'm letting the detainee go. Please let Mr. Moreau through," Mr. Clarke ordered Feyette. The general remained still before the door.

Troy trudged over to the man and waited impatiently. The two looked each other up and down.

"Please?" Troy asked sweetly between his teeth.

"By Mr. Walten's orders," Clarke said gravely.

Feyette stood his ground momentarily before finally stepping to the side.

"Good boy," Troy said mockingly before slipping through the sliding door into the detaining room.

"I wondered how much longer I would have to sit in this horrible, filthy place," Dovian muttered, looking over his shoulder to peek at Troy. A sideways smile crossed his face.

"Yeah, well, someone's been causing trouble, so I get to take you home now. Playtime's over." Troy bent down to remove the cuffs from Dovian's wrists. He cringed at the purple and black marks left by the restraints.

The Sorcēarian laughed. "You heard about that?"

"Kind of hard to miss the shattered glass that's supposed to be bulletproof."

Dovian stood, facing Troy. "Aw, but I only broke a couple of his ribs."

"Jeez, Dovian. Please behave yourself. These guys already think you're the cause of this whole mess," Troy whispered to the taller man.

"I've given them no reason to believe so. My attack was with reasonable cause."

"That doesn't matter. You can't just do that to police officers." Troy led the tall man through the door, standing between him and Feyette as they exited the room. Dovian held his hand outwards toward Feyette, waving his fingers impatiently.

"Your weapon will continue to be detained for further analysis," Feyette commanded in a deep voice.

Dovian glared heatedly at the general.

"Give him his staff," James ordered with annoyance.

Feyette huffed and opened the locker beside him, retrieved Dovian's weapon, and shoved it into his hands. Dovian gave the President a cockeyed smirk, to which he nodded in response. Rushing to the elevator, Troy punched the button for the doors, waiting in aggravation for it to climb the levels.

"Police officers are also not supposed to provoke," Dovian argued before entering the elevator. He chuckled as he rubbed his wrists. Troy frowned. "Funny…they thought that would keep me from attacking." He met Feyette's angry stare as the doors closed silently.

"You're going to be the death of me," Troy sighed irritably.

"Or, I could be your savior," Dovian stated humorously.

"What's that supposed to mean?"

"Hm." He smugly hummed. "You will see, I suppose."

"You make me nervous; you know that?" The soldier eyed the Sorcēarian and then directed his attention to the city surrounding the glass elevator. The scenery was already dark as the skyscrapers blocked out the sun.

"As every human should be."

"Stop it." Troy pointed a finger.

"What?"

"Your arrogance. You need to learn to socialize with people."

"You're surprised by my lack of social skills after being alone for thousands of years?" The Sorcēarian gave him a sly smile.

"Point taken. That's why tonight you're going to get practice!" Troy patted the other man on the back.

This time, Dovian frowned. "Where are we going?"

The door opened to the 60th floor, and Troy hurried toward Aria's apartment, adjusting the tie around his neck. "We're going to see the girls. It's Aria's birthday today. We're going to have a fun time, got it?"

"Girls, I like. Birthday parties, not so much." Dovian waited before the door as Troy knocked. The tall man fiddled with the hood of his long red cape. "Should I put this on?" he asked, sliding the garment over his head.

"No…why would you?" Troy gave him a weird stare.

"Is it not a ceremonial event?" Dovian gaped.

"Not the kind you're thinking of." He chuckled.

The door quickly slid open, and a bright, loud Ivory cheered, "Surprise!" She threw her arms in the air and gave a small hop. A triangular hat sat atop her wild curls as she blew loudly into a noisemaker. Then, her face held a look of confusion. "Oh, wait…I'm only supposed to say that to the birthday person."

"That's okay," Troy chuckled as he roughed up Ivory's hair, pushing the hat further to the side. "It was definitely a surprise."

A loud toot sounded from the kitchen area. Troy looked past the pretty blonde and smiled. Aria sat beside a half-empty bottle of Majestic with a lopsided grin as she blew raucously into her noisemaker. She, too, had a hat, which was uncharacteristic of her. Balloons and confetti decorated the apartment. The girls had been remarkably busy.

"Dinner is almost ready!" Ivory sang aloud, quickly padding into the kitchen to open the oven. "Did you know Aria's never used this thing before?"

"Now, *that* doesn't surprise me." The young man removed his jacket, placing it atop Aria's own on the back of a chair.

"Shush…I've used it once or twice," Aria grumbled.

"Couldn't wait to try it out, huh?" Troy tapped the bottle.

Aria rolled her eyes. "Ugh. Ivory's been drinking coffee all day. She made me take her downstairs to the store to buy decorations. I nearly had to drag her out of the place. She talked to every man that looked at her."

"Didn't get into any trouble, did you?" Troy asked with a serious tone.

"Shockingly, no. Just a lot of gawking."

Dovian, hood covering his features and staff in hand, remained in the doorway leading to the housing level's hall. Ivory closed the oven door with her hip and jogged to the tall man.

"Don't just stand there!" the blonde called out, grinning. She reached out to Dovian, her hips swaying from side to side as she grabbed his hands and pulled him inside. "Oh, your wrists!"

Looking at his bruised appendages, Dovian placed a hand over each wrist. In a matter of seconds, the darkened skin quickly brightened to its natural pale-white tone.

"This girl is inebriated," he stated in a dry tone. Ivory took the massive weapon from the man and set it beside the front door.

"Yeah. It's called booze." Aria widened her eyes. "You should try some."

"I do not think something that glows in the dark is safe to ingest," Dovian muttered.

"But your eyes glow in the dark." Ivory leaned forward, lifting the hood slightly on Dovian's head. The mysterious man stiffened under her scrutiny.

"You are not planning on ingesting my eyes, are you?" Dovian replied sarcastically.

"Ew! No!" She shoved away and returned to the kitchen, sipping from her glass. "If anyone here would eat someone's eyeballs, I'd say it'd be you."

Troy gave a loud snort of amusement.

"Oh, really? Why is that?" Dovian folded his arms, standing awkwardly in the center of Aria's living room.

"Duh! Cuz you're weird!" Ivory giggled. Aria matched the woman's laugh as she stared over her shoulder at the Sorcēarian.

"I suppose that is reason enough." Dovian shrugged finally. "So, what's in that stuff?"

"Awesomeness," Aria replied. "Here, have a glass."

"I warn you. I am…what is the term you humans like to use?" Dovian pondered a second before nodding. "A lightweight." He chuckled deeply, accepting the glass of neon blue.

After a couple of drinks, the group slowly relaxed, conversing casually. Troy and Aria told past war stories, some heroic, others quite humorous. They did an excellent job avoiding any tale that involved death or tragedy. Ivory listened intently, amazed at every word from the soldiers' mouths. Dovian also listened, not saying much other than a word or two to contribute. One would think he was bored if he didn't smile occasionally, proving he enjoyed their company.

After a dinner of natural roast beef—not the cloned kind—and vegetables, they moved on to the cake. Ivory proved she was an excellent cook and had made the dessert from scratch, a rare talent. Aria thought that perhaps Ivory was a baker. She decided to later search for any recently missing persons who had an occupation as a chef.

After an embarrassingly loud and obnoxious birthday song and a couple of cake slices, the event calmed as bellies were full. Troy and Ivory moved to the couch, watching the television, as Aria stared from the bar out the kitchen window, now revealing the night city skyline. Dovian played with the leftover frosting from his third piece of cake, swirling the pink and blue colors together.

"Damn!" Troy shouted over the noise of the television. "Aria, we're outta beer." The man waved the empty box in the air while Ivory moaned sadly.

"You drank all my beer?" The black-haired woman twisted on her stool.

Troy sat on the couch with his tie undone and hanging over his chest. His legs were propped on the coffee table and intertwined with Ivory's slender ones. "I'm gonna get some more, 'kay?" He rose from the seat, stretching noisily with a groan.

"Fine by me." Aria shrugged. She frowned at the empty bottle beside her. *'Boy, that tasty liquor disappeared fast.'*

"Can I go with you?" Ivory begged, crawling onto her hands and knees on the sofa. "Please?!" She was utterly oblivious to the seduction of her pouty pose and messy hair.

Troy gave the innocent woman a cockeyed smile. "Sure!"

"Troy…" Aria glared.

"Please, Aria! I promise I won't talk to strangers!" Ivory turned her attention to the other woman. Her large eyes shimmered in the light of the side table lamp while her small lower lip stuck out. The military woman sighed aloud. This girl sure knew how to play people.

"I'll keep her safe. Nothin' to worry about." Troy waved dismissively at Aria.

"Just…watch her closely, you got it?" Aria aimed a finger at the man, giving him her lecturing tone. Ivory squealed happily and leaped off the couch. Pointing her toes, she slipped on Aria's heels. Troy frowned as Ivory was now nearly a head height taller than him.

"Okay," he gave Aria the attitude of a teenage boy and wrapped his arm around Ivory's waist. "Wait till you see the liquor store! It takes up a whole floor!"

"Really?" Ivory's high-pitched voice squealed excitedly as the door shut behind them.

"Poor Ivory. Troy's going to try to mack on her so hard," Aria groaned, resting her chin in her hand.

"Is he always this stupid?" Dovian finally spoke.

Aria laughed. "Only when there's a pretty girl nearby."

The Sorcēarian sat quietly for a moment, twisting his fork. He looked at Aria, perplexed. "Then he must be stupid all of the time."

Aria tensed, feeling the heat rise to her face. What did he mean by that? Surely, Dovian had not just insinuated that she was pretty. Aria swirled the remaining blue liquid in her glass before drinking it. "Is it hot in here?" She cleared her throat. Suddenly, she felt self-conscious in her tight black dress. It was probably just the alcohol.

Dovian laughed. "Yes, it is, but only because I'm wearing much more than you." He raised his arms, showing off the long draping sleeves of his robes.

"You can take it off," Aria suggested. Then she blushed. "I mean…that sounded bad."

Dovian stared at her momentarily, purposefully making the woman uncomfortable. She shuffled in her seat, trying not to stare at his glowing irises. A laugh escaped her lips as Dovian continued to stare blankly at her.

"You know what I meant!" She shoved his shoulder.

Dovian finally moved, smirking at achieving his goal of making the woman nervous beneath his stare. He approached one of the cozy chairs and removed his heavy brass armor. First, he unclasped the neckpiece, which connected to the rounded spaulders on his shoulders. The large blue orbs on the sides matched the color of his eyes, casting a beautiful iridescence. Attached to the armor with small gold chains was a scarlet cape adorned with gold-threaded wings on the back, matching the symbols of Dovian's staff. He removed the items, lowered the large red hood from his head, and placed everything on the cushion. Next, he detached the armored waistband and laid the article down. He then glanced at Aria and smirked, undoing the gold hook-and-eyes of his red overcoat. After removing the garment, he loosened his black robes, revealing a white bodysuit. Dovian was incredibly tall and lean with tight musculature. His hood had messed up his silvery hair, the light shimmering golden specks throughout the strands. It surprised Aria how much younger he appeared beneath the heavy armor and cloak. He no longer seemed quite as intimidating.

Sighing awkwardly, Dovian returned to Aria's side, dropped onto the stool, tilted to the side, facing her, and rested his chin in his palm. The long black sleeve dropped, revealing an armband. The white undersuit covered the backsides of the man's hands, looping around his middle finger. A red symbol adorned the cloth, matching the color and shape of the tattoo on his face.

"Well, that was quite the peep show," Aria said.

Dovian grinned youthfully. Before, he appeared much more mature, bulky, and menacing. As he relaxed, he seemed only a few years older than her. Aria couldn't help but stare. The man was fascinating. Dovian shifted beneath her gaze, a slight hum sounding as he laughed.

"Isn't it a hassle wearing all that?" she asked.

"You get used to it after a while."

"You wear that every day?"

"Usually. I was required to wear this once I received my status. It's made of lightweight fabrics, so it isn't as uncomfortable as one may think." Dovian drank the last drop at the bottom of his glass. He frowned when he noticed it was empty.

"Your status?"

"I was Scarlet status. It means I majored in science technology. Humans called it magic." He gave a short laugh.

"So, you were a scientist?" Aria asked, intrigued by this discovery.

"A military scientist. I was trained with the staff and used my science to meld with my weapon. Everything I am capable of doing isn't magic. It's all very logical and real. Humans seem to dub everything they don't understand as magical." He rolled his head and eyes to the side. "Or sorcery."

"That's why you are called a Sorcēarian?"

"Indeed. It came from the word 'sorcerer,' obviously." Dovian shook his head. "But, once trained with my staff, and after I mastered all our science, I became Scarlet. That was when I received my tattoos," he ran a finger along his cheekbone, "and my robes as a sign of my status."

"What were the other statuses?" Aria asked, staring at the blood-red mark on the man's face.

"There was Gold, reserved for the highest of the Elders. They were masters of all the arts and sciences. Emerald was used for those who mastered the arts. Violet—" Dovian drifted momentarily. The look in his eyes became distant before flickering back to Aria. "Violet was often reserved for military leaders. It was usually given to some of the most prominent families who influenced our people. They often became Gold later in life. Then there were the primary fighters, typically Scarlet or Azure. Scarlet was involved in physical battles. Azure delved into espionage and intelligence."

"That's blue, right?" Aria asked, her eyes narrowing.

"Yes."

"Then, Euclid was Azure." The woman frowned. Dovian observed her before nodding.

"He was the best we had, top of the Azure class. He tried his best to earn a secondary status, but the elders had restricted him. As you have probably figured out by now, Euclid was considered a bad egg."

"I can think of better words to describe him." She gritted her teeth.

"How was the funeral?" he abruptly asked. Upon seeing Aria's face turn from angry to sad, Dovian regretted the question. The room suddenly felt heavy. "I understand. I shouldn't have brought it up." He scratched his head, the sleeve pulling down his arm once again.

"What is that?" Aria pointed at Dovian's armband, completely disregarding the last subject.

"This?" He showed her the underside of the item. "It's my library of sorts. Inside is every text I would ever need from the Sorcēarian libraries. It is also a documentation of human history, something that every one of my kind was expected to study. I can connect to all specialized databases and search your satellites if needed."

"You can hack our systems?" Aria raised a brow.

"Oh, most definitely. But, no worries, I have no need to cause any trouble with this information. It's only for educational purposes. And finally, it has a verbal translator." He clicked a few buttons, the item chiming as he turned to her and said something in Legacy. Aria grinned; it was such a strange language. After another click, he spoke, "I can speak any known human language."

"Any language?" Her interest was piqued. "Honestly, I haven't heard much of anything outside of English."

"Would you like to hear some others?" he asked. Aria nodded, her eyes lighting up. "Okay, let's start with 'hello.'" He clicked a couple of buttons and began his list. "Salve, hola, guten tag, konnichiwa, bonjour, aloha, šalom, nín hao, ahoj, ciao, hej, dydh da, Здравствуйте." And he continued, each word becoming stranger and more foreign than the last. Aria gaped at the man. She had never heard these words before. After a few more, he stopped. "There are many more, but you get the point."

"I had no idea there once were so many languages. Some people understand a few ancient languages, but it's rare. Some of that didn't even sound like words!"

"When my race came to this planet, there were roughly 6,900 known languages." He pulled up a three-dimensional globe. The Earth rotated slowly, flickering. "This is how your world used to look. Since then, some plates have shifted, and a few landmasses have expanded. Here," Dovian pointed, "is Ives. Long ago, it had a bridge connecting to the neighboring continent. Humans used to travel to it freely. They looked up to us and came to us for our technology. We should have been wary when they started asking about genetics."

"We came to you about genetics?"

"Yes." Dovian paused and then looked at the woman humorously. "Do you know what shares roughly 50% of your DNA?"

Aria shook her head, taken aback by his question. "Uh, I dunno. A cat?"

He pressed on his armband, and a holographic image popped up, spinning slowly. It was a banana.

"A banana?" Aria giggled.

"Precisely. You share half your DNA with a banana."

"That's just not right. Bananas aren't even considered living things. I mean, not like you and me. It's a fruit!"

"Strange, isn't it?" Dovian smirked. "But it isn't that farfetched. It may seem like you're closely related, but there's still a vast difference when you look at it beneath a microscope."

"I…I don't even know what to say to that." Aria eyed the basket on the countertop, staring at the yellow fruit. "So, what's the difference between you and me?"

"Every human shares 99% of the same DNA. That one percent can surely make a difference, correct?"

Aria nodded.

"Well, there isn't much difference between you and me except that I have a quad-helix, and you only have a double helix." The armband projected a double helix splitting in two, the bands twisting around each other. "With this DNA sequence, I can use and understand 100% of my brain and motor functions simultaneously. The second double helix, different from yours, is attributed to our massive intellect—more neurons and synapses firing, basically twice your brain capacity. My kind has an instinct with bodily-kinesthetic, logical-mathematical, rhythmic, and visual-spatial intelligence."

"So, basically, you're just way smarter than us."

"Well, the second double helix you lack pertains to our divinity." Dovian narrowed his eyes. "The reason we can sprout wings from our backs."

"You have a type of hybrid DNA?"

"Yes. We were made this way."

"So, you're a smart hybrid of a human."

"Um, kind of. You're more of a dumbed-down version of me. It's hard to explain these types of things to humans. You don't have the capacity to understand fully."

Aria wrinkled her nose. Dovian cringed, realizing he had offended her.

"But that is not a bad thing." He held up his hand. "It's splendid that you humans are not as smart as my kind. The world would be a far more dangerous place. In fact, that's why the Sorcēarians failed." He lowered his head, staring blankly at the countertop, drifting into his subconscious. His mouth set in a rugged, thin line, and he suddenly looked much older again.

"But you can't control what other people do." Aria tilted her head to the side, catching Dovian's empty eyes. He straightened his posture, returning to the present once again.

"No, you cannot. Some humans are evil. Those evil people are the ones who ruin everything for those who are good. Ivory, for example. She has no recollection of her former life. She's, for some reason, a clean slate. And right now, she is untainted. You can tell that she's an innocent girl. She has a good heart." Dovian casually ran a hand through his hair, messing it further. "But, through her perspective, she'll see the world for what it really is, and eventually, it will corrupt her. It will change her. Whether for the better or worse will be her decision. That's why you all have free will. From the beginning of time, before you were created, everything had the opportunity to become corrupt, and it's the evil that taints everything."

Aria listened intently. She had some idea of what Dovian spoke of.

"Why create evil in the first place?" she asked.

Dovian's eyes widened. "Your kind was innocent initially, but selfishness and desire ruined that. Deception is one of the biggest evils. Besides, how would you feel if forced to be a good person? Where's the fun in that?" Dovian scoffed. Aria sensed a slight bitterness from the Sorcēarian. "Perhaps you all could be mindless drones, but from the Other's perspective," he pointed toward the ceiling, "He wouldn't feel if it were true, correct?"

"I'm not sure I get what you mean." Aria flipped her long bangs out of her eyes.

"How about this? From a stranger's perspective, you could be utterly useless. You're nothing to them. They couldn't care less if they saw you one day and heard you were dead the next. Now, to someone who knows you, someone close to you, you could mean the world to them. It's funny how, from one person's perspective, you are not important or don't even exist. But, from another person's viewpoint, you are their entire world." Dovian spoke loudly, almost passionately, about the subject. "That's how He feels, except He knows everything. He hears it all—the hate, the pain, the joy, the laughter. Now, think about it. Would you rather have a world where you don't get to choose who you love, and others don't get to decide if they love you? Or would you want a world full of your own choices? You'll know when someone loves you because they made that choice, not because they were forced to believe that way. Understand?"

"I think so."

"There's only one who can see all the perspectives and still value everyone, even a banana!" Dovian pointed at the fruit. "And despite it all, you are loved. Everyone sins. In fact, Ivory has probably already sinned a thousand times since we met her!"

"What? That's ridiculous. That girl doesn't even know what sin is," Aria scoffed.

"It doesn't matter if it's an action or a thought. Anything counts." Dovian raised a finger. "If a married man thinks of another woman…in a sexual context, he has sinned! It doesn't matter if he's acted on it. If you think about it, you sinned it."

"Is that what they taught you?" Aria asked.

"It is the way." He smiled. "Everyone, alive or dead, who has ever existed, even I and my race, have all sinned, except for one man. And he is—" Dovian's enthusiastic lecture abruptly ended once the front door to the apartment slid open. A boisterous Troy and Ivory stumbled into the room, a pack of beer in each of Troy's hands and a bottle of wine, already open, in Ivory's.

"Jesus, Dovian. Are you preaching to her?" Troy gawked at the man.

Dovian's face lit up. "Troy deserves a cookie!" he declared.

Aria smiled at Dovian's joke, which was utterly lost on the other two.

"Oh, look. Dovian took his clothes off," Ivory mumbled, poking at the armor sitting in the chair. Troy's eyes glared momentarily in Aria's direction.

"We'll continue this discussion later." Dovian patted Aria's hand.

The woman twisted in her stool, smiling amusedly at her partner. "Hey, Troy. Know what 50% of your DNA is?"

Troy lifted a brow. "A frog?" He shrugged.

"A banana!" Aria picked up one of the fruits and revealed it to the man.

"Babe…I'm 75% banana!" He waggled his eyebrows. Aria gagged and dropped the yellow fruit back into the bowl.

"I don't get it." Ivory cocked her head to the side.

Aria met Dovian's eyes. "See, he's already corrupting the innocent," the Sorcēarian whispered.

Troy stuck out his tongue and blew a raspberry at Dovian. "Hey, I got an idea. Aria's got Click-N-View. Let's watch Skin TV."

"What's that?" Ivory beamed with excitement.

"Troy." Aria rested her forehead in her palm. *Leave it to that idiot to watch porn in front of a priest.'*

"Dovian's Portrait"

CHAPTER 11

Dovian shifted, his limbs dragging across the cream carpet of Aria's living room. The sound of glass crashing together jolted the Sorcēarian from his slumber. He sat up, alert, glancing at the kitchen area.

"Sorry," Aria mumbled. The woman wore her basic nightwear of shorts and a T-shirt. Her hair looked flat, the tips curling around her jawbone. She yawned as she gathered more glass bottles from the countertops and tossed them into the garbage chute.

"Ugh," a noise sounded from the couch. "I feel like I was hit by a truck…and then backed over again." The lump beneath the blanket groaned.

Aria sauntered toward the couch, water in hand. "Here." She tugged the blanket off Troy's body. He narrowed his tired eyes at the woman. "Don't glare at me. I'm giving you a Hydrate." She handed him the glass and a small pill. Aria turned to Dovian. "Do you need one?"

"Not sure I know what a Hydrate is, but I assume it's something to rehydrate the body after a long night of binge drinking," Dovian replied dryly.

"Yup. Works like a charm, too." Troy sat up, yawning and scratching himself.

"Too bad it doesn't give one charm," the Sorcēarian muttered.

"Hey, I'm classy," Troy argued.

"Right." Aria shuffled back into the kitchen. She lifted the bottle of Hydrate and shook it, alerting Dovian. He shook his head 'no' at her, and she shrugged, taking one of the pills.

"I don't suppose those help rejuvenate the liver as well?" Dovian said with amusement.

"We're seasoned alcoholics, Dovian. Our livers would fail if we didn't drink," Troy spoke proudly.

"Not sure that's something you would want to brag about." Dovian arose from his makeshift bed on the floor.

"Get in here and help me clean up this mess," Aria grumped, tossing more bottles into the trash.

"I'll help," Ivory's cheerful voice sang enthusiastically from the hallway. "Ooh, coffee." She grinned, snatching up a mug as she rounded the bar into the kitchen. Ivory's golden locks sprung in all directions. Her pale skin had a perfect sheen that seemed to shimmer along with her smile as the morning sunlight beamed across her face from the parlor window. She was a sight of near perfection, a view that made Aria cringe.

"Only one cup for you," Aria lectured, her tone sending the blonde's cheerful smile into a pouty frown.

"Wait, did she just come from your bedroom?" Troy lifted an eyebrow.

"Yeah, she was in my bed. Believe me. It gave me quite the start when I woke up next to another body." Aria shuddered.

"Aria's so warm!" Ivory stated happily, clasping her hands together. She received a weird stare from the other female.

Troy made his way to the kitchen, scratching his head. "That's surprising. Figured her cold heart would freeze you to death."

The dark-haired woman threw a banana at the man's face, which he effortlessly caught, much to Aria's disappointment. He gave her a crooked smile. His stare dropped to the dirty dishes beside the leftover cake on the countertop. "Holy crap, that's a lot of candles!" He hooted, eyeing the remains as he unpeeled and began eating the fruit.

"Shut up." Aria rolled her eyes.

"Why were there so many candles on the cake anyway?" Dovian joined the three.

An irritated growl came from the military woman as Troy laughed. "Cuz Ivory thought using individual candles rather than numbered ones would be fun. I didn't want any candles in the first place," she said.

Dovian recalled the birthday cake from the night before. It, indeed, looked as if it were on fire. He looked confusedly at the woman. "But it had far too many candles for your age."

Aria gave a loud laugh at his statement. "How old do you think I am?"

Troy chuckled as he picked up the sticky, half-melted sticks and tossed them into the chute.

"I'm a terrible guesser, but between your late twenties and early thirties. Am I wrong?" the Sorcēarian asked.

Now Troy and Aria laughed together.

"Aria? Thirty? Ha!" Troy hooted. Aria elbowed him viciously.

"I'm that far off?" the Sorcēarian asked.

"Dovian," Aria said firmly, "I haven't been thirty in a long time."

"How long is a long time?"

"Come on, Aria. Tell him." Troy winked.

The woman huffed and folded her arms. Speaking quietly, she uttered, "Fifty-two."

"Excuse me?" Dovian leaned forward, his eyes widening. "You didn't just say fifty-two."

"What's wrong with fifty-two? I'm still young!" Now, she was greatly perturbed.

"Has anti-aging technology advanced so well? Plastic surgery?" Dovian thought aloud.

"I didn't use plastic surgery!"

Dovian remained completely dumbfounded. Since when did humans look twenty years younger without any medical enhancements? He turned to Troy. "And your age?"

Troy shrugged shamelessly. "Fifty-five."

Dovian then looked at Ivory. "I don't know!" she chimed.

"Something is amiss here." The Sorcēarian rubbed his chin.

"Well, look at you, Mr. seventeen thousand years old," Aria grouched. "You don't look much older than we do."

"Yes, but I am immortal." Dovian pulled up the globe on his wristband. He stared at the spinning sphere, watching the axis turn. "Of course. That explains it," he spoke in a low tone.

"What?"

"You humans have torn your world up so badly that you've changed the axis and gravity of Earth. You live longer, don't you?"

"Average lifespan is one hundred and fifty," Aria said with a shrug.

"Common knowledge," Troy added.

"Not when we first arrived. Humans only lived to be in their seventies or eighties on average."

"Shit, that's around Mr. Clarke's age. Can't imagine him kicking the bucket anytime soon." Troy scratched his head.

"That's not a very long lifespan," Ivory said. She frowned at her empty mug. Aria glanced at the blonde and gave her a warning look.

"Water," she ordered. "Rehydrate yourself."

"Oh, I feel fine." The slender woman waved a hand.

Perhaps Ivory was an experienced alcoholic as well. She should've been hiding under the covers or hugging the toilet with the amount she drank the night before. Aria dismissed the thought as Ivory filled her cup with the clear liquid instead. Maybe she and Troy were getting old.

"And it would probably explain why you all seem much taller than I remember," Dovian mumbled. He scanned Aria's body. "Unless I have shrunk, you all appear to be approximately a foot taller than your ancestors."

"Foot?" Aria asked.

"Approximately thirty and a half centimeters. You Americans used to use the standard system rather than metric," Dovian quickly explained. "Inches and feet."

"Huh, weird." Troy cocked his head to the side. "How would that work? I mean, everyone's feet are different." He lifted his foot.

"Was that back in the cubits day?" Aria asked, amused.

Dovian smirked, pleased with her reference. "A little later, but close based on our current timeline."

Ivory smiled and giggled nervously. "I have no idea what you guys are talking about." Troy gave her a gentle pat on the head.

An alarm chimed as the kitchen window flickered, revealing Mr. Clarke's face covering nearly the entire wall.

"Aria," the President stuttered. "Did you all have a slumber party?" he asked anxiously.

Aria smiled. "Hi, James."

"Happy belated birthday; it looks like you all had fun, but I'm afraid I'll have to put an end to your festivities."

"You got a lead?"

"Indeed. We've had a team of scientists looking over the destruction sites. After much study and testing of algorithms, they discovered something remarkably interesting." Clarke's face dropped from the screen, replaced by a world map display. "Within the first week, all attacks had taken place along the same parallel, nearly wiping out all the bases and cities." A thick line running along the 33rd parallel trailed across the map. "We've lost all communications with Dai-Ni-Tokyo and the Beijing Province. As you and Troy know, the first attack occurred in the Jordanian area at the 66th I.R.B. Afterward, the strikes happened between the continents at alternating intervals.

"Attacks have wiped out our bases in the northern Britainia Congo and the Roswell Camp. Tripoli, Columbia, Dallas, and Phoenicia's city-states were nearly destroyed. The economic crashes have been devastating and felt worldwide. The San Diego fault line was also hit, submerging that side of the country in catastrophic floods. There was no warning, and there are no survivors." He paused, and everyone swallowed back the shock of the devastating news. One by one, the world's city-states blinked with red dots, a black line connecting each one.

"The next week brought on attacks at our base port in the lower section of Upper America and the Chadian I.R.B. in Britainia Congo. Then there was the attack on our base, which surprisingly wasn't nearly as devastating as it should have been, comparatively to the rest of the world, which leaves me slightly suspicious."

"That is odd," Aria agreed.

"I'm looking further into that matter. Next were Athenia of Russite and the Manitoba district north of Upper America. After analysis, we found that the distance between certain city-states, such as Columbia and San Diego, was roughly 3,300 kilometers. It's the same distance from the lower base port and Manitoba. All signs suggest the next attack will occur in Cherno of Russite, the same angular distance from the I.R.B. in the Britainia Congo."

Sure enough, the map reflected a particular pattern—blue lines connected to the continents, revealing equal distances between significant city-states.

"Of course, it's only an educated guess, but I'd like you four to leave immediately. I have your flights booked."

"All four?" Aria looked over her shoulder at Ivory. "But sir, Ivory isn't a trained soldier. You can't send her out in the field."

"I'm afraid she would be safer with you, Aria. Mr. Walten has shown some interest in both of your friends. It concerns me."

"What would Walten want with Ivory?" Aria unconsciously stepped closer to the other woman.

Ivory nervously glanced at Aria and the giant face of Mr. Clarke.

"I'm unsure, but trust me. If you leave that girl here, I fear he may turn her into a pincushion. He believes she has a connection to Ives and the events unfolding here."

"I…I don't want to be a pincushion," Ivory meekly squeaked.

Dovian watched the blonde with an unreadable expression. He was curious about what the young woman had been doing on his continent, but she certainly wasn't from his world.

"Can you at least shoot a gun?" Aria asked the trembling blonde.

"I, I don't know, but I will try. I would feel better with some form of defense." Her fingers trailed over the silver dog tag around her neck. "If this necklace is any indication, maybe I was trained in the military like you were."

"I'll continue running ID scans to determine your identity, Ivory. For now, I want you to stay close to your companions, got it?" Clarke stated.

"Y-yes, sir." Ivory nodded.

"Good. Your flight leaves in an hour. I suggest you dress warmly. Keep in contact on private channels. Call when you get in." The screen flickered to black before slowly fading into a busy cityscape of flurrying vehicles.

"Oh, my," Ivory whispered. "I hope I don't get in your way."

"Dovian can be your bodyguard." Aria patted the girl's shoulder.

"Bodyguard?" Ivory trailed her blue eyes to meet the tall man's matching stare.

"If those are my orders." Dovian gave a short nod.

"Why can't I be her bodyguard?" Troy argued, following Aria into the living room.

"Troy, I need you to focus. You'd get yourself shot if I kept you by Ivory's side."

"Tch, fine." Surprisingly, he didn't argue further.

A soft ding sounded from Aria's apartment door. Opening the side panel on the wall, she removed a large envelope. Inside were her and the others' documents for the flight, coupled with boarding passes.

"Paper?" Troy asked, fingering the pages.

"Yup, I certainly doubt Dovian has a DNAIS chip," she said irritably, handing the relevant papers to the Sorcēarian. "Don't lose these. You will be traveling as a civilian, got it? When asked, tell them your chip has been damaged. You are traveling to Cherno to have the item repaired."

"It says here that I am a citizen of Cherno." Dovian pointed at his identification papers. He frowned at the photo used for the document. "Do they always pick the worst photos for these things?"

"Yup," Troy affirmed. "But that's all right. Those people over in Russite are weird. You'll fit right in."

"What about me?" Ivory asked.

"Here are your papers. Say that you are traveling with Dovian, and your chip is also damaged. We are unsure of whether you have a DNAIS or not. We could run a scan, but James is afraid it'll alert the system, and Mr. Walten would be able to track your movements. It's best if you stay off the grid for now."

"I look happy in my photo!" Ivory grinned.

"You always look happy," Aria muttered. "Okay, we have less than an hour. Pack your shit. Let's get moving. Ivory, let's raid my closet. We'll have to buy you something better fitting when we arrive."

"You mean we're going shopping?" The blonde nearly squealed.

Aria sighed long and low, rubbing her eyebrows. "Yes." She flinched at the young woman's exuberant cheers.

'I'm going to shoot myself,' Aria thought.

Boarding the plane wasn't as troublesome as Aria had expected, except for one slight hitch. Due to the recent attacks, Cherno was under a State of Emergency and didn't allow any military personnel into the city. That meant that Troy and Aria had to act as a married couple. Mr. Clarke had even made up a fake background for the two, detailing the time and date of their marriage. They also shared the same last name, taking Aria's title—Ivanov—much to Troy's dissatisfaction. However, Dovian and Ivory seemed entirely at ease with their fake backgrounds. The two stayed close to one another. Even when boarding the plane, the couple had their arms interlocked.

"We're getting married," Ivory grinned, telling the careless official at the gate as he looked over their documents. She leaned forward, her chest nearly popping the buttons off her ill-fitting vest and blouse. "I'm so excited!"

Dovian remained as stoic as ever, letting the blonde drag him through the terminal.

Aria handed her papers over. "Trust me. It's not all that it's cracked up to be," she grumbled. Troy rolled his eyes before smirking and wrapping his arm around the woman's shoulder, shaking her.

"Ain't that the truth? But I tell you what! Wouldn't trade this gal here for nuthin' in the world!" he twanged.

"That was a horrible accent," Aria whispered after the documents landed back in her hand.

"Wait till you hear my Cherno accent!" He smiled.

The two trailed behind the other couple. Ivory leaned her head against Dovian's arm, pointing out and giddily talking about every little thing she found interesting or cute. You'd think the woman had never been outside the city before.

"Oh, look at the baby! It's so cute!" Ivory pointed at a passenger and her small child. The woman nervously eyed Ivory and the tall man she was with, shouldering the infant on the other side of her body. The two stuck out like a sore thumb with their tall stature, strange clothes, light hair, blue eyes, and pale skin. Freaks.

"Yeah, real cute," Aria muttered. She couldn't help but cringe at the horrible cry the infant made.

"Wait till you see what's in the diaper." Troy shuddered with disgust.

"You two are so hateful," Ivory scolded.

Much to Aria's disappointment, they took their seats in the back of the plane. Couldn't they at least be considered wealthy couples who could afford first-class seating? At least the flight was with America Plus, the fastest airline on the planet. She took the window seat, gazing over the endless browns of the dead land far below as they took off. Troy tiredly flipped through a digital magazine he had downloaded onto his DNAIS, chuckling as he listened to the constant one-sided conversation in front of him.

"And I told her, if you can't say anything nice, you best not be saying anything at all. I mean, really, can you believe her?" Ivory carried on, making up stories about other female friends and the drama in her life, talking Dovian's ear off throughout the four-hour flight. "And the animals! They were so strange! Never saw anything like it before!"

Aria scoffed. She was amazed Dovian hadn't vaporized the annoying woman into dust by now. Instead, he would only nod and chuckle lowly in response to her antics. The two certainly knew how to play the part. Aria eyed Troy, who snored and drooled all over himself, crumbs from his flight snack scattered across his chest. She wrinkled her nose and brought her attention back to the other couple. Ivory giggled as Dovian whispered in her ear. Aria's face flushed. She angrily elbowed Troy, waking him from his slumber, quickly folded her arms, and glared out the side window.

"Hrm?! What?" He sat up, hair in disarray. "Was I snoring?"

Aria ignored him.

"Aw, nasty!" He laughed, wiping his hand across his mouth. "Did you see that? Had a drool strand going all the way to my elbow!"

Aria closed her eyes, letting out a slow breath. "You are so disgusting," she muttered.

"Wow! It's so pretty!" Ivory chimed in. She had her face pressed against the glass, looking over the tundra on the earth.

"Pretty?" Aria replied. "That's not pretty."

"What do you mean?" Ivory leaned back to look at the dark-haired woman.

"God, Ivory, do you really not know anything?" she huffed.

Ivory sunk a little in her chair.

"That's a frozen wasteland down there, caused by nuclear winter. We've blasted that land so many times that it'll never melt. The entire world is nothing but desert or frozen rock," Aria explained.

"It's still pretty. Even if ugly things caused it," Ivory whispered.

Aria also sank into her chair, resting her chin in her hand. "There's nothing pretty about this world."

"Ives is pretty," Ivory argued.

"Not as much as it used to be," Dovian joined the conversation. "Now, it's covered in dark, violent storms."

"But the rain is pretty! Dark clouds are pretty! The orange hue the storms cast was so pretty against the green grass. Even dark things have their beauty. And there are living things there, right?"

"Some. Mostly ugly lizards," Dovian said.

"Aw, come on! Lizards are cute, right? At least the baby ones?" she asked.

"You are certainly no pessimist." Dovian stared down at the woman.

"What's the point of always dwelling on the bad? There are countless wonderful things in this world that so many people overlook. I think if more people tried looking for the beauty in things, there wouldn't be so much hate and misery," Ivory spoke avidly, her yellow eyebrows furrowing as she lightly slapped her fist against her other palm. Dovian watched the young woman with interest. Her words sounded familiar. Though it was a simple, optimistic idea, Dovian knew he heard them before.

"More humans…people…should live by that example. In fact, I know of one who could benefit from it." Dovian turned his head, eyeing Aria. She lifted her hand, signaling to him with her middle finger, and he smiled before turning his attention back to his blonde counterpart.

"I'll work on her later," Ivory whispered, "when we're shopping!" She clapped her hands together.

A loud chime sounded, interrupting their conversation.

"Welcome to Cherno District. The time is 20:00. We are in a State of Emergency. Everyone calmly depart the plane. Luggage inspection has already taken place. We appreciate your cooperation and patience. Thank you for flying with America Plus Airlines." The pilot's voice had a thick Cherno accent. Aria took note of the inflection and hoped Ivory had done the same. She wasn't concerned about Dovian.

"Thank you for choosing America Plus," Ivory repeated, making her 'r's sound hard. "It's kind of like talking with peanut butter in your mouth."

'Close enough,' Aria thought.

It took about twenty minutes before Aria's group made it through the checkpoint while their luggage moved down a conveyor belt outside the walls of Cherno. Due to the state of emergency, security checks occurred outside the city as a preventative measure to keep the threats out. These types of things always made her nervous. Someone could easily lose their belongings. Clothing and souvenirs were strewn all over as the contents of the passengers' luggage were carelessly dumped and dug through. Ivory impatiently hobbled from one leg to another as she stood to wait in line.

"What?" Aria asked finally, annoyed with the girl's fidgeting.

"The stores are going to be closed," she whined.

"Stores around here don't close 'til midnight; you'll be all right," Aria grumbled.

Ivory repeatedly kicked at the snow. Smiling, she bent down and made a small snowball. Aria gave her a sideways glance, watching as the naive woman raised the ball to her lips, her pink tongue sticking out to lick it.

"No!" Aria slapped the item from her hand. "Don't eat that!" She gave the frightened woman a stern look. "God!"

'Why is she so stupid?!'

"You can't eat snow off the ground, not in a place like this," Aria lectured her. Ivory sadly stared at the smashed snowball on the ground.

"Heavy luggage you have here." A security officer heaved the woman's baggage.

"We're women; what do you expect?" Aria shrugged, turning her attention to the Cherno man.

He opened the bag and shuffled through the clothing. "Lots of containers...."

"Makeup," Aria said with irritation.

"You women and your makeup. Always getting dolled up. You all would look better without it," he said with his thick accent.

"Appreciate the input." Aria snagged her bag as the man zipped up the items.

"Have nice day." He waved casually.

"Have nice day," Ivory repeated. Aria tugged on her arm, pulling her away from the luggage checkpoint.

Together, they met up with the two men. Troy had his bag shouldered as Dovian carelessly dragged his behind him through the muddy snow.

"Papers," another officer ordered.

Troy handed over his documents.

"Ivanov." The security official nodded. "Good, strong Cherno name."

"Damn right, it is. Anyone got a problem with it, I'll kick their ass," Troy mimicked the officer's accent.

Aria quickly shoved Troy out of the way, handing her forms to the officer.

"You married?" he asked, eyeing Troy. Aria nodded. "Good, I like him." He gently pushed her through the line. "Next."

Ivory cheerfully handed over her documents.

"You four traveling together?"

"Yes! We're getting married!" Ivory stated happily, in a nearly perfect accent.

"Love is in the air!" The officer shrugged. "Okay, good." He looked up at Dovian, and his face suddenly fell. "You getting married to this gangly?"

"Gangly?" Ivory asked.

'Oh shit.' Aria stopped Troy mid-step.

"Yeah, gangly," the officer repeated.

"Is there a problem?" Aria asked.

"No, no problem. Just a tall motherfucker. Better watch his back." Aria wasn't sure if the officer was trying to give good advice or was threatening Dovian.

"He can watch his own back, believe me," Troy said.

The officer looked at Troy and quickly handed the papers over to Dovian. "Welcome to Cherno."

"Спасибо," Dovian said curtly to the man as he followed down the line.

However, the officer kicked Dovian behind his legs before he could make it through, sent him to his knees, and carefully aimed his rifle at Dovian's head.

"You think you are being smart?"

"Whoa! What's going on?!" Troy rushed to Dovian's side, unconsciously reaching for the weapon he no longer possessed. *'Damn it.'*

"This man thinks it's funny to make jokes."

"What'd you do, Dovian?" Aria asked.

"I was merely saying thank you," Dovian growled through gritted teeth, his hands on the back of his head.

Aria grimaced with irritation. *'We do not need this. We do not need this kind of attention; we've already brought enough to ourselves without the police officials adding to the problem.'*

"He mocks my accent." The officer pressed the barrel of his gun against Dovian's head. Ivory watched, wide-eyed at the scene. Dozens of people stared in awe.

"Dovian…" Aria said in a warning tone.

"I was only trying to be respectful, speaking in one's native language."

"You insult us. Speak only English. You can get yourself killed."

It didn't make sense to Dovian. One used to be flattered when a foreigner tried to learn the native language of the country they visited. However, now it seemed to be considered an insult.

"Check his papers closely," Aria argued. "He's native to this country. It may not say it, but he's a studied linguist. He was only trying to be respectful of yours and his heritage."

The officer lowered his weapon, tugging Dovian to his feet. "You be careful. Words like that can get you killed. You look crazy 'nough as it is with your weird clothes and optic enhancers."

"Noted," Dovian replied, feeding the man a fiery glare.

"Come on." Aria tugged Dovian.

The Sorcēarian's face contorted into a scowl, and Aria shuddered. He looked downright pissed.

"You should be ashamed of yourself." Ivory pointed at the officer. Troy quickly pulled the woman with him.

"You can't do things like that, Dovian. I know you were only trying to be nice," Aria said.

"Your people are menaces."

Well, she couldn't argue with that. It certainly was an unpleasant welcome, but Russite wasn't the most pleasant of places. For the rest of the trek to the hotel, everyone remained silent.

Their hotel was positioned in a dark corner of the city. Aria and Troy didn't much care for the location or state of the building, but they were trying to be discreet.

Ivory thought it was beautiful, with its fluorescent lights playing off the icicle-laden windows. They retrieved the keys to their rooms. Dovian and Troy would share a place, while Aria and Ivory shared their own.

"Trade ya keys?" Troy asked.

"Not a chance," Aria replied, lugging her hefty baggage up the stairs.

"Heavy?" he asked.

"Yeah…got our rifles inside."

Hidden amongst all the tiny containers were the parts of Troy and Aria's weapons. The containers themselves made up the frames as the pieces snapped together. The bullets were currently in liquid form, and once set overnight in their moldings, they would be ready to fire. Thanks to Dr. Camery's detailed research, they were capable of formulating ammunition with electromagnetic static. When loaded into the weapon, the gun chamber would electrically charge the highly conductive metal. The speed and rate of spin on the bullets then created a miniature disruptive field, making it capable of piercing through the Faze Shields the monsters carried. Aria and Troy had no chance to test the new weapons, but Camery had reassured them of their success rate.

Ivory effortlessly carried her suitcase over her shoulder, humming a little tune. She didn't seem concerned with the weight of her bag, which was packed with her sniper rifle components. Aria thought it best to keep the woman away from the action on a rooftop, somewhere she would be safe. It seemed dangerous, especially since the rifle was still in the prototype phase and didn't yet have auto-aim capabilities. Still, Aria had told her many times not to shoot unless it was absolutely necessary and only if there were no humans near her target. They could always train her later. Aria hoped that no confrontation would occur at all during their stay.

After setting out the gun parts and filling the molds, Ivory had whined enough to break Aria's resolve. It was time to go shopping.

"Hi, Dovian! Want to come?" Ivory asked the brooding man in the hall. He held his staff, previously dismantled between his and Troy's luggage.

"Hell, no! Dovian's coming with me," Troy shouted from down the hall. "I'm buying the poor man a drink."

Ivory pouted slightly.

"Dovian. Put your staff away," Aria ordered.

"I'd prefer it to stay with me."

"You can't just carry that thing around; you'll cause problems."

"It could cause more problems if I don't have it." His eyes narrowed to thin lines.

"It's okay. He can take his pole," Troy interrupted.

"Troy—" Aria argued. He held up a hand to quiet her.

"If anyone asks, we can say he's one of those *roleplayers*."

"Roleplayer?" Dovian eyed Troy.

"Yeah, you look like a nut. We'll say you're going to reenact some World of Sorcery battle scene. All the nerds do it."

"If it allows me to wield my staff, then fine," Dovian muttered, walking away from the three.

Smiling, Troy mouthed to Aria, 'Oh, my God.' She rolled her eyes.

"Don't drink too much. We'll be back soon. I'm going to need one before the night is through," Aria mumbled, leading Ivory to the outdoors.

Troy waved to the girls and slowly headed to the hotel's bar area. In the back—the darkest corner of the room—sat Dovian, his eyes glimmering. The soldier made his way to the table, eyeing the area. Luckily, there were few people in the bar.

"Whatcha havin'?" Troy asked as he plopped roughly into his seat.

"Any type of ale that would put one in a better mood," Dovian grumbled.

"Whiskey?"

"A horrid choice…and I don't think that can be classified as a type of ale," Dovian said scathingly. After a moment, he continued, "Sure."

"Alrighty!" Troy slapped his hands together. "Yo! Barman!"

The rough-looking bartender lifted his head.

Troy winced under his furry-browed glare. "Two whiskeys?"

"No whiskey. Lots of vodka," the bartender replied.

Troy eyed Dovian, who shrugged.

"Sounds tasty!" Troy replied.

"Old Boris will fix you right up." The bartender nodded.

"Yay…Boris." Troy gave a thumbs-up. "I like this guy. Look at him…all lumber-jackey."

Dovian trailed his bored gaze from Troy to Boris. The man was stocky, big-armed, and with nearly no neck at all. His nose was broad and crooked, his jaw jutted out to the side, and his eyebrows were thick in one full line.

"He is quite hairy," Dovian agreed.

"Two vodkas." Boris slammed two glasses onto the metal table. "You start tab?"

"Yes, sir," Troy said.

"Good. I keep eye on you." Boris signaled, pointing to his eyes and then at Troy's. After a second, he then pointed to Dovian.

"Sounds good." Troy nodded slowly and then eyed the thick glasses on the table. He was expecting shots, not tumblers. "Eh, how much are these?"

"It's homebrew. Real cheap. Knock you on your ass," Boris replied, cleaning a few glasses with a towel that appeared less than sanitary.

"How I like 'em." Troy lifted the glass to his lips. The scent was strong, almost like a chemical cleaner, and his nose wrinkled as he gagged. It was going to be painful. He seemed fearful, holding the glass against his lips as Boris watched him.

Dovian slowly raised his drink. "Down the hatch?" he finally asked Troy.

"Down the hatch." They clinked their glasses together and poured the pungent liquid down their throats. "Oh, gah! It burns!"

"That…is horrendous." Dovian cleared his throat, a rather distasteful look on his face.

After several coughs and gags, the two men stared at one another.

"Good shit, right?" Boris asked.

They both gave a small laugh. "Yeah. Good shit, Boris." Troy signaled for another refill, which Boris gratefully obliged.

Deciding to take things slow on the next round, Troy and Dovian sat quietly in each other's company. Boris played some old tunes on the digital jukebox. The strange, nasally sound of the music set the tone for a lonesome atmosphere. Dovian sipped casually from the bitter liquid. A chime sounded from the opening door of the hotel. A young couple shuffled in, covered lightly with snow debris. They giggled quietly and made their way toward the bar. Boris busied himself with mixed drinks.

"Any idea where the attack will be taking place?" Dovian asked as the room filled with more noise.

"We speculate it will occur during the Stock Talks. Apparently, Vitaly Lebedev wants to buy out Elixis, one of the leading electrostatic research and development competitors. He already owns most of this city. The talks are supposed to be televised all over the world."

"And why would this man want to buy this company?"

"I dunno. Money. Elixis makes trillions of units each year. Can you imagine the amount of money and power one could receive by owning that company? It'd be like owning the biggest form of science the world has to offer," Troy lowered his voice. "Electrostatic technology is used for nearly everything. Militaries use it for force shields, ammunition, EMP weaponry, and hovercrafts. It's used for electricity, transportation, biomechanics, the medical field, and even something as little as holographic imagery. It's everywhere! If this guy buys out the company, he could easily buy out the entire world."

"That's a scary thought." Dovian glanced at Boris. The burly man was on his DNAIS, arguing with someone.

"Yeah, very scary. There's no balance anymore. We've known about the Stock Talks for a while now. Bio-Tech's been all over this intel for a long time. In fact, we were originally supposed to set up an operation—infantry and flanks—along the city's outskirts in case Lebedev was successful."

"You were going to start a war?" Dovian asked.

"Hell yeah. It helps balance the scales." Troy nodded. Dovian didn't look too pleased with this information. "But then those monsters showed up and ruined all plans for that. We'll have to wait and see now."

"Maybe the attack will occur before the talks conclude," Dovian murmured.

"That'd be nice," Troy paused, "Well, no, it wouldn't be nice. It would be nice if there were no attacks and Elixis kept their business in their own hands."

"I still cannot figure out why the monsters would attack during such a time. I had the suspicion that they only wanted to destroy things. This makes it sound like your military has figured out something useful and is not sharing that information with anybody," Dovian spoke softly, swirling the liquid in his glass.

"Hey, Mr. Clarke wouldn't hide anything from Aria and me. He wouldn't put us at risk like that."

"It's possible he isn't aware of the information either and is also being kept in the dark," he suggested.

Troy thought for a moment. What Dovian was insinuating was something unheard of. Why would Mr. Walten keep any secrets from President Clarke? Was something like that possible? Clarke did state that something fishy was going on in the upper side of Bio-Tech. He even warned Troy of his suspicions regarding Walten's behaviors.

"I dunno. You could be right. I just hope Mr. Walten realizes the grave mistake he could be making if he kept secrets from the President, who runs his company." Troy swallowed the rest of his liquid. Another chime at the door brought his attention to the bustling bar. When did so many people show up?

"Good, you're still here." Aria shook out her trench coat and tossed her hair, snow falling to the floor. Ivory stood beside her, shaking her furry-hooded head.

"That was fast," Troy stated.

"It's snowing pretty hard out there. Can barely see a meter in front of you." She shivered, her teeth clattering together.

"It's beautiful!" Ivory sang, jostling her bags from side to side between mitten fingers.

"You call something beautiful one more time, and I'm smacking you," Aria growled.

Ivory stuck her tongue out at the military woman, not caring that Aria saw. "Aria needs a drink," she said in a cross tone.

"Aria always needs a drink," Troy grumbled, scooting his chair to the side to allow the women to sit with them.

"Find something to your liking?" Dovian asked Ivory.

The woman had three colorful bags in her hands. She bit her lower lip, nodding happily.

"Yeah, she nearly broke me," Aria grumbled.

"Don't let her fool you. Not all of these are mine." Ivory grinned.

"Oh?" Troy glanced at the black-haired woman beside him.

Aria twirled the electric-blue tresses of her side bangs around her finger. "I maybe bought a thing or two."

"She bought underwear," Ivory blurted.

Aria glared at the blonde.

"The lacy kind," Ivory added.

Aria pressed her face into her hands. "Why don't you go upstairs and put on your new clothes? Show the boys what you bought."

"Okay!" Ivory spun on her heels and darted toward the staircase leading to the rooms.

"You're not going to try on your new items?" Troy asked mischievously. "To show us?" Aria lowered her hands, her green eyes shooting lasers at him. "No?"

"Order me a drink," she spat out sourly.

"Sure." Troy quickly scooted from his chair and headed to the crowded bar, flagging down the sweating Boris.

"Had fun, I presume?" Dovian asked.

Aria puffed out her cheeks, slowly breathing out. "Tons."

"She's quite the handful, isn't she?"

"You'd know; you were married to her for a day."

Dovian chuckled. The sound was low and hollow in his chest. "A little talkative, but she means well."

"Very talkative. She never shuts up. And everything is cute and beautiful. Bunny rabbits and rainbows," Aria scoffed. "I feel like I need a shower…to wash off all the cheerfulness."

"It's not all that bad, is it?"

Aria looked up at the Sorcēarian. His eyes were bright in the dark tavern. The light highlighted his features, a vivid contrast to the red tattoos on his eyelids—a look she had still not grown accustomed to.

"No. She's not bad, just annoying. I'm just not used to people like her."

"Maybe humanity could use a little amnesia." He chuckled.

"That would be nerve-wracking," Aria groaned.

"Not if you had it as well."

"You going to wipe my mind a clean slate?" Aria asked.

"Maybe, if I had the ability." He smirked.

"You don't have that ability? I thought you could do anything, Dovian."

She leaned forward, carefully eyeing the man before her.

"Oh, I can do lots of things, my dear."

"Like what?"

"Like—" he reached back for his staff. Aria gripped his hand.

"No staff. What things are you capable of doing without that weapon?"

Dovian leaned down, closing the gap to where their faces almost touched. Aria stiffened under his vibrant stare. "Those types of things are more personal."

"Personal?" she questioned, her voice involuntarily rising in pitch.

"If I were to do anything without my staff, it would require me to touch you. You see…" Dovian grabbed the woman's wrist and twisted it to raise her palm, "my body houses all the power I need. My staff acts as a conductor, allowing me to expel the energies the way I would need for combat." He moved his fingertip across the woman's palm. Tiny prickles of electric light sparked from his hand, trailing down his finger to her palm. The surge traveled down Aria's wrist, spiraling across her arm. It didn't hurt, and she found the sensation soothing. The blue lights swirled toward her shoulder, and she glanced up at Dovian, his eyes matching in intensity. Looking behind her, he quickly removed his hands from hers, the sensation dissipating altogether.

"One vodka—" Troy started. He stood beside the table, feeding Dovian a strange look. The soldier's crooked grin quickly fell as he turned his attention to a blushing Aria.

"Took you long enough," Aria muttered after a beat.

Troy's tense posture gradually loosened as he plopped onto the seat beside her, handing over the drink.

"Boris was in the middle of refilling the homebrew. Had to wait."

"Boris?" Aria asked, breathing a nervous laugh. "You know the bartender's name?" She did well to hide whatever strange thing she and Dovian had previously been in the middle of, acting oblivious to the fact that they were mere centimeters away only moments ago.

"Kinda rough around the edges, but I like him," he said.

"You always like those types."

"Hang out with you every day, right?"

"I'm not rough around the edges; I'm slightly frayed," she teased, drinking from her tumbler. She coughed. "Oh, God! What is that? Window cleaner?"

"Good shit, right?" Troy asked.

"No, terrible." Her face twisted as she took another sip. Aria nervously looked to the side. Dovian leaned back in his chair, arms folded. He seemed utterly detached from the others, watching the civilians in the room. His gaze then lifted to the stairs. The corner of his lips turned upward, and the militants peered in the same direction.

Troy whistled. "Take a look at that."

Ivory stood at the top of the stairs. She descended gracefully with a broad smile on her pale yet rosy face. Noticing every man in the room gawking at the fair-skinned woman, Aria suddenly felt sick. Who was Ivory? And why was she so damned perfect?

Adorned in fancy Cherno fashion, Ivory wore a yellow gathered halter, chain ties centering atop her chest with a white stony jewel. Above that, joined by golden bangles and more chains, was a tangerine-colored bolero jacket, gold imprints decorating the materials. Her middle was squeezed into a black leather corset, tailing with a golden ribbon over her backside. A tasseled belt wrapped around her waist, centered with a similar white stone. Matching leather leggings with a ridged texture covered her legs, along with knee-high laced boots identical to what Aria wore. It wasn't practical at all. She looked like a model.

Ivory crossed the bar, anxiously tugging her fingers. A tattooed woman with purple hair rushed to the blonde's side, grabbing her arm. Aria quickly jumped from her seat and ran to Ivory's side.

"Excuse me. I have to ask," the woman said. "What dye did you use to get that skin tone?"

"W-what?" Ivory asked.

Aria snaked her arm around Ivory's elbow. "Body Style by Chenar, dye color: Ivory," she quickly sputtered as she pulled Ivory back toward the table.

"She thought I had dyed my skin?" Ivory questioned.

"Yes, Ivory. You color your skin, dye your hair, and wear optic enhancers. Do not, under any circumstances, let anyone know that you are naturally—" she held her breath. *'Beautiful. Just say it,'* Aria lectured herself.

"Natural?" Ivory asked.

"Yes. No, you're not natural. I mean, you are, but you're not normal," she stuttered a moment before sitting the other woman and herself down. "People get jealous easily. They also fear strange and unnatural things. And, well, your pale skin and hair are very unnatural these days. You can't let people know it's your natural skin tone, hair color, or eye color, or they may attack you. It's for your own safety."

"O-Okay," Ivory whispered.

"Remember what happened earlier to Dovian?" Aria asked. Ivory nodded like a child. "That could happen to you."

"Okay."

Aria leaned back in her chair, sipping from her glass. She eyed the solemn woman beside her. For the first time, Ivory wasn't a basket of kittens. Aria suddenly felt a bit sorry. It wasn't Ivory's fault she was gorgeously different.

"Here." She handed the glass over to the blonde. Ivory gave it a curious look and then smiled, downing the rest of its contents.

"Oh. That wasn't pleasant," she coughed.

"Get used to it. Hang around us, and you'll be needing it," Aria said.

Aria then realized that if an attack occurred tomorrow, there was a good chance this was the last time the four of them could be alive together. It was the first time the idea had occurred to her. It did nothing to soothe her nerves either. But, if they did survive an attack, they would surely need another drink of Boris' horrible homebrew vodka. It was a good thing Aria packed an extra bottle of Hydrate.

"Ivory and Her BFG"

CHAPTER 12

Rustling leaves clattered against the stone pathway. The chilly air wrapped around Aria's body, twisting her thick coat across her knees. Echoes of her boots clapped loudly in her ears, puddles of water splashing underfoot with uneven tones.

"Are you ready for the show?" a male voice gently sounded from far, far away.

Aria wrapped her arms around herself; her hands clenched the black fabric of her sleeves.

"Look out! Everybody get down!" Voices from all around, echoing whispers in the woman's ears, called out in panic. "Honey?"

A gust of wind rushed past her, tousling her hair. Strands of black and blue streamed over her eyes, some sticking to her trembling lips.

"You have to get her out of here! Aria!" the pitches rose—a woman's voice screaming.

A thunderous boom, a vibration of noise, shook the stark landscape of brown and red leaves. The explosion heightened in volume, and Aria shook, falling to the side as a bright light engulfed her, turning everything white. A shrill shriek sounded, burning her ears. It lasted only a couple of seconds, leaving her in a silent black. Opening one jade eye after another, she slowly stood. She listened quietly to the new gurgling sound around her, looking side to side.

"Aria..." a choking voice whispered—a sound like death.

She froze, icicles spreading down each vertebra. Slowly turning while clenching her jacket, Aria shook in the cold that enveloped her. Her breath stopped as she saw a body lying face down on the stone pathway. A single ray of light in the darkness shined above her and the man beside her. She dropped to her knees, the pain sending shockwaves through her body as she quickly reached down and gripped the man's white dress shirt. Her knees were wet, soaked with the blood that covered the concrete. Slowly, she turned him over. Holes covered his torso, torn deep into the man's flesh. A murky, dark crimson spilled from the man's wounds.

His face contorted. He did not die peacefully. He looked terrified, with his mouth opened wide as if he had been screaming. Aria quickly recoiled, falling backward onto the stone. The cold promptly evaporated into desert heat. The landscape lit up as the streetlamps lining the brick road consumed the darkness. Stores and vehicles occupied the streets next to a theater, now set ablaze, with debris and bodies all around. The corpse before her trembled with a turbulent force, and everything exploded into crimson, shockwaves shaking the woman as she screamed.

"Daddy!" Aria shouted. She flew forward, her sheet falling from her chest. Darkness surrounded her; a soft hum came from the clock at the bedside. It was all just a terrible nightmare, one that Aria very much had not wanted to relive. Moaning quietly, she quickly wiped away the tears on her face. Self-consciously, she hastily turned her head to the bed next to hers. Thankfully, Ivory remained in a deep sleep, unmoving and entirely under the covers, reminding Aria of how dreadfully cold it was. Goosebumps lined her arms, and she shivered, her teeth chattering in the freezing temp of her hotel room. Eyeing the alarm clock beside her, she sighed. It was three in the morning.

One toe poked the wooden floor and then another before she planted her feet on the icy surface. With a swift tug and pull, she wrapped a sheet around her body and traveled to the heating unit beside the window. Aria gave it a swift kick, sending the device into a dull hum and shake as it sputtered back on, temporarily warming the room.

"Piece of shit," she muttered tiredly to the ancient technology and turned to the bathroom, snatching a glass to fill with water.

The light blinded her in the small lavatory. Her eyes were nearly slits as she turned on the freezing water. She glanced at her weary reflection and gasped, seeing two blue eyes attached to an enormous black mass behind her. A short yelp sounded, and she turned, dropping the glass in the sink. Nothing. There was nothing behind her. Aria exhaled long and low. Turning her gaze back to the mirror, she stared through the reflection at the ugly painting of blue flowers on the wall above the towel rack. Her nightmares had left her imagination a little wild. Still, she didn't hesitate to quickly yank at the shower curtain and peer inside before refilling her glass and leaving the room.

'Can never be too safe....'

A sudden, soft knock frightened the woman again. After giving a short jump, water sloshed over the sides of her tumbler and down her front. Aria tightly clenched her teeth.

'Damn it!'

Setting the glass down, she shuffled toward the entrance to her room, pulling the blanket tighter around herself. She opened the door and shuddered as she was greeted by a tall, dark figure, cerulean eyes gleaming down at her.

"Damn it, Dovian. You scared me," she huffed out.

He didn't wear his typical robes; instead, he donned only his skintight white undersuit. The light from the hall allowed no detailed view but gave him a sleek silhouette topped with an illuminating halo as it reflected against his pale hair. "My apologies. I thought I had heard some noise from your room and decided to check up on you ladies." His bright eyes darted to the sleeping lump on the second bed in the room—Ivory.

"Yeah, yeah, we're fine. I just dropped a glass in the sink," Aria stuttered.

Dovian stared at her momentarily, his dark face showing no emotion as he deliberated. "Very well; I'll leave you to your slumbers," he said after a minute.

"Okay," Aria whispered, avoiding his scrutinizing stare.

Dovian turned to walk away but hesitated. Something reflected in the light, grabbing the woman's attention. Lining Dovian's spine was a long, thin back apparatus. It was silver, molded to the shape of a spinal cord with two wings—one angelic and one demonic—attached to his shoulder blades. A couple of colored lights lined the center between the wings, blinking at random intervals.

"Aria," his deep voice droned, pulling her from her questioning thoughts.

"Hm?"

"…Sweet dreams." It sounded more like a request than a statement.

She gave him a sideways smirk and a raised eyebrow. "Yeah, um, you too." Giving a small wave, she closed the door to her room.

The area seemed so much larger in the dark. Her eyes adjusted quickly; moonlight flooded in from the cracks in the curtains as they swayed in the gentle breeze of the heater, casting white light against the two beds lining the wall. From the shadows, Aria watched between the moving, curtained gaps. Snowflakes dropped onto the streets and windowsill outside. Besides the shimmering moon, the sky remained black, a stark contrast to the bright golden lights of the city. Ivory was right. It was beautiful. She turned her attention to the sleeping body as it twisted in the bed. Blonde hair framed Ivory's pale face. The light from the window cast a beam across her slumbering features, reminding Aria of the sun. Surrounded by a vast amount of darkness, Ivory still shone brightly. Aria scoffed and shuffled her freezing butt back to bed, drinking from the icy glass of water. She hoped it would somehow lull her back into a more peaceful slumber.

Morning came fast. Luckily, no more nightmares plagued Aria the rest of the night—she didn't have a single dream, at least from what she could remember. It wasn't the most peaceful of sleep; the damn heater in the room seemed to flutter off as soon as it turned on, leaving her wrenching and fighting for warmth the rest of the night, but it was still better than long-ago memories she would rather forget.

She fidgeted, trying to muscle up some warmth as she sat on the rooftop of the building across from city hall, where the Stock Talks were in session. The hardest part of covert missions wasn't always keeping oneself from being spotted; it was sitting for hours in terrible weather conditions without any breaks, such as an icing blizzard. She set down her electrically charged rail gun, ECRG-15, and rubbed her hands together. The weapon whined, momentarily materializing visually against the snow before she lifted it again, her optical camo suit merging with the gun, pulling it back into invisibility. It wouldn't be so bad if she could wear her trench, but the dress coat wasn't capable of optical changes like her suit was.

"Anything on your end?" Troy asked through his mental chip.

"Not a damn thing," she replied.

Looking through her monocle camera, Aria zoomed in on Troy. Her thermal optics highlighted yellow around Troy's invisible form atop the roof opposite the building. She saw him give a casual wave, which she returned.

"Nothing on my end either," Dovian's voice chimed in. He was, unsurprisingly, capable of mental communication as well. Aria assumed it had something to do with his back apparatus. She turned her sights to the building beside her. His heat signature shimmered in a bright red, matching his robes. There were no doubts in the woman's mind that he somehow had his own built-in heater. He could even cloak with the use of his staff.

"How about Ivory?" she asked.

"She seems to be fine. I see her looking through her scope right now. She is waving at me. I did not realize her weapon had thermal imaging," Dovian said.

"I didn't think it did either," Aria muttered curiously, looking at the blonde who waited on top of their hotel roof in the distance. The colorful blip, with a red center and nearly blue-green outline, waved excitedly at the woman. Aria frowned. She greatly hoped Ivory wouldn't need to use her weapon. The 20mm, double-barreled sniper rifle was equipped with modified electromagnetic field disrupter ammo, EMFD, like Aria and Troy's weapons. It shot in double bursts and was nearly the same height as the woman. The gun's recoil could knock Ivory over, even when

mounted securely. The thought made Aria cringe. If the blonde weren't careful, she could quickly fire two shots in separate directions, despite nearly simultaneous bursts, with a kick like that. Nevertheless, it was better for Ivory to wait as far away as possible rather than up close and personal with nothing more than a measly handgun with auto-aim capabilities.

"How much longer till the talks are over?" Troy whined. *"I'm freezing my ass off."*

Checking the time on her DNAIS, Aria replied, *"Seems we got half an hour."* Her eyes fell on the giant screen outside the city hall, where they televised the Stock Talks. Hundreds of citizens lined the streets, watching the debates as they tended to their everyday errands. Many visited Cherno's convention center, where a massive science exhibition was in progress, which could mean more potential casualties. Surrounding the building were dozens of soldiers in heavy, top-of-the-line body armor. At least the Cherno military was on alert. However, it only made Aria's job much harder. If she and the others were caught, they'd be in serious trouble if not killed on the spot.

Thunderous applause sounded as Lebedev finally took the stage. He was a middle-aged man with grown-out dark hair and a graying beard. A furry ushanka cap covered his head with his city-state's emblem pinned to the front. The grey hat matched the color of his Cherno-style suit—trim-legged with a long dress coat.

"There he is. Everyone, be alert," Aria warned the others.

"My fellow Cherno residents!" Lebedev saluted. "I come to you this day not only as an investor of our great city but as a protector. As many of you have heard over these past few months, I have recently negotiated with Elixis Corporation, the mass contributor to electrostatic products. As a citizen born and raised in this great city, I want nothing more than to protect it and its citizens the best I can from future military onslaughts. As history tells us, our city was once uninhabitable, nothing more than a nuclear wasteland for thousands of years. That has all changed! Our home is again thriving; it is the largest in all of Russite! That makes us an easy target. I've heard rumors that some militaries have planned a surprise attack, unhappy with my negotiations to buy out Elixis. As it was in the past, mass conglomerates wish to own all advances in technology and biomechanical warfare. Some elitists want to take everything, own it all, own you! Corporations like in the United Americas. Corporations like Bio-Tech Military Corporation."

"Oh shit," Aria mentally called out.

"Well, enough is enough! I plan to buy out Elixis. Not out of greed, but out of safety for my people!" Cheers and shouts sounded as Cherno seemed to support Lebedev's actions. "So now, I tell you, today is the day Cherno will stand tall! Elixis, I make my bid to you."

Lebedev walked off the stage and removed an envelope from his breast pocket.

He graciously handed it to a plump man wearing an expensive navy-blue pinstriped suit. Bowing, Lebedev quickly took his seat. The accountant for Elixis, the stout man, whispered to the suits sitting with him at a round table. Lebedev smiled proudly; he seemed confident. After a few minutes of silent debate, the plump man handed Lebedev's and another previously opened envelope to a tall, thin, well-dressed man of a later age, the owner of Elixis, Martin Russo. Martin owned Elixis and maintained and partnered with many corporations in Athenia—a city nearly destroyed days ago. Athenia needed money to rebuild and flourish, and Elixis was considered expendable.

"Now, if there aren't any objections, I'd like to continue with the decision," Martin spoke in his native accent—his 'h's silent and consonants mixed—with hesitation. Lebedev looked over his shoulders and grinned. No one made a sound. "I 'ave 'ere, in my hands, two bids to buy out Elixis." At this, the crowd exploded into a noise of murmurs and whispers. Lebedev's face fell as he suddenly appeared ill. "Upon much deliberation, my staff and I 'ave concluded, based on the bid amount, to trade ownership over to Mr. Walten, CEO and owner of Bio-Tech Military Corporation."

"Oh shit!" Aria mentally screamed.

"Holy shit, Aria!" Troy shouted through his mental chip, giving the woman an instant headache.

The streets exploded with noise; a complete uproar had started. On-screen, Lebedev rose from his seat, pointing and shouting angrily.

"You traitor! You sell out! You betray your own country, Russite!" he cursed.

Martin Russo pocketed the winning bid and handed Lebedev's back. "My country was once something great until your people bombed it and reduced it to nearly nothing. We support our old allies, and as much as I was willing to help you because I do like you, Lebedev, in the end, the 'ighest bidder wins."

"H-how much? I'll raise it! Double it!" Lebedev reached for his checkbook, a piece of paper that could only be authorized by fingerprint and a drop of blood. "Anything; name your price! Just not that scumbag, Walten!"

Russo patted Lebedev on the shoulder. "I am sorry, but all of Cherno wouldn't even be a big enough trade." And he walked away, leaving Lebedev to sulk in his chair, tugging at his necktie.

"Aria, we're going to have a riot on our hands soon!" Troy shouted.

"Keep calm. If an attack is going to occur, now would be the time."

The screen flickered, changing the scene from Cherno's outraged city hall to Mr. Walten's private office.

"Fellow people of Cherno, Martin Russo, and associates, I proudly accept the new ownership of Elixis Corporation and vow to take the utmost care in further developing and growing the company. Lebedev, I appreciate your understanding, as it was nothing personal. As a business owner, you also understand the value of monopolizing what you can. But not for evil, as you apparently think I am, but for the chance to unite the globe and potentially conclude this never-ending war. Furthermore, money is money, and as I have plenty of it, I would gladly allow you a share in this organization if you were willing to split your resources with my companies in return." Walten gave a bright-toothed, insincere smile.

Mr. Walten was indeed monopolizing. Not only did he own nearly every corporation in the City of Fountains, but he also maintained dozens more in all the other city-states in the United Americas. Now, he tried to get his hands on Russite. He wanted to globalize his market and own as much as he could of what remained of the world. But for what reason? For what cause would a man want to own everything? Would it be for a peaceful solution? Or would it be for terrorism and intimidation? Aria was willing to bet on the latter. Mr. Walten wasn't exactly a warm and fuzzy type.

"You insult me by giving me an offer like that? For what? Nothing! You will eventually own anything I allow you a piece of. No, Mr. Walten. I will not play your games. You may think yourself swift, but I can see right through you! From this day on, we are no longer at peace with you. One more wrong step, Walten, and you may find yourself at war!" Lebedev screamed at the projection of Walten above the stage.

"You can bring as many soldiers as you want, Lebedev. My militaries alone outnumber your citizens. By the way, I think you have more important things to worry about in your current state of emergency." Walten winked sardonically before signing out, the screens flickering to black.

A loud explosion sounded from behind Aria, followed by the screams of terrified citizens.

"What was that?" Troy asked.

"Definitely an attack," Aria replied.

Turning, she watched in awe as a massive grey cloud funneled from the top of the convention center a couple of blocks away from Ivory. A multitude of shrieks spread through the streets, echoing in the vastness of the city—not human sounds. The monsters were attacking.

"Convention center!" Aria shouted.

"We're too far away! Damn it! Why would they attack there?" Troy roped down the side of his building, still cloaked from human sight. Aria followed his actions, signaling to Dovian, who was already halfway down the block.

"I don't know; why would they attack at all? I was so certain City Hall would've been the perfect target. Damn it. It doesn't make any sense!" Aria said.

"It makes perfect sense," Dovian joined in.

"How?" Troy asked.

"Science convention. Wonder what kind of weapon and defense technologies they have here in Cherno today," he responded sarcastically.

Maybe it was a little obvious once the strike began, but who would have guessed a nerd convention would have been the site of a massive, violent attack when more important and worldly negotiations took place a few streets away?

The three hidden individuals rushed side by side, dodging the already broken and bloodied bodies on the ground. Gunfire erupted, and the Cherno military was in action. Aria cocked her weapon and readied the first bullet in her chamber, the ECRG-15 humming an electrical tune. Rounding the corner, she quickly aimed and fired at one beast clambering on the outside wall of the giant marble building.

Twisting inside the barrel of the ECRG, magnetizing parts carried and spun the projectiles as they fired from the chamber, electrical bursts wrapping around them. One, two, three shots were fired at the beast. The first bullet crashed against its barrier, the second penetrated, and the third blasted directly into the creature's back, electrocuting its system, which allowed more rounds to pierce its flesh. Aria smiled, continuing her barrage of bullets from one creature to another. Civilians screamed and cried as they ran and leaped out of the way of the open fire. Some were gruesomely torn to pieces by the monsters, while the Cherno military took down others.

'Bastards don't even care if they kill civilians.' Aria glared at the careless soldiers surrounding the infrastructure. They were all panicked, shooting aimlessly at the flurrying beasts, their bullets not making a difference.

"EMPS! Use your EMPS!" she shouted.

One soldier heard her cries as he reached into a side pocket and tossed an EMP grenade into the pack, the blast temporarily bringing down the beasts. The bullets finally tore through their flesh, giving the Chernos a much-needed sense of victory.

"Keep throwing the EMPS, and don't stop firing! Watch out for civilians!" Aria continued shouting orders, still unseen by the Cherno troops. She looked around with hope, thinking they might win the battle.

Another massive explosion sent her flying against a nearby wall. Her Faze Shield clattered as bits of debris scattered through the air. Hot white seared her vision, and she faded fast into unconsciousness.

"Aria!" Troy shook the woman's shoulders, trying to wake her. "Aria!"

Everything spun. Her vision blurred as she tried to focus on the man before her. Finally recognizing his olive-green eyes, she sat up quickly, wincing at the sharp stabbing in her ribs.

"Are you okay?" he asked, his voice nearly drowned out by the atrocious screams and gunfire.

Turning her sight to the fallen men around them, she frowned. "Could be worse," she muttered. "Troy, you're bleeding."

"Eh?" he looked down and noticed dark red smudged with the camo of his uniform. "Not mine," he said after a moment, "at least not all of it."

"Dovian?" she asked in a slightly worried tone. Her attention then fled to a grouping of monsters attacking an invisible force. One by one, they were knocked back or disintegrated into ash.

"He's fine," Troy said. "Glad he's still undercover."

Aria then realized that she could see Troy. His optical camo no longer cloaked him. She looked down. Her uniform was also out, probably caused by the tremendous blast that occurred only moments before. Her face twisted into a look of confusion. That wasn't a typical mortar blast. Peering at the bodies by her feet, she realized they weren't damaged by shrapnel but were annihilated by massive lacerations that cut deeply through the thick metal of their body armor. A nostril flared as she gaped at one filleted individual, taking the brunt of the force.

"Wonder what caused it," Troy said.

A deep, low hum answered them, a sound that mimicked high-voltage electricity. A few meters away stood a gigantic beast, its black, beady eyes glaring as it bent forward, its clawed hands touching the rocky ground. It was taller than the creatures they had previously encountered and a bit bulkier. The talons were broader and greater in length, making it an even deadlier foe.

Click, click, clickity, clickity.

The talons snapped together, creating a sharp and ominous sound as the hum rose in volume. The clicking merged from singular taps to nothing but an oscillating, metallic clang, like fan blades turning against small pebbles. Hissing, drool slipping from the creature's angular teeth in generous heaps, it raised its arms and quickly threw them down, sending a shockwave toward the two combatants.

"Get down!" Aria shouted. She shoved hard against Troy, pushing away simultaneously to separate. She hit the ground hard, and a transparent wave of destruction passed between her and the man. Turning her shocked gaze back toward the creature, she saw its arms raised again, the terrible noise already commencing. Aria quickly pressed to her feet, her boots nearly slipping on the rubble. She tucked and rolled just as another shockwave churned her way, demolishing everything in its path, turning solid marble and stone into powder.

'So that's what happened to the bodies.' She thought morbidly about what could happen to her if she hesitated one more moment.

Gunfire erupted as Troy had enough time to aim at the beast before turning its attention to him. The slobbering creature screeched as it fell to its knees, ignoring the onslaught of miniature explosions traveling up its spine. Its body steamed at the wounds, cauterizing them as quickly as the bullets inserted into its flesh. Hot blood plopped onto the dusty ground. And then it tore after Aria, claws digging into the earth as it pulled viciously toward the woman. In less than a second, it was upon her. She barely had enough time to open fire as she toppled over, the pointed claws digging deep into the stone beside her head. Fighting with the beast, Aria pressed her feet against its abdomen and pushed hard, separating their bodies just enough so that when it snapped its toothy jaws at her face, it only missed by a few millimeters. Grimacing, she pushed against the creature again, finding enough space to twist her wrists and raise the barrel of her ECRG. Pulling the trigger, she blasted into the monster's chest. It screamed horribly, violently shaking as it fell to the side. Aria quickly rolled to her feet and aimed down, firing nonstop, not giving the thing a chance to breathe a single breath. She could feel the heat of its insides as it soaked her clothing. At close range, the bullets burrowed deep; it didn't stand a chance. Steam pooled out as the convulsing beast shrieked to its death, talons clicking violently against the ground.

'*Finally.*' Aria sighed, reloading her weapon.

She turned to find Troy, who handled a small group of monsters alone. His bullets, this time, took down the creatures effortlessly. Aria looked back at the brute she had just killed.

'*So, this was a roided-up version of the other guys,*' she pondered as she observed the battlefield. What exactly were these things? Were they monsters? Were they merely animals that lived underground? Aria doubted that. Or were they something more? Something she didn't yet understand. The thought made her shiver.

Aria turned to join Troy's side. Taking one step forward, she ran into an invisible force. One hand gripped her shoulder, and another snagged a wrist, keeping her from raising her weapon. She gasped as the figure fizzled like static, a quiet drone buzzing. In a flash, the body materialized, revealing long blue robes and a smiling face half-covered with raven-black hair.

"Euclid," Aria choked out.

A deep chuckle resonated within the massive man, and he turned her, locking her arms in place.

Lips grazing her ear, he whispered, "And the beast was taken, and with him the false prophet that wrought miracles before him, with which he deceived them that had received the mark of the beast...." He pressed her wrist against the DNAIS chip, and the woman reflexively dropped her weapon. "...And them that worshipped his image. These both were cast alive into a lake of fire burning with brimstone."

Aria gazed at the monster before her, noticing the beryllium-bladed talons and the hot, sulfuric blood pooling beneath.

"And the devil that deceived them was cast into the lake of fire and brimstone, where the beast and the false prophet are, and shall be tormented day and night for ever and ever." There was humor in his voice.

Aria squirmed under his grip. "What are you saying?"

"But the fearful, and unbelieving, and the abominable, and murderers, and whoremongers, and sorcerers, and idolaters, and all liars, shall have their part in the lake which burneth with fire and brimstone: which is the second death."

"These…these were people once?" Aria asked.

"This is what happens to a world forsaken by its God," Euclid snarled in the woman's ear.

"No," Aria said. "You, you made these things. You brought them here to wreak havoc."

"Are you sure about that?" A mocking gasp escaped his lips as he pulled Aria's hands together, trailing a golden-clawed finger across her cheek. "He comes."

"Euclid!" Dovian's voice boomed.

"I'll see you later," Euclid quickly kissed her cheek, "Gavin says hi." And he was gone.

Aria stood, chilled to the bone. What did he mean? What was he talking about?

"Did he hurt you?" Dovian gently grabbed the woman's shoulders, temporarily uncloaking.

Aria stared into space, lost in her thoughts, as her eyes quickly brimmed with tears. Euclid was wrong, wasn't he?

"Aria?" he asked more sternly.

She turned her gaze toward the Sorcēarian. Slowly, she shook her head.

"What did he say to you?" Dovian asked, his eyes narrowing.

"N-nothing. Nothing. Just some psychobabble." And just like that, she turned off her emotions and rushed toward Troy's side. Dovian hesitated but followed her, knowing that Aria was lying, and he had a fairly good idea of Euclid's intentions.

"Good, you're still alive," Troy uttered, never pausing in his constant barrage of gunfire. "These damn things just keep coming."

"That last one was a big one, stronger than the others." Aria joined in, aiming at a predator that tried to carry away a Cherno soldier. "Keep firing your EMPs!" she ordered the men.

"Who the hell is that?" one Cherno asked another.

"I don't care, as long as she is on our side."

Creeping through the doors and windows of the convention center, more of the disgusting creatures filed out. There was no way into the building. The monsters exited two to the one killed out on the streets. It was impossible. The Cherno military needed the same weapons as Aria and Troy. They required more soldiers like Dovian, more Sorcēarians.

"We won't last long at this rate! The Chernos aren't holding up well at all!" Troy shouted.

"Dovian! Is there a way you can send an electrical burst big enough to knock them defenseless?" Aria called over her shoulder. Dovian remained busy taking on a dozen at a time. The beings inevitably found him the most significant threat.

"Sure, let me get right on that," Dovian muttered sarcastically.

"Whenever you get the time," Aria responded, taking a friendly approach.

Two of the massive brutes, in a side-by-side formation, noisily exited the front doors of the building, their eyes already plastered to both Troy and Aria. Without hesitation, they simultaneously began clicking their talons. With double the force, the two could do some severe damage. Undoubtedly, these beings caused the loud explosions that started the fiasco.

"Troy," Aria called out with a warning tone.

"I see."

They both aimed, opening fire. The first couple of rounds bounced off the brutes' shields. Unconcerned, the two creatures lifted their arms and swung downward, sending a massive eruption toward Aria and Troy. The transparent frequency distorted the plane as it ate and tore away the landscape, funneling directly toward the two soldiers at an unreadable speed.

"Damn!" Aria cursed, jumping out of the way.

She and Troy both missed the brunt of the blow; however, pieces of glass and metal spiraled from the destructive force, cutting their bodies. The ear-splitting clatter was continuous, and the beasts followed through with another blow, one after another. Troy made his way over a broken wall from a nearby obliterated shop. Landing on his stomach, he covered his head as the surface shattered into a thousand pieces behind him, covering his form. Aria rolled, pulling up and around a nearby traffic post. The blast tore after her, the earth crumbling behind her feet as she sprinted toward a wrecked vehicle. Hopping over the car, she dropped and tumbled to the side behind a nearby garbage canister. A horrendous crunch sounded as the vehicle split into two pieces, electrical current crackling from the severed lines and wires. Aria didn't stop moving. She dashed around the dumpster, avoiding the vicious brutes' sights. Running along the side of the building, she dodged the flurry of gunfire from the last remaining Cherno soldiers and the other beasts swarming from the convention center. She heard it, another blast coming in her direction down the entire length of the building.

'Keep running; just keep running,' she mentally repeated.

Her hair stood on end as she heard the sickening plop of the wave hitting the soldiers behind her, chopping them to pieces, cutting even the enemy monsters into pieces. The brutes didn't care; they only wanted destruction and annihilation. The ground trembled beneath her footsteps. It would only be another second or two before the blast caught up with her, and she was running out of road. Before her, a giant pillar of the convention center had broken off, blocking the entire pathway. It was too tall. She couldn't climb it in time, and monsters funneled out of the cracks toward her. She was surrounded and had nowhere to go.

Invisible arms grabbed the woman, and she spun around, facing the obliteration that soared toward her. It exploded against a hidden force, blue light flooding around her in a spherical shape. As the energy concentrated toward the blast, scarlet robes appeared before Aria, blocking her view. Dovian pressed against the violent wave, his powers focusing on only the one task at hand. He groaned, teeth gritting as he gripped his staff. The crystal ball on top beamed with bright light, slowly eating away at the invisible detonating wave.

Aria lifted her weapon, firing at the other, more manageable, beasts around. She could at least fend off those while Dovian worked with the large, angry ones.

"We will have to figure out a better way of destroying these things," Dovian groaned. He finally expelled the destructive energy but looked a bit worn out. "I can't keep this up for long."

"Close range," Aria said. "The bullets are deflected easily from a distance, but if you can get close to those things, you can get deep penetration where the wounds won't heal instantaneously."

"But that still leaves the problem of getting close. They have a way of pushing the enemy back." Dovian joined her, expelling a few monsters. His blue eyes glared at the brute nearly fifty meters away. It hobbled slowly toward them, black eyes staring. Dovian readied his staff but halted. The second brute also rounded the corner, joining the other's side. "This is not good."

Aria turned her attention to the two massive enemies. They each brought their arms into the air, talons clinking together. Definitely not good.

"Dovian," Aria whimpered.

He didn't respond but gently pushed her behind him. She stood sandwiched between the downed pillar and Dovian's tall form. He held out his staff and mumbled in Legacy, the low tones bringing out more of the blue light from his staff. Aria gave him a worried look. What was he going to do? He could barely manage one of those blasts a moment ago. How was he going to take on two?

One of the brutes' heads unexpectedly exploded into a morbid mess.

Ba-Doom!

It was a deafening sound that immediately followed. The creature's arms dropped, but not a single burst of energy was dispelled. It plopped heavily to the ground, its rot-smelling blood soaking everything. The second monster watched, lifted its head, and shrieked angrily.

Sending the second creature's skull into a thousand pieces, another boom occurred.

Ba-Doom!

Aria watched, amazed. The sound was startling but also recognizable.

"Ivory!" she shouted, gazing toward the rooftops a few blocks away.

"Seems she has figured out how to use the weapon," Dovian murmured with surprise.

As the remaining monsters quickly scampered inside the building, loud shrieks and cries filled the air. More thunderous shots erupted, and Ivory continued her assault on the creatures. Aria instinctively covered her head, lowering herself to the ground. Dovian joined her side.

"Seems she's got a violent side to her." He chuckled.

Aria sighed, her nerves not yet calmed. From the two brutes that had attacked her and Dovian, the second one had previously been against Troy. Where was he now? Was he hurt? Was he alive? Aria quickly pressed against the node behind her ear.

"Troy! Are you all right?! Where are you?"

"I'm on the east side of the building! What is that noise? Monsters are falling left and right over here!" Troy shouted back, much to Aria's relief.

Aria eyed the walls of the building. The beasts scrambled back inside the structure in a frenzied panic.

"Ivory. Looks like she's scaring away the enemy. They are finally retreating," Aria said.

"Yeah, same on my side," Troy replied.

"Do you have a clear path to the building?"

"Yup."

"Okay. Get inside. Dovian and I will meet you on the opposite side; maybe we can corner Euclid and find out what he's doing here."

"Ten-four," Troy confirmed.

"Got that?" Aria asked Dovian.

"Ten-four," he replied humorously. The woman lifted her annoyed gaze to the sky.

Stepping cautiously over the fallen bodies, Aria and Dovian neared the side of the building where the pillar had blown away from the foundation. A massive hole lay within the wall above the broken marble. Dovian hoisted the woman up onto the huge rock. She kneeled, peering slowly into the large opening, weapon ready. After a moment, she turned back to Dovian and grabbed his hand, helping him up to join her side. They carefully slipped inside the building, Dovian lowering Aria to the floor before he silently dropped in behind her.

The convention center was in ruins. The tables and booths were strewn over the floor, some bent and broken. Hundreds of scientific devices were crushed or overturned, the owners' bodies similarly scattered and broken. In the center of the building stood a tall exhibit labeled 'Elixis' across the top. There, dozens of the nasty creatures lingered and watched as Euclid stood with hands in the air, murmuring.

"There he is," Aria whispered. "What do you think he's doing?"

Dovian's hands eagerly gripped his staff. "Opening a portal."

"A portal?"

"A means of transportation. That device beside him must be of some interest."

Directly next to Euclid was an enormous machine. A knocked-over poster stand lay beside it. The words, *Electrostatic Frequency Tuner: Not just top-of-the-line defense technology. Potential time machine? Journey to other dimensions? The merger of realms?'* were scrawled on the surface. The message only made the machine seem foreboding.

"That looks similar to a Faze Shield," Aria whispered.

"A really big Faze Shield," Dovian agreed with a nod.

Across the way, Aria spotted a shadowy movement—Troy.

"In place. I have a view of the bastard," he called over his mental chip.

"Stay cool. I don't want any of his pets getting in the way," Aria replied.

A loud pop sounded, and a distortion materialized above Euclid near the vaulted ceiling. Everything spiraled toward the center, and a wormhole opened. A large object began descending out of thin air from it, lowering toward the floor.

"What the hell is that?" Troy asked.

A cylindrical tube sandwiched between two metallic plates spewed from the hole. Inside the glass container was an enormous electric-blue orb; a loud, groaning buzz resonated from the pulsating ball. Rods from the plates sent energy waves back and forth, feeding into the sphere. Aria's eyes widened.

"Oh, my God…it's a reactor core," she gasped aloud. *"He's going to nuke Cherno,"* she mentally called out.

"I've got a clear shot! Let me take it!" Troy mentally exclaimed.

"I thought your people put an end to nuclear weapons," Dovian said through gritted teeth.

"We have. We only use nuclear energy in some city-states. However, they still cause meltdowns when taken from their reactors. Cherno is a city-state that banned any form of nuclear energy due to the massive amounts of nuclear waste and radiation buried deep beneath our feet. If that bomb goes off, he not only blows Cherno to oblivion but potentially the whole damned planet."

Euclid opened a second portal, quickly consuming the Elixis machine.

"Take the shot!" Aria ordered.

Not even a second later, gunfire erupted. The bullets didn't even touch the dark Sorcēarian as Euclid merely lifted a hand, the ammunition evaporating into nothing.

"And you thought I didn't know you were hiding in the shadows?" Euclid laughed wickedly. Thrusting his palm, the overturned makeshift wall Troy hid behind shot backward, knocking the soldier over and rendering him unconscious. Turning, he did the same motion, moving back the walls and tables near Aria and Dovian, revealing the two. They stood with weapons aimed. Aria fired without hesitation. Releasing a full clip, she dropped the mag and quickly reloaded another. Dovian halted her.

"Save your ammo," he said coolly.

Aria let out a shuddering sigh. Not a single bullet had hit Euclid. Arrogantly, he flipped his raven hair over his shoulder; his twisted smile wrinkled the tattoo lining his face.

"As much as I'd love to stay and play, I have a time bomb on my hands." Grasping at the thick cords connecting the spherical container to the black portal, Euclid pulled and tore the lines. "My dear, I bid you adieu. But first, where is your little blonde friend? Can't be too far away, can she?" Signaling to the beasts, he quickly closed the portal the Elixis machine had sunk into. "You have five minutes at best." He chuckled, disappearing.

'Ivory!' Aria's mind reeled.

Dovian didn't waste any time, instantly sending a shockwave that crashed against the creatures. He slammed his staff into a few others; their bodies scorched and scattered to ash. Aria followed closely behind him, watching the first portal sink slowly back into normalcy. She fired continuously into the nearing beasts, dodging and running toward the unstable core.

"Troy! Wake up!" Aria screamed into his head.

More gunfire greeted them; the remaining Cherno soldiers had infiltrated the building, finishing off the remaining creatures. Aria joined Dovian's side as he shouted in Legacy, and the portal hovering above the nuclear core halted its diminishing size.

"Quickly! We must lift it!" Dovian hollered. "If you can get it up high enough, maybe I can push it through the rest of the way before it closes." He quivered. His body was weak from continually expelling energy. "I just can't do both at once right now."

"Troy!" she screamed again, trying feebly to lift the hefty equipment. "It's too heavy," she groaned.

Scuffling from the shadows, Troy hurried the best he could toward the woman, wobbling while holding his head. "Stop shouting, please," he groaned. As if quieting her voice would help in a giant hall full of screeching monsters and relentless gunfire.

"Get your ass over here and help me lift this thing!" she growled.

"Hey!" Troy shouted to the soldiers, suddenly alert at the sight of the reactor core. "We need help!"

"Buddy, we all need help!" one soldier shouted over his shoulder. Seeing the core, the Cherno man twisted, tugging his partner. "Mother of…. How the hell did this get here?!"

"We'll explain later; just help us lift it high enough to get back inside the portal!" Aria yelled.

"It won't hold forever," Dovian groaned, fighting with the closing gap.

Together, the four soldiers picked up the core, barely able to move it any higher than a few centimeters. The ball in the center nearly doubled in size, pressing against the glass, and sent splinters up the surface.

"We need more soldiers!" Aria shouted.

"Hey! Help!" the Cherno man shouted to his colleagues. "Forget the monsters; we got bigger problems on our hands!"

One of the men halted his fire, eyeing something behind one of the exhibits. It had taken only a few seconds before he boarded and drove full speed ahead in a new-fangled forklift prototype. Frantic shouts sounded from all around. The other soldiers divided, half trying to help lift the core while the rest fired at the monsters that tried to attack the moving vehicle.

"Lift it as high as you can!" the driver cried, waving his hands as he neared the group.

Aria and the others heaved the item onto the prongs of the lift. It rose a moment later, lifting the core six meters into the air before the secondary arms carried it another five. The cab wobbled, threatening to turn over under the heavy weight of the rapidly growing orb. The soldiers quickly held onto the backside of the cab to add more weight to balance the machine.

"Hold it!" Dovian raised his hand. "Don't get the lift in the portal, or you'll be sucked up with it. Hold tight."

Quickly, Dovian released the gateway, the thing soon closing in on itself. Groaning, he raised the reactor core from off the lift, his staff's light carrying it into the portal just as it suctioned closed. A horrendous thunder erupted into the air for only a millisecond before everything fell silent. They barely escaped death. The world barely survived.

Dovian leaned against his staff, rubbing his forehead as Aria plopped onto her backside on the ground, sighing. The room fell into silence. All the monsters were dead, and Cherno was finally safe. However, she couldn't say the same for herself and her two comrades, as they were held at gunpoint. The dark-haired woman glared at the Cherno militants.

"What is this?" Troy asked in disbelief. "We just saved your asses."

A few of the soldiers traded anxious glances.

"Sorry, but we have no idea who you are. And your friend is quite suspicious with his…powers," one of the commanding officers stated. "Being in a state of military alert, outside militaries are forbidden within our city. As such, you are under arrest for violation of the code. We'll be taking you in."

"This is bullshit, and you know it!" Aria argued.

"Just come with us quietly. It'll make things so much easier, and we can speed the process up," the Cherno, who had helped with the lift, spoke up.

Aria, her face holding an unpleasant expression, reluctantly nodded.

"Weapons, please." The officer held out his hand.

"You're not getting my damned weapon," she snarled.

She eyed the forklift driver again, and he frowned, nudging his head toward his superior. Angrily, she shoved the weapon into the other man's hands. Troy and Dovian followed her actions, Dovian feeding a nasty, icy glower at the soldier holding his staff.

"You *will* be returning that," Dovian said in a seething tone. The soldier quickly nodded in response.

"Good. Now, this way." The commanding officer forced the three out of the building.

"Where's Ivory?" Troy muttered through clenched teeth.

"I don't know. Euclid said he was going after her," Aria whispered.

Dovian stared forward, marching with guns pressed against his back. He, too, worried about Ivory. With Euclid choosing her as a target, the young woman did not stand a chance. And what exactly would Euclid want with her anyway? There was something odd about Ivory, there was no doubt about it, but what made her so special? The thoughts left an unsettling feeling in the Sorcēarian's gut. Something wasn't right.

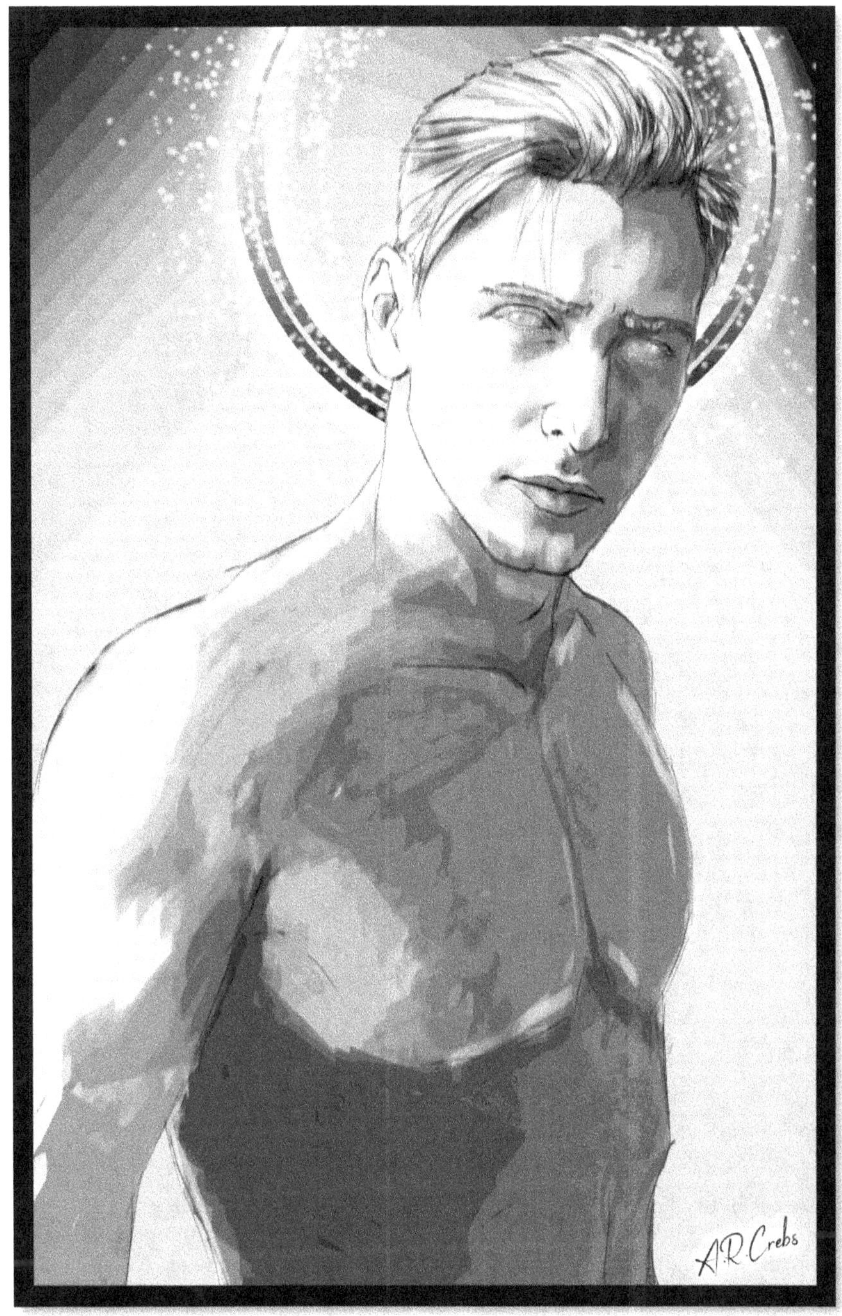

"Sweet Dreams"

CHAPTER 13

The loud music of the club pounded in Aria's ears. She swayed through the dancing crowd, looking about nervously. It wasn't her typical scene, but for the sake of Troy's birthday, she promised she'd be there. She already regretted that promise, seeing as she couldn't find her blasted partner anywhere. Self-consciously, she flipped her long hair over her shoulder. She hoped she looked all right. The women around her were decorated with glitter, neon tattoos, incredibly revealing outfits, and hair of all colors. She tugged on her tight halter top, pulling the item over her bare stomach. A hand slipped over hers, yanking her to the side. Instinctively, she readied to smack the perv who placed his hand across her belly, but she paused midway through, giving a shy smile.

"Gavin," she said sweetly. "I was about to leave. I couldn't find you or Troy."

"Am I that hard to miss?" he asked, spinning the woman so that she rested against his chest. Aria's eyes flickered to the surrounding crowd. There he was. Troy stood atop the stage, dancing with a group of electric-colored women beside the DJ. Gavin pressed against the woman's back, his mouth near her ear. "I spotted *you* from across the room." His warm breath gave her chills.

"Oh, please," she scoffed. The man smelled like whiskey and a cinnamon cigar, but it wasn't unpleasant mixed with the scent of his cologne. She shivered as he ran his hands through her long black hair, twisting it with her blue highlights. He piled it atop her head and lightly kissed her neck.

"I like this look," he murmured. "You'd look good with short hair. Show off that long neck of yours." She felt his smile as he nibbled her earlobe.

"Gavin," Aria gave a short laugh. Her green eyes flickered to Troy once again.

He had no idea the woman was there. Good, because she didn't know how he'd handle his friend's handsy behavior. Sure, she and Gavin had private moments, but they never showed affection publicly.

"But you look good no matter what you do," he whispered, his hands lowering over her abdomen again. He flicked her belly button ring with his thumb, giving a low, raspy chuckle.

"Gavin," Aria repeated with a stern tone.

"Aria," he teased mockingly. His hands lowered further, his fingers dipping into her tight black pants.

"Gavin!" She laughed, failing at sounding authoritative.

"You know this feeling?" he returned. "This feeling right now?"

"Hmm, yeah," Aria purred.

"You're never going to have it ever again."

"W-what?" She paused, slowly turning to face him.

Much to the woman's horror, blood covered Gavin's face.

"You'll never have this ever again. You know why? Because I'm dead, that's why. You ruined every chance you had at having any good memories." He looked angry and then hurt.

"Gavin?" she whimpered, watching the man as he gagged and choked.

"Aria!"

Quickly, everything turned black. The bright lights, the loud music, and the warm feeling of Gavin's body pressed against hers faded into nothing. Aria quickly opened her eyes. She sat in the Cherno military's holding facility, and a shiver ran down her spine as she felt the cold cement beneath her. The pale fluorescent lighting did little to brighten the gloomy room.

"You were dreaming," Dovian's voice intruded.

"Yes, I was," Aria huffed irritably.

"It wasn't a pleasant one," he stated.

"Whatever, I'm fine."

She ran her hands up and down her arms, trying to gather some warmth. Slowly, she trailed her fingers up her neck toward her chin-length hair. Gavin always preferred her short hair. Aria frowned, dropping her hands onto the cement. That night at the club was nearly fifteen years ago. It was one of her few memories closely resembling a normal life. Feeling a burning stare, she turned her gaze toward Troy. His expression was unreadable at first. Was he mad? Of course, he was. They were locked up for the remainder of the day and overnight while the world was in turmoil.

"You were dreaming about him, weren't you?" Troy finally asked in a low tone.

Aria scoffed. "Who?" She shrugged.

"You said his name," he muttered.

Aria tore her eyes away from his, staring at the cracks in the floor. "So what?"

Troy didn't push further. He gripped his knees, tugging his legs toward his chest.

"Your pilot friend?" Dovian intruded. Aria glared at the Sorcēarian.

"It's just a dream! It's not a big deal!" the woman growled.

"It's Euclid, isn't it?" Dovian murmured. "He's put ideas in your head."

"Don't know what you're talking about."

"You've been having nightmares ever since you met him, haven't you?" Dovian asked.

Aria remained silent for a moment. From her peripheral, she could see Troy watching her. "Yeah," she whispered finally.

"Don't listen to him. It's part of his tactic. Euclid specializes in mental torment. He likes to weaken the enemy by putting them in a poor emotional state." The Sorcēarian, sitting against the wall opposite the woman, leaned forward.

"I'm fine!" she shouted. "My emotions are fine!"

"Seems like it," Troy scoffed.

"Shut up, Troy," Aria spat angrily.

"I'm merely warning you. He's a master illusionist. He can easily plant ideas and images in your mind. I want you to know that whatever's going on in your head, don't believe any of it," Dovian advised.

"You make me sound like a nut."

"Gavin's death was not your fault. Don't let him use that as a tool against you."

"Can we just drop it?" she snapped.

Dovian leaned back and stared at the ceiling. He sighed in defeat.

The three remained in awkward silence for a few minutes. Dovian sat with arms folded and eyes closed. Aria wondered if the man ever slept. Troy fidgeted, playing with a loose string on his sleeve like a curious kitten. After another few moments, the woman sighed loudly. Talking was better than sitting and getting lost in her depressing thoughts.

"What exactly is 'fire and brimstone?'" Aria asked.

Dovian's eyes popped open. He stared at the woman momentarily, his lips parting as he pondered her question. "Where did you hear that?" he asked.

"Euclid said something about it," she mumbled. "They were cast into the lake of fire and brimstone where they were tormented day and night. Something like that."

"Revelation," Dovian said.

"Revelation?" Aria repeated.

"It's from the Bible, describing the end of days. Fire and brimstone are a description of Hell." Dovian frowned, seeing Aria's face falling into a dreadful look. "Is that what he told you? That your friend was in the lake of fire?"

"In a roundabout way, I guess," she whispered.

"Don't you dare listen to that man," Dovian snarled. "He knows nothing."

"But what if he's right?"

"He isn't," Dovian barked.

"How would you know?"

The room fell silent, and Dovian stared at the floor. "Because I know. I can tell."

"But how?"

"There are ways of seeing the light within individuals. He was a believer. That's all that matters."

"Oh, come on," Troy scoffed.

Aria and Dovian both turned their attention to the male soldier.

"Aria? You don't believe this, do you?" he asked. The woman stayed quiet, eyeing shamefully at her hands. "Don't listen to this crap! It's not going to help!"

"Why wouldn't it help?" Dovian asked, glaring at the other male.

"You're putting ideas in her head, giving her false hope," Troy argued.

"What do you mean, false hope?" The Sorcēarian's eyes narrowed.

"This whole mumbo-jumbo about an afterlife. We're soldiers. We see death daily. Why concern her with more thoughts about our dead friend? Make her worry about whether he's burning in Hell or living the good life in Heaven?"

"I didn't realize you were so close-minded on the subject," Dovian said, his tone unwavering.

"Do you hear yourself, Dovian? You sound like a madman."

"Madman?!" Dovian stood, and Troy followed his actions.

"I don't appreciate you filling Aria's head with these ridiculous ideas!" Troy shouted.

They stood nearly chest to chest. Troy was brave as he tried to get in the Sorcēarian's face. The top of his head didn't even reach Dovian's chin.

"Things are going on here that you simply don't understand, and you have the gall to stand before me and say that I am the madman when there is so much proof around you? Are you really that blind? Or are you simply scared?" Dovian asked.

"Scared? Of what? Dying? I've had thousands of chances to die. This is no different," Troy said indignantly.

"Those demons out there aren't any different?"

"Demons?! Those things…aren't demons!"

"Aliens, then?" Dovian chuckled.

"And that's more ridiculous than your beliefs? I'm supposed to sit here and think that those things are demons and that you are some angelic being with divine powers? If you were so powerful, then why can't you stop Euclid? Save Ivory?" Troy glared.

'Save Gavin?' The thought plagued him. If Dovian was what he said he was, would

Gavin be dead? If he were some ultimate being with supreme power, he should be able to bring someone back from the dead. He would have been able to keep Euclid from murdering their friend.

"Boy, I could send your body to particles without a moment's thought, and you stand here insulting me and my entire race?"

"As you insult me with your religious antics."

Dovian grabbed Troy, his hands twisting in the man's shirt.

"Then you better be scared. If those things get a hold of you, you will inevitably burn," Dovian said, his voice lowering to two tones as his incisors grew into sharpened fangs. His back rippled as it readied to sprout wings.

"Stop it!" Aria shouted. "What is the matter with you? Both of you? Why are you fighting?"

Dovian quickly rolled his shoulders, releasing Troy. The soldier pushed away, glaring.

"Troy, he is only trying to make me feel better; don't be offended by something you know nothing about." Aria pointed a finger at the man. Troy opened his mouth to argue, but Aria stopped him. "Shut up! Dovian! Don't…touch Troy." She tried to punish both men the best she could, but it didn't stop their hateful exchange of fierce looks.

Dovian huffed angrily. "I'm sincerely sorry about your friend. If I had known what we were up against, I would have tried my best to save him."

Aria eyed Troy. The man's face fell into one of solemnity. Was that what was wrong? Troy blamed Dovian for Gavin's death?

"I didn't say anything about that," Troy muttered.

"No, but I know you were thinking it," Dovian said crossly.

"What? You can read minds now?" Troy asked, tearing his eyes away.

"You are not a hard one to read. Your feelings are quite evident, even on the outside." Dovian folded his arms, leaning against the wall.

The room fell silent once again.

A loud slam alerted the three, followed by the sound of a furious woman. A Cherno soldier walked toward the large cell with Ivory beside him, wriggling in his grasp.

"I told you to let go of me!" she shrieked, elbowing him in the ribs.

"Ivory!" Aria stood, making her way to the cell door. Dovian followed her, giving a concerned look.

"She says you know her. Is this true?" the soldier asked in his broad accent.

"Yes, yes, we know her!" Aria shouted. "What did you do to her?"

Ivory looked a bit roughed up. Her mittens were torn, and the furry hat upon her head sat sideways. Her hair was in disarray, her eyeshadow smudged, and her corset had twisted and unraveled in the back. Aria quickly looked over the woman's clothing. Everything else seemed to be in place.

"She resisted," the soldier said in a seething tone. "She bit me." He lifted a hand and revealed a significant bite mark on his skin, each tooth evident.

"Ivory," Aria said with a lecturing tone as she checked the woman's clothing. She suddenly felt like everyone's mother.

"He pulled my hair," Ivory said, her eyes brimming with tears.

The soldier opened the door to the cell and roughly shoved the girl inside. "In you go. Anymore struggle, and I'll have you arrested and put on trial, you hear? Throw you in with the men," he growled, turning to leave. "Wait a few minutes. Lebedev wants to speak to you."

'Great,' Aria thought. "They didn't *touch* you, did they?" she asked, putting her hands on Ivory's face.

Ivory quickly shook her head.

"Ivory? You sure?"

"No, they didn't touch me," she said quietly.

"She's all right," Dovian murmured.

Aria trusted the man's instincts and dropped the subject. "I was worried about you. I thought that maybe Euclid had gotten a hold of you."

"No. I was busy watching from the rooftop when the soldiers surrounded me. They thought that I was in on the attack. I tried to explain, but they wouldn't listen!" Ivory said, nearly sobbing.

"It's okay. What's important is that you're safe, and that bastard didn't get to you." Aria ran her hands over the woman's arms, ensuring nothing more sinister happened to the poor girl.

"Euclid…he was after me?" Ivory asked, her hands shaking.

"Yes. Would you have any idea why Euclid would want you?" Aria asked.

"I, I don't know," she replied, her breaths growing heavy.

"Are you all right?"

"No, I mean, yes, not really." The blonde woman trembled, her chest heaving as she tried to catch her breath. Her eyes were like saucers as she stared blankly at the floor.

"Ivory?" Aria grabbed the woman's shoulders, giving her a look of concern. "What's wrong?"

Dovian neared them as Ivory began to hyperventilate. Troy approached the gate to the cell, calling out for help.

"I don't know," she gasped. "I was on the rooftops, and there was an explosion. Then there were monsters, and I don't remember the rest. Not until the soldiers showed up."

"You don't remember shooting the monsters?" Aria asked.

"I, what? Did I shoot them? No, I didn't." Ivory dropped to her knees.

"Ivory, calm down. You need to try to slow your breathing, okay?" Aria gave Dovian an alarmed look. The woman seemed to be shell-shocked.

"And Euclid. He's coming for me. He's going to kill me. He's going to kill me like the rest," she mumbled, her blue eyes glazing over.

"What?" Dovian sputtered, quickly crouching beside the blonde.

Ivory fainted, her limp body falling to the side.

"Oh!" Aria reached for the girl but paused as Dovian caught her. "Is she going to be okay?"

The Sorcēarian watched the unconscious woman in his arms, silent.

"Dovian, what did she mean 'he's going to kill me like the rest?'" Aria asked.

"I don't know," he murmured. The statement, however, sent chills down his spine. "She wouldn't know anything about his plans unless she had been in contact with him before we met."

"You think she's somehow associated with him?"

"I don't know. Euclid's up to no good, and I—" He became distracted as Ivory's eyes popped open, and her pupils dilated. Her hand gripped his forearm tightly, making him wince.

"Dov…Dovian," she gasped out. Her voice sounded foreign and unlike her own, the tone lower and more robust than her usual high, chipper pitch. "They are coming. He is coming. He is bringing the entire army, and he is going to kill us all. Do you understand?" She spoke firmly, maturely.

"Impossible." Dovian gasped, his face paling.

Ivory pulled herself up, gripping the man's scarlet robes. Gently, she placed one thin hand against his cheek. "Dovian, do you understand?" Her face wrinkled with worry. "You need to get out of here."

Shakily, he placed his hand over hers. "N-no. You…you don't know what you are talking about." He stuttered, his breath shaking. He closed his eyes as a shockwave of memories rushed through his brain.

"What is she talking about, Dovian? Is there going to be another attack?" Aria asked.

"What's going on?" Troy watched anxiously.

"You have to leave. Go." Ivory's faint voice broke as tears slid down her face.

Dovian took another ragged breath, tears threatening to stain his cheeks as well. "You, you're confused. You aren't…." He shook his head, refusing to believe the words came from Ivory's mouth.

"Go. Please." Ivory inhaled sharply and again fell lifelessly into Dovian's arms.

The Sorcēarian remained still. White shaking hands tightened their hold on

Ivory's body as his blue eyes stared at the corner of the room, wide with fear. A low moan erupted from the man, and he curled around the woman, rocking slowly back and forth.

Rain. It was raining. It was cold. Her touch was soft. Her eyes looked sad. He was locked in that cell, and there was no way out or any way to help her or cure her of her fright.

"The man has lost it." Troy gaped at the scene.

Aria's mouth dropped open with surprise. "What the hell just happened?"

"This isn't right. This doesn't make any sense," Dovian growled, shaking his head.

"What is going on?" Aria asked with an edge to her voice. "Are we under attack?"

"No," Dovian grumbled. "At least, that's not what that was."

"Then what was that?" the woman huffed, folding her arms. "If there's something you're not telling us...."

"It's nothing you would understand! It's…nothing I can understand." Dovian shook Ivory gently. "It doesn't make any sense. None of this makes any sense."

"You're telling me," Troy grumbled.

"Why would she tell you to go?" Aria asked.

"It's…it must be Euclid's doing. He's implanted some ideas into her head…or maybe my head. Whatever this is, it's something evil." Dovian quickly wiped his face, his demeanor returning cold and collected.

"I still don't understand," Aria said.

"Those words," Dovian began, "are some of the last I heard…." He fell silent.

Aria uncomfortably fidgeted as she watched him, shivering beneath the severity of his expression. "The last from someone you knew long ago?" she managed.

"Yes," he numbly stated, "from someone remarkably close to me."

"Are you sure? I mean, they were kind of vague words." Troy shrugged. Aria fed him a fierce look. "What? I mean, maybe she's simply confused or something. PTSD?"

"He is right, Dovian. She did say she didn't remember shooting any of the monsters. She could have blacked out through the whole ordeal and was just now remembering it. She could have gone into shock. It is a similar behavior for post-traumatic stress," Aria offered. It still didn't explain the strange voice.

Dovian held his silence for a long time. His wrinkled brow suddenly lifted, and his face calmed, looking less frustrated. "Perhaps you are right." He sounded defeated.

"Dovian?" a small voice squeaked from the woman in his arms.

"Are you all right?" he asked cautiously.

"I guess so." Ivory nervously looked from side to side. "Um, why are you holding me?"

"You don't remember anything that just happened?"

"No. I mean, I just came into the cell, and Aria asked me if I was all right. I must've blacked out or something. Low blood sugar?" she asked hopefully.

"Does this kind of thing happen to you a lot?" Aria asked. She wondered if that's how the blonde ended up at Ives in the first place. If she had some form of split personality, perhaps she could have wandered into a remote area unbeknownst to her. But it still didn't explain her complete amnesia.

"I don't know. I don't remember ever doing that. But then again, I don't remember anything more than the past week," she muttered sadly.

"What do you think, Dovian?" Aria asked.

"I am unsure. We must watch her closely and ensure she always stays nearby," Dovian advised. Slowly, he brushed a strand of golden hair out of the woman's face. "There's something mysterious about you, Ivory. We're going to figure it out."

"Okay," Ivory squeaked. She looked about uncomfortably at her awkward position and struggled to sit up. Dovian, shaking from his dazed state, helped the woman stand. "I'm sorry if I'm causing trouble." She poked her fingers together, shuffling in her boots.

"Just try not to go into crazy mode again," Troy said sarcastically.

"Is there a stick up your ass, or are you really just that big of an asshole?" Aria snarled.

"What?" he glared at her.

"Are you on your rag?" she instigated.

"Are you ever going to get off yours?" he retorted.

Dovian pinched the bridge of his nose. Children surrounded him. Apparently, being in the military these days was only considered a day job and never taken seriously. Things definitely weren't like they used to be. The two soldiers continued their argument, insulting and name-calling one another, as Ivory pressed against the wall, cringing from their words. The two had practiced their insults on one another many times before.

"You're a feeble-minded carpet-muncher," Aria snarled.

"Well, you're a rabid, scrotum-chewing bed-wetter!" Troy returned.

"Rancid ass clown!" she shouted back.

"Snooty gutter-slut!" he yelled.

"You're a brain-dead abortion survivor!" she quarreled, pushing against his shoulder.

Troy gave a cockeyed grin. Aria's face distorted as she tried to keep a serious expression.

"Abortion survivor?" he snorted out a laugh.

Dovian palmed his face, breathing slowly, trying his hardest to maintain his best behavior and avoid ripping down the facility's walls.

"Ahem," a male voice interrupted the four. Lebedev stood outside the gated cell; his expression was one lacking amusement. "You are the ones from the United Americas, correct?" he asked in his thick accent.

"Yes, sir," Aria confirmed. Straightening her posture, she gave a small salute.

"Mind telling me what you are in my city for?"

"We were sent here to investigate the recent attacks from the mysterious…military that's been infiltrating bases and cities around the globe. After a previous investigation, the projected attack route revealed that the next assault would occur in Cherno," she explained.

"And why not call and warn us of this attack?"

"Well, uh…you see…." Aria's lips twisted. "My company has tried communicating with yours, and, well, there was some speculation that your militaries may have caused the worldly attacks. And, seeing as Cherno was in a code red state of emergency, we figured you wouldn't let us in even if we asked."

"And what is this company you work for?" Lebedev asked, straightening his tie.

"Bio-Tech Military Corporation, sir," Aria spoke quietly. She suddenly wanted to become invisible.

"So, you are from the same company that just pulled the rug out from under my feet. The same company that has harassed my men outside the city walls for months. The same *company* accusing me of wanting to dominate the world."

Aria cringed. "Yes, sir."

"To me, it sounds like your military is the dangerous one. Mr. Walten is a power-hungry man. He's the one set to destroy this world, yet you come to me, thinking I am somehow related to this worldly evil surrounding us? If anyone's being suspicious, it is you!" Lebedev pointed accusingly at the woman.

"I know, sir, but trust me, we had no idea Mr. Walten planned to buy Elixis. In fact, he has no knowledge that we are here."

"A covert mission?" Lebedev's eyes narrowed. "One that even Walten knows nothing about?"

"The President ordered us to investigate Cherno. Originally, we were going to warn your military once we arrived, but at the last minute, we had to act as civilians to make it into the city. As suspicious as it sounds, we did not come here to sabotage the Stock Talks."

"I assumed you four were responsible for the attacks, but seeing as you helped remove the strange reactor core from the center of our city, it leaves me to question your actions. Either you are here to help end these attacks, or you are part of a more sinister plan," Lebedev explained. "Even though your actions saved Cherno, I cannot say the same for the people of Athenia."

"What do you mean? What happened to Athenia?" Aria asked. She and Troy traded worried glances.

"Merely moments after the attack here in Cherno, and supposedly seconds after you disposed of the reactor core, it was reported that a nuclear strike leveled Athenia."

"What?!" Aria yelled out in shock.

"Athenia was nuked?" Troy asked.

"There was a report of a nuclear meltdown at the facility. A reactor had gone offline. Operators of the facility called in a report of a giant portal opening and 'stealing' the reactor core. It was gone in seconds, only to return minutes later to detonate and send the whole city into ruins." Lebedev shook his head slowly.

"No! We didn't know! We had no idea the reactor core was from Athenia. We only did what we thought was the simplest solution—put it back where it came from. It was either that or let it level Cherno," Aria stammered.

Lebedev held up his hand. "And we all know that the consequences of that event would have been more devastating in the long run."

Aria sighed with relief. "I'm glad you realize that, sir."

"However, we still have an entire city-state that was destroyed, along with an essential business…Elixis. Now, I don't think an employee of Bio-Tech would set themselves out on a mission to destroy the one corporation their employer wanted most."

Aria grimaced. He was right. She and the others had just managed to destroy Elixis—the company Walten had just purchased. She saw a demotion in her near future or death by firing squad.

"So, does that mean we can leave now?" Troy asked impatiently.

"I want to know more about this technology in your weapons." Lebedev offered their freedom in exchange for their technology. "It seems you could deactivate those creatures' shields with those rifles. I am guessing you have met these things previously."

"Yes, sir. We first encountered these things at a base near Jordania. There, every man was slaughtered. We captured one of the beasts and performed an autopsy. I have a copy of the report on my DNAIS." Aria clicked on her wrist, the data streaming from her system to Lebedev's. "It's believed these creatures are capable of traveling through alternate dimensions through the use of their beryllium-based skeletal structure. They use Faze Shields to amplify the effects, which is currently under investigation as to how they received these mechanisms in the first place," Aria said.

"Sounds like your company is still involved somehow."

"It is possible the creatures received the items from bases scattered around the world. But that's all speculation at the moment," Aria murmured.

"And disabling their shields?"

"We use EMP technology. The EMPs wipe out the shields. Our weapons are formulated to pierce and send out electrostatic frequencies simultaneously, allowing the disabling of shields and making bodily contact."

"I want one of the weapons," Lebedev stated firmly. "We can backward engineer it."

"With all due respect, sir, you aren't getting my weapon. I'll allow you to keep one of the ammunition magazines for study, but you can't keep the gun. You would leave me defenseless, and as soon as we get out of here, we need to move to the next projected attack location."

Lebedev frowned, debating with himself. "We have been looking at the weapons while you've been here. We've run scans on the parts, and we should be able to piece together a prototype from the information we have. I will allow your weapons back. However," he pointed at Dovian, "yours is quite an oddity. We cannot get the item to break apart, even when pulled and pushed."

"The weapon is mine and mine alone. It is an extension of myself. No one else can wield it. And you had better stop trying to break it into pieces." The Sorcēarian stared menacingly at Lebedev.

"If you say so." Lebedev was at least smart enough to know not to argue with the mysterious man.

"Can we go now?" Aria asked, stepping from one foot to another.

"Where is it that you plan on going to?"

"I am unsure of our next target. I need to speak to James, I mean, President Clarke, before we go anywhere."

"I like Mr. Clarke." Lebedev nodded. "I am glad you take orders from him instead of that bastard, Walten."

"No offense to the business owners, but Mr. Clarke has risked his life repeatedly for his city. I would much rather lay my life on the line for a man as respectable as him than for someone like Mr. Walten, even if he owns us all," Aria strictly stated.

"No offense taken. I wasn't always a businessman. I once fought against Mr. Clarke in past wars. You are right. He is respectable. One hell of a soldier. Killed half my platoon in one strike once. Boy, was I angry." Lebedev laughed. "But I always wanted to meet the man under passive circumstances, play a good game of chess, and talk war strategies."

The Russites were an odd breed, that was for sure.

"He'd probably like that, sir." Aria smiled.

"How about this? You give Mr. Clarke a call. Get the detailed report of the recent attacks and a copy of your map projections, and then we'll talk about your release,"

Lebedev offered.

"We do that, and you promise to let us go, then we got a deal." Aria nodded.

"Good. I want as much a fair chance to win this war as anyone else. And believe me…I'm not going to keep any secrets. As much as I hate uniting with others, this is a time for people to stick together. These things are not human. We've got a race of monsters on our hands, or someone's military isn't playing by the rules." He eyed Aria severely. "And don't think that Bio-Tech is off the hook. The only involvement I want with the company will now be through you and Clarke only, understand? I want none of this to go to that bastard CEO, got it?"

"Got it," Aria agreed without hesitation.

"Good. Now, let's get you out of this dingy cell, shall we?"

To Aria's surprise, the meeting with Lebedev went much better than anticipated. Lebedev took an enormous gamble by setting them free, and she and her team realized his confidence in them. Soon after they came to an agreement, Aria and the others were allowed to return to their hotel, where she promptly called Mr. Clarke on her private line through her DNAIS. The private channels were always sketchy. It usually took a couple of tries to get the call through, let alone decent reception. James Clarke, however, must've been waiting impatiently on the other side. After the first ring, a harsh voice bellowed in Aria's ear.

"I've been waiting for hours. You were supposed to call me yesterday. I feared the worst," James Clarke's voice teetered with annoyance.

"I know. I'm sorry. We had a run-in with the Cherno military. They thought we were involved in the attack." Aria sat on her hotel room bed, talking with her fingers behind her ear.

"I had heard that they had some suspects. I figured you were captured. You're lucky you weren't shot on the spot, Aria. But, never mind that. The news is rolling with the destruction of Athenia. You know anything about that?"

Aria groaned, grimacing at the thought. "That man, Euclid, was here. He was in the process of stealing an Electrostatic Frequency Tuner made by Elixis."

"What would he want with that?" Clarke asked darkly.

"We're unsure. I feel it has to do with merging the realms," Aria said. She glanced at the frantic Ivory, who quickly packed her and Aria's bags.

"Merging of the realms?" James asked with a sarcastic tone.

Aria watched Ivory effortlessly take down her weapon into dozens of tiny pieces. "It's kind of hard to explain, sir. But we figure these things are alter-dimensional beings. It explains the reasoning behind quickly transporting from one location to another across the planet without detection."

"Whatever you say," he sighed, giving in to the absurd idea.

"We were in the convention center then, trying to stop Euclid. He had opened some type of portal and stolen the machine. At the same time, he had somehow pulled in a reactor core from a separate portal. It was unstable. He was planning on using it to destroy Cherno, and you know the possible damage that would have caused. Luckily, we pushed the bomb back into the portal from where it came," Aria paused. "Except, the portal was linked to Athenia's reactor. Once we put the core back into place, it went off. That's the reason why the city was destroyed."

"So, this guy was able to pull Athenia's reactor core out of thin air? You put it back into place, and it leveled Athenia?"

"Yes, sir," Aria said meekly. "But at the time, we had no idea where it had come from. It could have destroyed the entire world if it had gone off in Cherno. We had less than five minutes. It was the quickest solution."

"I understand that. I'm glad you were able to save yourselves and Cherno. There are always casualties in war; you know that. Though the death toll was massive, it was still less damaging than the destruction of Cherno and the entire world. Still, I have Mr. Walten high up my ass. He just lost the company he paid trillions of units for."

Aria cringed. "Yes, sir. I realized that."

"You had best get your asses out of there. As far as I know, Walten does not know your location, but he has promptly sent a team to investigate the attack. He somehow knows the attacks on Cherno and Athenia are linked."

"Why is he suddenly going behind your back on everything?"

"I don't know, Aria. It's got me concerned for sure. I'll keep playing dumb until I find out more."

"Any idea where the next projected attack will occur?" she asked.

"That's another point I wanted to talk to you about. There was an assault on Pierre this morning. We haven't heard much about it. It seems no one can make contact," Clarke's tone lowered.

"Did you know they would be attacked?" she asked with surprise. She received a concerned look from Ivory, which she waved away.

"They were on the projected route. We did send a team in to protect the city."

"And?"

"Nothing. We've heard nothing. We can only assume the entire team was lost."

"How is that possible?! The whole city? The whole military? Gone?" Aria shouted.

"It was a poor city-state, Aria. They couldn't fund the proper militia, and our team was unprepared. As you said before, they are used to fighting humans, not monsters."

Aria held her silence, debating on giving him the 'I told you so' speech.

"And you and Troy are the top soldiers of the company. What can I say? When paired together, you have the abilities equivalent to a dozen men."

"That's because we were trained by the best, sir." She smiled.

"Ha! Flattery, girl."

"I know, but it is true."

"If only I had a whole team with the work ethic of you and Troy. You know how to get down to business when it matters. I need more soldiers like you."

"Just keep them armed with EMP technology," she said. After some hesitation, she continued, "Sir, we had to work with Lebedev in order to be released."

"Lebedev? Are you mad?" Clarke shouted. "Walten will surely flip a lid."

"Or we would have been thrown in prison. Or worse. Just between you and me, we have a partnership with Lebedev. Walten's not to know about this. I had to share my weapon's technology with him, which worked wonderfully, by the way. Let Dr. Camery know."

"I will, and I will approve the advancement of funding for our fellow soldiers."

"Good. They need it," Aria said. "And Lebedev agreed to let us borrow his private jet to get to the next location. He also gave us a nice little armor package as long as we keep him in the loop. Lebedev doesn't want destruction, James. He wants the world to be safe."

"I get that. I want the same, Aria. Sadly, Walten owns and manages everything. I will do my best to keep things on the down-low, but please keep our top-secret technologies to yourself from now on," he spoke quietly as if someone else was listening. "But I'm okay with Lebedev. He was always a strong soldier. I always wanted to meet the man and tell him sorry for killing so many of his soldiers over forty years ago."

Aria laughed. "He would like that, sir. He mentioned playing chess with you."

"Chess? Oh, he's asking for punishment at that point," Clarke chuckled.

Aria smiled, feeling a bit relaxed for a change. James usually made her feel better.

"I'm glad you are safe. Please be careful from now on. I'm pleased Lebedev is sharing with you. Next time you are home, we'll have to get you better defensive technology. I've already put in a work order with the lab."

"Thank you, sir."

"Now, have fun in Saray, my dear."

"Saray?"

"Next projected city-state. The attacks are increasing in intensity and occurring closer together. I would like you to depart ASAP. Tonight, there is a peace conference being held in the city square. A treaty will be signed between Alijah Dizdarevic of Saray and Dario Benvenuto of Roma. They have been in a constant war for nearly thirty years and have decided to end all conflicts based on the recent attacks worldwide. The world is beginning to unify and realize that there are greater threats to humanity. We feel an attack may occur during that time. Euclid and his army do not want cities to unite. He'll most likely wish to drift everyone apart. With the world's capitals feuding, our armies can do little to protect each other from such violent attacks. Our goal is to ensure that the peace treaty takes place. With the help of Lebedev in the background and with the participation of Saray's military, perhaps we can keep Saray and Roma safe."

"I understand." Aria nodded.

"Call me once you are in place."

"Will do."

"And Aria," he hesitated, "stay safe."

"Yes, sir."

She ended the call, staring at the blinking numbers on her wrist.

"Where are we going?" Ivory asked, dropping the two large luggage carriers onto the floor. She huffed, wiping a blonde strand out of her eyes.

"We are off to Saray. We're going to need a lot of armor. That place has been nothing but a battlefield for decades."

"Sounds…lovely." Ivory frowned.

Mr. Walten stared at his reflection in the window of his top-story condo overlooking the City of Fountains. Slowly, he brought the crystalline glass to his lips, drinking the golden liquid inside. His caramel eyes moved to the shuffling reflection that entered the room.

"Tell me you have some good news for me," Walten said, quickly loosening his tie as he turned to face General Jeron Feyette.

"The Elixis scientists have arrived safely. They are currently setting up their equipment in the lab."

"About damn time I received some good news. I needed that building!" He slammed his glass onto his desktop and quickly refilled it. He didn't hesitate to drink the contents and fill it once again. "Doesn't matter," he sighed. "It's only a minor setback."

Jeron watched the CEO with emotionless eyes.

"I have my scientists. They have their notes. They will have to team up with Camery and rebuild the lost equipment. At least those menacing soldiers are out of the way now."

Jeron cleared his throat, interrupting the younger CEO's rant.

Walten turned his attention to the general, appearing shocked. "They are dead, correct?"

"We have not been able to confirm that, sir," Jeron answered in his baritone voice.

"What do you mean, confirm? Haven't the bodies been identified?" he sneered.

"So far, nobody has come up of unknown origin. The four had entered the city under false identities, so there would be no way to identify the bodies. Everyone's accounted for, and all are legal Cherno residents and military," Jeron replied.

"And I assume you checked the military offices and prisons?"

"Yes, sir. No anonymous individuals were mentioned in the reports."

"Damn it!" Walten threw his glass across the room. It shattered into a hundred pieces against his rich mahogany wall. "Surely, those beasts would have murdered them as they did to the men in Pierre. If not them, then the Cherno military, at least! I bet Lebedev is somehow involved in this secrecy."

"Would you like me to question Clarke?" Jeron asked.

"No. Let me deal with Clarke. I want your men to keep a close eye on all private forms of communication. We can't have those four ruining everything. I've already lost Elixis because of them. This is a delicate matter." Walten turned to Feyette. His golden-brown hair was a ruffled mess from constantly running his fingers through it. "I want those soldiers out of commission, you hear? I need that Sorcēarian and the girl brought back to me. Understand?"

Jeron saluted roughly to his advisor. Coldly, he replied, "Yes, sir."

"Ivory's Portrait"

CHAPTER 14

Aria watched out the small window beside her leather seat of Lebedev's private jet. In only twenty minutes, they hovered over Saray—a city of stone and rounded architecture. It was a harsh contrast to Fountains, having an old-time feel rather than modern. On the dull landscape of browns and grays, far below, she could see the blasts of gunfire and explosions of flame rupturing near the city's outskirts. Even though Saray was about to negotiate a peace treaty, they continued fighting. Most likely, the bullets would only cease after the papers were signed. It was pathetic. No one knew why Roma and Saray still fought. At this point, it was a matter of honor and reputation. A city-state didn't go up against the Romans, expecting them to turn their backs on a battle. Two bullheaded countries were up against one another, and without a conclusion through documentation, they could fight until the end of time. However, if they joined sides, Roma and Saray would undoubtedly be a force to reckon with.

Aria's gloved fingers trailed over the black helmet in her hands. Lebedev was more generous than he needed to be. He stocked the small group with their own sets of body armor and plenty of ammunition to help with the possible attack on Saray. And, with Saray being an ally of Cherno, Lebedev had also set up negotiations with the military's general to work with Aria and her team. No more sneaking around. The job should unfold much more professionally. Aria found it a relief.

Ivory sat in her chair, fidgeting with her breastplate. She had insisted on wearing her helmet throughout the flight, her face hidden. With the visor's technology, she watched the ant-like vehicles below up close with a data read on each one. Sporadically, her fingers pressed against the small nodules on the sides of her helmet, selecting the different view modes and various tools. Despite the exciting technology, she remained uncharacteristically quiet. Perhaps it was because she felt uncomfortable beneath Dovian's icy stare. He had a way of putting someone on the spot with eyes like that. Aria cleared her throat, gathering the Sorcēarian's attention. His cold eyes lifted to hers, his features relaxing a bit as he turned up the corner of his mouth into a gentle smile. Aria gave him a weird look, darting her eyes to Ivory. His smile flipped into a frown as he gazed at the other woman who looked out the window with feigned interest. Then, he lowered his head and gave a slight shrug. He remained concerned about Ivory's quick personality shift in the holding cell.

"Quite the battle going on down there," Troy's voice infiltrated the quiet cabin. He sat across from Aria, gaping out the window. He, too, wore body armor that fit his form perfectly in a dark gun-metal gray. His helmet rested in his hands. "Hopefully, we don't get dragged into it. We're here for more important issues."

"Lebedev said he spoke with General Kovacevic. They are to assist us, and we are not to be involved in their quarrel," Aria said, glancing at the giant blast that took out an entire flanking fleet. These guys didn't know when to quit.

"I won't hesitate to shoot one of the bastards if they so much as try to get in our way," he muttered.

"You'll have plenty of monsters to shoot, I'm sure," she said.

"Not exactly something I'm looking forward to, but this armor helps!" He moved his arms, testing the give and flexibility of his suit.

Aria smirked and returned her stare out the window. "We're landing. Brace yourselves," she mumbled, watching the cracked, busted runway near as they descended.

The plane rumbled intensely as the landing gear touched down, running over the bumps and holes on the paved surface. The group grabbed the armrests of their chairs, their bodies quaking violently. The jet turned and parked slowly near an old airport, the Saray military circling the vehicle.

"Come on, let's make some friends," Aria said, slipping on her helmet.

Outside, the land was dry and sandy. Wild winds kicked up miniature dust devils, spiraling around the filthy and tired Saraian soldiers. Aria and her entourage descended from the jet, weapons ready. A man in a tattered uniform with makeshift armor decorated in scribbles of hash marks and names neared them.

"You the ones from the United Americas?" he asked gruffly, a cigar smashed between his teeth. His voice didn't have the typical accent for Saray; he sounded American, possibly a mixed-race born in Saray or a defector. The man also looked as if he hadn't seen a shower in a week, his face covered in dirt and rough stubble. He was bald, a tattoo lining the backside of his head in an intricate design surrounding the military emblem of his city-state.

"Yes, sir. You Kovacevic?" Aria asked, shaking the man's large hand.

"Yes, ma'am. You the head of this investigation?" he asked.

"Yes. This is my partner, Troy." Troy signaled a small wave, his other hand gripping his weapon. Kovacevic nodded to the man. "Ivory." She pointed to the tall, slender woman.

"She your sniper?" he asked, eyeing the massive weapon in Ivory's hands.

"One hell of a shot." Aria nodded.

"And what's with him?" Kovacevic narrowed his eyes—one honey-colored, the other grey—as he puffed out his cigar smoke, looking Dovian up and down.

"That's Dovian. He's got his own strategies. It's a little unconventional, but you won't be disappointed," Aria stated. Dovian and Kovacevic gave each other a respectful nod.

"Don't need any armor?" he asked the giant man.

"I have my own." Dovian rolled his shoulders, his spaulders moving against his neck armor. The sorcerer was plenty capable of protecting himself. Besides, there wasn't any prebuilt armor in the world big enough to fit the man.

"Fair enough." Kovacevic placed the cigar between his teeth. "Come this way. We've cleared a path that will take you to the base where you will give your brief."

Following the general, they filed into a large troop transporter. It was massive, painted in brown camouflage with large artillery mounts on the front. This carrier was a hovercraft. This made for safe passage for its occupants as it could easily float over underground mines and Jumping Jimmies—a modified S-mine of the past with even deadlier sprays that could penetrate the heaviest of barriers and armor. Even old technology remained effective. Anything goes in war. As long as it killed enemies, it was useful.

"What's with all the hostility?" Troy asked. He swayed in his seat as the transporter avoided splatters of shrapnel.

"What? This? Oh, boy, this ain't nuthin'. You should have been here in '83. This whole place was nearly leveled. But we keep pushin' 'em back."

"This is pushed back?" Aria asked.

"Heh, they keep sending in their 'droids." Kovacevic laughed. "Damn bastards are easy to kill, but their sheer numbers can take out a fleet."

"Aren't you in the middle of negotiating a peace treaty?" Dovian questioned.

Kovacevic gave the white-haired man an amused look. "Son, I don't know where you come from, but war doesn't end. It keeps going. Sure, there may be days when things are quiet, but it all starts up again. Hell, our planet is evidence enough. Can't grow a damn thing out there in the wilderness. Can't imagine what fresh air smells like. All I know of is the scent of dirt, blood, and rust. Then there's the fresh, sterile smell of hospitals. Neither are pleasant; both make you miserable."

"I should consider it a blessing to have lived in a time where things were once peaceful." Dovian thought a moment. "And to know what fresh air and rain smell like. To have seen butterflies and flowers."

Kovacevic laughed. "You a flamboyant?"

"Flamboyant?" Dovian quirked an eyebrow.

"Yeah. A panty-wearer, giddy-ninny, sashay?"

Dovian kept his stern demeanor. Aria and Troy slowly sank into their seats, embarrassed.

"Gay?" Kovacevic added.

That word, Dovian understood. "Are you questioning my sexuality?"

"Talkin' of butterflies and flowers in the middle of a battlefield. I'd imagine there'd be better things on your mind." Kovacevic gave a humming chuckle.

"I can imagine fifty ways to kill you right now with that cigar before you even bat an eyelash," the Sorcēarian grumbled.

Kovacevic hooted loudly. "That's the spirit!" His amused eyes watched the aggravated Sorcēarian. "Aw, come on now. Don't give me that look. Just trying to get your blood pumping, that's all."

Dovian tightly gripped his staff, and his jaw clenched tight. "Call me whatever you want. I will not falter in appreciating the beauty in life, especially amongst carnage and bigotry. What I spoke of is what I fight for. Any other reason to fight is abhorrent. Besides, I don't see why it matters whether I am gay or not. My civilization was colorful in many ways despite what others want to believe."

The general's laugh slowly faded. He eyed the floor, twisting his rifle from side to side against the grated metal. "Naw, it really doesn't matter. All people fight and die the same regardless. And I can't say I ever seen a real rose, nor have I ever seen the rain, but I imagine it was once pretty great. But what I want to know is…how the hell have you ever experienced any of that." Kovacevic stared at Dovian. "I get the feelin' you aren't exactly a normal person."

"What was your first guess?" Dovian asked sarcastically.

"Well, I've been fighting for over fifty years and never seen anyone like ya. From what I can tell, your weapon is unique, something made from old technology. Based on your tattoos and getup, I'd say you were a soldier. And your eyes tell me you're much older than you look."

"You're perceptive."

Kovacevic chuckled again as he put out his cigar. "My great-grandpa used to tell me stories of some great soldiers from long ago. Now, don't call me a daydreamer, but I'd like to imagine you're somehow related to those stories."

Troy and Aria looked in Dovian's direction. He smirked at the general.

"Damn." Kovacevic clapped his hands. "Can't wait to see you on the battlefield."

As the transporter pulled to the camp, Kovacevic yelled through his DNAIS, "Get the troops pulled back for the evening. We'll need as many as we can get for our mission tonight. The Romans will have to entertain themselves for a few hours." He looked at Aria, staring at her green eyes through her lifted visor. He placed his helmet on his head. "Guard yourselves. We have a few meters to go before we're safe. There's a lot of gunfire goin' on close by."

The door slid open to the transport. A violent, torrential barrage of bullets and mortar blasts killed the peaceful silence. Aria flipped down her visor and signaled for the others to follow her, Kovacevic taking the lead. Two steps out of the vehicle, an explosion blasted nearby, covering her with dirt.

"Careful, now. Straight ahead an' we'll be safe an' sound."

"This is ridiculous. You have androids all over the camp!" Aria shouted.

She loaded regular ammunition into her weapon and fired upon the mechanized Roma soldiers that scrambled over the nearly destroyed barricades. Effortlessly, she and Troy killed a dozen androids before reaching the fortified metal building. There didn't appear to be any human soldiers fighting for Roma. That meant they had all been either pushed back or wounded. Droids were usually sent as a last resort to keep the opposite side busy while planning the next attack.

"In you go." Kovacevic flagged them inside the building as he opened the door. Filing in, Aria raised her visor.

"You think they're planning one last attack before the signing tonight?" she asked.

"Naw, I think the boys are just getting wound down. The Romans are probably too busy preparing a feast to feed their fat asses for the night. The fact that we're gettin' Dizdarevic and Benvenuto together in one room without hostility is reason enough to celebrate." He signaled to one of his men. "I said to pull in the boys! Send out our drones. It'll keep their bots busy for a few hours. Get some rest. We've got work to do tonight, serious work, too. So, we need our A-game, got it?"

"Yes, sir!" His soldier saluted before taking off in a run, hollering orders in his thick accent through his DNAIS system.

The racks were full of men and women alike—some dressing their wounds, others playing cards and smoking cigarettes. Kovacevic neared the center table, where a grouping of comps and vidscreens sat. Plopping into a seat with a loud groan, he rested his feet on a nearby stool.

"Okay, let's discuss plans for this evening."

"I assume you've heard about all the attacks around the world," Aria stated as she dropped into a chair opposite the man.

"Sure have. Monsters galore, I heard."

"More than you can handle and nothing like you've ever seen before," she said seriously. "We're going to need a full stock of EMP arsenals. Have everyone equipped with their defensive fields. Got any Fazes?" she asked.

"Something like it. Recipe'd up in our labs. Shock Wave distributors." He held up one of the devices. "Works in a similar fashion. Has a higher ricochet rate. Sometimes good, other times bad. If hit right, you can send a bullet flying back toward the target." He tapped the device, the item humming and then crackling as it puffed out a cloud of smoke. Kovacevic eyed the machine and tossed it over his shoulder. "Uh, that one's bein' worked on," he quickly mumbled.

Aria gave an unsure look at the sizzling device. "Interesting defense strategy. However, these creatures don't use bullets, but it should work well enough to protect against some of the blasts."

"What kind of blasts are you talking about?"

"They have a way of sending out explosive shockwaves. It's a little like a frequency attack. They have these large blades on their hands." Aria pulled up a screen from her DNAIS. A hand-drawn sketch of the monster appeared before the man. Troy smirked. Leave it to Aria to use her drawing abilities to her advantage in the war strategy. "These things, I call them Brutes, can create high-velocity vibrations that they can use as a traveling blast. They are big. Their claws are long, almost touching the ground as they stand. Once you hear the clicking of their nails, you had better move. The blast won't dissipate until it hits its target or something gets in its way. This strategy pushes our forces back, allowing for continuous attacks and rendering our ammunition ineffective, as they heal nearly instantaneously. Therefore, they are best taken down at close range. Render their shields useless through the use of EMPs and get in close. Another effective strategy is using heavy arsenal like sniper rifles." She nudged toward Ivory's 20mm sniper rifle. "These are our primary concerns right now."

Kovacevic listened intently, recording the things Aria said through his DNAIS. As she spoke, he moved tiny army men across his map of Saray.

"Now these guys," Aria pulled up a second sketch, "these are the regular ones."

Kovacevic gave her an amused look.

"I call them Brawlers. They are more of your hand-to-hand fighters. They like to bite, claw, and drag you away. They aren't very smart and don't seem to have any tactical plans outside of search and destroy, but that doesn't mean you should underestimate them. Fire the EMPs, and it should disrupt their shields and allow for standard attacks."

Running a finger against the screen of her DNAIS, she pulled up the third image. "These ones we've only come across while in Ives."

Kovacevic looked toward Dovian, chuckling.

Aria continued. "I call them Stilt-Men. They look different than the others in skin tone, having an olive-green tint. They are extremely slender and tall; their joints can snap backward. They are excellent at scaling walls, even better than the Brawlers. They also fight a lot like Brawlers, but I noticed they have long red manes of hair. At the end of the mane, there seems to be a pointed barb. However, I haven't seen them use these yet, but I would venture to guess you wouldn't want to be hit by one of them." She shuddered.

"Looks like a scorpion's tail," Kovacevic muttered.

"Exactly. I would assume it has a type of poison," Aria flipped the page, closing down her DNAIS.

"Interesting. You know of only the three so far?"

"Yes, sir. But I imagine we will run across more in the future. As we learn, they seem to adapt to make our lives more miserable."

"Sounds like a damn good time." Kovacevic lit up another cigar. "Anything else I should know?"

"The man leading the attacks is named Euclid. He is a Sorcēarian and is extremely dangerous."

"Sorcēarian, eh?" He eyeballed Dovian again. "Just like them stories."

"Just as deadly," Aria affirmed. "You can't touch him. Everything you throw at him, he deflects."

"Let me handle him," Dovian spoke up. "There's nothing you can do to stop him. Not with your technology."

"He's all yours, but I tell you what, you find that Euclid and get in a fight, and I'll send you a whole team for backup. Badass or not, he can't protect himself from an entire fleet of gunfire." Kovacevic pointed his cigar at the man. "You do some of that weird voodoo shit that I can only assume you're capable of, and we just may be able to get the upper hand on the bastard."

"That may work." Dovian nodded.

"Any idea why that asshole is leading the attacks?"

"We're unsure of his motive yet, sir," Aria replied.

"There is no motive other than wanting to see the entire world burn," Dovian interjected. "This man is capable of only nightmares. He wants to destroy everyone and everything. He will not stop until he does so. He will not halt until *I* stop him." Dovian's eyes dimmed, darkening as he brooded, lost in memories from long ago.

"Well, then, let's get that bastard tonight!" Kovacevic pointed at the map. "Here is where the signing will take place. Aria, I'd like you and Troy posted here and here." He pointed at the entrances to the building. "We got barricades already set up. You can sit up on the rooftops. I assume your armor has cloaking mechanisms?"

"Yes."

"Good. Now, you," he pointed at Ivory, "you'll be stationed in this tower. You see anything suspicious at all, you shoot it, hear?"

Ivory nodded quickly. The armor hid any form of expression, but Aria could imagine her look was one of fear.

"And you…" he paused, grinning at Dovian. "You are going to be back here." He moved a large piece to a facility marker on his map a few blocks from the city's center.

"You have a reactor," Aria stated numbly.

"Yeah, powers the whole city-state. It's underground, though. After what happened to Athenia, we can't be too careful. I want Dovian to keep watch from the tower opposite of Ivory's. You will have a view of the entire city. Below, my infantry will take a stand, guarding the whole facility."

"I want you to put a team inside, too," Aria said firmly. "Euclid can get inside without any of you seeing him. If he is to attack the reactor, I can guarantee he won't be walking through the front door."

"All right. I'll set up a team inside as well. They will surround the core. Sound good?"

"Great."

"I'll work out the guard posts surrounding the city square, where you should have plenty of backup. Now, I'm taking a significant risk movin' my troops inside the city. If, for some reason, that treaty isn't signed, Roma will not hesitate to attack. All my men will be inside, and Saray will be infiltrated."

"I understand, sir. We appreciate your cooperation. As such, Lebedev has agreed to have his troops back your forces. As we speak, they are setting up flanks on the mountainsides. They will be here in seconds if Roma pulls any tricks."

"Hot damn! You thought of everything. In that case, let's get a move on." Kovacevic stood from his chair and gathered his vidscreen. "The signing is at 20:00. Be at your posts an hour before. I will keep in touch." He pointed to his mental chip. "Tune in to frequency 141.12. You have a few hours; why don't you rest until then? There's some nice grub downtown. I'd offer you rations, but they aren't appetizing in the slightest."

"Sounds like a plan." Aria nodded.

"Good. I'll be here briefing my troops. If you need anything, let me or one of my men know. Just get your bodies to your posts by 19:00. I'll send troops out as soon as the briefing is finished." He turned on his heel and hurried across the giant hangar, calling for his troops.

"Everyone clear on what their positions are?" Aria asked.

"Yup," Troy sighed. It was second nature to the man. Just tell him where to be and when, and he'll bring his so-called A-game to the field. At this point, fighting a war was as routine as tying his shoes.

"I, I think so," Ivory stuttered, her first words since they left Cherno.

"Dovian will ensure you arrive safely at your post, and he will watch you from his tower, guaranteeing nothing happens to you. Got it?" Ivory turned her stare toward the Sorcēarian, and he quickly nodded.

"Oh, okay," Ivory whispered, fidgeting with her rifle.

Aria watched her cautiously. Something clearly bothered the woman.

"You hungry?" she asked.

"Always!" Ivory beamed a little too joyfully.

"Let's check out the *grub* in the square," Aria rose from her seat, stretching her back. Shouldering her weapon, she headed toward the transport facility. They would ride the monorail to the city's center—if it hadn't been annihilated yet.

Luckily, the tram remained intact and in perfect running order. Within minutes, the four smelled delicious spices and gourmet food in the center square. The inner city was the opposite of the military facilities outside the walls. Despite the obnoxious sound of gun and mortar fire, the streets were bustling with people. Aria had to admit, it was a little disturbing that the people went on about their everyday lives as the constant battle raged outside their walls. It was all televised on massive vidscreens throughout the city, too. The war was considered a game, nothing more than humans versus robots. Still, people died. And this was the way of life. It wasn't just Saray, either. The world partook in these useless battles—fighting for the sake of fighting, buying companies, and trading weaponry, all in the interests of power and money. Businessmen owned the world. There was no form of government, only chaos. Aria and the others were all toy soldiers used in a system of corruption to fill the suits' pockets.

Dovian watched in awe at the scene. People hollered and signaled for taxis. They bid on the streets for food, household items, and black-market weaponry while others stood in the middle of the road watching the news and battles on the giant monitors atop the surrounding domed structures.

A stray missile flew over the walls. Quickly, everyone darted under the protection of the side streets' overhangs. An explosion sounded, and rock and dirt sprayed over the buildings onto the streets. There followed a couple of shouts, mostly swear words, and the gesturing of hands. Only moments later did the people venture out to continue shopping and dining. Dovian's mouth hung in wonder; humanity had officially lost its mind.

Dovian followed Aria and Troy as they traveled through the crowd. He ignored the stares and grumbles directed his way. It seemed the people in this town had no respect for the military. He couldn't entirely blame them. What was the point of this useless fighting? Were thirty years necessary? What about the countless wars before this one? Wasn't it just a waste of money at this point?

He turned his attention to the blonde beside him. Ivory remained completely hidden behind the visor of her helmet. He frowned. Where was her cheerful disposition?

"Something is bothering you," he whispered.

"Me?" Ivory asked, turning her hidden face up toward the tall man.

"Yes."

"Oh. I suppose."

"You're not as chatty as you often are."

"Guess I'm feeling a bit tired today, that's all." She fidgeted with her gloved hands, the small armor plates clinking together.

"That's all?" He scrutinized her.

"You've been staring at me all day," she whispered.

"My apologies. It's just that I haven't been able to get a read on you all day."

"A read?" she asked.

Dovian paused a moment. "Usually, I'm good at reading people. You've been uncharacteristically silent today and a bit adrift. If something is on your mind, it is best to get it out now before going into battle. Distractions will only lead to you getting hurt or possibly killed."

Ivory didn't respond. She merely kept up her pace with the giant man.

"Do I bother you?" he finally asked.

"No! No, you don't bother me." She quickly shook her head. "I'm just not feeling well, I suppose."

Dovian frowned. His cold gaze darted to a small shop nearby, and he smiled. "Then perhaps a treat will help?" he offered.

"A treat?" Ivory lifted her head again.

Dovian grabbed her hand. "Something to cheer you up."

He led the girl to a café where tiny, intricately detailed pastries and truffles were displayed. Upon noticing the two, Aria paused and tugged Troy's arm.

"What are they looking at?" Troy asked.

"Chocolates," Aria replied dully. She met Dovian's vibrant eyes, and he cheerfully waved her over.

"Come look at these exquisite truffles." The tall man pressed a finger against the glass. The curly, peach-haired young woman behind the counter grinned.

"What about them?" Aria asked, folding her arms.

"May we purchase some?" he asked.

"Dovian, those are fifty units each," Aria stated sourly.

"I take it that means they are expensive?"

"Very," she replied.

Ivory gave a small whimper. "Oh, that's a pity. I've never had a truffle before."

She stared at the chocolates through the glass.

"Indeed, it is such a pity. It is probably the closest thing to Heaven on this entire planet." Dovian winked at the lady behind the counter. Her face turned a dark shade of red as she giggled.

"Come on, Aria. Don't be such a tight-ass." Troy nudged the woman.

"You pay for them, then. I had to fund a shopping spree the other night," she growled.

"You owe me for that sandwich incident," he pointed out.

Aria frowned.

"And you owe me for that stunt you pulled when you body-snatched me," he added.

'Damn it,' she cursed.

"Whoever is generous to the poor lends to the Lord, and He will repay him for his deed." Dovian grinned.

"Shut up, Dovian." Aria exasperatedly tugged off the armor on her forearm. "I'll take two truffles," she grumbled.

"Whoa, wait. I want one, too, missy." Troy grabbed her shoulder.

She glared at him, which warned him of his untimely demise. He fed her the biggest grin he could muster. Holding back her tongue, she turned to the peach-haired woman.

"We are having a special today," the woman gleefully spoke. "Buy three, get one free."

"Oh! A special!" Dovian grinned at Aria. "How lovely."

"Very lovely." Ivory nodded.

"Lovely, indeed!" Troy chimed in, clasping his hands together.

Aria clenched her fists, trying to keep calm. "Fine. Four truffles then," she sighed.

Happily, the woman bagged the chocolates in their decorative paper and placed them inside a small pink box with a heart-shaped seal. Aria nearly gagged when she lifted the pretty item. How ridiculous. She bitterly swiped her chip across the scanner and muttered a fierce thanks to the cashier.

"Half the cost covers the decorative wrapping," she grumbled as they neared a small table on the sidewalk.

"I think it's delightfully cute!" Ivory beamed joyfully. At least the woman's typical demeanor returned.

"Yes, yes. Delightful," Aria moaned. Daintily, she opened the package, slowly took each wrapped truffle out, and divvied among the four. She glared at Dovian as she handed him his. He smiled in return.

Slowly, Dovian took a small bite of the chocolate. He nearly melted on the spot. It had been thousands upon thousands of years since he even had a piece of chocolate as blissful as this. Troy put the whole truffle in his mouth, alarming the Sorcēarian.

"Dear God, Troy!" Dovian shouted.

"Mwat?" Troy asked, startled.

"Savor it! Don't simply gobble the whole damn thing in one bite, you ignorant cod!"

Troy quickly spat the item out into his hand and took a small nibble off the corner.

"You're so gross." Aria wrinkled her nose.

"What's the big deal? It's just chocolate." Troy shrugged.

"Not just chocolate…a little piece of Heaven. Nothing in the entire world comes close to the joys of Heaven. But this, this is the closest representation I can think of, so enjoy it. You, humans, need to slow down and enjoy the simple pleasures in life, not take everything for granted," Dovian snapped.

"Jeez, I didn't think it was that important," Troy grumbled, slowly eating away at his piece of chocolate. Why did he suddenly feel like a scolded child?

Aria took a tiny bite, watching Dovian as she did so. The treat had a slight crunch on the outside, but the inside was soft and cake-like. "Wow…that's pretty awesome." She giggled. "Not sure if it was worth fifty units, but it's good."

"It's the best thing I've ever had!" Ivory beamed.

"Heaven, right?" Dovian asked.

"Heaven," Ivory agreed.

"So…Heaven's made out of chocolate?" Troy asked.

Dovian glared at the man, slowly finishing his truffle. "It's made of things with wonder you can't even imagine."

"Guess we'll all find out someday, huh?" Aria quickly said. She grabbed the box and placed the paper inside. Standing, she stared at the trashcan beside her, weighing her options.

'Hell no,' she thought.

"What are you doing with that?" Troy asked her, following closely.

"I am not throwing this away, not after what I paid for it," Aria said.

Troy laughed. "So, you'll carry that pink box everywhere you go?"

She glanced at the pink container. Stopping, she turned to Dovian. "Here." She held out the item.

"What?" The Sorcēarian stared at the item with curiosity.

"Take this."

"And what am I supposed to do with that?" he dryly asked.

"You got that staff. Work up some magic and send this thing to my apartment."

He gave her a look that made her feel most stupid.

"I know you can do something with it," she huffed.

Troy looked over the woman's shoulder and then up at the sorcerer, his mouth open in amusement. Ivory stared at the tall man. Feeling on the spot, Dovian rolled his eyes.

"The things I do to entertain you children," he murmured sourly. Grabbing the pink box, he lifted his eyebrows sarcastically and uttered something in Legacy. After throwing his hands in the air, the item disappeared.

"Ha!" Aria folded her arms. "Knew you could do it."

"Yes, but it isn't guaranteed to be in your apartment. It may have landed in a dumpster somewhere else instead."

"You're an ass." She frowned.

"You had better not have wasted that pretty wrapping!" Ivory waggled a finger at the grown man. He leaned away from her gesture, pulling his staff with him.

Troy looked at the surroundings in interest, trying to spot something to busy himself with until his duty called. "Hey, a bar!" He tugged on Aria's arm.

"Damn it, man! You're an alcoholic!" she snarled.

"Not any more than you are," he argued.

"You have an hour," she sharply replied.

"More than enough time."

"We're going to drink before a mission?" Ivory cheeped.

"Why would you expect any responsible behavior from these two?" Dovian asked. Ivory giggled quietly.

"Shut up, Dovian," Aria grumbled.

Ivory giggled again.

"Such disrespect." Dovian shook his head sadly, gently placing his hand on Ivory's back and guiding her into the bar beside him.

The pub was clean, much to Dovian's surprise. Despite being packed full of people, the environment remained comfortable outside of the glares a few patrons sent his way. A small table occupied one dark corner and sat far enough away that people wouldn't be able to hear much of their conversation if they were quiet. Aria looked over her shoulder, pointing at the same seats he first noticed. He nodded in confirmation, and they took their places one by one.

"You're buying me a drink," Aria told Troy as she dropped into her chair.

"Bullshit," he said.

"Do it!" she snapped.

"Rawr!" he growled at her. "Chill out!" He swiftly moved to the bar.

"You have him on a leash," Dovian said in amusement.

"He needs a shorter one," Aria sighed.

The Sorcēarian chuckled, playing with the small candle sitting at the center of the table. He watched it, traveling far away again, lost in his thoughts. Aria furrowed her brow. Dovian was a rollercoaster of emotion. One minute, he joked with the others. The next, he fell into a pit of depression caused by unknown reasons.

"What are you thinking about?" she asked.

Cerulean eyes met hers. "You want to know?"

"Sure." She leaned forward attentively. "Let us in on a bit of your past. I know that's what you were thinking about."

"I'm that obvious?" he asked.

She scoffed. "I've been around soldiers most of my life. I know that faraway look. You're thinking about times that no longer exist."

"Indeed, I was." His tone lowered as he watched the flame. "The world has changed so much."

"Beer," Troy interrupted, handing out bottles to everyone at the table, the glass rattling against the surface. He noticed their somber faces and quickly plopped into his seat.

"How so?" Aria asked, ignoring Troy's intrusion.

Dovian breathed a laugh. "Oh, my dear, where do I even begin?"

"How about this? Why the seclusion?" Troy asked, putting his bottle to his lips.

"Seclusion?" Dovian watched the other man in interest.

"Yeah, from the rest of the world? You can't tell me that those little thunderstorms kept you locked up forever on that small continent," the male soldier said.

"No, they didn't. In fact, I used to travel the world quite a bit, but that was an exceptionally long time ago."

"What made you stop?" Aria asked.

Dovian frowned. "At first, people were kind. I was treated with respect most of the time. I used to give sermons, trying to restore humanity's faith and reassure them of better times. Then, I noticed a shift. Increasingly, people began to resent and eventually hate me. They thought I was a liar, a false prophet. The churches kicked me out, claiming I was a Fallen One. Pure beings don't fall from Heaven; only those tainted are cursed to live here. Then, the wars progressed. My people were no longer around to keep humanity under control. Sure, I'm a Sorcēarian, but what can one Sorcēarian do?" He slowly twisted his bottle, watching the liquid ripple inside the glass. "Besides destroy things." He sipped the brew.

"You say that like you're some monster," Ivory whispered. She leaned toward Dovian, the light flickering on her face like a campfire as she listened intently to the man's story.

"I never said I wasn't." He looked at her gravely.

"So, you just stopped going outside? Just like that?" Troy asked.

"Not necessarily. You see, I traveled for thousands of years. After a while, I was only wandering around in solitude. People eventually forgot about me, forgot about my race, and then they forgot the teachings. I watched them burn books, watched them burn churches. I was powerless. What could I do? I was labeled a madman. Many times, my life was threatened. I was doomed to sit on this planet and watch it slowly corrode into a pit of disgusting despair. The day I left…was terrible. It was when I finally realized how morbidly revolting humanity had become." Dovian stared into the grooves and dents of the metal table. In it, he saw his reflection—blue eyes gazing back up at him, much like they had the last day he had gone outside of his home.

"What happened?" Aria asked.

"There was a time when I tried to help the innocent ones, those that still stood a chance." He chuckled then. "I was a hero. I would save damsels in distress and help the elderly who had fallen and had no one to call. I brought food to the starving and helped children tie their shoes. It was a simple life but not entirely lonely. Some thought me to be their guardian angel. In a way, I was. I'm not sure what drove me. Maybe I thought it would counteract my sins and bring me closer to Him again. But one night, I heard the screams of a young woman. I watched from the rooftops as a man mugged and tried to rape her. I stopped him. How badly I wanted to cut off his arms, but I didn't harm anyone. Not since I…destroyed my kind. I turned to the woman. She was crying, cold, and wet as she lay in the rain. I asked her if she was all right. And she looked up at me with eyes holding so much fear. I remember that look, and it hurt more than any look I had received from a human. Because she was beautiful, and she looked just like *her.*"

"Her?" Troy asked.

Dovian gave a small smile. "Lanthe. She looked just like I'Lanthe. Her dark hair curled the same way. Her eyes were even a violet shade. Her neck was long; her skin was pale. And I couldn't stop staring. The woman screamed and pushed away from me. I guess I was frightening. She called me a freak and ran away. It hurt, more than anything, since the day I'Lanthe died…was murdered." His hands clenched as he watched the flame. "I suppose, in a way, I was hoping it was her. Maybe she had been given a second chance, was living another life as a human." He mockingly laughed. "That was when humanity began fearing me. I was tall. My eyes were abnormal. They started hating me rather than welcoming me and my faith."

"So that's when you stopped coming out? Because of this woman?" Troy asked.

"Not quite. It was a brief time later. Once again, I watched from the rooftops when I noticed a man in the middle of an act most vile. How humans can be corrupted so easily, I will never understand." Here, he took a long drink. "He had raped and killed a little girl. I didn't get there in time. As I grabbed and pulled him off her, her throat had already been slit. Her eyes…were like glass. She was cold and white, her brown hair soaked from the rain. Why it's always raining, I don't know. The worst happens when it rains." He took a shuddering breath. The other three watched in awe. "I couldn't control myself. The rage I felt. He had killed an innocent girl, had done horrible things! Men like that, they don't deserve life. They don't deserve any second chances! And just like that, like that…I…." Dovian's wild eyes suddenly dimmed, the ferocity momentarily leaving. "I snapped his neck."

Ivory gasped, holding her hand against her lips.

"It was the first time I had killed in nearly 10,000 years. But that wasn't the worst of it. The mother came outside and saw me standing above her child. She screamed. Such a dreadful sound. And it was like a knife cutting into my soul. This woman was the same woman from over fifteen years before. She had aged some, and her hair held some grey, but still, she resembled the woman from my past. I couldn't move. I couldn't do anything as she cried and screamed, holding her daughter. And there, at my feet, was her dead boyfriend, the man who had raped and killed her girl. She blamed me for it. She thought I had done it all. She cursed me, cursed me to no end. And then, as if a light had turned on in her mind, she remembered me. 'It's you,' she had said. 'You are the one who attacked me all those years ago.' She had somehow gotten it mixed up. Her memory failed her, making her believe I was the one who had attacked her all those years before. And then she thought I had killed her boyfriend and proceeded to rape and kill her daughter. I didn't protest. I said nothing, even as she pulled the gun from her jacket and shot me point-blank in the stomach. She left me to die in the rain as she ran inside to call for help. But what she didn't realize was that the wound didn't kill me.

"As I crawled through the mud, my blood poured out. I surely left a trail, but it quickly washed down the storm drains. I don't know how far I crawled before finding refuge behind a dumpster. There I lay, letting the wound bleed. I prayed I would die. I wanted to leave this horrible place. My powers were weak; I didn't even try to heal myself. I felt cold and, for the first time, so very alone. I heard nothing, heard no reply to my calls. He had undoubtedly left me. Would Hell be any worse? I didn't care as I watched the red soak through my clothing—the dark civilian clothes I had worn at the time to try and fit in. Funny how I wanted to fit in. Fit in with a world that was nothing like the one I belonged to.

"I stared at my reflection in the puddles around me, wondering the reasoning behind my worthless existence. Soon, the darkness consumed me. I thought I had finally died—a death of nothing but black, no memory of anything. It was a sad but forgiving death. But then I awoke. It was days later, a hot, sunny day. I have no idea how long I had laid there with no one stopping to help. Even the dumpster had been moved and emptied. That shows you how much the people cared. I was a muddy mess, covered in my own gore, but the wound had healed. And I was angry.

"He won't let me die. My punishment is to live forever. No matter what happens, I won't die. Slice my wrists, hang myself, jump off the highest peak of every cathedral, nothing. I am a cursed man. Some would think it a blessing, but not with the horrors I have lived through, not the things I have seen. I'm to live for all time. Only He gets to decide when I die. He left me. He left me to suffer. This world is my Hell."

Aria, Troy, and Ivory stared at the man. How terribly sad his life must've been. To see everyone that you love die. To watch the very existence of everything you were meant to protect become consumed by evil. What was his purpose? Was Dovian alive merely to live an eternity of pain?

"And no matter how I try to win this war, the *other's* eternal presence poisons the world. I'm not the only one chained to this planet." Dovian drank from his bottle.

"Who else?" Aria asked while Troy nodded.

Dovian scoffed. "And you don't even know the scripture!"

"Scripture? You mean this?" Aria asked. She dug into one of her side pockets and retrieved the small Bible. Dovian fiercely rose from his chair, the furniture slamming against the wall behind him.

"You have one of those?!" he asked incredulously.

"Yeah. It was on one of the men at the I.R.B.," Aria said. Dovian quickly snatched the item from her hands.

"How long? How long have you had it? And you didn't tell me? One of these still exists?! And you've had it this whole damn time?!"

"I, I didn't think it was that big of a deal," she stammered.

"Aria! This was what was burned so many years ago! Government oppression! Countless classic literature, educational, and religious texts were torn to shreds and burned in mass fires. Something like this shouldn't exist anymore. No, I mean, it should, but I had thought they had gotten every last one of them. To think it still exists." He flipped through the pages, his mood shifting to ecstatic.

"Of course, it exists. All the churches have them. Sure, it's rare. People don't usually own one, and it's nearly impossible to find any information about one outside the cathedrals, but they do exist," she reassured him.

Dovian's eyes widened. "Cathedrals? You…you still have cathedrals?"

"Yeah, Dovian."

"My God! The world has changed yet again!" He laughed, raising his arms into the air.

The bar shifted awkwardly, everyone's attention on the shouting Sorcēarian.

"Will you sit down? People are staring." Aria hid beneath her hand.

Dovian quickly sat, eyeing the thin pieces of parchment inside the leather binding. "Well, this version is completely inaccurate, but it gets the point across."

"Glad something has brightened your day," Aria grumbled.

"Do you not understand how momentous this is? This means there is still hope!" He slapped the cover, chuckling, his eyes creasing at the corners. Aria couldn't help but smile.

"Hope?" Troy asked. He stared at Dovian like he had grown a second head.

"For your survival! For your next life! You keep this, my dear. Read it!" He paused and tore out a large section. "Well, not this part. It's added indoctrinated nonsense. Humanity always meddles in things that they shouldn't." He quickly handed the book back to Aria. "It's about love, not hate. That, right there, is magic. Well, not the book itself but the words behind it." He looked at Troy. "You, too. Read it."

"Whatever." Troy rolled his eyes.

"Here, I'll let you burn these pages if it brings you joy." Dovian handed over the torn parchment. Troy grinned and took pleasure in burning the pages over the candle in the tabletop's center.

Aria thumbed over the engraved gold lettering on the book's cover. Was it really that special?

"C-can I read it, too?" Ivory asked.

"Yes! You should read it, too! The greatest book ever written!" He slung his arm around Ivory, shaking her gently. "I will save your souls yet. Even if it's the death of me!" he chortled.

"Yeah, well, my soul needs another beer," Troy said, quickly rising from his seat as he handed the burning pages to Ivory.

An alarm beeped from Aria's wrist, and she roughly grabbed Troy's elbow. "Hold it. No time. We've got to get into position. The signing starts in an hour."

"General Kovacevic"

CHAPTER 15

Saray's center square, an outdoor rotunda lined with pillars and deep-plum drapes, was filled with awkward tension as the signing of the peace treaty between Dario Benvenuto of Roma and Alijah Dizdarevic of Saray commenced. The square held a heavy silence as everyone waited with anticipation. Outside the city's walls, however, was a different story. Gun and mortar fire continued relentlessly, the booming sounds echoing against the buildings, giving the event a dream-like effect. It seemed neither of the CEOs would let up until everything was settled in writing.

Despite the supposedly joyous occasion, the event was regarded with little grandeur. All the tiny shops lining the rotunda were darkened, with no lights shining through the windows. Even the streetlamps dimmed to a low glow like candlelight. Thousands of spectators packed the streets, standing on their tiptoes to watch the two well-dressed men whispering on the small stage. Benvenuto and Dizdarevic sat on either side of a square table, forcing toothy grins. Between them were three candles and a piece of digital parchment—a thin monitor created to have an old-time look and feel. They continued whispering, not revealing much to the audience. The event seemed incredibly secretive. It was unknown whether it was because of the threat of attack or each city-state's unease with one another. Either way, it left an unsettling feeling within Aria.

The female soldier lay atop one of the barricades, completely cloaked from view. Eyeing the invisible Troy, a colorful blip on her radar on the opposite side of the ceremonial structure, she sighed anxiously. Something deep in her gut told her that this wasn't right. If there were to be an attack, she didn't feel it—at least not in this area of Saray. After trading a familiar nod with her partner, she turned her gaze to the two watchtowers at the city's perimeter near the nuclear reactor.

Dovian sat on the edge of his tower overlooking the entire city. The military occupied the streets and paths surrounding the reactor. Gently, the cool breeze whipped his cape. Icy eyes gleaming under the shadow of his hood watched the orange glow of the center square. Placing a long-fingered hand against the metal beam beside him, he leaned forward and glanced at the watchtower opposite him. Ivory stood rigidly next to her mounted rifle. From where Dovian stood, he could see her tremble as the wind tossed her golden locks. She didn't seem alert, which concerned the older man.

"Ivory," he mentally called out to the woman. He watched as she jumped and firmly pressed her delicate fingers against her throat.

"Yeah?" her quiet voice replied. Kovacevic gave her a throat mic so she could speak with the others. Her hands gripped the tiny buds inside her ears.

"Are you cold?" he gently asked.

"No," she answered, turning her head toward the Sorcēarian.

"Are you alert?" He narrowed his eyes.

After a moment, she replied, *"No."*

The giant man frowned. She remained distracted. Dovian momentarily wondered if it was he who made her uneasy. After some hesitation, he continued, *"You need to find a way to focus, Ivory. An attack can occur at any moment. I need you to be at your best, got it?"*

"I'm trying my best. I'm not used to these situations…at least from what I can remember." She sounded sad.

"Do you need me to come over there?" he asked.

There followed another long pause. Dovian watched the thin woman. She stared back; apparently, his cold gaze was visible to her. She gave a slight shrug and quickly stared at her feet, nervously shuffling as she shook her head. *"As lovely as that sounds, Dovian, I shouldn't let my distractions pull you down. I'll try my best to stay focused."*

A crooked smirk crossed Dovian's face. *"Keep your eyes open. If anything happens, I can be there in a flash. No worries."*

"Okay," Ivory's timid voice replied.

Dovian leaned back but kept a careful watch on the woman through the duration of the ceremony. He, too, had a nervous feeling, and he didn't know what caused it. Possibly it was several reasons—the fact that the signing was in progress, yet the war continued to erupt outside, that at any moment they could be attacked by Euclid and his demons, or that Ivory could become Euclid's prey or hurt in any way during the attack. He swallowed hard. Whatever happened, he simply had to prevent what felt like the inevitable.

Large vidscreens throughout Saray revealed the events of the peace treaty signing.

Dizdarevic and Benvenuto both stood. Placing a hand on each other's shoulder, they smiled more genuinely. Thunder raged outside the city-state. The war neared the walls. If it weren't Euclid's monsters, the humans would inevitably bring the city to its knees. Upon a table, the two men lit a large candle with each of their own—much like a wedding ceremony—symbolizing the joining of two cities. Then, they signed the digital parchment, the signatures large and swooping with dark-red ink. The two men stood tentatively in the center of the stage, slowly lifting their heads.

It was like magic. As soon as their pens finished signing the document, the barrage from the ongoing war abruptly ceased, filling Saray with an eerie silence. It was something the city hadn't known for over thirty years. It was nearly suffocating, heavy like a blanket. Dovian's ears rang, quickly adjusting to the lack of volume. His senses returned as a gusting wind brushed through the tower, pushing back his hood. It was simply amazing.

Dizdarevic and Benvenuto also seemed shocked by the sudden change in the dark, quiet city. Together they laughed and briskly shook hands. The city became alive with loud cheers and shouts. It was over; the war between Saray and Roma was finally over. The senseless combat, now perceived as a sport, had finally ceased, and the soldiers could finally go home to their families, relax, and enjoy the potentially beautiful city.

Thunder on the south wall shook the landscape. Dovian propped his hands on either side of the lookout walls, leaning over the side. Giant clouds of smoke littered the sky, billowing in churning, dark wisps. Then silence.

"The treaty was signed! Why is my city still being attacked?!" Dizdarevic shouted.

"It isn't my men! They immediately pulled out once the document was signed!" Benvenuto hollered back. He locked tense gazes with the other CEO and quickly lifted his wrist to speak into his DNAIS. "Why 'asn't the fighting ceased?" he growled.

A static screeched from the Roman man's earpiece, causing him to cry in pain.

"I-it isn't us!" an alarmed male voice sounded from the other end. Benvenuto quickly turned his frightened gaze toward Dizdarevic. The streets filled with gasps and shouts of distress.

Another rumbling boom collided with the south wall, sending a second cloud of dust. Dovian shivered in the chilly air, tensely watching as the structure holding back the violent storm cracked and splintered. Like scurrying ants, the soldiers rushed down the streets toward the reactor. Dovian picked up two heat signatures jumping from the barricades—Troy and Aria. Saray was dead silent outside the pattering of bootheels on the pavement.

Another pound sounded, causing the city to jump, followed by a monstrous groan, something new, sinister, and low. After the loud call, dozens of militants' bodies launched into the air, almost to the height of Dovian's tower, over the wall. The streets filled with screams as the barricade shattered, allowing an onslaught of monsters into Saray.

"Get your EMPs ready!" Dovian shouted like thunder. "Don't stop shooting!"

In seconds, the whole city became infested. War erupted again, gunfire blasting from all sides as the creatures spilled in like floodwaters. Crackling electricity violently surged from the hole in the city's wall. A temporary fence fed EMP currents from one side to another. It was an excellent defense as it simultaneously electrocuted the beasts and rendered them vulnerable as they passed through it. Their bodies dropped one after another in the firefight, and within moments, the pile of demon corpses was nearly the same height as the wall itself.

Just as it seemed the humans had the upper hand, the treacherous roar sounded again. Bursting through the hole in the wall—widening it more—a giant beast lunged at the frontline men. The EMP fence did nothing to stop it. The monster merely shook its head as the blue current temporarily shocked its system. It gave another low growl, turning its proportionately small head from side to side atop its thick, burly shoulders. Gunfire blasted into its hulking form, causing the thing's muscles to ripple and flex. Clasping its giant hands together, the five-meter-tall fiend swiped across the soldiers, sending their bodies into the air and crashing into neighboring buildings. As it gave another snarl through its wide mouth, its high nostrils flaring between two golden eyes, liquid fire spewed from the creature's mouth. Horrible screams came from the men as the fiery, putrid ooze covered them. After a couple more bursts of the monster's magmatic flame, it spun, gave another war cry, and darted with thick, stomping legs toward another flank.

Watching the hulking creature, Aria thought she might have to rethink her bestiary since she had already used the name 'Brute.' Another fire blast ignited Saray's southwest side as the monster spewed again. She and Troy watched with interest as they took cover around a building corner.

"How in the hell are we supposed to stop that thing?" Troy called out to Aria. They removed their cloaks so as not to get hit by friendly fire. "EMPs are doing nothing!"

"I don't know! Keep shooting until we figure out another solution!" Aria loaded a secondary clip to the front of her weapon. Taking a large sidestep, she rounded the corner and shot a grenade in the monster's direction. The projectile exploded against its chest but caused no damage.

"Holy shit!" she growled through gritted teeth. "He's not going down easily." She gave Troy an edgy look.

While Troy and she attempted to tackle the giant beast, the original I.R.B. creatures—Brawlers—lined the streets. It was chaos.

"Let me try a SABO." Troy slammed his secondary clip on the front of his rifle and followed the woman's previous actions, firing the bladed weapon at the enemy. Already focusing on the corner of the building Troy and Aria hid behind, the giant growled in protest as Troy's SABO barely nicked its chest. "Shit."

Troy spun, pulling Aria down with him, just as a pool of fire rained over them; most of the spew landed only half a meter away, eating through their barricade. Aria and Troy quickly wiped their armor, cleaning off the liquid debris. The two gave each other a frightened glance as the booming sound of the creature's footsteps neared their hiding spot. They simultaneously rolled to their feet. Aria twisted, firing a second grenade behind her as the beast rounded the corner and ejected its fire toward them. Dodging the molten blasts, the two soldiers darted to either side of the street. Aria gasped for air, her lungs filling with the suffocating sulfuric smoke. It was hard enough trying to run in the heavy armor. Sweat dripped down her brow, and her eyes narrowed, stinging from the flame's heat. She turned her sight toward her partner, who ran on the opposite side of the road. He was barely visible through the smoke. Casually, he'd toss a grenade or two behind him in an attempt to hold back the charging beast.

"Camo! Put your camo back on!" Aria shouted through her mental chip.

In a second, her partner disappeared, cloaking within the haze. She did the same, quickly turning around another corner and ducking behind a large garbage bin. Breathing heavily, she pressed against one of the many buttons on the side of her helmet. A respirator enclosed the front of her hood, filtering the oxygen. After a couple of puffs, she slowly stood. Smoke filled the alleyway, giving her no visibility. Even the garbage bin directly beside the woman was nothing more than a foggy silhouette. After pressing another nodule, her visor switched to thermal. Her surroundings appeared in yellow and red blobs. Giving another click, it all turned to sonar, dispersing tiny, inaudible blips into the surrounding area. Everything flickered to life, revealing a solid wall to her left, the bin, and a ladder high above her head. Quietly, Aria climbed atop the container and hopped up to grab the lowered rungs. She pulled up and gripped the second and third until she could plant her feet on the first. Agilely, she silently scaled the ladder and made a safe escape to the rooftop. Taking quick, quiet steps, she neared the street-side edge of the building. Something caught her attention on the roof across from her. A tall silhouette leaned against an air-conditioning unit.

"I can see you," Aria called out quietly.

The silhouette stirred, looking in each direction.

"Sonar," she muttered.

"Ah-ha. Good choice," Troy replied. His pale silhouette gave a small wave toward her.

"So, what are we going to do about that Spewer?" she asked.

"Spewer," Troy scoffed at her creative name for the giant. *"Haven't got a clue."*

"There's got to be something. A weak spot, anything."

"I didn't notice anything, but it's hard to see in this damn smoke." Troy gasped and then coughed.

"We need to get a closer look. Our best option, for now, is to use sonar. Once we're near it, if the smoke isn't too thick, maybe we can get a better look," she said.

"Give it a surprise attack?"

"Exactly. Come on, let's move." Aria turned to her right, looking at the building beside hers. *"Stick to the rooftops."*

With the help of the armored suit's muscle enhancers, Aria and Troy could jump twice as far. Leaping, they traveled from rooftop to rooftop, following the sound of thunderous footsteps and screams. After a couple of blocks, Aria spotted the enormous demon.

"Over here. On this side of the building," she called over to Troy.

"Well…let's test out this suit's attributes." The man rubbed his armored hands together.

"Troy," Aria said in an aggravated tone. *"Don't kill yourself."*

"Never, babe."

"Babe?" Aria tilted her head.

She watched tensely as Troy's form backed up. Giving a couple of nervous shakes of his hands, he took off at a full sprint, leaping from his rooftop, across the street, toward her building. Except he wasn't going to make it. He reached with his foot but missed, and his hands grasped out, his fingertips barely skimming the side.

"Troy!" Aria called out loud as she darted to the edge of the building. Leaning over the side, she sighed harshly, cursing at the man's stupidity. At least he wasn't dead, just clinging for dear life on one of the windowsills fifteen meters above the streets.

"Not too bad for a first try," he said humorously.

"Yeah, right. Don't try that again," Aria fumed.

"Scared, Aria? Worried about me?" he taunted as he climbed the side of the building like a monkey toward the rooftop.

"Please," she scoffed. *"It would be a waste of state-of-the-art body armor."* She helped tug him to his feet.

"Ouch," he said aloud, feigning hurt emotions.

"Come on. We're wasting time." She patted his shoulder and led the way to the opposite end of the roof.

Carefully edging toward the side of the building, the two crouched next to a small barricade. Aria pressed against her helmet, her vision changing to real-time. Troy did the same, scrutinizing the brutal being far down below. Its massive hand picked up a shorter man and squeezed his middle. Troy gave an audible sound of disgust.

"There's still too much smoke." Aria narrowed her eyes.

"We need to get closer." Troy looked over his shoulder. "If only there were some kind of rope or something up here."

"You really weren't paying any attention to the suit's tutorial, were you?" Aria stared at the man.

"What?" He rubbed the back of his helmet sheepishly.

Aria merely shook her head. Reaching into one of the square pockets of her suit's utility belt, she pulled out a long cord with a silver rod attached to the end. Troy followed her actions.

"It also serves as a zip-line," she instructed, pointing to a switch on one side of the rod. "Don't get your hand in the way of this end, though." She then gestured to the end that was not attached to the rope.

"Why?" Troy asked.

Aria quickly aimed the tool toward the floor. A blue laser sparked outward like a blade. The rod launched from her hand and buried itself deep into the roof's concrete at an astonishing velocity. She lifted her head. "That's why."

"Duly noted." Troy nodded.

He repeated her actions, and together they stepped over the barricade and speed-roped down the side of the building. Passing by the windows of each floor, they decided to stop only one level above the height of the Spewer. It continued its barrage, smashing and burning the bodies fighting against it, viciously roaring.

"Hey! O'er 'ere!" Kovacevic shouted with a cigar between his teeth. He was covered in black soot and blood smears and didn't seem fazed by the smoke surrounding him.

The Spewer turned, growling menacingly at the general. Kovacevic laughed, pulling the cigar out of his mouth. "Hot damn, you're a fiery one, ain't ya?"

Slowly, the beast circled, pounding heavily against the road. Its feet cracked the pavement with each step. Kovacevic mimicked the beast, growling in return.

"He's freakin' nuts!" Troy readied his weapon.

Kovacevic turned his gaze upward and looked directly at the two soldiers despite their activated cloaks. He gave a quick wink as he puffed on his cigar, weapon in hand. "Surely, you didn't miss those nasty growths on his back." He had a keen eye.

"Growths?" Aria gazed at the turning monster. With its back to the pair, they could see massive, glowing welts lining the Spewer's spinal column.

"Whoa, check out those puss pockets," Troy chuckled.

"Don't think they're puss pockets. I bet that's the fuel to his fire."

"Shoot first, ask questions later?" Troy aimed.

"Always," Aria replied.

Together, they opened fire, ripping into the enormous, bubbling warts on the creature's back. One pocket burst, sending the nasty ooze down the monster's dorsal side. A second and then a third also erupted. The Spewer twirled, howling in pain. With one swipe, its massive fist collided with Aria and Troy, sending them flying like rag dolls. Thanks to the cables attached to their waists, instead of splatting against a nearby building, they jolted at the extent of the rope's length and swiftly swung in the opposite direction.

To keep the Spewer distracted, Kovacevic fired into the creature's back. It spun and tore after him, running at varying speeds and zigzagging lines. The monster leaped, reaching toward the man, and Kovacevic jumped to the side, diving into an alleyway. The Spewer, giving a terrible howl, crashed into the side of an apartment complex. It created a massive hole in the building's side, and one after another, ten of the floors crumbled down upon it.

"Holy shit," Troy grumbled, holding his head. "I think your skull almost broke my skull."

Aria moaned loudly, reaching for the cord to lift her limp body. "You're the one with the thick skull, not me."

"Hey! You rookies goin' to sleep all day?" Kovacevic shouted at them.

Uncloaking themselves, Aria and Troy slowly lowered to the ground. The woman rolled her head and shoulders, her joints cracking in protest. Troy tried the same and winced. Yup, something was broken.

"Where's Dovian?" Troy groaned.

"He's dealing with Mr. Badass," Kovacevic answered, his voice barely audible over the gunfire consuming the city.

"Euclid? He found Euclid?" Aria asked. Her heart raced.

"Damn right, he did…and shit got *real*. I had to clear out. They were bringin' down the place," Kovacevic chuckled. "Euclid is a tough bastard, but he don't stand a chance."

"How can you tell?" Troy asked.

"Boy, that Dovian is one strong badass, if not a bit crazy. And, in war, crazy will get you far if you have the right amount of it. That Euclid chump, he's too driven by his lunacy. It blinds him. It'll be his downfall." Kovacevic stubbed his cigar and promptly lit another.

"Well, I hope you're right about that," Aria replied.

A familiar clanging hum alerted Troy and Aria. It took no thought to register where the sound came from or what caused it.

"Move!" Aria shouted, pushing Kovacevic back into the alley as a colossal shockwave drove past them. Troy dodged to the opposite alleyway, jumping behind a barricade.

"I take it that's one of those Brutes you told me about," Kovacevic said. He lay underneath the woman, her breastplate in his face as she pushed upward to look over her shoulder. He chuckled lowly. Aria looked down, her shocked expression turning into disgust as the man smirked at her with a quirked eyebrow. She quickly shoved away. "Now, don't feel the need to move because of me," he said with amusement.

Aria ignored him, aiming her rifle as she neared the corner of the alley. She noticed Troy across the way, signaling to her. Based on his gesturing hands, the creature was right around the corner.

"It's waiting for you," Troy said in a slightly haunting tone.

"Then shoot it, asshole."

Kovacevic waited, knowing she was speaking with her partner.

"And alert it of my hiding place? I don't think so," Troy scoffed.

"Then toss a frag behind it so it thinks we've moved to a new location. Distract it!" she snapped.

The woman suddenly jerked back as blood and brain matter splattered against the wall and pavement, interrupting their little argument. Next came the familiar deafening sound—*Ba-Doom!*

She turned her head upward. They were near Ivory's tower. Aria smiled and signaled with a raised thumb toward the blonde. She could see the rifle hanging slightly over the tower's edge. Ivory must have been watching through the scope.

Ba-Doom!

It sounded again, cracking against the wall beside Aria. The female jumped back. "What the hell?!" She jumped to the side.

Kovacevic grabbed the woman's shoulder. Aria turned and followed the man's gaze. Through a small window, Aria saw another Brute's now decapitated body lying in the center of the kitchen floor of the apartment they stood beside.

"Quite the set of eyes," Kovacevic mumbled. "Especially since there's no window on her side to see by."

Aria quickly left the alley and peered at the wall Ivory had shot through. Sure enough, there were no windows on that side of the building for the kitchen.

'What the hell is going on with Ivory?' Aria lifted her head.

Another burst from Ivory's sniper rifle sounded. A third Brute on the opposite side of Aria's alley went down, then one more on Troy's end. The thunderous blasts continued as the blonde went on a rampage, unleashing dozens of rounds on targets across the city.

"Damn. Remind me never to piss her off," Troy called out.

"Something is going on, Troy," Aria replied. *"She shot this one without even knowing it was*

inside the building."

"*X-ray scope?*" Troy suggested with a shrug.

"*Not that I was aware of,*" Aria replied.

"*Who cares? At least she's some help, right?*"

Troy was right. Ivory was a huge help. Still, something about her ridiculous accuracy didn't settle well with Aria. Ivory could easily be a trained soldier; they knew nothing about her. What if she was a spy or a traitor? She could've kept secrets from Aria and the others, though that assumption didn't make sense, seeing as Ivory could quickly pick off Aria and Troy at any moment. Still, loss of memory or not, there wasn't a human alive capable of effortlessly picking off monsters as quickly as Ivory was. Not a single bullet fired by the blonde missed its target.

A groaning rumble came from beside Aria and Kovacevic. The two slowly turned toward the rubble of the apartment building the Spewer had demolished.

"Get out of there! It's still alive!" Troy shouted.

"We've got to move!" Aria called over her shoulder to Kovacevic.

"Right with you, darlin'."

The two rushed from their alleyway toward Troy's. Giving an ear-splitting roar, the Spewer climbed out of the rubble with blood and liquid fire spilling from its body. As it struggled to its feet, parts of its flesh dangled from its backside, torn ragged from the explosions caused earlier by its magma sacs.

"Hurry, hurry, hurry-hurry-hurry!" Troy shouted, waving them toward him as he took off down the alleyway.

Aria and Kovacevic followed closely behind his bootheels. The pounding footsteps neared, rising in volume as the beast growled its death call.

"Split!" Troy shouted.

Troy veered left as they exited the alleyway, Aria took the center, and Kovacevic went to the right. Of course, the Spewer didn't want to slow down and only bothered with the easy route—following Aria. She knew its path, and right before entering the next alleyway, she dove, hitting the ground and rolling back to her feet to make a mad dash away from the creature. With its momentum, the Spewer couldn't turn in time. It ran past the woman and into the next alley, howling. Somewhere, Aria could hear Kovacevic's loud laughter.

'How could he find this amusing?' Aria thought, running as fast as her legs could carry her.

The earth started quaking. The Spewer decided to take a different approach, crashing through the buildings to catch up with the woman. Its bulky form smashed through the walls like paper with a quickening speed. Aria winced before the creature made contact, slamming through the walls beside her. Luckily, she slowed, sliding on her backside as it clipped her legs and sent her spiraling onto her side.

Something cracked in her lower back and hip. The monster could easily smash a person into a pulp with such force. Dazed, the woman painfully struggled to sit up, feeling the ground beneath her shake with each lurching step the massive creature made.

"Aria! Get out of there!" Troy screamed fearfully into her head.

Aria felt a tight sensation in her chest. As her vision focused, she finally realized the disgusting creature had lifted her into the air. It gurgled at her, hot ooze dripping onto her helmet and chest. The woman struggled, groaning as its fist tightly clamped around her.

"Troy!" she gave a raspy scream, feeling her insides would burst.

Gunfire erupted. Troy made a mad dash toward the woman and her captor. Screaming and shouting, he sent a barrage toward the creature. The bullets barely made the creature flinch. Another male hollered—Kovacevic. He joined in, shooting at the monster's backside and the last remaining sacs. Then, there was Aria's lifesaver—the sound of Ivory's rifle.

The Spewer howled, dropping the woman. Aria landed hard on her back, wheezing as the air rushed from her lungs. Troy was at her side in a millisecond, throwing hundreds of questions her way. He opened her helmet and stared into her glazed eyes. She was dizzy, the sounds of combat and Troy's constant questions numbing her brain. Aria tried focusing on the shrieking monster. The final sac bubbled, growing larger and larger. The beast stomped backward, attempting to gather its footing as it turned, looking upward at Ivory in the tower. A sickening plop sounded, and the monster's flesh began to boil and distend. It was about to burst and headed toward Ivory's stronghold at full speed. As it growled with an inhuman voice, the monster stumbled and crashed into the tower's lowest level as its body ballooned and burst into a colossal explosion of flame and magma. The stone and metal erupted into pieces. The hot liquid instantaneously ate through the support beams, and slowly the tower began to twist and fall toward the ground with Ivory at the very top.

"Ivory!" Aria tried to shout, but the pain was too much as the air escaped her lungs. She gasped.

Aria could see the woman, a tiny silhouette with a speck of blonde. Having removed her helmet during her sniping, it rolled across the tower floor, clattering against the stone. Ivory's hands gripped the sides of the lookout window in an attempt to stabilize. If she didn't fall out, the impact would surely smash her. At that moment, they were all surrounded by dozens of Brawlers, some already scaling the falling tower.

"Dovian! Dovian! Where are you?!" Aria mentally called out. *"Help Ivory!"*

Dovian watched from his tower as the giant beast crashed through the city's wall. Tiny prickles traveled up his spine as a familiar presence neared. The Sorcēarian, taking the ferocity of the new beast into account, stepped over the side of the tower and readied to take a plunge to dispel the creature before it could cause too much damage. However, he froze mid-step as his eyes locked onto familiar ones on the streets below near the reactor.

"Hello, Dovian," Euclid's low, silky voice rang out in Dovian's mind.

Dovian frowned, his large hands gripping the windowsill on either side of him. He drifted his gaze back to the fire-breathing monster wrecking Saray for a short second. Giant orange sacs trembled with each ferocious step the massive demon took.

'The two will surely notice the giant's weakness,' Dovian reassured himself as he caught Aria and Troy's heat signatures nearing the vicious beast.

Dovian quickly looked upon his enemy, Euclid, once again. He waited patiently for Dovian as he lightly trailed his gold-clawed fingertips down his face, his smile twisting crookedly. The sight of the raven-haired man was more than infuriating to the other Sorcēarian. Without hesitation, Dovian dropped from the height of his tower, thick wings of midnight black erupting from his back. He spiraled to the streets and then darted horizontally toward Euclid. Euclid disappeared into thin air when Dovian moved to ram against him. Dovian's body wrecked into the thick, fortified reactor door, sending the massive barrier to pieces as he broke through. He tumbled and rolled, his scaly wings folding to protect his body. He spun to his hands and knees, facing the busted entry, and met Euclid's amused gaze watching from the outside. Dovian growled lowly, his teeth clenching.

"My, my…aren't we angry?" Euclid chuckled, slowly approaching the scarlet Sorcēarian.

From behind Dovian came a flurry of shouts and the sound of weapons readying to fire. Twenty soldiers stood behind Dovian on the first level and platform with their guns at the ready, aimed at Euclid. The azure-robed Sorcēarian chuckled and shook his head. Two small flanks slowly descended the staircases on either side of Dovian, their assault rifles readied.

"Is this your backup, Dovian?" Euclid smiled. Dovian remained in his crouched position, watching his opponent with glaring eyes.

"Fire!" Kovacevic shouted from behind the group, his body guarding the small, armored door leading to the reactor core. Euclid's amused expression quickly fell.

Dovian immediately lowered to the ground. An explosion of gunfire erupted with all projectiles directed toward Euclid. A concussive shot, EMPs, and a couple of frag grenades were unleashed upon the madman. The room filled with smoke and glittering lights in seconds as ammunition ricocheted off the dark metal walls. Dovian's eyes never left Euclid's form. After a minute, the constant firing finally halted. They all stood in silence, at the ready, watching the clouds of smoke slowly clear to reveal Euclid still in one piece, his hand lifted with the palm out toward the army. Dovian could physically feel the disappointment and shock of the soldiers surrounding him. He, however, wasn't surprised at all. In front of Euclid's palm stood an invisible wall suspending hundreds of tiny bullets in place. The look on Euclid's face was one of discontent, his breathing irregular as a bead of sweat dripped from his brow. Dovian frowned, knowing Euclid's next step.

"You think this can stop me?!" Euclid shouted with anger.

Shoving his arm forward, the invisible wall protecting Euclid forced all the ammunition back toward the army. Dovian shouted; his staff clanged against the grated metal floor, releasing a protective barrier around him as the bullets zipped past. The militia crashed to the ground within one second, their bodies penetrated by their own ammunition. With eyes gleaming in contrast to the charcoal-grey metal and bright reds of the emergency lights, Dovian matched Euclid's cold stare.

"You underestimate me, Dovian. Do you think your soldiers can stop me? Do you think a *human* army can halt me? Don't you remember? Surely you haven't forgotten how weak the species is," Euclid taunted as he teleported to a soldier on the floor, pressing his boot against the man's throat. The soldier choked on his blood, his shaking hands gripping the black leather of Euclid's boot. Dovian quickly rose to his feet just as Euclid smashed the man's neck, crushing his airway.

"Damn you, Euclid." Dovian seethed.

"I already am," he said with a chuckle.

Dovian took a fighting stance, with his staff held firmly. Slowly, he rounded toward another fallen militant. Euclid watched him with disgust. Dovian crouched and pressed his fingers against the soldier's throat, never tearing his eyes from Euclid's. There was a faint pulse, but the man would die soon. He rested a palm on the soldier's chest, where he was fatally wounded. One of Dovian's black wings flickered to white, a stream of feathers dropping to the floor. Giving a small whisper, a tiny wave of blue light flooded from Dovian's hand onto the man's wound, the orb on his staff shimmering with matching luminosity.

"You can't heal them all," Euclid sneered.

"No, but I can try to save them." Dovian stood. The soldier beside him gasped for air, his eyes widening. As he caught his awareness, he rolled to the side and aimed his rifle at Euclid. "Leave him to me," Dovian said lowly to the man. "You tend to your comrades."

The soldier nervously licked his lips, looking uncertain about Dovian and Euclid. After a quick deliberation, he turned and ran up the staircase toward Kovacevic. The general was still alive. A bullet had passed through his shoulder, and a few others had grazed his arms and legs.

"Save them?" Euclid wrinkled a nostril. "I get your metaphors, Dovian, but they mean nothing."

"Trying to save them means everything!"

Euclid neared the staircase, his eyes watching the soldier Dovian had just saved.

"You leave them be, Euclid. Your quarrel isn't with them. Not as long as I am around." Dovian pointed his staff at the taller Sorcēarian.

"Oh?" Euclid returned to facing the other of his kind. "You want to be the protector of this race?"

Dovian swallowed thickly.

"You hesitate, Dovian. Is it because you finally see what I saw thousands of years ago? Disgusting, aren't they—living their lives to fight wars, only to kill one another? They care as much as I do about their own lives. All I am doing is speeding up their untimely demise."

"It isn't your job to do such things!" Dovian finally spoke, watching as Euclid slowly circled him. The white wing on his back rotted, the feathers dropping to reveal its black scales, as Dovian let his anger consume him once again.

"Then whose job is it, Dovian?! He left us a long time ago! Left them! Your job is finished; it was finished once you hypocritically destroyed your own kind, you traitor!" Euclid lunged at Dovian, gripping the silver-haired Sorcēarian's neck. Dovian winced as Euclid slammed his body roughly against the wall, his form sinking into the metal. "If you think our own race to be damned, then why do you think these horrendously imperfect ones deserve to live? Huh?" He pulled and then slammed Dovian into the wall once again. Dovian's hands gripped Euclid's wrist, his face contorting.

"Because…" Dovian gasped. His fingertips dug into Euclid's flesh, making the man grimace. "He told us to take care of them. It is our job. It always will be." A slight sound to the side alerted Dovian of the soldiers' presence. Slowly, the ones who remained alive retreated.

"It doesn't give you a reason to destroy us to save them!" Euclid yelled, his face centimeters from Dovian's.

"It is the reason! You all betrayed Him as much as we betrayed them!" Dovian bellowed.

"He left us! He abandoned us long before you or I were ever born. I wasn't given the decision, a choice!" Euclid growled, his teeth grinding together.

"Because you are not human! They were not born with the knowledge and understanding that we have. They were meant to be innocent. We were supposed to keep them that way!"

"They are no longer born innocent! They are evil! They all are!" Euclid spat.

"And you are any different in your desires?" Dovian retorted. "You, who are jealous of them, treat them like measly fleas. For what purpose? Because you want an excuse to act just like them?!"

"Shut up!"

Euclid tugged, throwing Dovian onto the floor. The scarlet Sorcēarian slid across the grated metal, slamming into the opposite wall, a huge dent molding into the surface. The raven-haired man neared Dovian with heavy footsteps. He reached down, and Dovian lifted his staff, the end ramming against Euclid's chin. Dovian quickly spun, wrapping the curved edge of one of the metallic wings on the top of his pole around Euclid's heel, tripping him. He then flipped his staff and aimed it at Euclid's head.

"We were never allowed to make our own lives, Dovian. We were damned, to begin with." Euclid, hair scattered over his eyes, breathed heavily.

"You damned yourself, Euclid," Dovian sneered, shoving the pointed tip of the golden demon wing of his staff against the other man's neck. Dark blood dripped across Euclid's pale skin onto the floor through the grate.

"The rules don't apply to us, Dovian! We can't merely believe it! As you said, we know too much, and too much is expected of us! It may have been easy for our Elders, who were originally pure, but what about us?! What about you and me?" Euclid gasped.

"We are a blessed race. We had specific rules, and you ignored them all!" Dovian growled, gradually pushing the point of his staff into Euclid. The dark man grabbed the ends, pressing against Dovian's weight.

Euclid growled through gritted and bloodied teeth, "If it were as simple as that, then explain I'Lanthe!"

Dovian froze. Slowly, pinpricks covered his entire body as an electric shock shivered down his spine. What was that? Did he hear Euclid correctly? Unknowingly, his mouth dropped open, his blue eyes staring into Euclid's once again, looking for any indication that the man had lied. Regardless of his precarious position, Euclid smiled in response to Dovian's expression.

'No, it can't be true. He is lying,' Dovian thought. Still, he saw no hesitation, no flicker in the other man's eyes to reveal that he was trying to pull a fast one.

"W-what?" Dovian finally stuttered.

"Oh? You didn't know?" Euclid laughed. He quickly swiped away the end of Dovian's staff, his body disappearing altogether.

Dovian grunted as Euclid rammed him against the metal staircase. He crashed through the steps, wrecking the platform as the support beams crunched underneath his weight. Euclid was atop him before Dovian could respond, planting his fists into his face. Dovian guarded the best he could. After receiving a few nasty blows, he wrapped his legs around Euclid's waist. Lifting his arms, he caught one of Euclid's fists and crossed to seize the other. Euclid pulled against his hold to no avail, and Dovian quickly rolled to the side and straddled him. He pressed Euclid's forearms against his throat and leaned in close.

"What do you mean?!" Dovian yelled, pulling and slamming the back of Euclid's skull against the floor.

Groaning, Euclid struggled beneath Dovian's strength. He may have been thinner and shorter than the other Sorcēarian soldiers, but Dovian always had incredible strength in his lean muscle. Euclid sneered, trying to kick the man off, but Dovian locked his feet against the other's legs instead.

"What?" Euclid gasped loudly. After a second's thought, he gave a raspy laugh. "You've lost your connection, haven't you?"

Dovian frowned, struggling against the taller man's push as he tried to free himself.

"You have! You've been forsaken! You've been left behind, and still, you wait for His disposal like a sad little dog!" Euclid cackled. Eerily, his humored features quickly dimmed to a critical look. "Which means you can't talk to the Elders. You can't speak to Him, can't speak to…her!" Euclid laughed again.

Giving more struggle, Euclid finally shoved Dovian to the side. Gasping, he took a deep breath and gripped his throat, quickly healing the wound on his neck. A slight hum rang from the pendant of his necklace. Once healed, Euclid quickly tucked the item into his robes. Turning to face Dovian, he felt a ton of weight crash against him as a bright flash sent him backward. Euclid slammed into the opposite set of stairs, the structure caving in atop him.

Approaching the rubble, Dovian growled, not finding Euclid anywhere. Turning, he quickly met the force of Euclid's invisible blow, which sent him back into the same wreckage. Euclid didn't let up, sending wave after wave upon Dovian, pressing him deeper and deeper into the floor until he finally fell through. Hitting every I-beam on the way down, Dovian dropped twenty meters to the bottom of the reactor core. His senses flooded with the deafening, quaking roar of the electric current and pulsating rotors that pumped the energy into various lines that distributed the power. Rolling to his hands and knees, Dovian held onto his side. A thick piece of rebar made a deep gash as he had fallen into the suspension lines.

The core room was massive, full of tiny cylinders of electric orbs marked with radioactive symbols and warnings. The silver and glass encasings reflected the blue energy like flashing strobes. Dovian's mind reeled at the obtrusive lights.

'Don't worry about me, Dovian. I can take care of myself. I'm more worried about you.' The soft vocals from a distant memory replayed in his mind as his fingertips focused energy into the deep wound in his oblique.

A soft whir sounded high above, and Dovian moved. Euclid drove violently into the floor beside him, the gridded metal sinking beneath his weight. He slowly turned his head toward Dovian, glaring.

"What, what happened to her?" Dovian winced as he stood, bringing his staff in front of him.

"You mean in the afterlife?" Euclid asked.

"You know what I mean, Euclid!" Dovian wanted to kill him so badly, to twist his neck right there, but Euclid knew something of immense value.

The azure Sorcēarian watched Dovian for a few moments. He enjoyed seeing his eyes glow brighter with impatience and anger. Euclid flipped his long hair over his shoulder, tapping a gold claw against his lip.

"I expected better of you, Dovian. I would have expected you to have known about her fate. But, how could you possibly know, especially since your Father has ignored you?" Euclid chuckled, ignoring the staff aimed directly at his head. "I can't blame you, Dovian. No one can. No one can blame you for not knowing that I'Lanthe is burning in Hell."

"You lie!" Dovian shouted. His black wings spread wide from his back, and he tackled Euclid into one of the cylinders; the electric current exploded against them. Dovian didn't halt; he gripped Euclid's robes about his neck and furiously pounded into his face. The sound was sick and forceful. After only a couple of hits, Euclid's blood stained his knuckles. Dovian continued his rage, choking the man. Euclid, for the first time, looked frightened. He was a master at toying with people's emotions, but he knew from long ago not to piss off Dovian. It had the opposite effect. Dovian's concentration may have seemed lagged, but his sheer rage and strength could leave him psychotic until he destroyed everything in his path, even if it killed him, even if it killed everyone. That is precisely why their race no longer existed.

Dovian continued pummeling Euclid. He paused only to lift the man, punched him again, kicked him low to bring him to his knees, and then grabbed his long hair and kneed him in the face. He grasped Euclid and threw him one after another into the various cylinders of the reactor. After destroying the tubes with Euclid's body, he sat atop the man again, sending his fists into his face. Everything melded together, lined with the icy glow of Dovian's eyes, as Euclid's vision blurred. Suddenly, the Azure man's ears burned with a horrible sound. It was a two-tone growl, a guttural sound from Dovian as he shouted in Legacy. His speech contained all the threats known to the Sorcēarians.

"You lie!" Dovian gasped out, his evil energies overtaking him. He needed to stop, or he would wipe out the entire facility. Looking over his shoulder, he found nearly every cylinder destroyed. The core churned violently, the energy growing wildly inside its confines. A loud whine vibrated within the room. Dovian finally let up, halting his brutal assault on Euclid's face. He looked down and felt his heart skip a beat. The man beneath him was unrecognizable. He did this. He did this to Euclid, a man he once knew, to a fellow Sorcēarian.

Still, Euclid continued his antics. If he couldn't destroy Saray, then perhaps he could get Dovian to do his dirty work with his rage. "She burns, Dovian, just as you will someday." Euclid coughed, gurgling on his thick blood as he reached into his robes, his hands gripping the pendant.

Dovian quickly rose. Preparing his staff, he lifted it over his head. It was now or never. Why waste time beating the wicked man to death when he could end it all seamlessly and effortlessly?

"Then I'll see you soon," Dovian murmured. His pale eyes stared into Euclid's.

"Dovian! Dovian! Where are you?!" Aria's voice mentally called out. *"Help Ivory!"*

'Ivory!' Dovian's mind spun back to his other reality. Up there, where the war continued with humanity, his friends were in danger.

"Better go save her, Dovian. Before the demons get her," Euclid gurgled.

Dovian looked down and swung his weapon. He could kill him then and check later to ensure the deed was done. As his staff swooped for Euclid's head, a tank exploded nearby, knocking Dovian off balance. In that split second, Euclid disappeared.

"Damn it!" Dovian cursed.

Lifting his wings, he didn't hesitate further. Dovian jumped back through the hole in the roof, into the main room where he and Euclid had begun their encounter, and out the broken door. He lifted high into the air. A finger gripped the camera looped around his ear, picking up several strange sounds and colorful life signs. The cityscape remained covered in thick smoke. Dovian's lungs immediately dried as he pulled in the sulfuric air. Rising even higher, he reached the height of his tower and caught a terrifying sight. Ivory's overlook quickly began to crumble and fall to the side. From his optics, he could pick up her form at the top. With a swift push from his wings, his body pulsated and moved at near lightspeed, a burst of noise following a second afterward.

It dropped fast, threatening to shatter into the dusty streets below. Creatures filtered into the building even as it fell, scattering to the top to capture Ivory. Dovian covered his face and prepared for impact. He crashed into the wall and exited the opposite side with Ivory in his arms. Pulling up, he caught the vibrant life signs of Aria and Troy and a third man. Aria's signal was not as colorful as the others surrounding her. Leaning to the side, Dovian turned and quickly moved through the air toward them. He slid harshly on the pavement, his feet planting into the ground. Looking down at the blonde in his arms, he sighed. Ivory was unconscious once again.

"Ivory!" he shouted, shaking her gently.

"Nice save, man." Troy patted Dovian's shoulder.

Dovian didn't pay Troy any attention. He checked Ivory's vitals, trying to get a read. Her blue eyes remained wide open; her pupils were pinpoints instead of dilated. Was she alive? Passed out? Why couldn't he get a read on her vitals?

"Ivory!" he shouted again with his deep voice.

"Dovian," Aria moaned weakly. At this, Dovian quickly turned his head. "Is she all right?" she asked.

"I am unsure," he mumbled.

Aria scooted across the ground, reaching out toward Ivory. Gasping, she held her sides and curled into a ball.

"Hey! What'd I tell you? Don't move!" Troy kneeled beside Aria. He gently placed his hands on her shoulders.

"You are hurt?" Dovian asked.

"No. No, I'm okay. Just make sure Ivory's all right," Aria groaned. Tears threatened to fall from her eyes. Why did crushed ribs have to hurt so much?

"No, she isn't all right," Troy grumbled. "One of those big-and-nasties tried crushing her insides."

Dovian abruptly set Ivory down. Troy traded spots with the taller man and checked Ivory's vitals, his calloused fingers pressing against the thin girl's neck. She felt ice cold.

"Let me heal you." Dovian gently grabbed Aria's body. "Take slow, even breaths, all right? Small ones," he said softly, his black wings growing back their feathers.

Aria nodded, breathing as instructed.

Kovacevic stood, rifle aimed. He slowly began picking off the demons that scampered down the street toward them. "We will be needin' some backup soon," he said.

Dovian nodded, acknowledging the general. He was relieved that Kovacevic was still alive and had gotten out of the way of his and Euclid's destructive battle.

"Are you feeling any better?" Dovian questioned. He ran his glowing hands over Aria's sides with his form crouched over her smaller one. Aria gasped, taking in a big breath of air. "Your lungs were punctured. Any longer, and you could have died."

Troy eyed Aria and gave her an angry yet concerned look. Her stubbornness could have gotten her killed.

"Thank you, Dovian," Aria gasped again.

He continued running his hands over her back, healing her fractured vertebrae. Finally, he removed her helmet and brought his hand to her face, his fingertips healing the minor scrapes on her cheeks and the massive bruise on her forehead. Aria observed him. A moment ago, he looked so angry; now, he looked peaceful as he healed her. That expression quickly changed, however, once he looked at Ivory.

"Is she awake yet?" he asked the man.

"No," Troy replied.

Troy and Dovian quickly switched spots, Troy grimacing as he gripped his side. Dovian quickly tugged him and pressed his hand against his ribcage. Troy didn't dare move, and Dovian healed the man's broken ribs in a few seconds. Once finished, the Sorcēarian immediately dropped to his knees beside Ivory. Troy and Aria immediately joined Kovacevic, helping him take down the mass of nearing enemies.

"Ivory?" Dovian asked, staring into the woman's wide eyes. She didn't respond. "Ivory!"

The woman gasped, her tiny pupils finally widening and thinning again as she focused on Dovian's face.

"D-Dovian!" She quickly rose, placing her palms on his cheeks. Her voice lowered as she spoke, "You're all right! I'm so glad you are all right! I was worried! So worried!"

"I'm fine. There's nothing to worry about." Dovian grabbed her petite hands and slowly lowered them. He gave her a small, uneasy smile. "Are you all right?"

"Don't worry about me, Dovian. I can take care of myself. I'm more worried about you," she said.

He froze. *'Don't worry about me, Dovian. I can take care of myself. I'm more worried about you.'* He replayed the old memory.

Mistaking his shocked look for one of disbelief, Ivory reassured him, her high-pitched tone returning. "I feel fine. Really." She nodded.

Shrugging his feelings away, Dovian gave her a worried look but finally nodded. "If you say so. Always let me know if you need any help, okay?"

"Okay." She bobbed her head again.

"We need a little help!" Aria shouted over her gunfire.

Dovian lifted his head and felt his heart sink. They were surrounded. Beasts filled the streets ahead of them, crowding the surrounding alleys.

"So, I take it that since you are here, Euclid should be finished off," Kovacevic uttered with his cigar in his mouth.

Dovian kept silent. Aria and Troy both fed him hopeful glances.

Kovacevic continued, "But seeing as these creatures are still surrounding us, I'm gonna guess that there's a possibility that asshole is still around."

Dovian lowered his head, his hood covering his face. He slowly pushed the nervous Ivory behind him. She was defenseless, her weapon now buried deep within the debris of the crushed tower, her helmet along with it.

"You would be correct in your second analysis," Dovian muttered.

"What?" Aria faced Dovian. "You let him go? Dovian!"

"I didn't let him go!" His icy eyes turned her way. His head remained lowered, but he was tall enough to reveal his glare to her, making the woman shrink. "I was about to end his life when you started screaming in my head. My choices were to either chase after him or save Ivory. Judging by the emotion in your voice, I'm sure you wouldn't want me to let her die."

Aria eyed Ivory.

"It's my fault. It's my fault Euclid got away," Ivory said, wringing her hands.

"No. It isn't your fault. It would be mine if it were anyone's," Dovian said firmly.

"It's fine. I'm sure we'll get plenty of chances to get the bastard. At least the whole city isn't leveled yet." Troy aimed and fired his rifle, hitting a Brawler directly between the eyes. "*Yet* is the keyword, though. How are we going to deal with them?"

Demons filled the streets and alleyways as far as the eye could see. There had to be at least fifty in the first square block, and it didn't include those still outside the city walls waiting to get through. Euclid had a never-ending army.

"Well, fight is all we can do," Dovian said. "Ivory…."

"Yes?" she responded nervously.

"Take cover behind the barricades. I want you to keep your eyes on me. If there is trouble, call out, okay? Don't let me get too far away from you." Dovian looked over his shoulder at the tall, slender woman.

"Okay," she said with hesitation.

"Take this. You will need some form of defense." Kovacevic handed her a small sidearm and a couple of extra clips. Ivory gratefully grabbed the items and quickly did as was told. She ducked behind a blockade, peering over the top.

"Let's do this," Troy said, his optical camera picking up multiple targets as he opened fire.

The creatures broke out into a sudden sprint, hissing as they scattered to the walls and rooftops of the surrounding buildings, all racing toward the small group. Where were all the other soldiers? Were they the only ones alive? The constant gunfire and monstrous calls drowned out any other noise within the city. The fire fogged the streets with a blanket of black smoke, making it impossible to detect the number of enemies filtering in.

The three soldiers continued shooting, catching many creatures at a distance. The demons that made it safely through the hail of bullets immediately sped toward Dovian. He stood, his legs slightly bent, one arm resting at his side as the other balanced his staff. Having no true emotion, Dovian watched fearlessly as three creatures lunged toward him. He spun once they were only an arm's length away, slicing away their appendages in one swipe. Following through, he sidestepped as a monster jumped past him, and he cut into another and kicked back at the same time to plant his foot against the other's skull and smash it against the concrete. He landed the back end of the staff into the face of another and spun the weapon down and around his arm to cut upwards into the creature's chin. Dovian continued fighting—swooping, turning, sidestepping, and jumping, brutally crushing the monsters' skulls into the walls and pavement.

Deep into the alleyway near Dovian, a loud clinking commenced. Two enormous vibrations distorted the visual plane, heading directly toward the Sorcēarian—Brute attacks. Dovian turned, catching sight of this, and dove out of the way. Twirling his staff, he formed a bright-blue barrier as the second wave crashed into him. The first vibration headed directly toward Ivory.

"Ivory! Move!" he roared.

The girl had detected the wave and dashed into the street as the blast disintegrated her previous wall of protection. However, as soon as she moved away from her barricade, the Brawlers moved toward her. Without fear, Ivory raised her handgun and fired at their heads. One, two, three. They all fell. Dovian sighed with relief. At least she could defend herself for the time being, but as the countless creatures neared, he feared they would be in fatal danger soon.

"I'm running out of ammunition!" Aria shouted. Troy quickly reached into his pack and handed the woman one of his last remaining magazines. Dovian watched the pair trade similar glances before returning to business. They, too, feared what was to come.

"I've got a couple of grenades left once I run out. But after that," Kovacevic puffed on his diminishing cigar, "all I got is my smokes. And even then, there's not enough for all of us."

Dovian would have to step up his game. They all depended on him.

'Got to do it, Dovian,' he told himself.

He jolted, as did the others, as a dreadful howl wailed at the end of the block. It called out again, the sound of crackling flames nearing them. As they feared, it was a Spewer. It plodded slowly, spitting fire on either side of the street for a whole block before it noticed the small army of five before it. Tiny golden eyes narrowed, and the beast tore off in their direction, growling and howling, alerting every creature of their position.

"You handle the small ones. I'll take on this one," Dovian said, running toward the beast.

The two collided, and Dovian brought the colossal beast to its backside. For a few minutes, the two scuffled. The monster grabbed Dovian's cape, tugging him back onto the concrete as he blasted away at its face with his staff. Dovian tucked and rolled back onto his feet and then jumped gracefully to the side just as the massive being laid its fist into the ground beside him. Dovian ducked, throwing handfuls of energy toward the creature's back, blasting the pockets lining its spine. The Spewer howled, the fiery liquid eating its flesh. As it struggled to stand straight, Dovian mimicked its movements, stepping left and right, planting blasts on the rest of the sacs before placing a final one into the base of its skull. As he did so, the two Brutes that had destroyed Ivory's barricade neared his position, tossing invisible forces his way. He quickly dodged the blasts and turned toward his party, knowing they were out of ammunition and the Brawlers had closed in on their position.

Dovian looked over his shoulder as he ran. The Spewer bubbled and rippled, its skin stretching out as it began to glow a vibrant red and orange. It was going to blow. Dovian smirked. The two Brutes were on either side of the Spewer just as it exploded, its mass taking out the two beasts, sending their bodies into pieces that splattered across the walls of the buildings on either side of the small street.

"Ivory, watch out!" Aria screamed at the top of her lungs.

The warning was too late to reach Ivory's ears. When the beautiful blonde turned around, a monster had buried its clawed hand deep into her abdomen. Ivory's eyes widened with shock. She trailed her bony hands over the demon's own, down to its wrist. Black eyes with no pupils stared menacingly into hers. It gave a low hiss as drool dripped from its ragged teeth.

"No…." Dovian spun with his staff in hand, on guard. His eyes enlarged, his skin crawling with dread. Frozen, he watched the scene unfold, his mouth gaping. He charged to help the woman the next instant as the Brawlers surrounded her. Giving a quick cry in Legacy, Dovian reached over his shoulder beneath his cape and pressed solidly against the top of his back apparatus. Instantly, a high overtook his mind, feeding into his emotions. Dovian gave a low growl as his wings fluttered, the black scales shimmering in the firelight surrounding him. Pulling his hands out to the sides, he grasped at the air, tugging the flame that consumed the buildings into swooping streaks that flowed from the palm of each hand. Swinging, he brought the fire down like a whip upon the creatures surrounding Aria, Troy, and Kovacevic. The demons shrieked, falling to ash. Giving another whirl, he harshly brought the violent, raging flames upon the circling enemies that reached for Ivory. Giant, vivid waves washed over the demons' bodies, turning them to dust. Dovian turned toward the blonde, ready to destroy the creature with its clawed fist buried deep within her middle, but paused.

"Urgh," Ivory made a low growl before her face twisted into a grimace of not pain but anger. Her armored hands gripped the monster's arms. She squeezed tightly, the force cracking and splintering the beryllium bones of the wild creature. The veins bulged, and the muscles and tendons tore. It screamed, writhing as it tried to escape the sudden pain, but she would not let go. Ivory gently pulled the long claws from her body. She spun in a half-circle, dragging the creature over her shoulder. Letting go of the demon, it spiraled through the air fast and landed hard against a lamppost nearly five meters away. It smashed rather unpleasantly with a loud crack.

"What the…." Troy halted. He watched in awe, trying to understand what he had just seen.

Ivory leaned forward, her hand on her stomach. She turned to Dovian and grabbed his hand. "Hurry! Heal me!" she pleaded to him with enlarged eyes. Dovian nodded, unsure as to what to say. Ivory should have been dead. She should have bled out. He gaped at her as she forced his hand over her wound. Staring at him with a feral intensity, she waited for his flow of power. "Dovian!" she shouted. She looked to the side, watching the others approach.

"Right." He nodded out of his daze. After a moment, a slight blue aura transferred from his hand over her stomach. She closed her eyes, feeling the energy soar throughout her body. A quiet sigh whispered past her pink lips, and Dovian watched her in wonder. He had been afraid moments before but was now unsure what had happened.

"Done." He cleared his throat, which broke Ivory from her relaxed daze. Tentatively, he removed his hand, staring at the broken body armor that revealed the pale skin of Ivory's belly. There were no scars or hints of blood. Ivory appeared to have nothing more than a hole in her suit. He ran his hand over her stomach again, mesmerized. Ivory anxiously tugged on her fingers.

"Uh…thanks," she murmured.

"This isn't right," Dovian whispered, his glowing eyes staring into hers. She fidgeted under his intense stare.

"I know. Just…don't tell them," she sputtered before Troy and Aria arrived at their sides.

"What happened?! Are you all right?!" Troy asked. He looked Ivory up and down as he grabbed her shoulders and tugged her from side to side.

"How'd you avoid that attack?" Aria narrowed her eyes. The blonde shivered beneath her glare. Aria suspected something, and it made Ivory nervous.

"Uh, I…I was just lucky, I guess," Ivory trembled in her speech.

"It narrowly missed her internal organs and main arteries," Dovian helped. "There was a small puncture in the intestines, but it was nothing my energy couldn't cure.” His tone was unwavering, yet Aria didn’t believe him.

“Wow…you’re somethin’ else, Dovian.” Troy gazed at the Sorcēarian.

“Just like the stories,” Kovacevic added.

Aria eyed Dovian. He avoided her gaze, and she knew. “Right. Well, be careful next time,” Aria said in a warning tone. “You won’t be very helpful to us dead.”

“I’m sorry,” Ivory whispered.

“As much as I’d like to celebrate, I think we still have things to worry about,” Troy muttered as he looked over his shoulder.

The line of creatures only grew, refilling the streets. It was impossible. With the soldiers out of ammo and Dovian already exhausted from using his energies, they were doomed. And to make things worse, another loud howl sounded in the distance, followed by a second closer one. More Spewers were on the way, and judging by the shouts and the sound of destruction flowing down the blocks, Brutes were also on the attack. Perhaps they’d survive if all they had to deal with were the Brawlers. However, the reality seemed like a never-ending nightmare that would bring them death.

“I want you all to stay close together. Find protection under a barricade. I’ll have to take care of these things.” Dovian reached for his back apparatus again, fingers twitching nervously. “Actually, find some shelter in one of the buildings, preferably deep underground.”

“What are you going to do, Dovian?” Aria asked.

“Something I haven’t done since my entire race was obliterated,” he hesitantly said.

Flashes of imagery from Ives flickered in Aria and Troy’s brains. The two looked at each other, their mouths open. Whatever he had planned could level the whole city of Saray. Aria sensed Dovian’s nervousness, sweat dripping from his brow, the first time she had seen him reveal any weakness or doubt.

The Sorcēarian lifted his arms and unclasped the cape from his armor, revealing the silver apparatus lining his spinal cord. He quickly handed the massive red cloth to Aria. He then pulled off the top of his coat and black robes, letting the upper half hang over the metal belt around his waist. Closing his eyes, Dovian began pulling on his apparatus. His muscles flexed beneath his skintight white undersuit.

“What are you doing? Removing it?” Aria spoke up. “Dovian?”

“I told you to find shelter!” he shouted.

“No, we’ll find another way. What if you kill yourself? What if you kill us all?” she asked.

“There is no other way!” Dovian turned, giving her a look of desperation. “I have to try.”

“Come on!” Troy tugged on Aria, pulling her toward a shop where Kovacevic had kicked in the door.

"No! We can't leave him out here!" she argued.

"He can handle himself!" Troy struggled with the woman. "Goddamn it, Aria! You aren't in control anymore! This is a time when you need to retreat!"

Aria met Dovian's eyes. He nodded at her and began snarling, again pulling at his back apparatus. His fingertips dug underneath the ends of the metallic wings on his shoulder blades. Aria didn't exactly know what the device did, but it looked painful as it began to separate from his skin on the edges, blood covering his fingertips. Dovian never returned Aria's stare, and she finally let Troy pull her inside.

Ivory appeared panicked. "Will he be okay?"

"Yeah, he'll be okay," Aria affirmed, leading the girl to the basement of the building.

Filing in one after another, they rushed to the basement window, looking up at Dovian, who struggled with the apparatus. The two Spewers neared him, only meters away. Giving up and pressing the buttons on the device instead, Dovian lifted his staff and began throwing the last of his energy at the creatures. Brawlers littered the streets, the alleys full of Brutes, and Euclid remained nowhere in sight.

A loud rumble filled the air, and just as the two Spewers readied to spill their guts onto Dovian and set him aflame, they burst into nothing.

"What the hell was that?!" Troy shouted. He stared upward in awe with his face nearly pressed against the small pane of glass.

Dovian did the same, watching the skies with a genuine smile. Aria stared in awe. Did he know that they were coming?

Another rushing rumble sounded, and the alleyways lit up with mortar fire. Heavy artillery fell from the sky, obliterating the Brawlers. Dovian remained on the streets, helping in the fight. He sent pulse after pulse toward the creatures, shoving them into thick piles to be annihilated by the air fire overhead.

"It's Cherno! They sent their reinforcements from the mountains!" Aria cheered, hopping on the balls of her feet. Due to the endless chaos, Aria had forgotten about the Cherno military sent as a backup in case things went awry during the signing. The Roma military had its reinforcements as well. Their best bombers, with precision aiming, blasted away at the enemy. Within seconds, the war had made another turnaround. Euclid's beasts didn't stand a chance.

A gushing roar sounded, and water rushed over the sides of the buildings, extinguishing the many fires in Saray. Aria and the others waited, watching the demon hoards diminish. Within half an hour, everything fell quiet, and the whole town smelled of sulfur and ash. Saray may have nearly been destroyed, but it still stood.

Aria, Troy, Kovacevic, and Ivory slowly ascended the stairs from the cellar. Once outside, they found the streets full of noisy civilians and military personnel. Cleanup started immediately, and so did the celebrations. It was surreal. What if Euclid attacked again once they all had let their guard down? Kovacevic dismissed the question after receiving an update that the reactor was empty. Euclid's location remained undetermined; the same went for the reactor core. What Euclid wanted with it was unknown, but there were no reports of any nuclear blasts that had eradicated other city-states. Luckily, Saray had their reactor backed up with traditional methods, the procedure set up in case Euclid stole the core. At least Saray wouldn't be having a nuclear meltdown. Using Saray's natural gas reserves, everyone would have to live by old-fashioned standards. Sure, it was costly, but it could always be worse. Saray could've easily met the same fate as Athenia.

"There you are," Troy said.

Dovian neared the group. Black soot covered his face—drenched with sweat and water. He gave them a faint smile, though he looked utterly exhausted.

"How are you feeling?" Aria asked, handing the man his cape.

"Like I just fought a war," he said unenthusiastically. Flapping the fabric, he twirled it about his body and quickly fastened it.

'Ah, there's sarcastic Dovian,' Aria thought. She frowned once she caught him staring at Ivory.

"And you are all right?" he asked the blonde-haired woman.

"Just fine." She nodded quickly, staring at her feet.

"Well," Kovacevic rubbed the back of his neck, "it's been fun, kiddos, but I still have lots of work to do. Got to count how many men I have left." He began to walk away but paused. "You know, I always thought I had the best war stories, but tonight…tonight tops 'em all! From now on, I can say I fought alongside a Sorcēarian." He chuckled.

Dovian gave him a single nod back with respect.

"Hope to fight alongside you again someday, son." Kovacevic lit a fresh cigar, puffing out white clouds. Thanks to the fires, one would think he had enough smoke inhalation for the night.

"Hopefully, nothing of this magnitude," Dovian replied.

"Aw, keeps you young." He smiled. Kovacevic eyed Aria and Troy. "You kids keep yourself safe. Stay together. You make a strong pair, though you may want to work on your arguing." He winked.

Aria gruffly folded her arms.

"Get some rest. You all look like hell." Kovacevic gave a small wave with his cigar before finally walking away from the group, yelling into his DNAIS. The action never stopped with the man.

Dovian watched Ivory, who stared at the wet, scorched pavement. She intensely avoided making eye contact with anyone. Troy yawned loudly, ignoring the intense glare Aria gave the Sorcēarian and the suddenly awkward silence that befell them. They remained that way momentarily, listening to the cheers lining the streets and the music playing from the small shops and bars. One thing was for sure: Saray didn't let a little war get in the way of their lives.

"Come on. It's late," Aria grumbled. "We have to find a hotel." She turned about-face and walked away. Troy followed quickly after her.

"Okay," Ivory managed to say above a whisper. She could feel Dovian's stare burn into her back as she followed.

Dovian waited before joining them, his thoughts searching for a reasonable solution. Ivory looked like a soft, gentle woman, but what had happened earlier didn't make sense. There's no way a human, let alone a frail-looking one like her, could snap a monster's bones and toss it like a piece of trash. Not only that, but Ivory didn't *feel* right. Dovian had covered many wounds before but knew her injury was fatal. She shouldn't have lived through it. He looked down at his hand. No blood. There was no blood from her wound, and her stomach had felt hard, too hard. She also felt cold. There was no doubt about it; Ivory was hiding something, and Dovian had a fairly good idea of what her secret was.

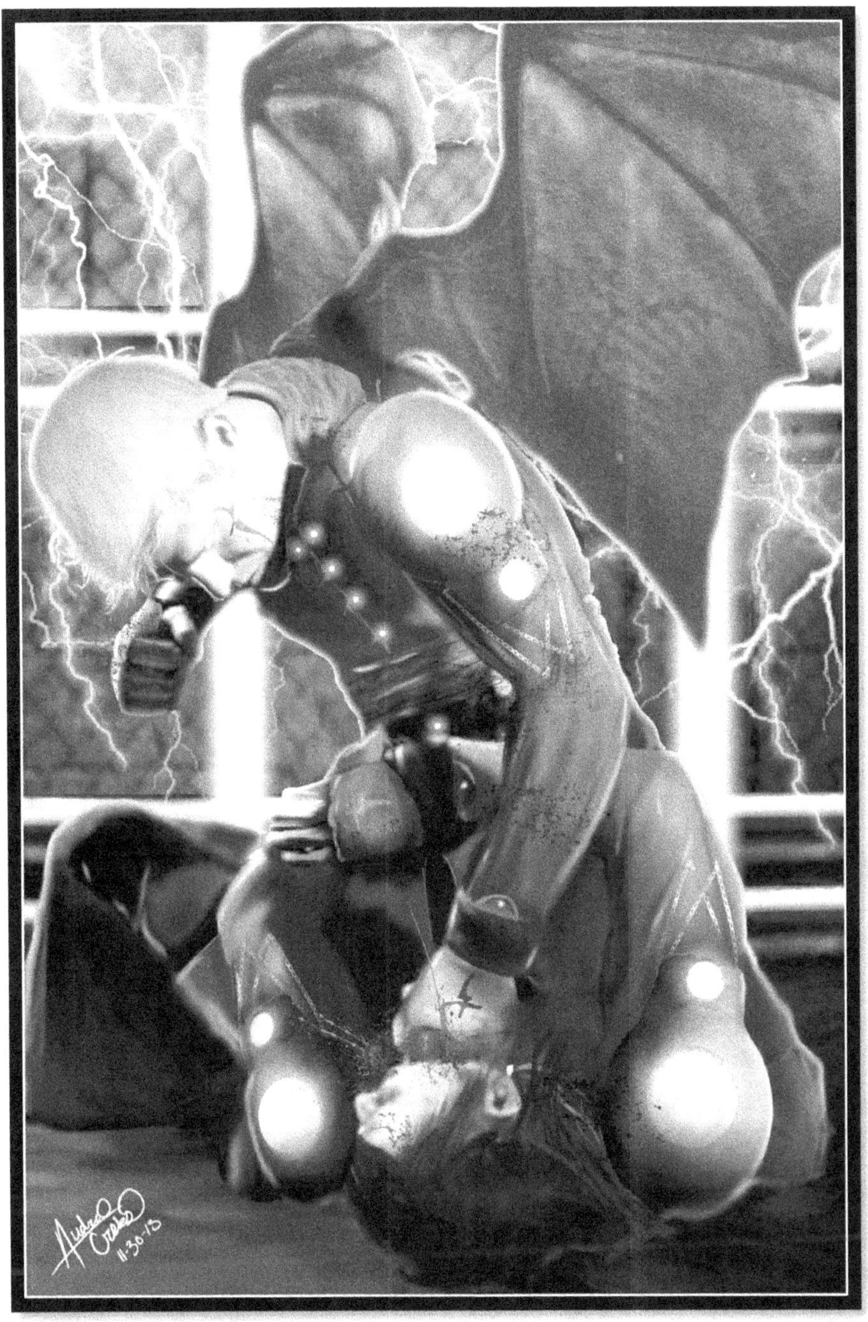

"Scarlet"

CHAPTER 16

Dovian plopped roughly onto his overpriced hotel room's old, floppy mattress. He sighed, the sound loud and low in the almost silent room. The murmur of voices echoed among the surrounding streets along with the various sounds of traffic, cats mewing, sirens from afar, and the occasional crash of glass breaking on the concrete. The party in Saray was finally dying down. The low moan sounded again from the Sorcēarian.

"What a tragic race…" he hummed, his voice coarse and empty.

The man covered his eyes, shielding them from the light that hung from the ceiling fan. The bulb had no cover and wobbled back and forth as the blades whirled in slow circles. There was a creak, probably the building settling. Dovian had noticed more than a few cracks and holes in the foundation. But who was he to complain? He lived in the ruins and rubble of an ancient race for thousands of years before Troy and Aria came along. Troy, however, did mind. He threw a tiny fit about their destination, and Aria promptly hushed him. She had muttered something about keeping cover, being inconspicuous. Dovian had chuckled. Anywhere you go with a Sorcēarian, you will be noticed. It didn't matter how much of a rat-hole the hotel was or how discreet the location was.

There was a knock at the door—probably not the sound of the hotel settling. Dovian ignored it. He took a deep breath and relaxed, closing his illuminating eyes. The hollow sound repeated, even louder than the last.

"Dovian, open up." It was Aria. Her voice was even duller as it called from behind the hollow metal entrance. Dovian decided to wait for a minute longer, one more second to piss off the woman, so her voice would saturate with annoyance.

"Get off your ass and open this door."

The door swung open with a violent force. Dovian leaned against the frame, rubbing his messy, glittering hair. He yawned and eyeballed the woman in front of him. Her tiny fist was about to strike against his chest, the approximate location where the door pounding had earlier taken place.

"Can I help you?" he drawled out long and low. Aria dropped her arm but kept her glare fixated upon his.

"What happened earlier?" The woman's tone was painfully dull.

"…Earlier?" The lanky man blinked, shrugged, and shook his head simultaneously. The gesture did more than irritate the woman.

"With you and Ivory," Aria grumped. She folded her arms and leaned against the outside doorframe.

"Oh, that." Dovian tapped a finger on his chin for a moment and thought. At least, he pretended to. "She was wounded—"

"Right. And…" she hissed.

"And," he nodded, "I healed her." Dovian reached for the door and readied to shut it in the woman's face, but her hand slapped against the surface, the sound like a ruler against a desk, and kept it in place.

"There's more to it than that! I saw you! What happened? What are you hiding? I swear to God if she—"

"I wouldn't swear to Him." Dovian leaned forward, pointing upward at the ceiling as he rolled his eyes to look in the same place. "He doesn't take kindly to such things."

"Like I care," Aria growled, her teeth gritting together—perfect square pearls grinding against each other. Her jawbone set out to the side, and the muscles twitched with her anger. It made Dovian smile.

"But you should." The Sorcēarian leaned downward, his elbows propped against the door and the frame. "You see, you already have it in bad with 'The Man.' Any type of atonement would do you good."

"I'm not here for your holy talk!" Aria raised her chin, showing she wasn't afraid of the self-proclaimed deity.

"You want my opinion?" his voice was a low whisper. Dovian stared directly into Aria's eyes. Now she was becoming uncomfortable. He liked it. He liked to watch her tense beneath his gaze.

Aria remained firm, her eyes not tearing from his, even though she wanted to look away. The fact was she couldn't. His eyes were always mesmerizing, but they seemed more intense than usual. They glowed with a brilliant hue that was more heavenly than the stars. His radiant orbs could lure a person and ensnare them, and that's one of the things that bothered her the most. He was like a predator. He was like a deep-sea trench creature trying to entice her with live bait, and that's what she felt like—prey. She felt like she had walked into a trap. Dovian had been in more than just a sour mood this evening. He had seemed downright murderous and insane thanks to the energy his back apparatus fed into his nervous system. But still, she wouldn't let him smell her fear.

"Only on the question that I previously asked," Aria replied. She stepped forward, resting a shoulder on the inside frame of his room. Now he couldn't shut the door in her face. At least he'd have to shove her out and then close it, which Aria wouldn't doubt he would do. His usually peaceful behavior toward her was now nonexistent.

"I think that you are jealous," he coldly stated. He received a brow raise in response. "And you're angry."

"Obviously, more than angry," she said with a lethal tone.

"It's all because you've lost control of the situation. You see, you're a full-bred military woman. You have the power, you have the authority, and you have the skills. The problem is you're in unfamiliar territory. You're not dealing with humans, men with weapons more powerful than they can handle." He leaned in even closer, their noses almost touching. "You're dealing with more than you can handle. It's all over your poor, little, overconfident head. The military has you spoiled. You may have been drug into this war with me, but I bet more often than not, you spend most of your time inside your haven, spitting orders and playing the strategy game with maps and toy soldiers. I bet you feel no remorse for those you send out to die, not caring about numbers but only results. Staring at the computer screens and watching the digital figures disappear like some videogame, you send out drones and robots to do the cleanup so that all of you at headquarters don't have to deal with the reality of it all. And, in the end, you get the paycheck, the awards, and the ceremonies. At the same time, those who survived dirty work attend the memorials and funerals to say their final goodbyes to family members, friends, and comrades. I bet you wear that symbol proudly." His icy eyes rested on her shoulder patch. "High status," he said with the same bitterness and sarcasm Aria often heard from the civilians and military personnel on base.

"Don't you dare criticize me!" Aria shouted. "I've seen more war than you can imagine!"

Dovian cut in before she could say more. "Oh, really?!" His volume rose to her level. He snatched her by the arms and dragged her into his room, slamming the door behind her. With a quick pound, he had her pinned against the wall with his arms locking her in the tiny space. "Enough to see an entire race ethnically cleanse itself?! Enough to see the world end nearly three times?! Enough to watch everyone you know and love vaporize and disintegrate between your fingertips? Did you see any of that? Have you experienced a full war in the first person? Were you the cause of any of it? Did you solely end a war? No…I don't think so. I don't believe you've seen what war can do to a single civilization."

"I've been born and bred in this age of death and war!" Aria said.

"But you didn't know what it was before!" he retorted. "You only know of results."

"The results of your wars!" she alleged back.

"Brought on by your race!" Dovian hissed with spitefulness. "A horrid, disgusting race!"

"At least my race has found a way to keep itself alive!" Aria caught her breath as Dovian gave her a look most grave. Even she knew she had gone too far with a remark like that.

There followed a long silence between the two. The sudden awkwardness of their positioning made the air harder to breathe. Dovian could have sworn he heard the skittering of a runaway cockroach. Aria waited to see what would happen next. Would he say anything more, or would he just kill her right then and there? He lowered his gaze; the conversation had ended. Dovian would spare her that one mistake. But Aria's initial question remained unanswered.

"This has nothing to do with the question I initially asked," Aria spoke up, but her tone had somewhat softened.

"Ivory?" Dovian raised his head. "You want to figure out what Ivory's all about?"

"Yes," replied Aria.

"The initial question which brought my previous answer—jealousy."

"What jealousy?!" Aria shouted. "Can't you take anything seriously?!"

"The jealousy of not having control over the current situation, not knowing who or what Ivory is, knowing that there's something beyond your knowledge. And it's the fact that I was there to save her, and I'm the one that knows her little secret. Ivory, the pretty girl who shares a secret with the Sorcēarian, the magical sorcerer from the little books you read as a child. We share a bond that you don't understand, and you're mad because you can't figure it out. Maybe it's just the fact that she's prettier than you. She's naturally different. She doesn't need the hair dye, makeup, tattoos, and optic enhancers. Ivory's a beautiful woman, and I know how human women behave. It doesn't matter what rank you hold. You're still a woman. Perhaps you're all in a tizzy and want to find something wrong with her to feel justified when you accuse and alienate her." He was low-blowing her.

"This is ridiculous!" Aria threw up her arms, but Dovian swiftly caught them.

"The fact that your face turns red every time Troy so much as glances at her gives you away. He acknowledges every curve and batted eyelash from any other woman but never gives one look your way unless you hound him. You do keep him on a short leash," Dovian said.

"And you're not worried about the fact that Troy may hit it off just right with Ivory?" Aria pursed her lips together. "I've known that man my whole life, and I know when he has a chance and when he doesn't." She scoffed, giving in to the Sorcēarian's petty game.

"And what do you think?" Dovian almost purred.

"It has nothing to do with our mission. I'd tell him to keep his hands to himself. And I noticed more than a few glares from your eyes, Dovian." Aria pried her arms free from the giant's hands. "You keep changing the subject to something you're more interested in. You don't like Troy at all. He's got game; I'll admit that. He knows how to get what he wants. And you're sexually frustrated after fifteen thousand years of alone time and have suddenly been thrown into a mix of humans, half of which are women! And I've noticed your eyes fall upon me more than once. I think you, sir, are the jealous one."

"Don't make me laugh," Dovian scoffed.

"You're saying that you're not jealous?" Aria questioned.

"No...*Aria*," Dovian said her name in a way no one had before. It rolled from his lips with the accent and proper pronunciation of Legacy. It almost gave the title a whole new meaning.

There came a silent pause as Dovian eyed her. He ran a hand up and down her cheek, a least-expected gesture. Aria's throat made a squeak as she swallowed nervously.

"I'm not denying my jealousy; you see, I'm not a perfect creation either. I, too, have my sins." He trailed to her collarbone. "I was denying that you think I've even looked in your general direction with any sexual interest." He smirked, watching her mouth drop open like a dead fish. Still, he remained close. With a low whisper, he continued, "You realize, Aria, that you and my kind, together, are the perfect recipe for disaster. As much as you've apparently read and fantasized about my race, you can't live a fantasy with me. My kind and humanity are not meant to be together. It only ends in heartbreak." He frowned.

It was true. Dovian's people weren't supposed to intermingle with the other species. It was impossible to live a happy life with another whose lifeline seemed to last as long as a day compared to a Sorcēarian's. Dovian saw this more than a few times, his friends falling for the charming, petite human women. Humans were small, fragile, and had an adorable ignorance and blushing shyness regarding the mysticism of the sorcerers. Little summertime crushes were what Dovian had called short-lived romances. He repeatedly warned his friends about keeping their hands off the delicate ones.

However, the relationships never lasted long, at least not for the Sorcēarians. Still, to the humans, it could have been a lifetime of them waiting and falling continuously over these beautiful warriors. Some Sorcēarians toyed with human emotions, luring them in for a quick ride or two of fun. It ruined the person's soul, leaving them vulnerable and hurt. There were many tears, suicides, and even murders. Families were torn apart, and some Sorcēarians were banned from traveling to the outside world. Jealous husbands and boyfriends would attack the Sorcēarians. Women would die during childbirth, unable to carry the offspring of such a magical being. But it wasn't just the humans who suffered. Many Sorcēarians took their own lives on account of losing their mortal loved one, either through breakup or death. Some couldn't stand to watch something they genuinely loved age so quickly and pass like the changing of the seasons.

Orin, one of Dovian's closest friends, had been caught in a summertime crush. Her name was Elizabeth, ordinary and nothing special, but Orin thought it to be the most beautiful name he had ever heard. He quickly was torn by his love. Dovian remembered when his friend stated that he could see her age every passing second. While he remained youthful, she grew older, new wrinkles and lines emerging on her face every day. It hurt Orin to watch a human woman go through her typical life cycle, and he couldn't handle it. Finally, unable to observe her age further, he told her that he was leaving. Elizabeth was devastated. She begged him not to go. Orin had lied to her, saying that he had to go to battle and that he would come back to her if he lived, even though he didn't plan to come back either way. In the end, Orin couldn't keep his promise to Elizabeth even if he had wanted. Dovian shook the thought from his head. He didn't wish to take another ride down memory lane.

"You cocky, arrogant asshole," Aria growled, her voice tearing him from his sudden contemplation. She ran into him, shoving him away from her. "I'm through talking to you!" Her finger pressed against his chest. "You're just a sad, lonely old man taking his anger and bitterness out on a 'weaker' species. If you think you're so much better than us, why don't you return to your ruined civilization?"

She opened the door to Dovian's room, paused, and turned around, running directly into his chest. Did he have to follow so closely? She noticed he caught her to keep her from falling over. '*Oops*,' was the word that went through his mind for showing any amount of falseness to his hard exterior. Aria smirked, catching his gesture.

"Ya know what? I think you're just lonely and scared of being abandoned, and that's why you're still here with us. You like to act like you're better than us, but you're nothing more than a weak soul who would give anything to have someone by his side. That's why you keep arguing with me and changing the subject. You're so bored, and you need the attention." Her words sputtered from her mouth at light speed. "I bet you'd love to have your way with Ivory and me." She pressed firmly against him. "But I'm not as weak as you!" she snarled through her teeth.

The door slammed with an ear-shattering splinter as Aria left the room. Dovian's ears rang as the silence of the room grew overwhelming. He stood, watching the door. Angry for losing control of the verbal battle, he returned to his lumpy mattress and carelessly dropped, his face smashing into the thin pillow. A muffled, irritated groan erupted from the man. Not only had he made himself angry, but he also somehow allowed himself to get sexually frustrated. Next time, he'd have to be sure to slam the door in the woman's face.

Aria stomped down the hall, out into the hotel's dining area, where Troy sat at the bar with a bottle of his favorite booze. She jumped onto the barstool, spinning around in a half-circle as she barked an order for some whiskey.

"Someone looks like a pissed-off monkey." Troy watched the fidgeting woman.

"Shut up!" Aria shouted heatedly at the man.

"Jeez! And needs to get laid." Troy took a long, hard suck from his bottle. Aria glared at him as she grabbed the glass from the bartender and took an enormous gulp.

She thought, *'Honestly, Troy, you have no idea.'*

The two sat silently next to each other. Every so often, Aria's attention would fall on the man beside her. He didn't acknowledge her but watched the vidscreen above the bar instead. The man chuckled, his eyes vibrant in the bar's dim light as a commercial played, showing a thin female scantily clad in the most expensive form of lingerie. The smaller the underwear, the higher the cost, it seemed. Aria darted her eyes from Troy to the screen. Was he really that repulsive?

Once the commercial was over, a frown set on his face, his olive gaze dropping to his empty beer. He signaled to the bartender and continued gaping at the screen, still not acknowledging the woman sitting next to him. He gave a confused stare upwards as a team of scientists blabbed about their research during a previously recorded convention.

"I do believe that the solar flares are the cause of the recent electric bursts that have plagued our satellites as of late. After years of study, I have concluded that the sun's magnetic reconnection is increasing exponentially. The solar arcades are ever-increasing within the areas of closely contained loops of magnetic lines of force, creating an enormous helix of a magnetic field that is unconnected with the others. The quicker the loops, the more the helix grows, sending out multiple coronal mass ejections. But as it grows larger, the loops grow faster and closer together, but the flares are slowing down. This is causing a massive amount of energy to build up. I predict that an enormous ejection will occur in the upcoming month. It could explode at any time, leaving us with the largest flare in nearly 20,000 years and potentially annihilating our satellites and obstructing all energies on Earth."

"What the hell is this shit?" Troy asked as his face twisted with disgust.

"When do you predict the massive ejection will occur?" another scientist questioned on screen.

"Judging by the rate and speed…around the end of December," the previous scientist replied. "Possibly the twenty-fifth if my calculations are correct."

"Aw, ruins the holiday season, doesn't it?" Troy asked mockingly to the television. "Hey! Can we change the channel?"

Looking up at the scientists on-screen, the bartender shrugged and carelessly pressed against the controller on his side of the bar. The channel on the television switched over to a game of football. Even though the world remained in complete turmoil, the civilian lifestyle continued, and humanity's favorite pastime was sports. Because of the small number of cities in the world, every city-state received broadcasts of each other's games. From home, Troy could watch the matches of Cherno and Saray; likewise, they could watch the sports native to Fountains.

A scoreboard flickered on the screen with flashy effects, revealing the mascots of the two teams. The Fountain Arrowheads were up against the Mile-High Mustangs. In the center of the artificial field, robots adorned in gold and red took one side, while blue and orange stood on the other.

"Now that's what I'm talkin' about!" Troy laughed, drinking his beer. "Wonder if the kicker will lose his leg again this week when he punts?" He finally looked over at Aria.

Resting her elbow on the bar, chin in her hand, her face lacked amusement.

'Yup, a complete idiot.' Aria sighed heavily.

Troy's enthusiastic expression faded. He turned his attention back to the screen. "So, where's Ivory?" he asked.

"In her room. She said she didn't feel well." Aria played with a chunk of ice in her glass.

"Don't blame her. That thing tried to make a shish kabob outta her," Troy said. "Dovian did an excellent job patching her up."

"Yup," Aria murmured, drinking.

'What's her problem?' Troy's brow furrowed. Aria was always pessimistic, but lately, she had been downright pissy about everything, and he couldn't help but feel she directed the brunt of her hostility toward him.

They sat quietly next to each other, except when there was a touchdown or a bad call, and then Troy became vocal.

A blur of red caught Aria's attention. Looking to the side, she noticed Dovian had come out of hiding and dropped into a chair in the corner of the dining area of the small bar. His smoldering gaze aimed at her. Casually, he gestured to the seat beside him. Lifting her glass, Aria slid from her stool, the chair spinning in a circle, and joined the Sorcēarian. Troy continued his rage, yelling with the bartender at the referees.

"Stupid machines!" Troy scoffed, totally unaware of his partner leaving his side.

"Having an enjoyable time?" Dovian asked smoothly, his hands resting in front of his face, elbows sitting on the tabletop.

Aria rolled her eyes like usual. "Hardly. Troy isn't much of a conversationalist." She dropped into the seat beside the tall man.

Dovian chuckled, his hardened exterior temporarily lifting. After a moment of silence, he took a deep breath. "I'm sorry, Aria. I haven't been myself tonight."

Aria quickly turned toward the Sorcēarian, her face appearing shocked. "It's okay. I didn't help much by arguing back with you."

"Things are much different than they used to be." He stared at his hands.

"I can't imagine all the things you've been through, Dovian. Besides, after being alone for so long, I bet it's a little overwhelming to suddenly be in a world surrounded by war and ignorant humans." She breathed a small laugh, letting him know that there were no hard feelings.

"I still find it hard to believe that your race has advanced this far and hasn't destroyed itself yet. Since I've been alive, your kind has risen from the ashes, moving from simple farmers to high-tech soldiers and annihilating yourselves three separate times. It's why I stopped caring in the first place and locked myself away on my island. Being around humans again is, indeed, very overwhelming but not necessarily unpleasant." He looked at her, giving her a wry smile. Aria's breath hitched as she was drawn in by his glowing eyes once again. "Do I make you nervous?"

"What? No. No, why would you think that?" she asked.

"You just look a bit tense, that's all." He smirked.

"If you couldn't tell, I'm always a little tense," she joked.

"I've noticed," he said with a laugh.

More yelling commenced from the bar, interrupting the couple's conversation. Troy high-fived the bartender as the two hooted and hollered. Aria and Dovian watched the celebration momentarily. She frowned as she watched Troy's jumping form.

"Is there something wrong?" Dovian asked.

"No, I'm fine." She quickly tore her eyes away from her partner.

"Can I make an observation?"

"Sure," she said with caution.

"It seems you've been a bit edgy toward your friend lately."

"Am I that transparent?" Aria asked. She watched Troy again, her expression blank. "I don't mean to be. I think it's just stress. We've both been exhausted. And I know he hasn't been acting like himself either. Not since Gavin…." She stared at her glass, twisting it slowly between her fingertips.

Dovian noticed the woman's forlorn look. "You all three were very close, weren't you?"

"Yeah," she said quietly. "Troy and he were best friends. They were nearly inseparable whenever they had time off from their work. They'd known each other for over thirty years. I know it hurt him a lot, losing Gavin."

Dovian leaned down, catching her blank stare. "And what about you?"

"Me and Gavin?" She laughed, her eyes instantly tearing up, glimmering in the pale light. Dovian's face fell at her sudden distressed expression. "Um," she started, looking away from the man, "we were, uh, good friends, too. I've known him for about as long as Troy has."

Dovian watched her carefully as if analyzing her. Aria noticed, sighed, and finally shook her head.

"Guess I can tell you. It doesn't really matter anymore…now that he's gone." She sniffled, trying to hold back from crying. So badly, she wanted to appear strong and not like a weak child whenever somebody mentioned Gavin. Her fingers unconsciously trailed to her kitten necklace. "Gavin and I actually used to be more than friends. God, we tried so hard to hide it. I knew Troy would kill him if he found out, but honestly, I don't see how Troy wouldn't have known. Gavin told him everything. They were worse than a couple of children when it came to keeping secrets." She giggled.

Resting on her hand, she continued. "We, uh, first met when I was twenty-five. It was at Chester's. Troy had always talked about him, so I already knew a little about him. If anything, I expected him to be a ladies' man like Troy, and he was. But he was still different than Troy. There was something about him that was more charming." Her eyes faltered once again on the soldier at the bar. "Of course, I was young and inexperienced when I first met Gavin, and I fell for his relentless flirtations. As much as I tried to remain professional, that damn boy kept pushing my buttons until I finally gave in and dated him. After that, we kept meeting, but we always kept it a secret from Troy and the others. I think Gavin wanted to shout it from the rooftops. I, however, wanted to keep it low-key. I had just been promoted to high-status. I had an image to uphold, you know? Besides, I was terribly busy, too busy for commitment. Also, who knew when I would die in the heat of battle? As much as I gave orders to troops, I also saw my fair share of fighting."

"You feared to get too close in case one of you were to die," Dovian murmured, understanding her side of things.

The woman nodded, letting out a breathy scoff. "Yeah. Stupid, right? I mean, look at what I have to show for it!" Her lower lip trembled. "This damn cat necklace?"

"You have memories. That's important," Dovian offered, suddenly feeling like a heel for bringing up the subject.

"Yeah, but how many more memories could I have had? If only I had just admitted that I was in love with him and wanted to be with him." She shook her head and took a sip of her drink. Setting the glass down, she let out a small breath. "There, I said it. We were in love. I guess you can call it that. I mean, don't couples meet in the middle of the night? All I'd have to do was message him, and in a heartbeat, he'd be at my doorstep. He even had the code in his DNAIS to get into my apartment. Troy hadn't even had a code to my place at the time, and we were partners! But…God, I miss those nights. They were so simple, so content. He'd come over sometimes and watch television with me on the couch. We didn't need to talk. We'd just sit there. Sometimes he'd hold me. Other times, we'd drink coffee and look out the window of my kitchen, watching the lights of the passing cars. Then, we'd go to bed. He'd hold me all night. No matter how much I would protest, he'd insist on holding me. He was so good at sneaking out, too."

Aria faded out momentarily, remembering the nights Gavin would visit. He was loyal to her in the past. She closed her eyes, thinking. It seemed like yesterday when she was hiding under her covers, crying quietly. A small chime had sounded on her DNAIS. It was Gavin, wondering how she was doing. They hadn't spoken in a couple of weeks. She had told him, quite shortly, that she was fine, but he didn't fall for it. He was the only man who could read her like a book. In minutes, he was in her room. Seeing her distressed, he jumped under the covers and quickly gathered her into his arms. It took much prying to get the woman to finally answer and tell him that it was her birthday and that no one had remembered. To make her feel better, he gathered her up and took her to the kitchen for some coffee. As Aria sat by the window, Gavin dug through her kitchen and made, to the best of his knowledge, a birthday cake. It was horrible, tasted like salt, and was lopsided. Still, it was the greatest thing Aria had ever received. Gavin, having never known her birthday until that night, never forgot the date and proceeded to give her something small every year.

Aria continued fiddling with the cat charm around her neck. "But there was one morning…he slipped out, and Troy caught him. I'm not sure what happened, but after that, things changed."

"They changed?"

"Yeah. I mean, Troy acted fine, but Gavin kept his distance. I don't know why. I figured that maybe I had done something wrong. But, every time we happened to be together alone, Gavin would pick up right where we had left off. I think he, too, was scared. We both agreed to keep our distance. I followed our rule more than he did. There were a few times he tried to bring our relationship, or whatever you want to call it, to light in public. I always refused, though. The older I got, the more I distanced myself from him. In our line of work, you have to worry about that other person. They could get dragged into the firefights. They could be held hostage by the enemy. Or I could have died, and he would have been devastated. I don't think he would have been able to handle that." Aria sniffled. "He would have blamed himself for it."

"Do you blame yourself?" Dovian asked.

She stared at him, lost in thought. "Yeah, a little. I don't know what I could have done to save him from Euclid, but I can't help but think how different things would have been if I hadn't pushed him away for so long."

"Even if you hadn't pushed him away, you think he would have let you go to Ives alone?"

Aria lowered her head, a ragged breath passing her lips. "No. He would have been there at my side…which means he would have died either way." That was a terrible thought. Aria didn't want to think that no matter what, it was predestined for Gavin to die the way he had.

"You don't know that. But you also can't change it." Slowly, Dovian placed his hand on hers. "But you don't have to be sad about it. Gavin may be gone by your terms, but he really isn't. He's still here. He's still around."

"He…is?" Aria asked, her reddened eyes lifting to meet Dovian's.

"Have you been reading your book?" he asked her.

"Um, yeah," she said, feeling a bit thrown back by his question.

"And what have you learned from it?"

"Well, I know about the end when the judgment occurred. Those that had succeeded were carried off into Heaven. Those who failed, the ones who were supposed to go to…Hell, we were given a second chance. The angels came down," she eyed Dovian anxiously, "which, I guess, is what you call the Second Fall, and they took charge of watching over humanity. They were supposed to make sure we remained innocent, but sin always strikes back, and humanity failed, giving in to temptation again. And since your race is no longer around…" she spoke carefully, unsure how to continue.

"We failed," he helped.

"Unless the Golden Prophecy has yet to occur," she added.

"I'm surprised you know so much," he said with interest.

"I've read it some, even when I was a little girl. My parents both worked at a University. They used to take me to the church for educational purposes. Kind of like Gavin." The woman's expression fell, remembering the pilot.

"Trust me, my dear. You don't have to worry about him. Keep reading the book. You'll find much more in there to help you with that." He patted her hand.

Aria timidly laughed, and a couple of tears finally dropped down her cheeks. She swiftly wiped them away with her sleeve. "I really hope you are right, Dovian."

"Of course, I'm right." He sat upright, tugging on the front of his robes. Aria chuckled again, this time a bit more genuinely. "I'm a Sorcēarian. I know what's best."

"Oh? Is that so?" she asked, giggling as Dovian firmly nodded.

Troy looked over his shoulder, hearing the sweet, foreign sound of Aria's laughter. He gave the two a curious look, watching Aria and Dovian trade jokes. He hadn't seen her laugh like that since Gavin was around. The military man gave a look of disapproval before turning back around to face the television, ordering another brew.

"And what about Troy?" Dovian asked, catching Troy's stare from across the room.

"What about him?" Aria asked in return, a bit sour.

"You've known him a long time, correct?" He cleared his throat and returned his attention to the woman beside him.

"Oh, yeah, since we were kids. My parents died in an accident when I was about nine." She paused a moment. "His mother died when he was young. His father raised him, but he was in the military as well and was killed in action when Troy was eleven. We were both then given to the army to be trained as soldiers. James was our instructor. He taught us everything we know. Once we were teenagers, we were assigned partners. He thought Troy was a good fit for me. Don't know where he got that idea," she scoffed mockingly. "But we've been together ever since."

"It certainly has formed an unusual bond," Dovian said humorously.

"Yeah," she agreed. "But why all the questions? I feel like I'm being interrogated." Self-consciously, she wrapped her arms around herself, placed her feet on her chair, and drew her knees to her chest.

"My apologies. I'm only trying to get to know my...*partners* better." He straightened his posture.

"So, what about you?" she asked, running a hand through her midnight hair.

"Me? Oh no, I'm far too boring." He waved at her dismissively.

"Aw, come on! I just told you some of the most private things about me; it's my turn to hear about you!" She relaxed in her chair once again.

"No, no." He shook his head. Aria narrowed her emerald eyes, and he chuckled. "Okay. Just one question, though."

Her face fell. She had hundreds of questions for him. Slowly, her brain ticked between each one repeatedly. Then, her eyes flickered with curiosity. Dovian immediately knew what she would ask, and his expression changed to one of dread.

"Who's I'Lanthe?" she asked.

"Nope, not that one. Any question but that one," he said, trying to hold an amused expression for her sake.

"Oh, come on!" Aria protested.

"All you need to know is that she was close to me. That's all," he said quickly.

"You were in love?" she asked, holding the tip of her tongue mischievously between her teeth.

Dovian glared at her, his blue eyes baking into her skull. Aria shuddered.

'*Okay, wrong question to ask.*' She frowned.

"You're no fun, Dovian." She folded her arms again. "Okay, fine. Tell me about that thing on your back."

"My apparatus?" He looked over his shoulder.

"Yeah. What's its purpose?"

"Well, this helps me keep my emotions under control."

"I find that hard to believe," Aria said, smiling.

"Why?"

"Dovian, you're an emotional landslide!" she blurted. She quickly covered her mouth.

"I am not!"

"How many emotions have you gone through in the last hour?"

Dovian feigned to ponder carefully on her question. "You want me to count? Let's see. Boredom, anger, lust, sadness, amusement, contentment." He listed the emotions on his fingertips, counting each one.

"Excuse me?" Aria leaned toward him. "Did you just say lust?"

Dovian lowered his head, smirking. His messy silver and gold hair gleamed under the faint light hanging over their table. His eyes suddenly became much brighter, the glow radiating off his eyelashes. There was the smoldering look again, the one that made Aria nervous. She locked in place, her heart pounding.

"Did I?" he asked, baring his perfect teeth in a crooked smile.

"Thought I heard you say it," she said quietly.

The broad grin remained plastered on Dovian's face, making her return a similar expression. Truthfully, Aria was quite beautiful when she wanted to show it. Sadly, she didn't smile enough; years of training and a harsh life had brought about a near-permanent scowl on her face.

"I don't think I did," he lied, his smile growing.

"You did!" Aria pointed at him, laughing.

"It must be the dark energies I released into my system earlier," Dovian said with amusement. "This button back here controls my negative emotions. If I release it a little, I can be useful in battle as it feeds into my rage. However, it does have its side effects."

"Oh? What kind of side effects?" she asked with peaked interest, using a playful tone.

"It tends to leave me feeling rather dark. I tend to do irrational things. I don't think clearly," he said in a low tone. Slowly, he lifted his hood over his head. His eyes brightened, the light cascading over his cheekbones and tattoos.

"And what happens if you press the other button?" she asked, unconsciously chewing on her lower lip, curious about Dovian's strange mood.

"It helps suppress my sinful nature. Keeps the balance," he said, still hiding under the shadow of his hood.

"So why not suppress it if you're worried about your behavior?" she asked.

Dovian watched her for a moment. She stirred beneath his scrutiny. He kept his expression unreadable, the tight muscles in his chiseled jaw twitching slightly.

"Because I'm having far too much fun watching you squirm." He grinned.

'What?' She quickly sat back in her chair. Aria played with her hair nervously, pulling it behind her ears, revealing her long neck. She anxiously twirled her bangs around her finger.

"I'm not squirming." She shook her head.

"Aria," Dovian leaned forward, resting his hands before his face.

"Yeah?" she asked quietly. It was suddenly hard for her to breathe. She felt like she had just gotten in trouble for something. Thirsty, she reached for the glass beside her, but it was empty. Her hands couldn't keep still, playing with her hair, necklace, and fingers.

'Like a trap,' she thought.

"Do you have any idea how hard it is to sit next to you, knowing all of your thoughts?" he asked in a deep tone.

"What?" she gulped. He was joking, right? He couldn't read her thoughts.

"Oh, my dear. I'm only fortunate you don't know what I'm thinking right now."

'He can read my thoughts? There's no way!' Her mind spun. 'Don't think of anything. Think of nothing!'

Dovian's eyes thinned as he observed her like a predator.

'Curse him and his amazing eyes!' She grimaced, now aware of how much she talked to herself in her head. If he could read her mind, he knew how much she liked his tattoos, his lingering stares, and the deep tone of voice as he spoke in Legacy—especially how he had said her name earlier in the foreign dialect. 'Shit!'

"It's also quite amusing," he murmured, his piercing stare never leaving her.

His sleeves slid down to his elbows, revealing the tight bodysuit underneath. Aria cringed again. The other night, when he had checked on her, he wore only his skintight suit. Surely, her mind had reeled over his fit physique. Aria groaned, hiding behind her hands, listening to the rumble of Dovian's laughter.

"Why? Why would you tell me this?" Aria whimpered in embarrassment.

"Because it's funny."

"It's funny to embarrass me?"

"Troy and Gavin are both right. You are quite cute when you get frazzled."

"Cute?!" she growled.

"Don't know why more men don't throw themselves at you," he said, enjoying the red tint on her face.

"As I said before, it's dangerous. Plus, I'm too busy to meet new people," she stammered as she quickly listed her excuses.

"Well, that's certainly a waste of flesh, isn't it?" He raised an eyebrow.

"I can't believe you just said that. Are you allowed to say that?" she asked incredulously.

"I was born on this earth just as you were. I'm capable of the same sins."

"Yeah, but you're special and holy and stuff." She waved her hands at him, trying not to get locked in his heated gaze.

"I'm not Jesus," he mused.

Aria sagged in her chair. "Ha…" she said, lacking enthusiasm. "You had to throw that one in there, didn't you?" He kept up his intense stare. "Please, stop that."

"Stop what?" he asked, slowly leaning closer to her, his hand sitting on her knee. Small electric prickles started to surge, tickling her kneecap and thigh. He was desperately trying to seduce her.

"Dovian!" she shouted as her eyes enlarged.

Leaning toward her, Dovian placed his mouth beside her ear. With a warm breath, he whispered, "How about we discuss more of my apparatus and its horrible side effects upstairs in my room?"

Aria stared at Dovian in disbelief. Was he serious? He couldn't be serious. He had to be messing with her, playing a rather cruel joke. She swallowed thickly. Before she could answer, he rose and grabbed her hand. Roughly, he tugged her from her seat and led her through the dining area and up the staircase. Aria's heart pounded in her chest. When was the last time she spent the night with a man? It had been far longer than she'd ever like to admit, and now Dovian knew thanks to her running brainwaves, which was horribly embarrassing.

"W-what are you doing?" she stammered as she let him pull her toward his room.

"You know all too well," he quickly said as he unlocked the door and shoved her inside, holding her against a wall. The door slammed behind them. "And you've already answered me about fifty times in your head," he whispered.

Aria gasped. She felt like she would have a heart attack. Her trembling knees threatened to give out as the Sorcēarian grabbed her wrists with one large hand, pinned her arms over her head, and quickly descended upon her lips, kissing her.

The loud cheers from the bar were unheard by the others in the hotel. Troy jumped to his feet, high-fiving his new friend.

"Your bots know how to play a good game." The bartender patted Troy on the back.

"We got some of the best, that's for sure! Hey, Aria!" Troy spun toward the table where he had last seen his partner. "We won…." He quickly deflated. Aria was gone, and so was Dovian.

"They left a while ago," the bartender said gruffly, washing the glasses at the bar.

"Well, it's been a long week. I'm sure she was exhausted," Troy said.

The bartender laughed. "She will be in the morning."

Troy gave him a strange look.

'What's that supposed to mean?' he thought.

"Well, it's long after closing time," the man said.

Looking at his wrist, Troy groaned when he saw the time. "Didn't realize it was so late." He patted the barman on the shoulder and then paid his tab. "Thanks for the beer."

"No problem. Next time you're down, we'll catch one of Saray's games."

"Sounds good!" Troy pointed at the man, smiling.

Heading up the stairs with heavy footsteps, Troy looked over his shoulder at the table Dovian and Aria had occupied. He couldn't shake the strange feeling that something was off, but he wasn't sure what it was.

A loud noise tore the man from his brooding thoughts—the sound of something heavy falling over. A couple of voices followed the noise, one female.

'Aria!' Troy recognized it immediately. Panicked, he darted up the stairs and halted in the middle of the hall. She sounded like she was in trouble. He waited beside her door, listening for the cries again.

"Oh, my God!" Aria's voice shouted, followed by her loud, cackling laughter.

Troy froze, feeling chills shudder down his spine. Slowly turning, he faced the closed door to the room from where the sounds came.

'No way….' Troy gaped open-mouthed at Dovian's room, listening to the breathy sounds and laughter. Shocked, he remained in the center of the small hallway, staring at the golden numbers. Maybe he had the numbers switched in his head. Perhaps he was confused about which room was hers. She was watching television. It was something shocking and possibly humorous.

'No, you damned idiot,' he cursed at himself. Then, there was a deep voice. Sure enough, Dovian was in there with her.

Troy suddenly felt sick and tired.

'Who cares? Who cares if she's in Dovian's room? She's an adult. She can do what she wants.'

Troy ran his hands through his hair, quickly making his way to his room. What

Aria did was her business, not his. Besides, he constantly lectured her about getting out and meeting people. She was a hermit, and it was about time she had a little fun.

Closing the door behind him and quickly dropping onto his back on the bed, Troy covered his face with his arm, trying to ignore the sharp pain of his looming headache. He scoffed loudly in the silent room.

"A little fun," he said sarcastically.

'I didn't mean with him,' he sourly thought.

Now he understood the bartender's little joke, and it still wasn't funny.

"The Kiss"

CHAPTER 17

The stone floor felt ice-cold in Dovian's cell. Cracks lined the walls. Tiny streams of light twinkled from inside the surface as spells kept the room intact and indestructible. The Sorcēarian sat underneath the small, barred window, head hidden in his arms that rested on his knees. Outside, thunder rolled like a freight train, shaking his body. He listened quietly, waiting for the horn to blow, to signal the war that was about to begin. There was nothing he could do, nothing to save his people, nothing to protect her. His friends and family had betrayed him, locking him up in the dark, dingy cell. Tiny splatters of raindrops pelted against the stone windowsill and onto his body.

"Dovian?" a female voice alerted the man. It surprised and pained him to hear her voice, a sweet melody in the darkness.

He abruptly rose, rushing to the metal bars. The poles surged with energy; an unbreakable spell sealed him inside. Gently, he placed his hands over her gloved fingers as she safely gripped the gate.

"I'Lanthe," he whispered to her.

She looked frightened. Dovian knew it wasn't because of her own safety, but she feared for his. Her violet eyes shimmered in the darkness, her pale-pink lips forming into a small smile. She had a terrible time trying to hide her emotions.

"You're all right! I'm so glad you are all right! I was worried! So worried!" Her eyes brimmed with tears as she spoke to him. She lifted her hands, cupping his face as she looked into his eyes.

"I'm all right," he reassured her, slowly lowering her hands from his face. Placing a small kiss on her knuckles, he tried to smile.

"They are coming," she sputtered quietly. Dovian's eyes widened. He knew they were coming, but as the words fluttered from her mouth, he realized he was unprepared. No one truly was. "He is coming. He is bringing the entire army, and he is going to kill us all. Do you understand?" Her expression remained hard as she spoke slowly to him.

Dovian stayed silent, his mind churning, trying to figure out how to stop the war before it began. His stomach flip-flopped. There was nothing he could do, not while he was locked up in this cell. He couldn't stop the inevitable.

"Dovian, do you understand?" Her face wrinkled with worry. "You need to get out of here."

Dovian shook his head. "L-Lanthe, I—"

"You have to leave. Go," she said louder, her eyebrows lifting. "Go. Please." Her hands gripped his tightly.

"I cannot leave this place, you know it," Dovian said finally. She shook her head, tears dripping down her rosy cheeks. "I'Lanthe, you need to hide. In my room, there is a way out. There's a hole beside the bookcase. It's small, but you can fit through it. It leads to the tunnels. Take them; go to the vacation home…."

"I can't do that." She shook her head again, staring at the floor. Her dark curls spiraled over her shoulders. "I have to lead my men. I can't abandon them."

"No! Lanthe, no! You have to get out of here!" Fear was now evident on Dovian's features as reality finally began sinking in.

A loud alarm sounded in the distance, sending shivers down both of the Sorcēarians' spines. It was a terrible noise, reserved only for the holy—a tumultuous blaring of a thousand horns. It was starting.

"Get out of here!" Dovian frantically shouted.

Gasping under his outburst, I'Lanthe cupped his face once again. She gave him her most charming smile. "Don't worry about me, Dovian. I can take care of myself. I'm more worried about you."

"No!"

"Find a way out. Get out of here. I want you to fly away. He'll kill you as soon as he finds you. He's probably on his way right now. I need you to live, Dovian. Please." I'Lanthe leaned forward, pressing her soft lips against his carefully between the bars. Dovian quickly wrapped his arms around her waist the best he could. Thunder growled, the wind howling along with it. Bright lightning flashed, and she tried to pull away, but he held her firmly against the gate. "Dovian, let go."

"No, not unless you promise me that you'll get to safety." His glowing orbs stared into hers.

She watched her feet. Hesitating entirely too long, she replied, "I promise." She gave him a worrying look.

The horns blared again. She jerked from the noise.

"I have to go!" I'Lanthe pulled away.

"Get to safety!" Dovian shouted.

"I love you," she whispered, quickly turning and dashing away into the shadows.

Dovian watched her, his heart threatening to burst from his chest. She was lying. I'Lanthe wasn't going to leave. Bound by her duties, his love would find her place on the battlefield.

"Lanthe!" he shouted. The name echoed down the stone and jeweled halls of the empty tower.

With a jerk, Dovian's eyes popped open. He let out a loud moan and lifted his head, finding himself in his small hotel room in Saray. Sighing, he lowered his head and halted, watching the body beside him.

'Aria….' He relaxed, staring at her slumbering form. Gently, he pulled her hair behind her ear. She groaned and mumbled, her arms twitching. It appeared nightmares plagued her as well. Dovian lightly placed his hand on her head and closed his eyes. *"Shhh…everything will be all right,"* he whispered into her mind. Sighing, the woman twisted into a more comfortable position, lying on her belly.

Dovian sat up in the bed, scratching the back of his head as he returned to the present date. Looking at Aria again, he realized that this was the first time he had slept through the night since the others had found him. He gave a tiny smirk. Aria was a good sleeping pill.

After a moment, Dovian rose and traveled to the bathroom, readying a warm shower. The sound of the rushing water awoke the slumbering Aria. Groaning, she twisted and turned a few more times before fully becoming aware of her surroundings. She gave a long stretch and sat up, squinting eyes searching the room.

'This isn't my room,' she thought with momentary confusion. With a sharp gasp, she grimaced. *'Oh, crap!'*

Quickly rising from the bed, she looked from side to side, seeing her clothes scattered all over the room.

'Crap!' she mentally shouted again.

The door to the bathroom opened, and Aria jumped. Out stepped Dovian with a towel wrapped around his waist. He had another on his head, drying his shimmering hair. His biceps flexed as he moved the cloth; the tips of the wing tattoos lining his shoulders and arms had a fluttering illusion. Aria must've made a sound because the man looked up, catching her stare. She quickly looked down and noticed that she was naked. Squeaking, Aria quickly tugged the sheet over her body, her face burning with embarrassment. Dovian gave her a sheepish smile.

"Nothing I haven't seen before," he said humorously.

Aria gripped the cloth tightly. She made a funny face as Dovian gathered her clothing, tossing the items on the bed for her. He watched her with amusement as she pulled the articles beneath the blanket and shimmied into them until she had her pants and top on. It was impressive how women could dress and undress in secrecy. He remembered I'Lanthe removing her bra without taking off her robes first. The thought of I'Lanthe made him tear his gaze away. He began to feel remorseful for his behavior.

'You're not an animal, Dovian,' he lectured himself.

Aria tugged her boots on one at a time, her sweater hanging over her small hands. She gave Dovian a sideways glance as a pink hue covered her cheeks.

'Wonder if he's always reading my thoughts.' She stared at the Sorcēarian. Dovian glanced up at her and fed her a gentle smile. *'Yup.'* She outwardly sighed.

"Listen, Aria," Dovian muttered. He stood in the center of the room with his arms folded across his bare chest. Feeling awkward, he looked off to the side, staring at nothing.

'Shit, here it comes,' she thought. It was impossible not to think about anything when the man was around. Still, an inner monologue was always better than blurting every thought out loud.

"I wanted to apologize for last night. I honestly wasn't behaving like myself. I know it isn't an excuse. I gave in and wasn't acting very gentlemanly." He frowned, glancing at his clothes on the floor.

"You're apologizing?" Aria asked. "For what?"

"For…well…we…." he stuttered, having difficulty finding the right words.

"For sleeping with me?" she asked.

"Yes. I pushed myself upon you, and it was entirely unnecessary. I'm sorry. I shouldn't have done that."

Aria sat on the bed, feeling a bit hurt. She understood what he meant, but it still didn't leave her feeling good about herself.

"As I said, I lost control. I used my apparatus last night during the battle. The residual energy left me vulnerable and weak," he tried explaining.

"What is that?" Aria scoffed. "The Sorcēarian's way of saying, 'Jeez, I was way too drunk last night and didn't mean to have sex with you?'"

Dovian cringed. It did sound like that. "That's not what I meant."

Aria stood. Her face was either beet-red from embarrassment or anger, Dovian wasn't sure.

"No, I know what you meant. Don't worry about it. Not a big deal." She quickly headed for the door, wincing. The first few steps hurt, making her hobble—as if she weren't embarrassed enough.

'You just keep flirting with me every chance you get and then regret it. Makes sense.' She inwardly cursed for thinking at all.

"I'm sorry. I shouldn't have done all of those things," Dovian replied.

"Will you stop apologizing?" She twirled, facing the nearly naked man once again. "You are making it worse. There is nothing like continuously being reminded of how sorry someone is for having any sexual interest in me. I get it. It wasn't very holy of you. Whatever." Aria suddenly felt like crap. Why did it always end up this way? One-night-stands were always a bad idea. She wished she had just gotten up and left before Dovian finished his shower.

"Please, Aria. I'm not saying I wish I hadn't done it. I am only apologizing for my behavior because I feel like I pushed myself on you."

"Did it ever occur to you that I actually enjoyed it, Dovian? You read minds, right?" She glared at him.

"Yes, I know, but still…verbalizing a thought is more important. People think things all the time but wouldn't always outwardly express them."

"You thought it, you sinned it, right?" she said sarcastically.

"This isn't ending up like I was planning."

"No, Dovian. How did you expect me to respond to that?"

"I don't know." He grabbed the side of his head. It had been so long since he dealt with a woman with sporadic emotions.

"You don't know? You know everything! You're always reading my thoughts!" she shouted.

"Not all the time, Aria. I'm not simply tuned to your brain continuously. Only when I want to."

"So, right now, you're not in my head?" she asked.

"No. If I were, I probably wouldn't be screwing this up so badly." He smirked.

Aria stared at him, not looking amused.

"People's thoughts are just constant background noise. I can concentrate on one thought and focus on it. I shouldn't have done it to you. It wasn't fair. That's why I'm apologizing. I feel like I've taken advantage of you." The tall man sighed irritably.

Aria began to feel a tad bit bad for her emotional outburst. The whole thing was awkward. How was she going to handle this from now on? They were partners trying to save the world.

"You didn't take advantage of me, Dovian," she said quietly. "In fact, I enjoyed it. I just don't want you to worry about it anymore. We've got work to do. This can't distract us. It's no big deal. It didn't happen, won't happen again, all right?"

Now, she was shutting him out, turning off her emotions like she had done with Gavin. Dovian frowned.

"Aria," he started.

Aria's wrist chimed, and she quickly looked down. President Clarke was calling.

'Thank God, a distraction,' she thought.

"Yeah?" she asked, pressing against her ear.

Dovian's shoulders sagged.

"Uh-huh," she said. Giving a small wave, she opened the door and walked the hall. She quickly let out a breath of air, glad to be out of that suddenly very stuffy room. However, she didn't miss Dovian's disapproving stare as she dropped the subject and escaped the situation.

'Whatever, we'll talk about it later…the next time we're at a bar and he decides to seduce me again.' She smiled at the idea.

As she neared her room, Troy left his. The man gave her the nastiest glare she had ever seen.

"Did you hurt your leg during the battle last night? You seem to have a limp," he said sarcastically. As he walked by, he added, "You could have Dovian patch it up for you. Bet he'd be willing. Just take off your pants and show him where it hurts."

Aria glared back, giving him the middle finger as she entered her room, Clarke rambling into her ear.

'Okay, so Troy obviously knows. What else can go wrong?' Aria sighed, slamming the door shut behind her.

"Are you listening, Aria?" James asked.

"Yes, sir, Roma," she affirmed. So, she wasn't listening completely, but she got the gist.

"But come home first. I have some gifts for you."

"Can we afford to come home, sir? Aren't we short on time?" she asked, grabbing her toothbrush from her suitcase.

"I can have you home and back to Roma by tonight if you catch the next flight out of Saray," he said.

Aria looked at her watch.

'Holy shit, 10:00.' She frowned with her toothbrush in her mouth.

"You'll need to hurry, though. You have less than an hour and a half to get to the airport. I'm sending confirmation for your tickets right now."

"Mm-kay," she grumbled, brushing her teeth.

"Oh, Aria?"

"Hm?"

"You'll be landing on the Underbelly," Clarke said reluctantly.

Aria spat into the sink. "Underbelly? Why?"

"I'll explain everything once you are here. Meet me by the transport elevators outside the airport."

"Okay," Aria said cautiously.

"Be safe. Try to remain inconspicuous once you land."

"Roger."

She ended the call and stared at her reflection. Were they in trouble? Was James in danger? Aria couldn't help but feel that Mr. Walten was somehow involved.

Getting to business, Aria took a quick shower and then shoved all of her belongings into her suitcase. Inconspicuous meant no armor. Some of her belongings were left behind to make room for the massive amount of armor and weaponry. After fussing with the luggage, she went to the dining area. Ivory and Troy sat at a corner table. The two seemed to be having a good time. Troy was gesturing like usual, and judging by his expressions, he told a funny story. Ivory kept giggling, her eyes creasing as she held a hand to her lips. Troy noticed Aria, his energy faltering momentarily. She gave him a strange look.

"So I said, 'That's not what you use a turkey baster for!'" Slapping the tabletop, he laughed, Ivory giggling with him.

Aria smirked, having heard that specific tale a few times before. She set her luggage down and took a seat beside Ivory.

"Oh, Aria! Good morning! Did you sleep well?" Ivory politely asked.

"Bet she did," Tory murmured, sipping his coffee.

Aria scowled. He certainly was trying to get on her bad side this morning.

"Better than I have in years," Aria stated with a broad smile. Troy rolled his eyes. "How about you?"

Ivory beamed. "Like a baby! At least, I think babies sleep peacefully. They certainly look like they do!"

At least Ivory was in a good mood.

"Got a call from James," Aria changed the subject.

"Oh? Where are we going next? Do we get to ride on another plane? I love planes!" Ivory grinned.

"Well, the next attack is supposed to occur in Roma, but we need to make a quick trip home first. So, you'll get to have a lot of experience on the plane today," Aria grumbled. Ivory squealed with delight.

"Why are we going home?" Troy asked.

"He said he has some gifts for us, but the weird thing is…we're landing in the Underbelly."

"Why?" he asked with confusion.

"Not sure. He said he'll explain when we get there. I dunno. This doesn't feel right. I think something is going on; I just hope James isn't in trouble," Aria said, pouring a cup of coffee.

"If anyone's in trouble, it'd be us," Troy grumbled. "I bet that Walten bastard is the cause of this private meeting."

"That's what I figured, too." Aria looked at her watch. "But we need to leave

ASAP. Flight leaves in less than an hour."

"Holy shit!" Troy quickly finished off his brew. "Why didn't you tell us sooner? Come on, Ivory. We gotta pack."

"I already have!" Ivory beamed.

"We need to be inconspicuous, so pack your armor and dress civilian," Aria called out to the man as he rushed toward the stairs.

"Dandy." He paused. "Guess I'll tell Dovian, or does he already know?" he asked, trying not to sound bitter.

"He doesn't know," Aria murmured.

Troy didn't say anything but continued up the stairs.

'Is the entire day going to be this awkward?' Aria inwardly sighed.

The whole day was extraordinarily awkward. Dovian embarrassed Aria by insisting on bringing his weapon aboard the flight, to which all the security officials came to reprimand him. Dovian merely slammed the staff together and condensed the rather large device into a small box, the wings forging into a handle to which he stated, "It is my carry-on."

Then, the seating arrangement on the flight left Aria and Ivory sitting next to each other, which wouldn't have been bad except that it left Dovian and Troy sitting beside one another. Aria would have offered to trade seats, but she didn't want to sit with either of the men. Still, Troy and Dovian's tension was quite apparent. The two barely said a single word to each other. Truthfully, the men were pissing her off. They both were acting like children. She especially expected better from Dovian, someone over seventeen thousand years old.

"I can see Fountains!" Ivory shouted a few hours into the flight.

'Thank God!' Aria sighed heavily.

She noticed Dovian looked her way and wrinkled her nose. *'Stop reading my thoughts!'* The Sorcēarian quickly looked away, a smirk on his face. *'Bastard,'* she added. She noticed his smile promptly fade.

The flight attendants rushed to their seats as the aircraft descended toward the bottom of the center plate that held up Fountains. From her position, Aria could see the upside-down buildings hanging from beneath the city. The structures were all made of metal, built to withstand the gushing winds that suctioned under the plate to cool the reactor core and feed into the wind-propelled energy.

From above, Fountains was a beautiful city of white, silver, and blue with expanded platforms of green grass and small trees. It was one of the most beautiful city-states in the world. Underneath, however, was a stark contrast. Being the more impoverished district of the city, the Underbelly was dirty and dank, never receiving enough sunlight even to create small pastures of green. Because of the forceful winds, many buildings didn't even have windows—the few that did were small and made of thick panes of bulletproof glass, emitting tiny white lights in the dark structures. A deep black hole lay underneath it all, used for mining precious natural resources and water.

The plane jolted, catching the gusts. From the speakers overhead, the pilot's voice warned of turbulence. It took a few minutes before the jet's quaking subsided as it sped to the side of the center plate that housed the airport. After landing, Aria and the others rushed to gather their things, Dovian returning his weapon to its natural state, and made their way into the terminal. Thanks to the recent attacks, the security checks were longer than necessary, as the city was on red alert. Once outside the airport, Aria sighed with relief. James waited patiently for them beside the giant transport elevators that led to the upper city.

"Aria!" James quickly approached the woman, his arms open.

With a little bounce in her step, Aria rushed to the President and set down her luggage to return his hug.

"I'm so glad you are all right. I worry about you day and night, you know that?" he asked.

"I'm fine. I've got a good team," she said, looking over her shoulder.

"Indeed, you have. I heard you're quite the sharpshooter," Clarke said to Ivory.

"I try my best, sir," Ivory replied with a grin.

"And Troy. How have you been faring?" Clarke asked, noticing the young man's distant expression.

"Just fine, sir. Busy as hell, but that comes with the job description, right?" Troy forced a smile.

"It does." Clarke nodded. "And I can only assume you've been extremely helpful, too." He looked up at Dovian.

"I try to do what I can," Dovian replied.

"He's been accommodating," Aria added.

'I bet he has,' Troy thought bitterly.

Dovian gave the soldier a sideways glance.

Aria continued, "I don't know how many times he's saved my life."

"And mine!" Ivory chimed in.

"Well, I'm glad you have decided to join their side, Dovian. Any help we can get is most appreciated." Clarke then cleared his throat. "Now, I bet you're wondering why we are here."

"I am curious." Aria nodded.

They remained in the central core of the upper and lower city and were encased entirely within one giant superstructure that stretched the whole expanse of Fountains. From the small windows, they could see the massive hole far below. It was menacing, threatening to swallow the city whole.

"Truth is—Walten is pissed. If he catches wind that you are in the city, he'll send a team out immediately to detain you." Clarke stood at attention as he spoke. "He seems to consider you all enemies as you are responsible for the attack on Athenia. He has branded the four of you traitors."

"What?!" Aria and Troy shouted at once.

"That's bullshit!" Troy growled.

"Oh, my," Ivory gasped, her hands clasping over the dog tag hanging around her neck.

"I've tried explaining, but he won't listen. He wants someone to blame, and you are the only tangible thing he can get his hands on." Clarke looked upon Dovian. "I also fear he wants something from Dovian. I'm unsure why, but he has also expressed an interest in Ivory."

"Am I in trouble?" Ivory asked.

"I would like you to remain close to Troy and Aria," Clarke told the woman. "They're the best. I trust you'll be safe at their side."

"You also have me, remember," Dovian said to her. Ivory quickly bobbed her head.

"But what about our channels?" Aria asked. "They could be monitoring them."

"I've been using my private channel. It has the highest encryption. Walten doesn't even know about the line," Clarke reassured her. "As such, I would like you to leave immediately. There's a private plane departing in a little over an hour. Stay well-hidden and remain close to the airport at all times. You are going to Roma. I'm not sure why they would attack, seeing as Roma doesn't have a nuclear reactor, but the festivities start later tonight."

"Festivities?" Troy asked. "To celebrate the peace treaty signing?"

"Precisely. Roma will have a masquerade ball tonight to kick off the celebrations. It'll be the perfect opportunity to go in covertly to see what Euclid's up to. The festivities are supposed to last all week. It's the first time they've been able to hold their tradition in decades. Originally, all of the world's elitists were invited to attend, but since the attacks have been wiping out city-states left and right, Roma is still in a state of red alert. This means there won't be many people of value outside of Benvenuto attending, and he won't give his celebratory speech until tomorrow night at his home, where the grand ball will take place. It would be the perfect time for Euclid to strike. But, as I said, there is no reactor. And with the daily attacks, I am unsure why Euclid would infiltrate tonight since Benvenuto won't be addressing the public until tomorrow…unless he plans to take out masses during the masquerade later this evening." Clarke rubbed his forehead. "This guessing game is a little mind-numbing. There is also the possibility that he'll attack elsewhere since we've interrupted his plans twice now."

"No," Dovian spoke up. "He will continue as planned. What day is today?"

"Saturday," Aria answered, looking at her DNAIS.

"It's the day of the Sabbath. Euclid will not attack today," Dovian said. "He will continue as planned tomorrow."

"How can you be sure?" Aria asked.

"Rules are rules. Evil or not, you don't mess with the day of the Sabbath. People have been struck down for less," Dovian explained.

"But I thought Sabbath was on Sunday," Troy said. So, he did know a little something about the faith.

"No, not traditionally," Dovian replied. "Trust me. He'll attack tomorrow. Besides, I doubt he's healed from yesterday's fight." He unconsciously squeezed his hands into fists.

"Just to be safe, I'd like you all to leave on this afternoon's flight to get away from this place and as far away from Walten as possible," James advised.

"We will." Aria set her alarm.

"And take these with you." Clarke pointed to a few heavy crates. "I've already got them tagged and ready to board the plane. They have plenty of new ammunition for you to use, even a few grenades. Also, Camery's got some new reinforced suits for you to wear. They have the highest form of defensive shield I've ever seen— Plasma Shields. These shields have a dual-layer plasma helix. The shields pull in ambient energy. The shields squeeze particles together as the energy intensifies, creating a rebound effect. It's like Saray's technology but only stronger. Ivory, you have a new weapon. It's more stabilized than the last and has cloaking mechanisms like Aria and Troy's. Dovian, he developed something for you as well. Not sure if it'll be of use to you." Clarke lifted the lid to one of the crates. Grabbing an item, he handed it over to the Sorcēarian.

Dovian gave the item a curious look. It was circular and almost flat. A glass-like gem adorned the center, making it look like a pendant. Small lines decorated the outside of the jewel. "It's a frequency tuner. Looks like a top model."

"What's it do?' Aria asked.

"It should help me tune into different frequencies, allowing me to teleport as Euclid does." Dovian flipped the tuner over, scrutinizing it. "Interesting piece of technology. It almost looks Sorcēarian in nature. I'm curious as to how he developed it."

"You'll have to ask him that. I don't know a thing about it." James held up his hands.

Dovian twisted the gem in the center like a dial. His form twitched and vibrated. Dovian disappeared from the group's center with a flash and then stood directly behind Clarke. "Works well," he said.

"You may want to be careful where you use that thing. I think a few people noticed." Aria folded her arms. She looked at the hundreds of citizens walking through the pathways. A few gaped at them with interest while others quickly walked away, glaring over their shoulders.

Aria flinched as an arm shot out, and a long piece of paper dangled before her face. It was a flyer for one of the churches in the city. Swiftly, Aria snatched the item from the stranger's hand.

"It'll be a good message this week. Always is," the man said. He was about Aria's height and appeared to be similar in age to Mr. Clarke, having peppered hair himself. The man also wore thick-rimmed glasses, which was rare since most people had surgery to correct their vision. Most likely, the man was too proud for an operation. Most people in the Underbelly had some differences compared to the citizens above. Here, instead of fearing the variations, they embraced them. The people on the underside were much more united than those above.

Aria eyed the pamphlet once again. Listed on the bottom was 'Roy's Printing Press.' Something even rarer was the use of paper. It was considered wasteful, and things such as printing and parchment were no longer useful. Leave it to the Underbelly to use something from ancient times in a world of technology. It was their way of "sticking it to the man." Though the things the underside people did hadn't always made much of a difference, let alone any sense, Aria wouldn't judge. They at least remembered their roots and had consideration for history.

"Been a long time since I've seen a church," Aria muttered.

"A church?" Dovian asked, his eyes lighting up.

"We have one of the most beautiful down here!" Roy beamed enthusiastically. "And the pastor is great! You'll be surprised; why don't you give it a try? Won't hurt."

"No, thanks," Troy grumbled.

"I would like to see it," Ivory cheered.

Roy gave the tall, busty blonde a wide-eyed stare. "See? Can't say no to a pretty gal."

"We do have plenty of time," James said. "And it has been a terribly long time since I've seen the one down here."

"You'll love it! The sermons are great, and they are televised all over the city." The man was humorously animated, if not a little bit neurotic. He gestured toward the numerous screens lining the tops of the buildings down the side streets. "If you notice, the Bibles in the cathedral were printed in my shop! My family has been printing books for generations. There's something about holding a real book: its smell and how it feels in your hand!" Roy sniffed the newsprint. "You can't get that with your digital books, no way! If it weren't for that dadgum technology, my family's business never would have gone under. After years of sitting empty, I used my life savings to get this thing up and running again."

Aria gave the man a strange look. Only in the Underbelly would something like Roy's business be able to make money.

"People here like to gossip, so I started my own newspaper! Who doesn't like hearing about all of the news that's been going on? I tell you, those darn elitists up above are trying to withhold information from the people! It's wrong! People care more about the celebrities on their shows than how their money is being spent. I mean, people have to speak up. They got to let their leaders know who's in charge!"

"So, what do you think about the events happening worldwide?" Aria asked, interrupting the man's little rant.

"Demons!" he said with no faltering whatsoever. "It's those dadgum demons that are causing all the trouble. It's getting close to the end. I ain't joking!"

Troy held a hand to his forehead. Was this man serious?

"You're one of those conspiracy types, aren't you?" Troy asked.

"You're an idiot if you don't believe it. Now, I'm not saying all those strange conspiracies are true, but I can say that some are, and something funny is happening around here. I think the demons are in charge, always have been. Those suits up there, controlling all of our money, making all of the rules, they are controlling them!" The man pointed upwards, swinging his arm.

"Interesting theory," Dovian said with a crooked smirk.

Roy's eyes bugged at the sheer monstrous height of Dovian. "I don't mean to sound rude, but you're the tallest dadgum man I've ever seen!"

"I get that a lot." Dovian frowned. "So, where is this church?"

"Just down the block and around the corner." Roy pointed.

Turning, Dovian looked upward, noticing the massive buttresses and points of the gothic-style cathedral. He gripped his chest, gasping in awe.

"Beautiful, ain't she?" Roy asked.

"Most beautiful thing I've seen since I've left home," Dovian murmured. He walked away from the group, eyes on the cathedral, mesmerized.

"Home?" Roy asked.

"Ives," Dovian muttered as he strolled away.

"Ives?" Roy pushed his glasses further up his nose.

"Um, thanks for the information, Roy," Aria said quickly before trotting after the Sorcēarian. Ivory and James did the same, not wanting to lose track of their party. Troy heaved a sigh, following the others, trailing behind.

"Wait...Ives?!" Roy asked again, staring at the scarlet-robed man who had already walked to the far street corner, turning toward the church. "Can I interview you?!" Roy shouted, quickly lifting his old-fashioned camera to take a group picture, but he was too late.

Beautiful was an understatement. The cathedral was remarkable in architecture. The peaks nearly touched the digital cloud ceiling of the enclosed city. The sharp angles twisted and poked outwards, creating a stunning yet eerie effect. The doors were massive, made of wood and old metal. The structure looked like it came straight from ancient history—straight from Ives.

Even Troy stood gaping at the giant cathedral, his mouth hanging open. "Would not want to be the one who had to design this thing," he muttered quietly.

"It's fantastic," Dovian whispered. He looked like a kid in a candy store.

Aria's eyes darted to the men standing outside the entry doors and the sides of the building. They wore shiny silver armor, purposefully given an old-time design. Helmets, with pointed wings for ears, hid their faces, and white cloths adorned with long red crosses hung loosely over their torsos. They were called Soldiers of God and were a privately funded mini-militia whose only job was to guard and protect the cathedrals. Many wealthy men put a lot of money into preserving the last of ancient history's faith. Their leathered hands squeaked as they squeezed their large rifles. They saw Dovian as a threat as he neared the church, his hands touching the stained-glass window. One guard in the front slowly approached the group.

"What's your purpose here?" he gruffly asked.

"We came to watch the sermon," Aria replied, trying her best not to use a lethal tone with the man.

"The doors have already been closed for this sermon. You can watch from the outside," he said.

"Outside?" Dovian asked in disappointment.

"Can you at least let him in? He can stand and watch in the back," Aria suggested.

"Sorry, I can't do that."

Dovian frowned.

"There isn't one seat you can give to him?" Troy asked with disbelief.

"Hey, I said no. It means no. You're not from around here, are you? I can tell by your clothes. You're one of the up-siders. Churches down here fill up fast. Can't you tell?" The soldier pointed behind the group.

The streets were full of civilians, all staring upward in anticipation at the vidscreens. It was incredible. The city seemed to stop just for the sermon. In their hands were the small pieces of parchment handed out by Roy. The unity this side of the city had was inspiring.

"What's the matter?" An older man dressed in regal robes approached them.

"Sir, you should be inside. It isn't safe out here." The soldier quickly readied his guard, two others running up to join either side of the pastor who stood beside them.

"Son, I grew up in these streets. I'll be fine. Now, what is the matter?" The older man seemed incredibly kind and gentle. His blue eyes were abnormally pale, indicating why he lived below.

"These people wanted to sit in on the sermon, but I told them we were already full."

"Pish-posh!" The older man waved at the soldier. "I cannot turn away a group needing prayer."

"I understand if you are full, but could you at least let our friend inside?" Aria asked, pointing at Dovian.

The pastor turned, facing the Sorcēarian. Giving a loud gasp, he immediately dropped to his knees. "My God!" he shouted, his eyes enlarging.

"Sir! Are you all right?!" the soldier asked.

"In all of my years…" the old man stammered. He quickly gestured a cross over his face and torso. Dovian observed him with an unreadable expression. "I never thought I would actually come face-to-face with a *real* Soldier of God!"

Dovian bowed his head slightly, remaining expressionless.

The other soldiers quickly followed the pastor's gesture, falling to their knees and pointing crosses over their bodies.

"You, you are a Sorcēarian, are you not?" the old man gasped. Aria feared he would drop dead at any minute from a heart attack.

"That I am," Dovian replied.

"Oh, Lord!" the old man wheezed again.

A couple of shocked cries and murmurs filled the streets as the civilians whispered to one another, the alarming message quickly traveling through the streets that there was a Sorcēarian present.

"I would like to sit in on your message if you don't mind," Dovian said.

"M-m-my message?" The pastor laughed. "My boy, I don't deserve a presence such as yours. Please, I would like to ask that you lead in today's prayers."

Dovian smirked. "It would be an honor."

"Oh, wonderful!" The pastor promptly stood. "Quickly! We must get ready! There has been a change in plans. Mr. uh, Sir," he stuttered, looking for a proper title for the Sorcēarian.

"Dovian," he offered his name to the old man.

"Dovian!" he shouted. "My good friend, Dovian, will lead the sermon today. And, please, allow his friends front row seats."

The pastor placed an arm on Dovian's back, slowly leading him up the small flight of stairs toward the entrance. Two militants pulled on the massive doors, majestically opening them for the Sorcēarian and pastor. The other soldiers guided the rest of the group in a similar fashion. Aria quickly looked over her shoulder, noticing Troy had not followed.

"Are you coming?" she asked, pausing.

"Naw." He waved at her. "Go ahead. I'll wait out here."

"Troy, you can't be out here alone." Aria descended the staircase and approached the man. He stared at the church, his expression slightly distressed. "Come on. What's wrong?" she asked.

"Nothing. Just go ahead. I'm not really into this kind of thing." He kicked at the cement with his boot, avoiding her stare.

Aria looked back at the others; they were impatiently waiting. "I'm going to stay out here with him. I don't want him to be alone out here. In case something happens, at least you'll be safe in the church."

"Should I stay, too?" Ivory asked nervously.

"No. Go ahead. Sit with James. It'll be okay. I'll be just outside the door watching on the screen," Aria reassured the other woman.

"Come on. You can sit with me." James wrapped his arm around Ivory's. "Those two will be all right."

"Okay," Ivory said slowly.

Quickly, the doors shut behind the small group. Aria shivered. The murmurs flooding the streets were a little overwhelming. She could also feel thousands of eyes upon her and Troy. 'Those who were friends with the Sorcēarian.'

After a couple of minutes, the screens turned on. Modern-style music began playing through the loudspeakers surrounding the corners of the streets. The live band used ancient instruments and had no electronics to change their voices while singing music with religious undertones. The songs were unlike anything Aria and Troy had ever heard before, but the townspeople knew them by heart as they sang along. It was more than a little strange. Aria felt like she had stepped onto another planet. Troy scoffed and folded his arms over his chest. He thought it all was a joke.

"My fellow people! I have glorious news today! As some of you have already noticed, God has graced us with an amazing gift! Today another will lead our sermon. But not just any man, but a Sorcēarian! That's right! The last remaining Sorcēarian from the forbidden land of Ives! He has come out of hiding during this time of turmoil that plagues our dreadful world to help humanity! Only a kind and blessed soul such as his can save us from the demons that have infested our land!" the pastor spoke through a tiny microphone wrapped around his ear. "Ladies and gentlemen, I present to you, Dovian!"

The streets filled with cheers and shouts as Dovian walked on stage. He seemed entirely in his element as he stood in front of the massive stained-glass window at the pedestal.

Troy wrinkled his nose. *'They're already idolizing him.'*

Dovian started. "It's been a long time since I've preached to you. In fact, I must apologize. I have lacked in my responsibilities for the past few thousand years. You see, I once had given up hope for your race. It's a terrible mistake that I should have never made, but I couldn't see the light at the time. Humanity has always been shrouded in darkness. When one goes looking for that light and can't seem to find even one small flicker, like a candle, he tends to lose hope after a while."

The crowd fell silent, eagerly looking upon the man in the scarlet robes. He watched them momentarily, his eyes showing uncertainty. "But now, by being here today, I see that I was wrong. Underneath this city is an entire civilization hidden by darkness, treated as outcasts. Seeing all of you here today reveals that you are even greater, shining brighter than the darkness that threatens to swallow you whole. My great-grandfather used to tell me, 'if you can find one man who believes, then the city is worth saving.' Belief is the keyword. Do you see? It isn't about living a good life with good morals. Sure, it helps, but in the end, it doesn't matter if you don't believe it. We are all sinners. Yes, I am included in that category. I was born on this earth just as you were. You all need to understand that it doesn't matter how many rituals you partake in. They are useless. There are no loopholes. No one is any more deserving than the last. Only one thing matters…and that is whether or not you believe. Whether or not you love." Dovian lifted his hand, pointing at the enormous cross hanging above him. "Have a little faith," he said with a gentle expression.

All around the outside, people surrounded the church. They gaped at the Sorcēarian on the vidscreen, their eyes glittering with hope as he spoke. There wasn't a single space left on the entire city block. It seemed that every civilian of the Underbelly spectated the live feed. It was history in the making.

"You don't really believe in this crap, do you?" Troy finally spoke up, watching Dovian from the outside.

Aria gave him a look of disbelief. "It's not crap, Troy," she said with irritation. "It's kinda hard not to believe when you have a living Sorcēarian on the stand!"

"Oh, come on! Bullshit," Troy said in a sharp tone. Aria was blown away. Was he going to argue with her in front of the crowd while Dovian preached his sermon?

"The fact that he's thousands of years old is an anomaly. And what about those monsters out there? Explain those!" she said.

"That's exactly what they are—monsters! And yes, Dovian is an anomaly. He's some crazy guy with some weird genetic anomaly that allowed him to live without aging for a long time. Or, for all you know, he can be a crazy man feeding us lies! We have no proof that he's thousands of years old."

Aria gawked at Troy, astonished. Was he serious?

"But what about his intelligence? His science…or magic-like abilities?" she asked.

"Magic? It's like he said, Aria, it's science. He's smart, sure, but still crazy! He's had years to develop stuff like that. He could be from another military, infiltrating Bio-Tech for all you know. He could be a traitor, a spy." Now he was just grasping at straws.

"I can't believe you're questioning this," Aria said, keeping her voice down. She grabbed Troy's arm and led him away from the crowd, toward a small alleyway unoccupied by civilians. He didn't struggle with her. He at least had the decency to argue in private, as if he hadn't embarrassed her already.

"I can't believe you…believe this! Aria, the no-bullshit kinda gal, falling for this man's brainwashing!" he shouted once they were in the clear.

"Brainwashing?! You sound like a conspiracy theorist, Troy!" she growled back.

"Conspiracy Theorist?" He raised his eyebrows, showing he was offended.

"Yeah…like how the military brainwashed you? You sound like those people on the streets trying to shut the militaries down."

"And you sound like a gullible fanatic," he retorted.

Aria's mouth twitched into a crooked smile. "You know what it is? You're afraid of the truth, aren't you?"

He scoffed at her. "What truth?"

"The possibility that there may be something more to all of this."

"Like what? That there's a God? Something that no one's believed in for thousands of years? It wouldn't have fallen through the cracks if it were true!"

"Then explain all of these people! You can believe in aliens, but you can't believe in this?" she asked, her anger rising.

"You want to know what happens when you're dead? Nothing! Nothing happens! You just die!" he shouted at her, making her flinch. Aria had never seen him so angry, and it frightened her.

The truth was—Troy was scared. He was afraid of many things, but none of them he would admit. In a couple of weeks, his entire world had turned upside-down, and now everything in his happy, little lifestyle was being questioned.

"But where's the harm in believing? I mean, if nothing happens, nothing happens. No harm done. But what if something does happen? I don't want to think about what the rest of eternity would be like if I had the opportunity to simply believe in something and had forsaken it all for my own ego," she said spitefully, her eyebrows knitting together.

Troy stepped forward, making the woman lean back against the wall. His eyes widened. "Ego? My ego?"

Finally getting more than irritated with her partner, she stepped forward, matching his angry tone. "Yeah. You don't want to admit that maybe you're wrong about something."

"Damn it, Aria! Ever since Dovian showed up, you've been acting like a lunatic!

You're living in this crazy fantasy world! Not to mention, you're sleeping with your priest!"

His last statement blindsided her. "Excuse me?" she asked, dumbfounded.

"Yeah. You're going to believe that hypocrite?"

"He's just as guilty as you and I. He's not perfect," she defended Dovian.

"No, but you sure do seem to think he is," he sneered. Troy turned away, running his hands through his hair.

"Is that what this is all about? Dovian? You're jealous of Dovian?" she asked in amazement.

He quickly spun back around to face her, his expression livid. "Jealous?! Aria, who you screw is your own damn business. I just don't want to hear about these lies he's putting into your head. And you know what? *You're* the one who's scared. You're the one who's afraid of dying. You can't simply let go. People die. There's nothing you can do about it. Stop holding onto the past. This stuff is idiotic and nothing but a huge waste of time. We should be out there stopping whatever those things are, not sitting in Bible study." He turned again, beginning to walk away.

'Oh, hell no, is this argument over? Aria seethed mentally.

She pushed away from the wall. "Idiotic? So, now I'm an idiot? Why? Cause I have an open mind? Because I read books? There's so much more to life than killing people and watching TV!" she screamed, no longer caring if anyone overheard their shouts.

Troy faced her, pointing a finger at her chest. "And you think you're better than me? Cuz you read books? Cuz you sit there by yourself in your sad, little apartment reading about things that don't exist?" His tone was bitter and icy, cutting deep into Aria's heart. "There's an entire world out there full of people, Aria. And you're missing it all because you feel so goddamn sorry for yourself. Maybe, if you weren't such a know-it-all bitch all the time, you'd find something to live for. You wouldn't have to worry about this life-after-death bullshit because you'd be living in the *now*." He glared at her, unmoving, ready for her reply.

Aria's mouth gaped open, twitching as she tried to form her words. Her eyes glimmered with tears. "And what about our parents? What about Gavin? You don't want to think that there's a possibility you'd see them again?"

"Why worry about Gavin now? You never gave a damn when he was alive." Troy halted and stared at the ground, avoiding the hurtful expression he had just caused Aria to have. He took a deep breath, trying to calm down. "Listen, you believe what you want to believe; just don't try to drag me into your hypocritical, sad lifestyle." He gave her one quick look, his eyes narrowing with hate. He turned away from her once again.

"You asshole!" Aria shouted. Bending over, she picked up a crushed soda can.

Crying out, she lugged the piece of trash at Troy, the item hitting him in the back of the head. She jumped as he spun around, his enraged expression like nothing she had ever seen. Glaring, he pointed at her again. She stared, matching his angry gaze the best she could.

"You may not be a lady, but I'm still *not* going to hit you. But, if you do that shit again, I will punch you in the face, got it?" he said, his jaw clenched.

"Fuck off," she barely managed to utter as tears filled her eyes.

Giving a rough wave with his arm, Troy walked away into the thundering, cheering crowd. A small whimper erupted from Aria as she leaned back against the stone wall. Slowly, she slid to the ground, her hands covering her face as she gave in to her emotions. She sobbed, the sound hidden by the constant cheers and praise the civilians gave.

'He hates me. He really, truly hates me.' Never in her life had she felt so alone. A tiny wail escaped as she cried, "Why am I such a fuckup?"

"Waiting"

CHAPTER 18

Loud applause and conversation roared throughout the streets of the Underbelly, suffocating the sounds of Aria's sobs and shaking breaths. She remained in the dark alleyway during the celebration, hidden from any bystanders on the streets. Her knees were tucked against her chest as she covered her head, wishing she could disappear and go home back to a time when things were normal. She gripped her black hair and tried to stop the harsh cries heaving from her chest. Not only was she embarrassed, but she felt like a child. Her self-disgust only made her pain worse as her brain mercilessly flickered through every terrible memory she had where she lost someone she loved. It left her feeling empty and alone. Her self-pity consumed her, and her more practical side cursed her for appearing so weak and helpless. It was time to grow up.

'Stop feeling sorry for yourself,' her mind lectured.

"Aria?" The voice belonged to Mr. Clarke. "Aria, my dear, what happened?"

The woman suddenly stopped her cries and lifted her head, wiping at her tear-streaked face.

"N-nothing," she replied harshly.

Clarke chuckled. "You're a terrible liar. Your face gives you away, regardless."

Aria frowned, staring at her boots. James crouched beside the woman, placing a hand on her shoulder.

"Something I need to know about?" he asked her.

"No," she replied meekly.

"Tell me anyway," he replied softly.

Aria turned her head toward the older man, her face contorting as she sobbed again. "Troy hates me!" she squealed.

Clarke gave her a look of shock. "What? My dear, whatever gave you that idea?"

Taking a couple of shallow breaths, she replied, "We had a fight. We've been arguing a lot lately. I don't know. Ever since Gavin…he's just been different."

"I'm sure he's only stressed just as you are. Neither one of you took Gavin's death well. Truthfully, I was quite shaken by the news as well. But to say that Troy hates you is a bit of a stretch. He needs you now more than ever."

"How do you know? You didn't see the way he yelled at me." Aria folded her arms, still feeling quite unprofessional while talking about such a private matter to the president of Bio-Tech. But then again, James was the closest person she had to a father. Besides, he wouldn't let her go quietly. The only solution was to spill her guts now or wait in the alley all night until she gave in.

Clarke sat beside the woman, groaning a bit as he did so. Neither one of the two noticed the silhouette watching from the end of the alley.

'You're a damned asshole.' Troy glared at Aria and Mr. Clarke. His anger, however, was directed at himself this time. He had returned a few minutes after the argument to apologize to his partner but was too late as Mr. Clarke had beat him to her side. It was an understatement to say he felt awful about what he had said to Aria. Troy had succeeded in only taking his anger out on her, and her quiet sobs were like a stab to his own heart as he realized he had only caused her more unnecessary pain. Watching Clarke run his hand over the woman's back as she quietly talked to him was more than enough. He'd have to deal with her later. Clarke was better at comfort than he was anyway. Besides, being near Troy was probably the last thing Aria wanted.

His expression faded to one of regret, and he slowly turned away from the alleyway, nearly running into Dovian's chest as he did so. The two men stood awkwardly, staring at one another for a few moments. Dovian finally tore his eyes away to peer at the two sitting in the alley. As he returned his attention to Troy, the soldier stepped around the Sorcēarian, not saying anything. His expression and energy gave everything away. Dovian had a fairly good idea of what had transpired between Aria and Troy. He also walked away from the scene, not wanting to interrupt the much-needed conversation.

"I know because I watched you two grow from small children to the wonderful adults you are now," Clarke replied. "Sometimes, the ones that are closest to you are the ones who can hurt you the most. I seriously doubt that Troy meant a single unkind thing he said to you."

"I don't know about that. I've never seen him like this before. I think I finally did it. I pushed him away for good this time." Aria sniffled, her crying fit finally under control.

"Ridiculous. He's loved you since the day you both met," James said humorously. Aria scoffed. "No, he hasn't!"

"It's true! I'm not lying. Trust me; you'd know if I were." He looked down at Aria as she stared up at him, waiting for him to continue. "He asked me the first day he saw you, 'who's the girl with the pretty black hair?' I told him, 'that's Aria; she's new here.' He said that you were beautiful and didn't look like you belonged at Bio-Tech, and he firmly stated that he would protect you. Then he said I couldn't *ever* tell you that he said that, or he would shoot me. I think he was serious about it, too, but that was so long ago, I don't think he'd worry about it now," James chuckled.

Aria remained silent, not quite believing what the man had told her.

"And from that moment, I knew it was best to have Troy always at your side." James nodded.

"Why?" Aria asked.

"Because, who will protect you better than someone who loves you?" James asked with amusement. A red hue tinged her cheeks. She suddenly wanted to hide. "How many times has he saved you?"

Aria pondered a moment. "Too many to count," she quietly replied.

"And what about you? How many times have you helped him?" Clarke questioned.

'Well, there was the time I almost blew his head off in the 66th I.R.B.' She cringed at the thought, but she understood what Clarke meant.

Aria sniffed, dabbing her nose with her sleeve. "He's all I have left." Staring at her hands, she shook her head. Clarke watched her, frowning at her distress. "And he may have thought that at one time, but I don't think he does anymore," she added.

"M-Mr. Clarke?" Ivory's voice interrupted the conversation. Clarke swiftly looked over his shoulder at the tall blonde, revealing Aria sitting beside him. "Oh, I'm sorry. I didn't mean to interrupt. I-I couldn't find anybody. I got worried."

"It's all right, Ivory," James reassured the young woman. "I was just talking with Aria, that's all."

"Are you all right, Aria? You look awfully sad," Ivory stated the obvious.

Aria slowly and audibly blew out a deep breath. "I'm fine. Only tired, that's all." She stood, dusting off her backside. "Come on, let's find the others."

"Call me if you have any further troubles, you hear me?" Clarke said under his breath as he and Aria joined Ivory's side. Aria, frowning, gave a short nod.

Walking into the massive crowd in the streets, Aria finally didn't feel like the entire world spotlighted upon her. She and the other two slowly made their way through the bustling horde, which faced one direction. It made it easy to locate Dovian, the object of everyone's attention. Underbelly civilians surrounded him, and he appeared slightly distraught as each person asked their eager questions and pleaded with him to heal their genetic disorders while others wanted autographs.

"Dovian?" Ivory chirped.

Her tiny voice, though quiet, was easily picked up by the Sorcēarian's ears. He quickly turned his attention to her and then said to the crowd, "I'm sorry, but I must go. I have much work to do, and if you'd like me to help defend your race against these demons, I'll have to leave now." Swiftly, he dodged the many hands reaching out to him and made his way to the others' sides. "Quickly…" he said with distress, leading the way toward the side streets where Troy watched from afar.

Troy pushed away from the wall he leaned against and quickly joined them. He locked eyes with Aria; the expression he held was pathetic and puppy-like. She twisted her mouth, trying not to give in to his apologetic look.

"The private plane leaves in a little less than an hour. I already have everything set up, so you can go straight through customs without any trouble. I want you to call me as soon as you land in Roma," James advised, his authoritative tone returning. "We'll discuss further details once you arrive."

Aria nodded.

"Ivory?" A small and unfamiliar voice called out over the roar of the crowd. "Ivory?!"

The group stopped and turned to face a young woman rushing toward them, barely out of her teens.

"Oh, my God! Is that really you?!" she shouted. The girl looked highly distressed as she trotted toward them, her blue eyes wide with shock. Her hair was a tangled mess of blonde that bounced with each step she took; she had pale skin, and her frame was tall and slender. She wore an oversized pastel-blue knitted sweater that hung off one shoulder, tattered jeans, and colorful sneakers. Her small hands gripped a locket around her neck. The resemblance was more than a little alarming. The girl was the spitting image of Ivory. "It's impossible! You can't be Ivory!"

"Who…who are you?" Ivory asked nervously, and her hands clamped over the small dog tag hanging from her neck.

"It's me, Fiona. I…I'm your sister," the girl replied with matching anxiety.

Ivory gasped, holding a hand to her lips. Everyone else in the group had similar, stunned expressions. Was the young woman actually Ivory's little sister? Could they possibly figure out Ivory's mysterious past?

Pulling at the locket, Fiona opened it and apprehensively revealed a holographic photo. Sure enough, the woman in the picture looked identical to Ivory.

"But," the girl shook her head, tears welling in her eyes, "it can't be you. You can't be Ivory. You should be dead. I watched you; I watched you die. I watched *her* die."

"Die?" Ivory's voice pitched higher with her confusion.

"It's just, you look so much like her! I'm sorry. I just had to be sure I didn't see a ghost." Fiona shook her head again, wiping her eyes as she turned away from the group.

"Wait!" Aria called out to the girl. "You know Ivory? You really know who she is?"

"You mean her name *is* Ivory?" Fiona nearly stumbled over her own two feet.

Ivory quickly nodded, lifting her dog tag to reveal the simple name engraved on the metal plate. Fiona looked at it carefully, her mouth gaping open. Though she was tall, she only stood as high as Ivory's shoulder.

"This doesn't make sense. You were never in the military." Fiona frowned. "Who are you?"

"I, I don't know. I don't remember any of my past. At least, nothing more than a week ago," Ivory replied.

"You…you died over a year ago," Fiona said.

Dovian locked eyes with Ivory. She quickly looked away from the large man.

"How can she be dead? She's standing right here," Troy asked. He was just as confused as the two girls.

"I'm not lying. I have the ashes at home! They're on a shelf beside the window, Ivory's favorite place to sit. It's the only window in the entire house," Fiona said.

"How?" Ivory asked. "How did I die?"

Everyone remained silent, watching the young woman.

"As I said, it was over a year ago. We went to the movies. To see that show about the butterflies. You always liked those silly, light-hearted films. But when we were walking home, we were attacked." Fiona covered her mouth, letting out a soft cry. "It was a group of men. They…." She looked upwards, trying to keep her tears from falling. "Uh, they didn't like how different we were. They called us names, and then they started throwing trash at us. One of the men grabbed me, and you tried to step in. It was then that…they beat and raped us, then tried to kill us. I, I survived." She lifted her golden curls on one side of her head, revealing a large, round scar. It was a bullet wound. Fiona had survived a shot to the head. "But you…you didn't make it. I had to cry out for help, but no one ever came. Finally, I had enough strength to crawl to the police station a few blocks away. By the time they got to you, you were long gone. There was no way to save you." Fiona frowned, staring up at Ivory with saddened eyes. Hesitantly, she pulled Ivory's hair to the side, revealing a matching scar on the right side of her head. Fiona gasped, tears falling. Dovian's hands reflexively clenched.

Fiona quickly stepped back. "They sent your body to the crematories. We were given a jar a few days later, and we had a small funeral for you."

"We?" Ivory asked, suddenly feeling dizzy.

"Dad and I…and a couple of our friends," Fiona answered.

"Mom?" Ivory asked with a quivering voice.

Fiona lowered her head. "Mom died a long time ago. She was attacked, too. It's why dad never wanted us to go out alone."

"Dad? Where is he?" Ivory asked. Her face held a blank expression as she placed a small hand on Dovian's shoulder, trying to regain her balance.

"Are you all right?" he cautiously asked.

Fiona shook her head from side to side. "Dad died a few months ago…terrible mining accident."

Ivory gasped, her eyes wide and pale, the pupils quickly shrinking in size. Giving a loud cry, she sprinted from the group toward the nearest building.

"Ivory!" Aria shouted along with Fiona. Together, the whole group followed the frantic woman.

Squeezing through the sliding door of a small restaurant, Aria and Fiona worriedly looked for the runaway blonde. Dozens of eyes laid upon them; dozens of others faced the opposite direction with concerned expressions.

"Bathroom," Aria sputtered, quickly running toward the back of the building.

Pushing through swinging doors, they entered a small bathroom with rock-inlaid floors. The countertops were made of reflective metals, the mirrors lined with faux gold and brilliant lamps. Though it was a small facility in the Underbelly, the bathroom was relatively clean and classy. They had entered one of the high-end restaurants, which was much to Aria's relief as she found Ivory unconscious in the middle of the public restroom's floor.

"Ivory!" Aria shouted, slamming to her knees to check the woman's vitals.

"What happened to her?" Fiona gripped her long sleeves with anxious worry.

"She does this from time to time. Now that we know what happened in the past, it's safe to say the bullet wound may have caused her amnesia and blackouts." Aria gently lifted Ivory's head and placed it in her lap.

"Is she going to be okay?" Fiona asked. She began to cry, pacing back and forth.

"Yeah, yeah. I think so." Aria shook the unconscious woman carefully. "Ivory." She glanced nervously at the sister. "Ivory!" she shouted.

Ivory's form began violently convulsing, and her mouth opened wide as she sputtered a harsh gasp. Fiona screamed, covering her face.

"Damn it! Get help! We need help!" Aria called out. "Dovian!"

Fiona quickly trotted toward the exit, her arms waving in the air as she stuttered to a halt before the door abruptly slammed open. Dovian, palm outstretched across the door's surface, held it against the stone wall. His eyes quickly dropped to Ivory's convulsing form. He swiftly approached the women.

"Hey! You can't go in there! That's the ladies' room!" someone shouted from the restaurant.

"Can it! We've got an emergency here!" Troy's voice sounded from outside the bathroom, where he kept watch.

"She's having a seizure," Dovian murmured, quickly tearing at one of the cloths hanging from his black robes beneath his red coat. He hastily rolled the fabric between his hands and placed it in Ivory's mouth. "Hold her jaw," he ordered. Aria promptly complied.

Ivory continued shaking, her blank eyes staring at the ceiling lights. Fiona stood in the bathroom corner, bawling, holding her sleeve-covered hands over her mouth.

"Ivory!" Dovian shouted, his hands glowing with blue light. He gently placed one hand on her head, the other behind her neck. "I need you to calm down. Calm down, Ivory."

Dovian closed his eyes, concentrating on the power coursing through his hands. He tried to visualize Ivory's brain to find the scar tissue, the misfiring neurons. Nothing, he couldn't sense anything. And he was alarmed by this.

"Ivory!" he shouted.

The tremors caused the poor blonde to make horrible moans. After a few more seconds of aggressive tremors, Ivory's arms shot out to the side, violently shoving Dovian against the countertop behind him. The Sorcēarian's large body crushed through the metal surface before dropping to his elbows and knees, his staff clattering to the floor. He winced, reflexively placing a hand on his back.

"Don't you dare touch me!" Ivory's voice boomed with a foreign tone. She quickly stood, pointing an accusatory finger at Dovian. "You loathsome, disgusting monster! You are a disgrace to our race! How can you do this? How?!"

"I…I'Lanthe?" Dovian gasped. His face held a look of both terror and shock.

"My name from your lips is like poison! You treacherous bastard! What have you done with Dovian?" she growled with eyes dark with hate.

Aria joined Fiona's side. Together, they watched the strange interaction unfold.

"What are you talking about? It's me. I'm Dovian," he said, slowly rising. Gently, he held out his hands toward the woman. "You're talking to Dovian."

Ivory gave him a skeptical look. They both stood rigidly still, watching each other with great caution. In the blink of an eye, she placed her boot underneath the staff and kicked it upwards, holding it in her hands. She quickly spun the weapon and aimed it directly at Dovian's head. He watched her with fearful eyes.

"And how do I know you're not one of his illusions?" she asked, breathing in slowly. Her jaw clenched tightly in anger.

"His illusions?" Dovian thought momentarily. Giving a small gasp, he made the connection. "Euclid? You think I'm one of Euclid's illusions?"

"Don't say his name! It's disgusting!" Ivory spat.

"No, I'm not one of his illusions. Lanthe, it's me, Dovian. I'm here, right now, standing before you," Dovian spoke slowly.

"Lanthe…" she repeated quietly. "Only Dovian and my closest friends call me Lanthe." Her eyes widened then. "But how?! Euclid has you locked up in the tower! How'd you escape?! How'd you get here?" She ran up to him, dropping the staff, the item clanging loudly within the stone and metal room. Desperately, she touched his face and shoulders.

Dovian looked down upon the woman. Ivory's eyes searched his features. Her questioning expression quickly turned into one of recognition. He watched with a hopeful smile, his heart pounding in his chest.

"Dovian!" she shouted, wrapping her arms around his neck. She held him tightly. "I can't believe it's really you. I was so afraid he was going to kill you!"

"He didn't kill me; I won't let him," Dovian whispered. He took a deep breath and stared at the ceiling, feeling overwhelmed.

Ivory quickly pulled away. "But why are you here? I told you to run away! You have to get out of—" She looked to the left and then the right, taking in her surroundings. "…here."

'No….' Dovian swallowed hard.

Ivory looked up at him. "Where am I?!" she asked with fear.

"Lanthe…." Dovian reached for the woman.

"Don't touch me!" Ivory shouted, stumbling backward. "Where am I?" She looked over her shoulder at Aria and Fiona. "Who are you?!"

"Lanthe, please!"

"No! No! This isn't right!" Ivory dropped to her knees, holding onto her head.

"Lanthe!" Dovian kneeled beside the woman.

"My name isn't Lanthe!" Ivory's small voice shrieked. She glared at Dovian, her blonde curls falling over her face. Her eyes were wild and mad.

Dovian halted, feeling his body freeze. He lost her. He lost I'Lanthe once again.

"Why do you keep calling me that? My name is Ivory!"

Dovian gaped at the blonde. His expression twisting into a look of sorrow. Ivory continued her glare, her eyes fixated upon his.

"Ivory?" Fiona asked quietly, interrupting the toxic silence.

Ivory spun, her angry expression quickly fading into one of joy. "Fiona!" She stood and embraced her sister, holding her tightly.

Aria stood in the corner, watching Dovian. He looked lost as he stared at the floor, sitting on his knees. If she didn't know any better, she'd guess he just had his heart broken all over again. The man's hands shook, gripping his robes. Aria waited for a response, anything from the Sorcēarian, but he remained on the floor, unmoving.

"Dovian," Aria whispered, taking a step closer to him.

Shocked, he looked at her. His usually vibrant eyes were nearly white, their electric blaze extinguished.

"Aria," he whispered, wiping at his face. "Back to reality, eh?"

"Was that her?" she spoke softly, helping lift the man. He felt extremely heavy in her grasp.

"I don't know. I thought it was," he murmured, watching Ivory and her sister hug.

"How is that possible?" she asked.

"Your guess is as good as mine." He raised his hood, shrouding his face in shadow.

Quickly, he picked up his staff and headed for the door. Aria started after him but halted, unsure how she would help the bizarre situation. As Dovian reached the exit, Troy's body slammed through, crashing into him. The two crunched against the stone wall, falling into a heap on the floor.

"Concussive shot!" Troy gasped with his hand pressed against his chest.

"Get to cover!" Aria shouted at Ivory and Fiona.

Pointing his staff at the door, Dovian shouted in Legacy, the sound booming in the small room. A large blue field erupted in front of the door, protecting the group from the sudden onslaught of gunfire. He helped Troy stand. "Are you all right?" he asked.

"Fine. Just had the wind knocked out of me," he coughed. Catching Aria's questioning look, he added, "Looks like Feyette's team found us."

"Shit!" she shouted.

They were unarmed. They had no weapons. The items were all in crates waiting to be loaded onto the plane.

"What are we going to do?" Fiona asked, cringing at the sound of the bullets.

"Make our escape," Dovian replied. Aiming his staff opposite the bathroom, he fired, and the stone blasted outwards. One by one, they filed outside, Dovian taking the rear. "Take cover immediately; we don't know—"

Plop! Boom!

Dovian froze, knowing the sound before he heard the horrifying screams from Ivory.

"FIONA!"

Fiona's thin body had been penetrated in the front by a sniper's round. Judging by the massive blood splatter on the wall behind her, it tore through her back, instantly killing her. Her lifeless body lay on the ground, and her blonde hair splayed across her face. Dark crimson pooled around her, soaking her pastel-blue sweater.

A small hand rested outstretched in Ivory's direction. Her locket lay open on her chest, the holographic image of her older sister flickering.

"NO!" Ivory reached for the young woman, struggling in Troy and Aria's grasp. "Fiona!" she painfully shrieked.

Another blast erupted, cracking against the wall's surface only centimeters from Ivory's head.

"We have to get to cover!" Troy shouted.

Ivory struggled a second longer.

"Dovian!" Troy shouted as he tugged on the fighting blonde's arm.

Dovian, eyeing the sniper on the church's rooftop, waved a temporary spell, casting a bright light around their general area to prevent the shooter from seeing them. He spun and tightly gripped Ivory's shoulders.

"Move! Now!" he ordered her.

"Fix her, Dovian. Fix her, please!" Ivory pleaded with him.

The words were identical, once again, to those from Dovian's past. He struggled with the memory, gritting his teeth as he fought with the blonde.

"I cannot. She is already gone," he said slowly.

"No! She isn't!" Ivory refused to listen to reason.

"She is! I cannot heal her now! She is gone!" Dovian hollered. Gripping the woman's chin, he forced her to look up at him. "I'm sorry, Ivory. There is nothing I can do. She is dead. The shot killed her instantly."

"No…" Ivory whispered, her lower lip trembling. Dovian ran a hand through her hair, keeping eye contact with the hysterical woman.

"She felt no pain. Now, please, you will kill us all if you do not move on," he said sternly.

Ivory tried to tear her eyes back toward her little sister. Dovian forced her to look at him again.

"Now," he ordered.

She finally let him pull her away from the body. The four quickly made their way through an alley and down a couple of blocks from the restaurant.

"Where's James?" Aria asked.

"He was outside. I don't know if they got to him," Troy replied.

"Damn it," Aria cursed.

"We have no weapons." Troy ran a hand through his hair. "We have no goddamn weapons!"

"I have one," Dovian said.

"We don't even know the number of soldiers there is. He could have the whole army for all we know," Aria snapped irritably.

Ivory sat against the wall, staring to the side, emotionless.

"I can take care of them. What other choice do I have?" Dovian asked.

"Die…you could die," Aria scoffed.

"I told you…I can't die." He smirked.

"Still doesn't mean I want to test it," she replied.

"Die…" Ivory murmured.

The three looked at the woman with worried expressions.

"They will all die," she said darkly.

"Over here!" a shout sounded from above.

"Cover!" Aria shouted.

They all darted to the sides. Dovian sent up a flare, hiding them from the enemy soldiers' view. Loud footsteps neared their location. Cocking weapons sounded, and within seconds, intense flashes from the soldiers' Ignition Rifles blasted down the alley, erupting in bright explosions against the surface of the walls and dumpsters. Aria and Troy crouched behind one large container, hands covering their heads. The rounds exploded and crystallized into tiny shards that rained against their bodies.

Ignition rounds were a nasty type of ammunition explicitly used by Feyette's unit. The ammo was like capsules of liquid fire. The containers exploded and instantly cooled upon impact, sending splintering shards into the target. It was nearly impossible to clean out a wound once hit by an Ignition round; the fragments were often so small that they were unseen by the human eye.

"We're totally going to die," Troy coughed, covering his mouth with his leather jacket. He tried not to breathe in the crystalline dust filling the air for fear of cutting up his lungs. Aria covered her face with a magnetized, form-fitting shroud that clipped to her ears. The electric-blue material hung before her face. The fabric magnetized with a tap against the gems in her earrings, tightening over her nose and mouth. Troy followed her advice, pulling his hooded mask over his face from the back of his military undershirt.

A loud shriek sounded, echoing amongst the chaos. It was Ivory.

"Was she hit?" Aria asked.

"I don't know; I can't see a damn thing in this bright light," Troy answered.

From the opposite side of the alley, Troy and Aria could hear the shouts of the soldiers as Dovian fought against them. Judging by the sound, he directed the military away from the two. Gunshots fired from above—sniper rounds. There followed a massive crash behind Aria and Troy as the body of one soldier fell against the dumpster they took cover behind.

"Shit!" Troy jumped. He looked up at the outstretched arm that was dislocated from the shoulder joint and dangled limply over the side of the canister.

Aria narrowed her eyes, inspecting the large hole in the man's torso. He took a shot point-blank in the chest.

"It's Ivory," Aria said. "She's taken one of their weapons."

Rapid-fire sounded continuously for a few minutes. Troy and Aria waited impatiently behind the dumpster, feeling utterly useless. Never in their life had they seemed more like amateurs since starting the dreadful mission at the 66th I.R.B.

"Die! You are all going to die!" Ivory shouted from the rooftops.

"I sure hope she isn't killing civilians," Aria mumbled.

"I don't think she's hit that point of crazy yet," Troy said with little doubt.

"You didn't see her freak out in the bathroom. She took Dovian down and was ready to kill him if needed." Aria glanced at her partner.

"Are we the only sane ones in this entire war?" Troy asked.

Aria's brow wrinkled. She never even thought about that. For the first time, she and Troy seemed like ordinary people.

"Die!" Ivory screamed again.

"Someone, please stop her!" Dovian's voice called out mentally to Aria and Troy. *"Ivory, listen to me—"* Dovian tried speaking to the blonde.

The bright light that flooded into the alleyway began to dissipate, finally allowing the two soldiers to see. The sight was not pretty. Broken and battered bodies filled the alley. Half of them had large holes in their torsos. Ivory was on a rampage, killing every soldier on sight, which delighted Aria, but apparently, she had lost control by Dovian's standards.

"Ivory!" Aria shouted.

"Up top." Troy pointed, catching the yellow and orange of Ivory's Cherno-style clothing.

Aria climbed atop the dumpster, avoiding the fallen soldier's body. She reached for the rungs of the ladder that led to the rooftop. Quickly, she and Troy ascended to the top. Peering over the edge of the building, Aria met the sight of the barrel of Ivory's weapon.

"Shit!" She ducked down just as a blast erupted into the building behind them, narrowly missing Aria's skull—the first time Ivory had ever missed.

"Did she just fire at you?" Troy asked.

"Yeah!" Aria wiped her forehead. "Ivory!" she shouted. "Ivory! Can you hear me?"

Silence filled the air.

"Ivory, it's me, Aria! Put down the weapon! Troy and I will get you to safety, all right?"

Still no response.

"I'm not sticking my head up there again," Aria whispered, looking down at Troy.

"Damn it. She's lost it." He quickly descended the ladder, sliding down the sides. "Now, we have the entire world against us."

"Not entirely," Aria said, following him.

"Dovian, Ivory's out of control. She almost shot me in the head." Aria pressed against her mental chip.

"I know; she shot me," Dovian replied.

"She shot you?!" Aria mentally screamed. Looking down at Troy, she spoke aloud, "She shot Dovian!"

"Holy shit!" Troy shouted, helping to guide her off the dumpster. "Is he okay?"

"Are you all right?" Aria asked.

"Just have a hole in my side; no big deal." Even Dovian sounded mentally fatigued.

"Damn it." Aria rested her hand on her forehead.

"What?" Troy asked. "What'd he say?"

"Just have a hole in my side, no big deal," she mimicked the Sorcēarian.

"Damn!" Troy tried to suppress his amusement. If it didn't kill Dovian, it didn't mean it didn't hurt. "So, what are we going to do?" he asked.

"How about this, for starters?" A male voice intruded.

General Feyette stood a couple of meters away from the couple. His hand gripped his side, blood dripping from a large wound that Ivory evidently caused. "You're coming with me to headquarters. You will be detained until further notice. Your investigation is over."

"The hell it is!" Troy shouted, stepping in front of Aria.

"Dovian, we've got trouble. Feyette's here," Aria alerted Dovian. She waited a few moments but received no response. *"Dovian?"* Now, she began to worry. What if Dovian wasn't all right? What if his wound was fatal? What would happen if Ivory shot him in the head?

Feyette looked amused, crookedly smiling as he pressed two fingers against the back of his ear. He stood for a moment, having a silent conversation with his soldiers.

"I want you to alert your blonde friend. She's coming with us," Feyette said.

In that instant, a group of four soldiers rounded the corner, each one gripping Dovian's arms and shoulders, dragging him across the rough cement. His body was limp, blood dripping in generous heaps from his middle onto the ground in dark splatters. His already pale skin was pure white. He appeared lifeless. One of the soldiers held his staff, inspecting it as they walked.

"Dovian!" Aria shouted.

"He can't hear you," Feyette chuckled.

"What did you do to him?" Troy asked.

"Nothing. Thanks to your little, rabid friend, he was dead when we found him." Feyette gave a crooked smile.

"No!" Aria gasped. It wasn't true. Dovian said it himself. He couldn't die.

"You're lying!" Troy shouted.

"Am I?" the General asked. Slowly, he tugged his sidearm from its holster. Turning, he approached the Sorcēarian. He stared at Dovian with dark eyes. "We don't need him alive. The autopsy alone will tell us more than we can imagine. Not only that, but with our cloning capabilities, we'll be able to use his blood, whether or not it courses through his veins." Feyette turned to the side, looking at Troy and Aria both. He raised his arm, took aim, and shot effortlessly at Dovian's head, the blast making direct contact with his left temple, blowing out the other side in crimson streaks. The soldiers carelessly dropped the Sorcēarian.

Aria screamed, covering her mouth as she dropped to her knees. Troy remained standing, guarding her. His chest heaved as he took deep breaths and watched the blood pour from Dovian's wounds. With a twitch, his teeth ground together as he tightened his jaw.

Dovian had told them he couldn't die, but he also said that, in the past, Euclid only perished once he was decapitated. Troy wondered if a shot to the head would be the equivalent.

"Prepare for evac," Feyette ordered his troops.

Aria stared at the downed Sorcēarian, her shaking hands covering her face. If Dovian were dead, there would be no hope for survival. The world was doomed.

"Dovian, wake up. Please wake up. Dovian!" she mentally called out. Still, he remained unmoving.

Feyette stood rigidly, with his fingers against his ear. He turned his gaze toward Aria from beneath his military hat, and Troy caught the gesture. The general continued his silent conversation for a few more seconds before nodding. "So sorry," he began, "but there's been a change in plans."

Feyette lifted his pistol once again, aiming it at Troy. "Mr. Walten has informed me that you two are no longer needed. I am to relieve you of your duties…permanently."

"You bastard!" Troy shouted. He stepped back, sheltering Aria even more. "Run…" he whispered to the woman, his eyes never leaving Feyette's. Aria gaped at her partner. Was he serious? She wasn't going to abandon him and let him die alone. "Run, Aria," he growled.

Feyette chuckled and aimed low at Aria's head. His finger pulled back on the trigger. And as soon as he did so, Dovian's arm shot outwards, snatching his leg. He pulled Feyette off balance, and the shot went wide, banging against the dumpster beside the woman. Feyette went down hard as Dovian tugged him to the ground. Pressing a hand against his chest, Dovian teleported and reappeared behind the soldier holding his staff. He kicked him in the back of the head, grabbed his weapon, and spiraled, cutting across two of the other soldiers' chests in one fluid motion.

The bodies limply fell onto the concrete. As Dovian made his attack, two eruptions sounded, and the other two enemies' torsos exploded out their backsides, hit by Ivory's rounds. Dovian aimed his staff at Feyette's head, glaring at him with fierce, glowing eyes.

"H-how?" Feyette stammered.

"It's a secret," Dovian snarled.

A second later, Ivory dropped to the ground, weapon in hand. She smirked at Aria and Troy.

"Are you sane now?" Troy gaped at the blonde. She appeared to be normal for the time being.

"All part of the plan," Ivory whispered, winking.

Aria sighed, folding her arms over her chest. "Next time, let us in on the plan!"

During the attack, Dovian had time to communicate with Ivory mentally. They formulated the plan silently to one another, quickly devising a way to fool Feyette and his men. At least they knew that Walten had plans to clone Dovian's DNA. For what purpose, they weren't sure, but the most logical reason was to create an army of Sorcēarians or genetically-modified soldiers. Still, they didn't know what was so special about Ivory.

Feyette lay on the ground, hands raised in defense against Dovian's staff.

"What do you want with Ivory?" Dovian asked in a grave tone.

"She's quite extraordinary," Feyette replied, glancing in the blonde's direction. "Couldn't let that little brat ruin our plans."

"You killed my sister! For what?!" Ivory asked, pressing the barrel against Feyette's cranium. "What the hell is so special about me?!"

They all remained still, waiting for the general's answer. When he gave none, Ivory cocked the weapon, ready to fire.

"I've got more than one round left. How many brains do you got?" she fervently asked.

Dovian smirked at the young woman's fire.

Feyette frowned, his eyes darting from Ivory to Dovian. "Okay, don't shoot," he grumbled.

They waited impatiently.

"You see…you are special because—" Feyette's eyes darted to the digital sky, then he smiled. It was the same arrogant, crooked smile he gave when he thought he had the upper hand with Troy and Aria. "That information is classified," he said smugly.

A black cord dropped between Dovian and Ivory from above. Wasting no time, Feyette snatched up the rope, and he was tugged upward at light speed toward a cloaked aircraft. Ivory quickly aimed and fired, the round catching the man's leg just before he disappeared. A burst of red painted the side of the invisible craft. The severed limb dropped, twirling through the air, and plopped against the concrete a few meters away. The sky flickered in distortion as the jet upped its thrusters and flew fast and far away from the Underbelly.

"Damn it!" Troy cursed.

"Got his leg," Ivory said a bit too cheerfully.

"And it was a good hit." Dovian nodded, eyeing the appendage.

"Aria!" It was James Clarke's voice. *"Are you there?!"*

"Yes! Are you all right?" she replied.

"I'm okay! I'm at the airport. Quickly! Get your asses over here ASAP! I have your jet ready for takeoff! We don't know when Feyette will show up with reinforcements."

"Roger that, sir! On our way now!" She turned to her team. "We've got to move out! Clarke's got the jet ready! Be armed and ready!" Kneeling, she grabbed one of the Ignition Rifles. Troy followed her advice.

Tactically running through the streets, Aria and Troy safely led the group toward the airport. Luckily, they were only a few blocks away. They could board and evacuate on one of the fastest jets to Roma within minutes.

At the last corner, Aria spun and looked to the right. Troy took the left. Together, they scoped out the airport. The sight was dreadful.

"Careful. Watch your twelve," Dovian mumbled, pointing straight ahead. Troy and Aria quickly retreated.

An entire fleet of militants marched from the entrance of the airport. They lined the front of the facility. There was no way in without getting caught.

"James, we have a problem," Aria stated mentally.

"Already on it. Wait a moment," James replied.

Aria and the others waited impatiently as the soldiers neared their position. They all had weapons at the ready and aimed down the alleys and corners of the airport. They even searched the fake plants outside the entrance. Within moments, Feyette's men were only meters away.

"Come on, James…" Aria whispered.

Like an answer to her prayers, someone launched a grenade in the general vicinity of the militia. It signaled the start of the rebellion. In seconds, the streets were full of the Underbelly's civilians, all armed to the teeth with antiquated weaponry. Even the Soldiers of God acted, their rifles blasting accurately at the enemy soldiers' heads. Soldiers of God were flawless fighters, few and far between compared to the regular militaries. They were a valuable asset, and Aria was proud to have them on her side.

"Anyone who's an enemy of the Sorcēarian is an enemy of humanity!" one person shouted.

"They are against us all!" another screamed.

"Down with the system!" a third rallied.

Whether it was for Dovian and his friends or the sake of the Underbelly, the people weren't going to let Feyette's men go without a fight.

"Go! Move! Get to terminal 5!" James shouted to Aria.

"Roger!" she replied.

Signaling the others, she rounded the corner, giving cover fire as they darted inside the airport. The battle continued inside, the thundering of ammunition nearly deafening. The security guards at the facility helped cover the four as they made their way to the terminal. Aria and the others sprinted down the halls, firing when necessary. They jumped over the staircases, tucking and rolling as they landed. Ivory seemed to do the same without any issues, just as expected. More civilians crashed through the facility's doors as they neared the proper terminal. A violent uprising had started between the lower plate and the upper plate's military—Walten's private army. It was unheard of and, yet again, history in the making.

"Are you there?" James asked.

Aria darted into the terminal marked with a 5, explosions bursting around them. Some shrapnel hit one of the bulletproof windows, cracking its surface. The airport began depressurizing, allowing the high-velocity winds to gust through. The long corridors of the facility acted as a funnel, pulling in the harsh winds. The force knocked Dovian back, and he struggled to slip into the terminal's tunnel. The others looked back, calling out to him. Taking two thumping steps, he pulled himself in with the help of Ivory, his cape whipping behind him.

"Aria?!" James shouted.

They rounded the corner, the aircraft's door open as the engines purred loudly. With pounding footsteps, they raced inside. Once all four were in, the door slammed shut behind them, and the aircraft instantly pulled out, turned, and sped away from the center plate, high into the air.

"In!" Aria finally replied. *"We're in!"*

"Thank goodness…." James' frequency faded momentarily. They were pulling away too fast. *"Call…Roma—Ugh!"*

'What was that?' Aria felt her heart jump.

"James! James?!" she mentally shouted.

There was no reply.

The radio at the front of the jet crackled with static. "The President's been hit! I repeat! The President's been hit!" A frantic voice called through the channel. After a few minutes, there were no more alerts as the jet was already one hundred kilometers away.

Aria's blood felt like ice. Was James okay? She glanced at Troy, who held a similar, troubled expression. She ran her hands over her face, massaging her skin where the tight shroud had earlier been.

"We'll be in Roma soon. I'll call him then," she said tiredly, trying not to worry.

"Dress Civilian"

CHAPTER 19

Roma was a vast city decorated with marble statues and pillared buildings that touched the sky. The maroon banners, which waved in the chilly December air, hung from the streetlamps, connecting one side of the city to the other from a center joint where the festivities would later occur. Roma was one of the few remaining city-states that held onto traditional celebrations and culture. The citizens readied for the masquerade to celebrate the end of the thirty-year war. Some already donned intricately decorated masks and dress clothes. With the people were a multitude of androids—artificially made to look like humans but still lacking the necessary features to have them mistaken as such. Androids were often used as servants, but they weren't always considered simple tools as some of the robots also wore similar masks and seemed eerily as excited for the night's events as the humans were.

Roma was a highly technologically advanced city-state and the top-rated city in the world for beauty. Because of the use of solar and wind energy as a form of power, there were no reactors to operate the metropolis, which meant no reactor cores for Euclid to steal. Because of its natural energy form, Roma was also the cleanest city-state in the world, with Fountains in a close second. Besides its sanitary ways, Roma's pride and joy rested in its mechanical androids. Over three-quarters of Roma's military were robotic and drone-operated, significantly reducing human casualties from the constant warfare.

"Welcome to Roma. Your luggage has already been retrieved and will be placed in your rooms. We have your suites reserved. Please see the front desk for your key numbers." A robot bowed to Aria and her group as they exited their cab and neared the entrance to the massive gold-encrusted hotel.

"Wow…luxurious." Ivory gawked at the monstrous facility before her.

"Better than Cherno and Saray, that's for sure," Troy agreed.

Aria shook her arm, trying to get better reception on her DNAIS as she tried for the fortieth time to call James Clarke. Her brow furrowed as she groaned in irritation.

"Don't forget about tonight's festivities! The Pendant Hotel is the key point of interest for the night. We'll have live bands playing for the masquerade in our ballroom. Also, a massive feast will be held in the town's center before the dance! Free for all!" A female-voiced droid happily bounced as she spoke to the small group. She handed a pamphlet to Dovian.

"Thank you…." Dovian eyed the machine cautiously. He slapped the pamphlet against his hand as he looked at his surroundings. Roma had changed a lot from the last time he had ventured to it, but it still held some familiar aesthetics—stone, marble, Renaissance-inspired architecture, and an overall artistic theme.

"Anything?" Troy asked Aria.

"No…I can't even get a signal through." She frowned.

"It's all right. I'm sure he's okay." Troy shoved his cold hands into his jeans. A frigid gust tugged his military jacket and whipped through his chestnut hair.

"Hope so," she muttered, slowly climbing the steps of the Pendant Hotel.

The lobby of the hotel was extravagant. The marble floor twisted with specks of sparkling gold. The vaulted ceiling was covered with an ancient painting depicting strange scenes of people floating in the sky, individuals wearing drapery and robes, and a centerpiece depicting a nude man casually reclined with a finger pointing outward toward another finger belonging to an older man with long silver hair and a beard. Many wouldn't recognize the significance, but Dovian did.

"My God…they turned the Sistine into a hotel." Dovian stared at the ceiling in disbelief. He felt like crying at the sheer dreadfulness of the idea, let alone seeing it with his own eyes.

"State your names," a droid ordered from behind the front desk.

"Um, Ivanov. Aria Ivanov." Aria, distracted from her DNAIS, looked up at the clerk.

"No name in database."

Aria looked at Troy with confusion.

"Clarke," Troy tried.

"Twenty names with 'Clarke' in the database. Please state your first name." The droid clicked and beeped as it ran its program.

"James Clarke," Troy sighed.

"Denied. No 'James Clarke' in database," the droid replied.

"That's strange." Aria's forehead wrinkled. "Can you try Courtney Clarke?"

"One 'Courtney Clarke' in registry. Party of four."

"That'll be it," Aria said. "He must've kept our names off any systems in case Walten did some searching," Aria whispered to Troy.

Courtney was the name of James' digital secretary, named after his late fiancé. They never married; the woman, pregnant with James' child, had died in a plane crash caused by the Cherno military days before the wedding. It was a safe name that few knew about, one reserved for such situations.

"Please scan your DNAIS." The android pointed to the scanner beside it.

Troy and Aria quickly swiped their arms across the scanner.

"Two do not have DNAIS systems. They are damaged," Aria said.

"My apologies. I see that now in the special notes section of the registry. You will have to swipe your cards to access your rooms." The robot quickly dispensed two cards. "For security purposes, scan your thumbprint." The robot pointed at the scanner.

Ivory quickly scanned her finger. The receptionist then handed her a card.

"Next." The robot turned to Dovian.

Dovian hesitated, watching the robot with skepticism. He noticed Aria's glare and quickly complied with the request.

"Welcome to Roma. I hope your stay is joyous," the robot monotonously said. A chime sounded, and a new message fell through its speaker system. "Attached to your DNAIS or keycards is your Pendant Hotel ticket! You have access to all the extraordinary events of tonight's masquerade! Enjoy your fill of wine and tasty delicacies at tonight's ball!"

"Thanks," Aria muttered, leading the group to the massive, maroon-colored staircase with golden guide rails.

Taking the ornate elevator to the top level, Aria was awed by the beauty and size of the hotel. She and the others had the whole floor to themselves, divided into four rooms. She paused before the curtained window at the end of the hall. Through it, she could see the entire vastness of Roma. The day was already fading into night. The pale orange of the setting sun cast a beautiful glow against the silver, gold, and maroons of Roma. As the light faded, the artificial candles inside the streetlamps flickered aglow. Aria wanted to cry. It was the most beautiful thing she had ever seen in her entire life. James knew that she had always dreamed of traveling to Roma. She had gotten close several times in battle but never reached the city's walls. Quickly stiffening her twitching mouth, she sniffed and strode to her room's door.

"Well, James certainly spared no expense on this trip," she spouted, a small laugh escaping her.

Knowing that Aria was a hopeless romantic, Troy caught her trembling expression as she quickly swiped her wrist across the scanner on her door. The others slowly made their way to their rooms.

"Uh, I guess we should get ready for the masquerade," Aria mumbled, turning to the group. "We don't know what Euclid will do if he attacks. I want to be alert, even if he doesn't plan to attack tonight. We must keep our eyes peeled. The masquerade will keep us hidden. Meld with the people and try not to stand out. Dovian, I know that will be hard for you. I'd like you to keep watch outside for most of the night."

Dovian nodded to her.

"What about me?" Ivory asked quietly.

"You don't stick out quite as much as Dovian does. Keep close to Troy and me throughout the night. If anything happens and we get separated, get to Dovian," Aria advised.

"Got it." The blonde nodded.

The four stood quietly outside their rooms.

"Well," Troy cleared his throat, "let's check out our rooms! The dance starts in a couple of hours!" he cheerfully said as he looked down at his wrist.

"Sounds lovely!" Ivory clapped her hands.

Aria nodded and quickly entered her room, closing the door behind her. Blowing a puff of air out from between her lips, she stared at the enormity of her majestic suite. She moaned, laughing quietly. Her bed was monstrous, large enough to fit three people. With the burgundy curtain pulled aside, a window that spanned an entire wall overlooked the city. The room had a small silver and gold kitchen and a hallway leading to a spacious bathroom with the fanciest automated shower she had ever seen. The hotel room was as large as her apartment. In the center of it all was a giant marble statue of a man in the nude. He stood contrapposto, an arm holding a sling over his shoulder with his head turned to face Aria as she entered the room.

She smiled. "Hello, David."

Carefully walking up to the statue, she ran her hand along the thick pane of glass that encased the masterpiece. She narrowed her eyes at the gold plaque on the pedestal of the figure. The woman couldn't help but roll her eyes as she looked at the artist's name.

"Artist: Michelangelo or Da Vinci. Records of origins have been lost."

"Michelangelo," she scoffed. "Come on, people." She smiled.

Aria's father may have been a history professor with greater knowledge than average, but Aria's mother was an adept artist and musician. Hanging in her mother's studio was a poster of this exact sculpture. She would tell Aria all about the classic artists of the ancient past. She also owned many old books that were once considered illegal; therefore, they were incredibly valuable as all the others were burned long ago. Now, the items sat safely on Aria's bookshelf.

Twirling toward her bed, she noticed the luggage resting beside it. Casually, she hoisted Clarke's baggage he had prepared for her onto the mattress. She curiously opened the item and squeaked an excitable laugh. She removed a cobalt blue garment, letting it unfold as she lifted it.

It was a dress, the most elegant of its kind. It had cap sleeves and a tight drop-waist bodice lined with sparkling jewels that crossed the middle and twirled into a gathering on one side of the chiffon-tiered fabric that flowed to the ground. Aria's eyes dropped to the v-cut neckline. She shifted the dress, and its iridescent fabric sparkled in the light. It was more than beautiful. James definitely spared no expense.

Underneath the dress was a black filigree mask intricately woven with spiraling designs. Matching blue gems sat at the center, slightly above the eye holes at a pointed tip. Attached was a handwritten note.

'Have fun at the masquerade.

—James'

"James," Aria whispered with a small smile. He was doing this all for her. In the middle of the most dangerous mission of their lives, the riskiest of humanity's wars, he thought of her and indulged in her childish fantasies. Aria frowned, her hand trailing over the jewels on the gown.

"I hope you're okay," she whispered sadly.

"You did what?!" Sapphire shrieked.

Her shrill voice made Mr. Walten jump in his leather chair.

"With the rebellion and all…I, I had no choice!" the man stammered.

"You had no choice? You had no choice?!" she repeated. "You called out your military, fine, but then you summoned my pets to do your bidding?! You're lucky I don't kill you right now!" she screamed, the sound distorting over the speakers of Walten's vid-com.

"Please understand my situation!" Walten pleaded.

"Understand *my* situation, Mr. Walten," the child said lethally. Her grayish-blue eyes glared at him through the vidscreen. "You can order around your soldiers any time you like, but you are *not* to touch my pets, understand? You roused my demons on the day of the Sabbath and killed thousands! Even a priest! You, sir, are most certainly cursed now. His eye is surely upon you for stepping over the line. Even I know better than to attack today!" The child was livid, and, for once, Walten was glad he remained locked up safe inside his office away from her. "Since you decided to make this asinine move, His eye is most certainly looking upon me now!"

"B-but isn't that what we wanted? We wanted Him to notice?" Walten asked.

"NO!" Sapphire shouted. After a second, her expression relaxed. "No, not yet. We have a very delicate procedure to follow, Mr. Walten. I cannot have you interfering again. If you do, I will see that you reach the afterlife prematurely. Understand?"

Walten stared deep into the hellish eyes that watched him through the monitor. How a small child could scare him so much was unknown. The man swallowed thickly.

"I, I understand," he said quickly.

"Good. Now, find Clarke. He's only caused us trouble since the beginning. I want you to dispose of him…now!" Sapphire quickly pounded on the armrest of whatever she was sitting on, the screen abruptly fading to black—the room filled with a humming silence.

Walten licked his lips, his hands shaking as he poured a drink. A sudden sound brought his caramel eyes to the front of his office. Appearing out of thin air, Euclid and two of Sapphire's beasts stepped out of the shadows. The creatures sat on their haunches like dogs with large chains wrapped around their necks. The shackles were gripped firmly in one of Euclid's hands. He smiled crookedly at the CEO of Bio-Tech.

"Well, shall we?" Euclid asked.

"I'll show you what room he is in." Walten quickly downed his drink.

James Clarke lay in his bed inside a small, sterile hospital room. He tiredly gazed at the vidscreen, watching as the news replayed the events of the morning attack on the Underbelly. Military and monsters alike destroyed the civilians down below. As far as he could tell, there were very few survivors. The screen flickered with horrifying images of dead bodies strewn throughout the streets—soldiers, men, women, and children. No one was spared. The camera panned up toward a small girl with dark hair. Her tiny hand sat outstretched as she lay on her belly.

James, with closed eyes, shook his head, frowning. Slowly, he struggled to press the remote to turn off the screen. The image of the small girl reminded him far too much of Aria. He turned his head, looking out the small window beside him. He was on the upper side of Fountains now, unsure how he had gotten there.

Eyeing the glass of water beside his bed, he reached for it, wincing at the sudden pain that shot through his shoulder. He looked down at his wrapped chest. A bullet had torn up his right side. Judging by the wrappings, it had gone straight through. He sighed heavily, dropping his head on his pillow. Sweat beaded on his brow, dripping down his pale skin. He had been shot many times in the past, but this wound felt worse than all the others. He noticed the many specks of blood on his chest, looking at the dressing again.

'Ignition round,' he calculated mentally.

The bullet had broken and splashed against his shoulder and chest, burrowing tiny splinters of liquid shrapnel into his body. It would take weeks to push out the miniature pieces.

A scream sounded from outside his room. James quickly turned his head toward the door, eyes wide. Listening carefully, he picked up another dissimilar shriek. He recognized it from the security feed from the 66th Intel Reconnaissance Base. Frantically, James tugged at the needle in his arm and the cords taking his vitals. Leaping from his bed, he pressed a finger against the bedside monitor, silencing the alarm before it sounded. He quickly reached into a small closet, pulled out his dress coat, and slid it on, gritting his teeth as he moved the wounded shoulder.

Gunshots sounded, making the man jump. Breathing heavily, he watched as soldiers passed by the small window of his room's door. There followed a couple of quick shouts. Gunfire echoed in the dead silence of the facility, and then more terrified screams echoed down the halls.

Looking carefully through the glass, James saw a small group of soldiers standing alert at the edge of the hall. One held up a fist, halting the other two. Cautiously, the soldier looked around the corner. In a flash, his head disappeared, a large splatter of red splashing against the opposite wall. One of the nasty beasts followed around, clamping its jaws against another soldier's neck. The third soldier opened fire, unaware of the Sorcēarian that rounded the corner.

James gasped, pushing away from the door. As hard as he could, he elbowed the electronic mechanism for the door, locking it in place, and darted to the window. He tugged it open and firmly planted a foot against the protective screen, breaking and pushing it outward.

A scream close by alerted him. Peering over his shoulder, he saw the glass on the door smeared with crimson.

James quickly grabbed onto the sides of the windowpane and slid onto the thin ledge outside. He could hear the door to his room burst open, the heavy item slamming against the floor. Clutching a pipe secured to the outside wall, he pulled and spun away from the open window to the left. One of the creatures flew out, a claw swiping at his pant leg, and toppled over the side of the building, falling nearly two hundred meters toward the bottom of the city. Wobbling, James looked straight ahead, avoiding the sight of the fifty floors far beneath him.

Automated rail systems carried thousands of vehicles around the city buildings, zipping by the President at unbelievable speeds. Slowly, he shuffled to the side, his bare feet curling around the edge of the stone ledge. His hands pressed against the wall's surface, guiding him. If there was one creature, there were sure to be others. And he saw the Sorcēarian. There was no doubt he was the one leading the beasts.

"Grayson, are you there?" James called out through his mental chip, slowly shimmying across the side of the building. Gusting winds threatened to pull him away from the surface, the breeze catching onto his jacket.

"Yes, sir."

"Quickly, as fast as you can, get to the upper level in your car." James winced as blood began to ooze through his bandaging.

"The car, sir?"

"Don't ask questions! Drive your car by the floor where my room was located! I'm outside on the ledge!"

"Coming, sir," Grayson quickly replied.

Clarke wobbled, feeling light-headed. Approaching another pipe along the wall, he gripped it firmly, narrowly avoiding a freefall off the side of the building.

"Going somewhere?" Euclid's voice called out.

Gasping, James looked toward the window to his room with glassy eyes. The raven-haired man sat on the windowsill, legs dangling over the side. His elbow rested on a bent knee as he watched James with interest.

"You stay back!" James ordered, his authoritative voice shuddering.

"You don't look so good," Euclid said with a chuckle.

James tried shuffling to the side again, momentarily letting go of the pipe. He quivered, quickly losing balance as his knees began to buckle. He reached with his wounded arm and gripped the line again as his feet slipped from underneath. James' free hand grabbed his hurt shoulder as he held on for dear life, crying out in pain. Dark stains dribbled through his bandages, the rich blood pouring down his chest and side.

"Don't mind me. I enjoy watching your distress. It looks like you're going to do my job for me," Euclid said with amusement.

"Bastard!" James spat, growling as his hand slipped down the pipe.

"Like a worm on a hook," the Sorcēarian sneered. "This is so easy. Don't know why Walten wasn't brave enough to do his own dirty work." Euclid stared at the golden claws on his fingertips.

"Walten?" James gasped for air. His knuckles were white as he struggled with both hands to lift himself back up toward the small ledge.

"Oh, I said too much." Euclid feigned a gasp. "It seems your boss wants to get rid of you with more than a pink slip."

"I knew it! Walten's the cause of this! Why?" James asked, slowly sliding down the pipe.

Euclid watched him cautiously. "Why not?" he callously replied.

"What's that supposed to mean?"

"Why not destroy the race that has forgotten about their God? Why care about a race that a God has forgotten?" the Sorcēarian scoffed. "It's a pathetic cycle. You both are too selfish to appreciate one another. I don't know why *He* would bother with your kind anyway." Looking at James as he struggled with his grasp, Euclid jeered. "So weak!"

"Says the man whose own race couldn't keep itself alive!" James retorted, chuckling lowly. He locked eyes with Euclid. The Sorcēarian's amused expression quickly fell. Starting to rise, Euclid halted. James' hands slipped once more, and his mocking smile faltered as he let go, falling.

"Fool!" Euclid shouted, laughing. His hair spiraled in the harsh wind surrounding him.

James dropped a couple of floors, his body slamming onto the top of a car. He rolled and grabbed the open window in the roof as the vehicle pulled back into traffic and sped away. He then dropped inside, saluting Euclid with his middle finger.

"Damn it!" Euclid snarled. His blue eyes darted from side to side as he tried to follow the single black vehicle that melded with the thousands far below. Standing, he prepared to leap after the President but cursed again as he couldn't keep track, even as a Sorcēarian, of the ridiculous numbers.

"Where to, sir?" Grayson asked.

"Somewhere isolated and safe," James replied, panting. He opened his jacket, looking at the blood-soaked bandages. "How's your patching skills?"

"Not as good as my bedside manner, sir," Grayson replied dully, looking at the President through shaded glasses.

Troy sat at the bar of the Pendant Hotel. Inhaling, he took a long drag on his cigarette, the blue embers shimmering against the gold-plated surfaces around him. He puffed out slowly, a small white cloud passing by his lips as he lifted his glass. Drinking, he eyeballed the vidscreen over the bartender's head. A banner scrolled across the display, mentioning the attack on the Underbelly of Fountains. Roma took the news lightly as they had bigger plans for the night, primarily highlighting the peace treaty between its city-state and Saray and the current festivities—another banner scrolled by, speaking of James Clarke's disappearance.

"Shit," Troy muttered, taking another drag. "Aria's going to flip out."

"I'm sure he is okay," Dovian called out from behind the man.

Troy's body went rigid.

"Is it okay if I join you for a while?" Dovian kindly asked. "There's too much noise in the ballroom, and my room is strangely uncomfortable right now," he said, remembering Caravaggio's massive painting of 'Judith Beheading Holofernes' that hung on his bedroom wall. He unconsciously shuddered.

"Not my bar," Troy replied. He winced, noticing how dickish that sounded. "No, I don't mind," he corrected.

Dovian sat beside the soldier, twisting as the stool rotated. He glanced at the screen and then at Troy. The man eyed the Sorcēarian in return.

"Want one?" Troy asked, holding up a cigarette. Dovian stared at it. "It's the real stuff. Doesn't have any of those nasties in it."

"Didn't know you smoked," Dovian replied, taking the offered cigarette.

"Don't do it often. If so, it's gotta be this kind. Shit's expensive, though. This pack took up about a quarter of a paycheck, but it's worth it." Troy shook his small box. "Has a nice taste to it, and it helps calm the nerves."

Dovian placed the stick between his lips and mockingly patted his nonexistent pockets.

"What are you doing?" Troy asked.

"Lighter?" Dovian followed.

Troy leaned forward and tugged on a small cap covering the end of Dovian's cig. The item sizzled and then lit up in a vibrant blue.

"Don't have to light them, man." Troy gave the Sorcēarian a strange look.

"I take it I don't blend in very well," Dovian stated, taking a quick puff as he talked.

"No, not one bit," Troy chuckled.

"I'll have to work on that," he replied, cigarette squeezed between his teeth. After a pause, his eyes widened with amusement. "Oh, wait. How about this?" he asked.

Reaching into his scarlet coat, he tugged out a beautiful porcelain mask. It was white with silver and red detailing, gold lining the eyeholes. With a crooked smile, Dovian placed the item on his face, the matching red and gold-flickered feathers on the right-side wobbling as he did so. A chuckle vibrated in his chest as he blew out a puff of smoke.

Troy snickered, relaxing a bit. He shook his head. "Still creepy. How about ditching the robes?"

"Mm, mm," Dovian mumbled, taking a drag. He breathed out slowly, holding the item between his fingers. "Robes gotta stay."

"Ah, that's right. Makes you a chick magnet, right? Chicks dig the robes," Troy said with amusement.

Dovian frowned. He stared at the cigarette between his fingertips. "Troy, I've been meaning to speak with you," he said in a severe tone.

The russet-haired man grimaced. He knew where this conversation was going.

"About Aria," Dovian continued.

"Listen, man. I don't care about that, all right?" Troy said, swirling his liquor in his glass.

"But I do. I shouldn't have done what I did. I know there's no excuse for it, but I didn't mean to cause any trouble between you."

Dovian shook his head when the bartender asked if he wanted a drink. Troy signaled for a refill.

"Between us? Nothing is going on between us. We had a small fight, that's all. It's fine now. We're cool." Troy shrugged, avoiding Dovian's stare.

"So, what happened between her and I had nothing to do with the fight you two had?" Dovian asked, doubt saturating his voice.

'Damn it. He sounds like Dad.' Troy stared at the vidscreen.

"No," Troy quickly replied. Looking to the side, he watched Dovian's blue irises. Growling, he continued, "Okay! Maybe a little, but it's not necessarily because she slept with you!"

"Then what is it?" Dovian asked, intrigued.

"It's because of your stupid religion!" he said a little too loud. Quickly fixing his mistake under Dovian's scrutiny, Troy lifted his hands. "Not stupid, it's not stupid. I'm just frustrated by it."

"What is it that frustrates you?" Dovian asked.

'I really don't want to talk about this right now,' Troy groaned mentally.

"I don't know. It's just…how are we supposed to believe it? I mean, there's no proof!" The soldier's teeth clenched tightly around his cigarette.

"Have you read the book?" The silver-haired man puffed.

"Well, no."

"You should read the book."

"I don't own a book!"

"Borrow it from Aria."

"She's reading it."

"When she's finished."

"But…I…." Troy tried looking for more excuses.

"Why don't you tell me what's really bothering you, Troy," Dovian said, looking at the other man with an unreadable expression.

"I'm freaked out, okay!" Troy ran his hands through his hair, messing it in all directions. He growled in frustration. "Your damn religion scares the hell out of me!"

"As it should," Dovian mumbled.

"See? Then you reply with something like that. How am I supposed to feel?"

"How about you change your way of thinking," Dovian suggested.

"What do you mean?"

"Don't think of it as a religion. It's not a religion. It's the truth. Take it literally; don't try to read between the lines. That's where humanity struggles. They try to find loopholes and alternate understandings. They use it to manipulate and twist truths. Just believe in it."

"In what? That there is a God? That I may die and go to Hell because I didn't believe, because I didn't have the tools to even learn about this stuff? That everyone I know, Mom, Dad, and Gavin, could be in Hell right now? That's not comforting," Troy said with a sarcastic tone.

"Don't worry about them. You've had the tools. There was a church lying right below your city. Aria's got the best tool, and you just tried making excuses as to why you won't educate yourself. That's even worse, having some knowledge and neglecting it in spite."

Troy quickly downed his second drink as soon as the bartender placed it before him. He reached into his box and pulled out a second cigarette, ripping off the tab in the front. He breathed in deeply.

"You're a good man, Troy. There's no doubt about it, but that isn't going to save you," Dovian said. "You need to be strong, to believe. If anything, you better believe these monsters are more than just monsters. You make one bad move, and it could be your last. Believe in the real threat. If not for you, then do it for Aria."

"For Aria?" Troy asked. His interest was piqued.

"Hell is a separation, Troy. Can you imagine being in a faraway place, separated from the ones you love the most? Imagine losing that one person you care about most in the world and never being able to see them again for all of eternity. Can you imagine that? Do you know that pain? Even the worst pain is unimaginable if it comes true. Is that a gamble you're willing to bet on?" Dovian asked. His tone was not gentle. His expression was severe, making him appear more menacing behind the mask.

Troy glanced at the tall man beside him, his throat constricting at the possibility that he could make the worst decision of his life by refusing to believe.

But, where's the harm in believing?' Troy thought, remembering Aria's words from earlier that day.

Could he imagine a fraction of the possibility? What would it be like to be separated from the ones he loved? Troy hadn't thought about it. He always assumed he was alone ever since his father died. His mother had passed when he was young, and though he never knew her, he still missed her.

"I've already lost Gavin," Troy murmured. "That was one of the worst moments of my life."

Dovian watched Troy, intently listening as he spoke.

"And who knows what's happened to Mr. Clarke. I will be upset if he's dead, but he's not as close to me as he is to Aria. If he died, she would go ballistic. I'd be all she'd have left." Troy looked down at his hands that had clasped around his glass. "She's the only reason I got through Gavin's death. As long as she was around, I was able to carry on." He paused, lost in his thoughts, finally realizing an alternate point Dovian was trying to make. It was Aria. She was all he had left. Sure, there were acquaintances and his little black book of numbers, but none of those people knew him inside and out as Aria did.

"It's Aria," he said finally. "If I lose Aria, I lose everything," he muttered, his cigarette bouncing between his lips. "We grew up together, trained together, have been partners for as long as I can remember." He chuckled. "I was even there for her when her stupid, fat cat, Xena, went missing." Troy chuckled, shaking his head.

He noticed Dovian's interest in the subject and continued. "She had gotten it as a birthday present from Mr. Clarke when she was sixteen. It was black and had green eyes. He said it reminded him of her. Years later, when we were on a mission, we had to leave in a hurry, and I guess Aria left her window open. When we returned, Xena was gone. We never saw the cat again. Aria was so devastated by it; you'd think that her parents had died all over again. I think she was holding onto that cat, using it to replace the loss she felt from seeing her parents die right in front of her." He twirled his cigarette between his fingers, watching the blue embers create an illusionary circle.

Dovian continued listening and allowed Troy to take the conversation to a different level, for which the soldier was thankful.

"I was lucky, you know? My mom died when I was a baby. My dad died out in the field. I didn't have to see their bodies. Apparently, Aria's father had shielded her with his own body, taking the full brunt of the mortar that landed only a couple of meters away. She was pinned beneath him and some debris for an hour before anyone found her. The only thing she could see the whole time was her mother reaching out for her, slowly bleeding out."

Dovian's eyes narrowed as he watched Troy. The soldier closed his own, frowning.

"It's so damn terrible, isn't it? There really is no hope for humanity," Troy grumbled. "And you want to know the sickest part of it all?" He lifted his gaze back toward the Sorcēarian. "That day, when Aria's parents were killed, the mortar that was let off was fired by James Clarke's own hands. He was given some bad coordinates, and the fire landed in the civilian area of the theatre where Aria and her parents were watching a play. It was a play Aria begged her parents to take her to…for her birthday. Guess that's why he feels so protective of her."

"My God," Dovian finally spoke, holding a hand to his porcelain forehead.

"Not fair, is it?" Troy asked.

"No, it certainly isn't. And I know where you're going with this, but please believe me when I tell you, God had nothing to do with that," Dovian said lowly.

Troy scoffed. "No. Everything that happens is just bad luck, all caused by humanity's stupidity and greed." He sucked on his cigarette. "We're damned. Always have been. That's why God left in the first place. And we're all on our own now. But I'll keep her safe, no matter what. I bet my soul on it," Troy chuckled. After a moment, his smile faltered. "If I haven't lost her yet."

Dovian sagged in his chair. "You think that argument has the potential to ruin your relationship? You've never been in a real relationship before, have you?"

Troy gaped at the other man curiously.

The Sorcēarian sighed, the sound low and hollow. "It's not about what you say that hurts the person the most. Sure, at the moment, it hurts, but it's more about what you're leaving out, not saying, that can pour salt in the wound. Everyone argues. The question is whether or not you want to give up and have that argument be the final conversation you had, or if you want to fix that mistake and make an effort so the other person can understand how you really feel. Too many people give up too early. If you are willing to give up, then fine, give up because you're not worth her time. But, if you want to fix it, you had better hurry up and fix it. You can only leave a wound untreated for so long before it starts to fester, and that isn't love."

Troy sat stiffly on the barstool, staring at the ice cubes in his tumbler.

"She's incredibly important to you," Dovian said. It wasn't a question but a statement.

Troy nodded slowly.

"You say that you'll protect her, but don't forget to protect yourself along the way, okay?" Dovian rose from his chair, patting Troy on the shoulder.

"Nice pep talk, Dovian," Troy said. The Sorcēarian glanced over his shoulder. "Guess I'm a little slow at recognizing these sorts of things."

"Better late than never." Dovian nodded, giving the man a gentle smile. Looking at his wristband, he said, "You should get yourself dressed for the party."

"Aw, gotta put on my dancin' shoes," Troy muttered with his cigarette between his teeth. "Hey, Dovian!" he called out again, swiveling on his stool.

The Sorcēarian looked back with a questioning look on his face.

Gesturing to Dovian's mask, Troy said, "You going to take that thing off?"

"No," Dovian refused. Tapping on the porcelain, he gave a sideways grin. "I think I'll keep it. The chicks dig it."

Troy shrugged, "I dig it," he said jokingly.

Dovian chuckled and turned, giving a small wave as he slowly took the stairs to the elevator. The noise level of the hotel had risen tenfold. He could hear instruments tuning from the massive hall and the garbled conversation of dozens of excited guests. Looking up to stare at his golden reflection in the elevator doors, he smirked. The naivety of his human comrades was quite amusing. And here he was playing matchmaker between the two best soldiers of Bio-Tech. His smile faltered. But what about him?

'It would never have worked out between us, my dear,' Dovian thought. He closed his illuminating eyes, reflecting on the night with Aria. Vividly, he remembered her touch, her smell, her laughter in his ears, and, most importantly, the sound of her breathy moans. Dovian chuckled, opening his eyes. 'But thank you for the memories and the small fantasy in my otherwise dreadfully realistic world.'

The soft chime of the doors opening tore the Sorcēarian from his thoughts. Entering, he pressed against the number of his desired location. He watched, indifferent, at the blinking lights on the many floors of the Pendant Hotel. Once on his level, the gates pulled open again, giving him another gleeful ding. His impassive expression fell further as he noticed a nervous Ivory standing and knocking frantically at his room. Slowly, he made his way toward the woman.

"Looking for me?" he asked quietly.

"Dovian." She turned to him, her pale face covered by a silver decorative mask adorned with orange jewels. She wore a beautiful gown of yellow and silver, tight around her top and billowing out at her waist with a transparent gossamer, the fabric sparkling with tiny gems. Matching silk gloves covered her arms. The woman tugged on her hands. Her blue eyes, offset by dark eyeliner, stared at him fearfully. "We've got to talk."

Sensing her unease, Dovian couldn't help but swallow hard. It was a discussion he was sure they needed, but one he wasn't quite ready to have. Shivering under her icy stare, Dovian carefully moved around her, unlocking the door with his keycard and thumbprint. Pushing the surface, he held out a palm, gesturing for her to enter first. Ivory quickly strode into his room, staring at the carpet. While lost in her thoughts, her blank expression looked upon nothing of interest. A tense silence filled the room, nearly consuming her. For the first time, she felt like she was in a foreign place, somewhere she did not belong. The sound of the door closing made her jolt, and her hands wrung once again.

"What would you like to talk about?" Dovian asked after a minute.

Her chest heaving, Ivory finally turned to him. "I'Lanthe. We need to talk about I'Lanthe."

Like being doused in ice water, Dovian froze, feeling bumps covering his skin. "And what, exactly, do you know about I'Lanthe?" he mustered.

Caving into her anxiety, she shouted, "I don't know! I don't know anything about her!" She was distressed, her eyes brimming with tears. Grabbing onto Dovian's coat, her lips trembled. "The only thing I know about her is her feelings for you."

Dovian stiffened under the blonde's proximity. He stared down at her, his mouth gaping as he tried to form words. "H-how does she feel about me?" he asked after a moment.

Ivory's grip on his clothing loosened, and she looked away, staring at the floor again. Her mouth twitched, and she took a deep breath. "She loves you. She loves you so much, and it hurts. I can't explain it. I don't know how any of this is happening. All I know is, being around you hurts so much."

Seeing her desperation left an all too familiar sting in the man's chest. Dovian's brow creased with concern as he gently grabbed her small wrists. She winced then. "Dovian, you are hurting me!"

"I hurt you?" he asked, quickly releasing her.

Ivory unconsciously rubbed an appendage, staring down at her gloved fingers. "N-no. That's not what I meant." She rested a palm on her chest, closing her eyes.

Dovian flinched, grabbing the side of his head as another painful memory flooded his senses. It was a distant memory from a time he argued with I'Lanthe.

It was a terrible day, one full of aches and regret. He had grabbed I'Lanthe tightly, pulling her at the wrist toward him.

"Dovian, you are hurting me!" she screamed.

He quickly let go, watching her with a sorrowful expression.

"I'm sorry," he muttered, rubbing her wrists.

"That's not what I meant," she whispered, placing a hand against her chest. "I don't like seeing you like this. It hurts."

Dovian sighed, trying to thrust the memory from his mind. Ivory looked at him once again. She noticed his anguish and frowned.

"I don't know who she is or why she's inside me, but I know she loves you more than anything and misses you so much." A small sob crept from her mouth. "And it's affecting me! I don't know what to do! I've been sitting in my room, all alone, and I have no clue what these feelings are or whose they are!" She quickly turned away, clenching her fists before her mouth.

Dovian reached for her, his shaking palms resting on her shoulders.

"I don't know what's going on! Who am I? Why do I have these terrible memories? They are full of so much pain!" she cried out, her hands covering her face.

"Lanthe…" Dovian whispered, his hands running down her arms.

"No!" Ivory quickly pushed away. The man looked at her, his face holding a hurtful expression. "I'm not I'Lanthe! Don't call me that!"

"But what other explanation is there? Who else can you be?" Dovian asked.

"Ivory! My name is Ivory! I am my own person!" she shrieked.

"Then why do you have memories that do not belong to you?!" Dovian asked, his blue eyes glimmering in the pale light of the hotel room.

Ivory trembled at the man's booming voice. "I don't know, okay?" she responded, slowly backing away.

"Ivory! Who in the hell are you?" he asked firmly, gripping her arms. He tugged her close, watching her intently with narrowed eyes.

She shivered under the man's intense stare. He was oblivious to his mask, which hid his features, making him even more mysterious and terrifying. She gripped his arms in return; the two held onto one another. Her breaths remained uneven as unknown memories flooded her system, causing her to flinch.

Love.

Passion.

Regret.

Fear.

Sorrow.

It all hit her like a tidal wave, and Ivory began to shake, trying not to give in to the emotions that did not belong to her.

"What?" Dovian asked. "Please, tell me what you are thinking."

"No," she whispered, refusing to look him in the eye.

"You are the only person, the only human, I've ever met that I cannot read," he replied. "It scares me not knowing what you are thinking, not knowing what you are hiding."

Ivory finally tore her blue eyes up to his. She gaped at him, her wrinkled brow hidden behind her mask. "You can't read me?" she asked.

"I cannot read your thoughts. I've never encountered this before. Not since the Sorcēarians were still alive."

"I'm not a Sorcēarian."

"Then what are you?" He sounded irritated.

Ivory stared with narrow eyes. He returned the same intense look.

"I can't explain that to you. Besides, I already think you have a good idea," she said, swallowing thickly.

"I have my hypothesis," he whispered, "but I still cannot make any sense of it."

Realizing that they still held onto each other, Ivory pulled away. "Neither can I," she replied. "One minute, I'm awake in a strange land with all of you staring at me. Next, I have emotions and memories I've never had before. I'm seeing you and recognizing you, and I know I shouldn't know you. And then…" she paused, her hands gripping the dog tag around her neck, "I'm scared. Scared of what I really am, of what I will become."

"And what, exactly, is that?"

"I don't know. I have no idea. All I know is that I'm scared. I'm afraid, and I have no way to explain it," she whispered.

"Your sister said that you were dead. Do you think that has anything to do with it?" he asked.

"It probably has everything to do with it, Dovian," she said bitterly, folding her arms. "But I don't know why I woke up in Ives. I have no clue as to how I ended up there. My memory only stretches as far as when I first awoke with you all around me."

"Maybe she's communicating through you. Maybe you are I'Lanthe."

Dovian placed a hand on Ivory's shoulder once again. She flinched, turning to face him.

"And that's exactly what you want, isn't it, Dovian?" she asked sourly. "You are wishing and hoping that I am your lost love! That's all you care about, isn't it? It's the only reason you've shown me any kindness!"

"No, that's not it," he disagreed.

"The only reason you've shown me any interest or care is because of your desperation to talk to I'Lanthe once again. It has nothing to do with me! The actual me!" she said, her tone rising in volume.

Dovian gaped at her, trying to form words. In a way, she was right, which filled Dovian with self-disgust. Still, it didn't mean he cared less for Ivory as a friend or comrade. He genuinely did care about her safety and well-being. Also, he needed to find out how she knew anything at all about I'Lanthe, about a woman who was long ago forgotten to history thousands of years ago.

"You don't care about *me*. Ivory! You only care about your past!" She threw her arms in the air. "The only people who care about me are now dead! I don't exist! I'm dead, too! I'm some stupid shell of a person with some ghost in it—a ghost that you wish I would pretend to be!"

"I didn't say that," he alleged.

After losing to her depressing thoughts, Ivory whispered harshly, "Who is to say that I am Ivory? Fiona said it herself; I'm in a jar on some shelf somewhere. Ashes!" she growled in frustration. "I'm dead, Dovian! I don't exist! Am I even real? Am I even standing here?!"

"You are here," he replied quickly, trying to settle the woman down. "You are here. You are standing here, real, in the flesh. You are your own person."

"Am I?" she asked skeptically. "Do you really believe that, Dovian? Is that what you really want?"

Ivory glared at him, her pupils thinning to tiny dots. Dovian stared back; the sudden silence was nearly suffocating. However, his hesitation lasted too long, and Ivory shoved past him and walked toward the door.

"Ivory!" he called out, facing her.

"You said it yourself, Dovian, when we first met. An imitation is never as good as the original. I'm never going to be as good as the real thing—as Ivory…as I'Lanthe," she said in a sad tone, her voice cracking.

"Ivory, please. You are just as important as the next person," he tried to explain, but she wouldn't have any of it.

"Don't call me Ivory. That name no longer belongs to me, either," she hissed, pulling open the door. "I'm just some shell with no identity. I belong to no one. I am no one."

Dovian reached toward her, his mouth opening to speak, but she shut her eyes and walked into the hallway, closing the door firmly behind her. He stood in the room's center in silence, his hand slowly falling to his side as he stared at the peephole on the door.

Beep-beep. Beep-beep.

His alarm sounded, signaling the start of the masquerade. The others would be in position soon, which meant he needed to stand guard outside. Alone.

'Always alone. Always screwing everything up,' he thought.

Then he wondered why he didn't bother trying to fight this battle alone, away from all the distractions and drama of the humans. Was it really worth being surrounded by them and their constant problems? Did having the others around benefit him in the grand scheme of things? Weren't they only an interference, something that merely got in the way? Why was he with them? Why did he hopelessly cling to Aria, Troy, and Ivory? Was it because he was lonely and desperate for interaction? Was he dead set on finding I'Lanthe once again?

The answer was simple—yes. Dovian wanted others around him. He wanted a tiny sliver of joy and amusement, pure emotion in his life. But, in the end, did any of it matter?

His mouth set into a thin line. Letting out another deep groan, Dovian rubbed his forehead, his fingers running along the painted lines of his mask. He stared at his reflection in the glass that covered one of the many paintings in the room. Behind the disguise of red and gold, his blue eyes glimmered with a chilly expression.

He watched himself in silence, feeling the weight of the world shift from shoulder to shoulder as he pondered the current stresses in his life.

Was any of it worth the effort?

"There Can Be No Darkness Without Light"

CHAPTER 20

Aria stood off to the side of the grand ballroom, watching with casual interest the many couples dancing in the center of the room. At least two thousand people crammed inside the magnificent hall. More champagne-sipping guests, all laughing and talking noisily behind their shimmering masks and overpriced garments, filled the lobby. As the dancers twirled, sparkling lights glinted from the glittering chandeliers of gold, silver, and crystal against their jeweled ensembles. The music droned with a classical rhythm underlying pulsating beats from the suave band upon the stage. The musicians used cybernetic hand instruments, electronics, and optic DJ systems. Technically, the event felt more like a classy, costumed club.

"Drink, miss?" A kind but slightly uptight-looking man offered drinks from a silver tray.

"Thanks," Aria said, quickly accepting a glass of bubbling champagne.

He smiled and walked away, moving to other guests. Aria fidgeted uncomfortably in her blue dress, trying her best to avoid the stares and wolfish smiles from the men lining the opposite wall. She was not in her element. Sipping awkwardly from her glass, she turned to look out the large window near the corner she was closest to. With a squint, she could see a shade of red through the blackness of the night. Probably picking up her thoughts, Dovian turned to look back at the woman, his crystalline eyes glowing in the darkness behind his shimmering mask. She smiled at him but couldn't read his expression through the glass, distorted by the reflections of the lights and ornate decorations from inside. She did, however, hear a small whisper in her mind.

"Beautiful." It was quiet but in Dovian's calm tone.

Unconsciously, she fed him another shy smile. He turned away, lifting his hood, and Aria couldn't help but feel that there was something the matter with the man.

Returning her attention to the ball, she shifted her glass to her other hand, her eyes wandering from mask to mask. Finally, she looked over her shoulder at the bar—no Troy.

'Where is he?' She frowned.

A flicker on the vidscreen above the bar alerted her. Watching from afar, she read the banner sweeping across the bottom of the display stating James Clarke's disappearance. Her body went rigid, her heart thumping in her chest. Following the report was a series of unsettling scenes revealing the destruction of the Underbelly.

"James…" Aria whispered.

"Don't pay any attention to that; we'll deal with it later," Troy's voice echoed in her mind.

Eyes darting around the room, trying to catch a familiar face behind an unknown mask, Aria looked for the man. Glancing up toward the golden elevator, she saw the form of a man unclasping the buttons around the wrist of his dress shirt. He rolled the sleeves slightly over the top of his stark-black dress coat, revealing tattoos on his forearms. The suit had a slim fit, hugging his frame as he descended the stairs and adjusted his dark tie that sat partially hidden beneath a matching black vest. To top it off, he wore a black porcelain mask. Silver lined the eyes and mask's edge, meeting a single cobalt blue gem in the center of his forehead, matching the color of Aria's dress. The clean, sleek look of the man's suit was slightly off-balance with his facial hair and messy brown locks.

Aria smirked, catching his nervous expression as he strode toward her.

"I like the suit," she said with amusement. "You clean up well, Troy."

Luckily, he wasn't hard to pick out from the other people in the crowd. His posture gave him away, if not for the cocky grin he always had on his unshaven face.

"Eh, it's the suit." He shrugged casually. Relaxing a bit, he quickly snatched her glass and set it on a side table, then he grabbed her hands and pulled her toward the dance floor. Placing a hand on her hip and clasping his other in one of her own, he gave her a look-over.

Truthfully, Troy had never seen Aria dress up for anything outside of funerals, and for those occasions, she always wore her little black dress. Now, she was dolled up in bright blues, the color matching the streak in her pulled-up hair. Her dark strands spiraled toward the back and spiked out slightly as they piled on her head. A slanting piece of her bangs fell over her mask, attempting to cover one of her green eyes highlighted by dark makeup. Troy never realized she even knew how to make herself up, not that she needed to. She was pleasant to look at. Still, Aria didn't know that.

"You look magnificent," he said quietly.

Aria's mouth twisted into an expression revealing that she believed differently.

"In fact, you're the prettiest woman in the entire room," he said. "Not lying."

She gave him an awkward smile before mumbling a thank you, avoiding his eyes.

"That's why everyone's staring at you," he whispered, closing the space between them as they casually danced to the music.

Aria lifted her head, looking around nervously. "They are not," she said quickly.

Troy chuckled, his fingers moving between hers. After a moment of silence, Aria finally grinned again.

"Nice mask," she said. Finding his olive-green eyes helped calm her nerves in the crowded room.

"You like it?" he asked. "It had feathers in it, but I tore them out."

"Troy!" Aria slapped him on the shoulder.

"No, seriously, I looked like a freakin' peacock!"

She giggled. "You don't even know what a peacock is."

"I've seen a picture once." He chuckled, the sound merging with hers. Troy watched her as they danced between the other couples. "You should smile more. Not to sound like one of those assholes who tell women to smile, but I like it…because it means you're happy."

On instinct, Aria frowned.

"No! I said, smile! Not frown!" He poked the side of her cheek, forcing another giggle from the woman. After a second of listening to her melodious laugh, Troy leaned in close and whispered, "See? It suits you very well."

He pointed to the side where a large mirror hung on the wall. Aria twisted her head, looking at the reflection of her and Troy pressed against one another. She didn't notice her smile but looked upon her and the man so close. Each of their hands clasped together. One of her palms sat on his shoulder, and his other rested low on her hip. And she noticed the broad smile on his face as he looked at her with eyes that showed appreciation. Biting her lip, she turned her attention back to him and smiled.

"What does? You being so close to me?" she asked.

Troy quickly tore his eyes away from the mirror, gaping at Aria with a shocked expression. There was a slight hitch in his breath as he began to speak but then paused. She giggled. Troy was never speechless; it was certainly a first.

Lifting a palm, he placed it gently against her cheek. "I think that suits you very well, too," he said quietly.

And, for the first time, Aria didn't know how to reply. Was he serious? Usually, he joked about things like that, but seeing the look in his eyes told her differently. Troy often reserved words like that for other girls, not her. But this was the first time she had ever heard Troy say something so sweet with such an earnest look.

"Are you kid—" she began to speak.

"Shut up," he whispered, leaning down to kiss her.

Aria's body tensed at first to the feel of Troy's lips upon hers. A flurry of thoughts dashed through her mind. A million 'what ifs' and a hundred 'buts' crashed together, and as Troy added a second hand to cup her face and gently deepened the kiss, she didn't care anymore. None of it mattered. Nothing mattered. It was the first time she felt like not giving a damn about anything. She wrapped her arms around him, suddenly needing him more than ever.

"Why don't you kiss me like that?" a woman articulated aloud to her significant other.

Troy hummed a laugh, his mouth still pressed against hers. He pulled away but still held Aria against him. Hearing the other woman's protest made her blush, heat rising to her face. Aria peered apprehensively at the man, slowly running her hands down his back to sit at his waist. Her fingers trailed over something strapped to his lower back.

"Is that your gun in your pocket?" she asked with amusement.

"Yup, the latest Bio-Tech model in handguns—a .50 caliber Liberty Eagle with Ignition rounds coupled with EMP vibrations," he said.

"Love it when you talk dirty," she growled.

Troy chuckled. "Are you armed? Can you even hide a gun in that dress?" he asked curiously.

Aria grabbed one of his hands and placed it on her thigh. Troy flushed as she wrapped her leg around his and lifted slightly, causing the dress to part at a slit. Eyes flickering in the bright light, she guided his hand up her thigh to her small, holstered gun.

"Oh, I really like this dress a lot," he muttered.

"Mini Liberty Eagle," she whispered. "Want to know where I keep the extra ammunition?"

Troy nearly choked, his face turning beet-red beneath his mask. Aria gave him a mischievous grin. The low tone of the massive, antique grandfather clock chimed at the close of the slow song, noisily beating twelve times for midnight as the DJs prepared the next tune. Troy moved his hand, scratching his head as he cleared his throat.

"Would you like a drink? I think I need a drink," he quickly sputtered.

Giving a small laugh, Aria replied, "Sure."

Parting slowly, he winked. "I'll be right back."

As Troy walked away, rubbing the back of his neck, Aria remembered the people surrounding her. She shivered slightly as the warmth of Troy's body disappeared. Funny, she had felt so bold only moments before. Now, she felt utterly self-conscious as eyes darted in her direction from jealous wives and curious men. Aria stepped back, intending to leave the massive group and return to her lonely corner, when she bumped into someone. She gasped, feeling two hands steady her.

"Having fun?" a familiar, warm voice whispered in her ear from behind.

Aria froze, recognizing the tone instantly.

'It isn't Gavin,' she reminded herself. She closed her eyes, feeling a hand run across her stomach. A sharp claw dug into her cheek, trailing delicately against her face so as not to blemish her skin.

"Euclid," she hissed, knowing it was he who teased her.

She struggled, but he quickly locked her in place from behind. With a hand lifting to grip her face, he trailed his claw over her cheek again, a bit harder.

"You know, I can kill you so easily in this room, and no one would even know," he whispered, gripping her wrists tightly together. "He would never know. I can drag you far away from here and be on another continent in seconds. He'd never see you again."

Aria gritted her teeth, trying to pry free from his grasp. She could see Troy standing at the bar, ordering the two drinks.

"You could be mine," he whispered harshly. A hand gripped her waist, pulling her against his chest. "Forever."

"Fuck off," she spat.

Growling, he tightened his grip on her wrists, bruising them. "You stand no chance. You've never stood a chance. Give up your fight."

"Never."

"Then you will die a horrific death, and I will make sure he sees the whole thing. But before I do, I'll make sure you watch him endure the worst pain first. He will suffer as I cut him limb from limb and chain him to a wall in pieces, making sure to keep him alive long enough for me to do the same to you!" Euclid placed vivid mental pictures of his horrifying promise into Aria's mind. Each image made her heart skip a beat, leaving a sour taste in her mouth. Euclid laughed, the sound creating more fear within the woman as she watched Troy turn and lock eyes with her. "I will paint the walls red with your filthy blood."

Troy first noticed Aria's pale and frightened expression, and then he saw the towering silhouette behind her. Dropping the glasses of champagne, he reached behind him, gripping the weapon that hid underneath his dress coat. He darted into the ballroom, but his footsteps moved in slow motion as Aria endured Euclid's horrid laughter in her ears and felt his wet kiss against her cheek before he released her and disappeared. She instantly pulled the small gun from her thigh holster and scanned the room for the azure Sorcēarian.

"Are you all right?" Troy asked, planting a hand firmly on her shoulder.

"Euclid's here. We've got to find the others," she said, her authoritative voice returning.

The hallways seemed to narrow, creating long, thin, dark tunnels that stretched toward the orange glow—specks of color—from the windows that appeared so far away. Ivory stumbled, her delicate hand shakily grasping for the wall. The textures scraped against her skin, causing pinpricks. It was cold, but she didn't feel cold. Something inside her told her it was. The wall was icy, the surface rough, and the exterior was painted in dark maroon with gold spirals. Her vision soared toward the small light, her pupils shifting, trying to adjust to the darkness. She felt dizzy; she felt sick. But she couldn't remember ever feeling sick. She couldn't remember the last time she was ill. What did 'sick' feel like? Did it feel like this?

Ivory shuddered, her head dropping as she remembered lying on a large bed with satin sheets. The cloth was softer than anything she had ever touched. The fur blanket that sprawled over the top was thick and fluffy. It kept her warm in the stone room where billowing curtains blew between marble pillars from an open wall. The soft trickle of rain dripped onto the floor and echoed splashes as the droplets fell into the giant fountain in the garden outside. The air had a sweet smell from the wet orchids. A low rumble of thunder sounded, and it was soothing.

'*No, not my memory.*' Ivory frowned, trying to suppress the sadness that consumed her.

She stumbled, falling from one corner of the hall into the wall on the other side. A loud gasp erupted from her lips as her hand gripped her chest. Was she dying? Was this what death felt like? She couldn't remember the last time she died.

"No," she whispered. She reached out toward the light in the window, still hearing the rain. Was it raining? Did it rain in Roma?

She could remember the feel of the rain. It was cold; the heavy droplets were almost painful as they crashed against her body, the trickles tinkling against the metal of her heavy armor. She felt numb. She couldn't move her fingers. Involuntarily, she twitched. She touched her stomach with a shaking hand, feeling the warm red liquid that gushed from her wound. It was a painful wound, and she remembered feeling the life pour out of her.

"No," Ivory mumbled again. "Not mine."

Her body locked into place. She couldn't move, could only stare upward at the dark sky and watch the rain fall toward her. After a flicker of bright light and a roar of thunder, a black-winged mass shot from one of the towers. She felt utterly hopeless then, her heart breaking into two. Another burst of light fired out, and the clouds filtered a speck of white light. It spread, eating the whole sky, and spewed down toward her. Within seconds, all her pain and fears dissipated. And all she felt was nothing.

"Not my memories," Ivory whimpered, falling to her knees.

Everything was dark. The pale-orange glow from the outside world flickered through her warped vision. The booming music sounded far from her ears as she listened to the raging storm outside, the water hitting the windowpane only an arm's length away.

"There can be no darkness," she whispered, "without light."

Her body twitched again, causing her back to arch painfully. A loud groan erupted from her lips, and Ivory fought again for control over her body, control over her memories.

"And the one who brings the light can extinguish the darkness," a foreign voice whispered in the woman's mind. *"Because you cannot have one without the other. There's got to be a delicate balance. If you let one consume the other, then it destroys."*

Ivory moaned; her seizure worsened. She stared at the ceiling but couldn't see it. Everything was black, and the orange glow was gone. Darkness consumed Ivory. As she twitched, her mind was lost, her vision gone. She was an empty vessel convulsing in the center of a vacant hall inside a hotel. She felt nothing and had no awareness. Therefore, she did not feel the hand on her shoulder, could not see the wicked smile, the glowing blue eyes, nor hear the dark laughter that spewed from Euclid as he lifted her off the ground.

"I told you, you cannot escape me. Run all you'd like. You'll never get away from me," he whispered harshly, staring at the trembling blonde in his arms.

"Drop her!" Aria's voice shouted from down the hall.

"Release her now!" Troy's voice boomed.

Before Euclid could even acknowledge the intruders, he felt multiple rounds blast into his dorsal side, the ammunition splattering and then burning hundreds of tiny splinters into his flesh. He turned slowly, ignoring the searing pain that ate away at his backside. He gripped the blonde tightly, his golden claws digging into Ivory's pale flesh.

With white teeth showing, he growled, "You cannot win! Your petty weapons are no match! I will only heal just as I always do!"

"Let her go!" Aria shouted.

"Never," he snarled. Slamming his hand against his chest, Euclid abruptly disappeared with Ivory, leaving Troy and Aria alone in the decorative hall. Thunder rumbled violently.

Dovian stood outside the Pendant Hotel, watching the clouds slowly shroud the stars. He could hear the drone of the strange music, a sound he never expected to hear in the traditional form of a masquerade. But then again, he hadn't been to a gala in thousands of years. He was surprised the humans even understood the ancient festival. Glancing over his shoulder, he saw Aria dancing with Troy. For the first time he had met her, she looked genuinely happy. He was sorry he couldn't say the same for himself. His mind settled in its darkest recess, reminding the Sorcēarian of once peaceful but now agonizing times.

A flicker of light alerted the man back to the night sky. Thinning his bright eyes, he blinked as a raindrop splashed against the porcelain mask on his face, dripping onto his pale skin. He breathed deeply, feeling a reminder of home as the humidity rose, creating a wet, slightly sweet smell. A dull thunder rolled in the distance, and more drops fell from the sky, clicking against the cobblestone walkway he stood on. It was peaceful and fitting for his mood.

A small laugh alerted Dovian. He looked to the side, catching a wandering couple as they traveled, drunk, into an alleyway. Moving his sights over the expanse, he noticed how barren the outside was. The Sorcēarian walked away from the hotel, taking large, slow steps toward a pole with a giant lantern.

'There can be no darkness without light,' he thought, remembering a passage from the second book his people routinely memorized.

Dovian tightly closed his eyes, remembering I'Lanthe's words from long ago.

"I believe everyone has a little bit of both. No one can truly be consumed by one or the other. I don't believe anyone is truly 100% evil."

Dovian sighed, feeling his depression sink further. "My dear, you were so wrong," he mumbled.

Thunder clapped again, and Dovian gripped his staff, his knuckles turning white. He grimaced, eyes closed, and choked out a painful cry as the rain brought back horrible memories.

He remembered I'Lanthe laughing. Her voice held a high pitch, echoing against the walls of her private garden. He chased her indoors and watched her leap onto the bed to hide beneath the covers. The smell of the orchids was as vivid in his memory as in real life. He remembered the feel of the smooth cloth of her satin sheets as he tickled her through the blankets. She screamed a shrill cry mixed with laughter as he mockingly attacked her. The crisp air made his nostrils tingle with the smell of spring showers.

Dovian shuddered. The memory faded from her giggling shriek to nothing but a horrible scream. His mind flashed with gruesome images of death—bodies lining the red-stained grass as far as the eye could see. Atop a mountain of corpses lay one familiar form. Her body seemed drained, her skin white, the violet tattoo on her cheekbone looking like a dark scar blending with the red smears of blood. Lavender eyes stared blankly, their usual glow now dissipated. Ice-cold, her dead body was nearly weightless as he lifted her, holding her tight.

"Damn it," Dovian cursed through closed teeth. The emotions that should have eventually faded into nothing were replaced by physical pain. He groaned, and his eyes closed as he tried to keep his knees from buckling.

Another memory flashed. I'Lanthe's brown curls were a mess underneath her large helmet, sticking to her face and neck. As hard as Dovian tried, she made no breath; she did not move, and her eyes held no more light. Her soul had left, gone far away. Dovian whispered to her, his mouth muttering in Legacy, praying for her to return, but nothing happened. He instantly became disconnected from the heavens; from that day forth, even God had nothing to do with him. He couldn't feel Him, couldn't hear Him. It was a new separation, and Dovian was more like the cursed humans. I'Lanthe was gone, too. His largest fears were then realized, and he could do nothing. He screamed. It was a feral sound. That day, all of the light of his world had extinguished.

"Lanthe," Dovian groaned, dropping to his knees.

The Sorcēarian kneeled in the center of Roma, rain soaking through his robes as he remained lost in his unbearable memories. A low cry sounded from him as he lost his battle. A shaking hand struggled to hold his staff upright. The robed individual hung his head, grimacing in pain, wishing that he could forget the past. He wished none of it had happened. He wished he had made a different choice. But there was nothing he could do now. The ordinary life that he once knew, one that was peaceful and happy, had been destroyed. He had taken it all for granted, just like everyone else. If he had known what his fate would have been, would he have done things differently? Would he have done more to save her? To save his people?

Dovian cried, tearing the porcelain mask from his face. The item clanged against the stone ground, shattering to pieces. Nothing, nothing could hide his remorse. Nothing could make him forget the horrors of his past. It was what he deserved— a life of misery. This life was his living Hell, separated from everyone and everything he once loved.

"I'm so sorry, I'Lanthe. I'm so sorry," Dovian gasped.

He remained on his knees underneath the pale-orange light. He didn't care that he was soaked to the bone. Nothing mattered at that moment. All of it—the memories and pain— stemmed from Ivory and her strange amnesia. There was no way Ivory could know about any of his memories unless she was I'Lanthe.

'It's impossible, Dovian. I'Lanthe is dead, long dead.' The thought made him groan. *'But so was Ivory. She's supposed to be dead.'*

Dovian's chest popped as his heart began to pound with hope. What if she was I'Lanthe? What difference would it make? What would it mean? Dovian still had too many questions and not enough answers, but the thought gave him a sliver of hope. Maybe he was given a second chance, an opportunity to make things right again.

Twelve chimes called out mournfully from the massive clock tower at the edge of the street. Dovian lifted his head, his hood falling. The rain washed over his face as he watched the lightning flash across the sky. Whatever happened, he couldn't let Ivory out of his sight, especially when Euclid was after her. Remembering this, Dovian stood. He had to find her.

A raid siren signaled in the distance. Dovian looked in the direction of the noise, frowning. Roma was in a state of alert from an attack. The enemy, Dovian was sure, wasn't human.

A hiss came from the right side, and Dovian spun, weapon at the ready. He watched with glaring eyes the alleyway from which the sound came. Waiting, he listened to the clicking of talons against the stone. One by one, the sounds increased, surrounding the Sorcēarian in all directions. Dovian walked, slowly dragging the staff behind him as he looked straight ahead, listening, waiting for the first attack.

He assessed his situation.

'First, one will attack from behind. As it does, a second will try to attack from the opposite direction as I turn. The two on the sides will be sure to move in simultaneously, both attempting to take me down at once—one reaching for my head, the other my legs.' He processed the thought in a millisecond, spinning with his staff. He cut across the first beast that leaped for his skull and pushed behind him with his other palm, sending a blue burst of light that knocked the second creature out of the air and onto its backside. As he followed through, he cut along the third that had jumped high from the left side, hit the middle of the returning second, and then met the wingtip of his staff on the side of the final beast's face that tried to take out his legs. Dovian ended in a crouching position, waiting for the next move.

'Rooftops,' he thought.

As the creatures launched from the buildings, Dovian kept up his effortless fight. Side to side, he dodged the demons' attacks. He followed through with energy blasts and slices. Within seconds, he had a dozen killed, the corpses surrounding him. He continued relentlessly, listening to the sirens from afar.

What exactly was it that Euclid planned on stealing? There were no reactors. What energy source would he need? And what, exactly, did he plan to do with all his nuclear power? He could've easily destroyed the planet numerous times by now. But Euclid did enjoy playing games.

A hum sounded a couple of meters away. Dovian turned with his staff aimed at the black distortion in the physical realm. A static charge pulsated, and the hole enlarged, bursting outward to reveal Euclid. Dovian charged toward the other Sorcēarian but abruptly paused once he noticed the body in the Azure man's arms— Ivory. Her eyes remained closed; she was unconscious.

"She's mine now, Dovian," Euclid taunted.

"No!" Dovian shouted, aiming at the man once again.

"I'll let my friends deal with you." Giving a hearty laugh, Euclid pressed against his chest. The portal behind him opened again and quickly consumed him and Ivory, taking them far away.

"Dovian!" Aria's voice interrupted the sudden silence that followed Euclid's departure.

A sharp stabbing traveled up Dovian's spine and spread throughout his body. His back arched, and he gurgled; the familiar feeling of warm, thick blood traveled up his throat. He slowly looked down, seeing the massive claws that penetrated his middle. A loud crack from Troy's weapon echoed in the night, the bullet shattering the Brawler's skull. It quickly fell to the ground, tugging abruptly from the Sorcēarian's body. Dovian coughed, the coppery taste filling his mouth. His shaking hands covered his wound as he slowly dropped to the ground in a heavy heap.

"Dovian! Dovian, are you all right?" Aria screamed, her hands shaking the downed man's shoulders.

"He'll be all right, Aria," Troy reassured her. He placed a hand on Dovian's chest, looking into his fading eyes. "I mean, he lived through a bullet to the head, right?"

Aria placed a hand on Dovian's cheek, whispering to him. The sound was distorted in the Sorcēarian's ears, blocked out by his choking noises as his lungs tried to collapse under his shattered ribs. Dovian gurgled, his body quaking as he reached for his staff, nails scratching at the stone. Troy quickly placed the weapon in his hand. Aria watched Dovian with fear; she looked pitiful and helpless as the man struggled in the middle of the street.

He gave a quiet mumble, and an intense blue light moved from one hand to another, the glow consuming the massive hole in his body. A sickening crunch sounded as his ribs returned to their rightful place. Dovian gave a large gasp and rolled over onto his hands and knees. Heaps of blood stained the ground, falling from his wound as he took deep breaths, mumbling in Legacy. He tried to hasten the process, holding one hand in the front and another in the back, his foreign language hastily traveling past his lips. After a few moments, he dropped into a sitting position and sighed, trying to regain his strength.

"Are you okay?" Aria asked after a minute.

"Yeah, fine," Dovian coughed.

"That didn't look very fine," Troy murmured.

"It doesn't feel good, I'll tell you that much," he grumbled, letting another blue light trail over his abdomen from his fingertips. "But I'm not dead."

"Guess that's worth something, right?" Troy asked.

Dovian fell silent. Slowly, he climbed to his feet. "I must follow him," he said with a weak voice.

"Follow him? How?" Aria asked.

Dovian quickly looked at the small device strapped to the inside of his scarlet overcoat. He had Mr. Clarke's gift—the frequency tuner. With a quick twist of the knob, Dovian disappeared.

"Wait! Dovian!" Aria shouted.

She and Troy took a couple of steps toward the center of the square, looking for the missing Sorcēarian. A howling wind rushed, the rain coming to a halt in a few final sprinkles. After roughly thirty seconds, Dovian reappeared, looking much healthier than he had only moments ago.

"That was fast," Troy said.

"Glad it was for you," Dovian muttered, catching his breath. "Took me days to catch up with him."

"Days?" Aria asked.

"Time is different on the outside. It isn't as you perceive it now," he explained. "I couldn't do anything, though. I was greatly outnumbered, and Euclid detected me nearby and closed the gate, taking Ivory with him."

"Where did he take her?" she questioned.

Dovian paused. He looked at the two soldiers beside him with heated eyes. "Ives."

"Oh, I Really Like This Dress A Lot"

CHAPTER 21

Dovian sat beside the window of his hotel room. He watched through the night the rushing shadows of the human Roman soldiers. Apparently, during the short attack on Roma, Euclid had managed to steal the entire robotic force, leaving the city-state with only a quarter of its militia. With his army of demons, two reactor cores, a massive Electrostatic Frequency Tuner, and an entire robotic military, Euclid only grew stronger with his arsenal. And that was without knowing what else he had obtained from the city-states that Dovian and the others couldn't travel to. Even now, the humans had nothing, not even the knowledge of his plan. Why didn't Euclid blow the planet to pieces? What was the purpose of slowly eating away at the city-states' resources?

Dovian closed his eyes, thinking of his journey through the alternate dimension using his frequency tuner. First, the tuner itself was based on ancient Sorcēarian technology, which meant Camery had some dealings with Euclid, but for what purpose and how? Why create the frequency tuner in the first place, especially when Euclid had one of his own? At least, Dovian assumed Euclid remained armed with his weaponry of the past.

Having traveled onto Ives before Euclid shut the portal, taking Ivory and himself into the physical realm to his hidden base of operations, Dovian stopped by the old cemetery. He didn't have to dig much to discover that Euclid's body was missing. As he suspected, the other Sorcēarian was alive again, but the question was, how? Was there someone else pulling the strings? The thought was quite an unpleasant one.

'You've been given extraordinary gifts. Why not Euclid?' Dovian thought wearily.

Upon further investigation of the ancient burial ground, Dovian had his heart broken again. As much as he disliked it, he traveled to I'Lanthe's tomb. It was left untouched, the same as the day he made it outside of being a bit overgrown with foliage. Still, the purple orchids blossomed. Timidly, he had pushed back the entry into her crypt and nearly doubled over with disappointment to find her sarcophagus locked and still occupied with the silhouette of her corpse. So, who was Ivory? What was her connection to I'Lanthe if she wasn't I'Lanthe herself?

He left with more questions than answers. But one thing was certain—Euclid had died once; he could surely die again.

Shortly, Dovian and the others would have their chance to find some answers. Once the morning arrived, they would set out to Ives. It could be their final battle, the one that saved or destroyed humanity. Either way, Dovian had a crucial decision to make. In the end, would he make the right choice? Would he be able to make up for his past mistakes? Would he be able to save what he fought so hard to protect, what he sacrificed his entire race to save? After all this time, was that sacrifice even worth it?

The Sorcēarian frowned. The spiraling questions created a static in his brain, leaving a heavy weight on his chest. He would have to wait and see.

Morning came quickly, the sun rising before Dovian even made it to his bed. The crisp pinkish-orange light crawled over the tallest peak of the skyscrapers, shining across his pale face. Slowly opening his heavy lids, the new day left an unsettling sensation deep within the man's gut. He sighed heavily, exhausted yet incapable of sleeping a single wink—not like he would have the opportunity now if he even wanted to. Rising from his chair, he grabbed his staff, watching the pulsating colors of the rising sun meld with the grays and reds of the city. He spun, his scarlet cape fluttering behind him as he took quick, large strides to his door.

Entering the hall, he looked to his left at the sound of two other doors closing. Troy and Aria looked equally tired in the morning light, each wearing their full-blown Fountain body armor of shimmering grey. Across their chests were the insignia for Fountains—a blue outline of an eye with splashes of water for eyelashes, a single tear dropping into their high-status symbols of a triple-bladed sword. None of them wanted to waste any more time; enough had been squandered at too high a cost so far in this war, a war that seemed horribly one-sided.

No one uttered a single word. Aria swiped her wrist across the door, watching Dovian. Troy did the same, taking eager strides to meet up with the Sorcēarian. They only eyed one another as the three met with tired and worn expressions. It seemed morale was dangerously low now. As much as Dovian wanted to lift the humans' spirits, no motivation came as he looked at the closed door to Ivory's room. Strangely, the hotel seemed hollow and empty in the deathly silence. Dovian lowered his eyes to the floor, feeling oddly out of place.

"We must move," Aria said, breaking the stillness.

"By what manner are we traveling?" Dovian asked quietly.

Troy glanced at the woman beside him. She quickly tugged off one of her forearm guards and dialed into her DNAIS. The hallway felt stuffy.

"Grayson," she said after a few seconds. Her tense face finally relaxed. "Let me talk to him."

Troy's shoulders lowered, his stiff position relaxing at the sound of Aria finally contacting someone on their side. Lately, it seemed it was them against the entire world. Nothing was worse than finding out that the corporation he and Aria devoted most of their lives to serve had suddenly branded them traitors and wanted their heads on a platter for trying to save humanity.

"James!" Aria shouted. She quickly turned away from the group. "I've been trying to reach you since we left! Why didn't you contact me?" she lectured the man. "I don't care if you were shot fifty times and fell a thousand meters from a window! You call me! Where are you?"

Troy smirked. Only Aria could get away with giving the President her motherly tone.

"No, we're fine. Well, except for Ivory. She's gone." Aria cringed. James' voice was loud enough that the two men could hear.

"What do you mean she's gone?" James Clarke shouted.

"Euclid took her. He took the robotic army, too. Roma's virtually defenseless."

"This isn't good, Aria. I need you to stop him, no matter the cost. We're running out of city-states in this world. With his arsenal, I fear his final attack will occur soon. I need you to figure out his plan, get Ivory away from him, and prevent his next attack. I'm no longer safe at Bio-Tech, so I cannot get you any projected locations. I cannot tell you of my current location," he quickly spoke, most likely afraid of the call being traced.

"Ives," she replied.

"Ives?"

"He's in Ives. I know this for a fact. Dovian tracked him down," Aria said.

There was hesitation in James' reply. "Aria, I want you to be careful with the Sorcēarian, got it? They are dangerous people. For all you know, he could be in on this plan. I know he's given no reason to make me believe so; he's been very faithful to you so far. Still…my gut tells me otherwise."

Aria eyed Dovian. His bright gaze met hers as if he had listened to the conversation.

"I don't think it will be a problem, sir, but I will keep myself prepared," she said quietly.

"Good. Now, I'm running out of time. A Hawk is heading your way. It will take you to where you need to go. Keep in contact. We'll have to keep conversations in short bursts, though. We cannot risk being detected. We have both sides against us, Aria. Resources will not be easy to obtain."

"Got it."

"Take care."

The phone call terminated, and the digital numbers flashed on the screen. With Grayson's security technologies, no one would have been able to pick up the call. If they did, it still wasn't enough time to track the location; at least Clarke would have sufficient time and smarts to know when to move to a new position. Things were getting scary. James may have been a fantastic soldier in his prime, but he hadn't seen the field in many years. He was rusty, and old age had caught up with him. Aria sighed. At least he had Grayson.

"Well?" Troy asked, tearing Aria from her thoughts.

"He's on the run from Walten. James had a run-in with Euclid, and the bastard's working with Walten as we expected. James is in hiding now. We'll have to be careful about contacting him from now on." She ran a hand over her DNAIS on her wrist, staring at the tiny chip embedded in her skin. "He's also got a Hawk on its way to our position. It should be here soon. It will take us to where we need to go."

"So, it looks like we're back where we started." Troy rubbed his armored hands together. "Really screws with the perspective of everything."

"We can't think like that. We had no idea what we were dealing with then," she said.

"I should've done something to prevent all of this," Dovian murmured.

Aria and Troy stared at the Sorcēarian. He had a rather gloomy expression.

"I've wasted so many chances, so much of my life. My carelessness has only caused the loss of more lives in the long run. You two should have never been brought into this battle in the first place." He faced them. Once again, Dovian appeared like the day they first met—older, mysterious, and angry. "This is my entire fault. This is a battle that I should be fighting alone."

"You can't fight this battle alone, Dovian," Aria stated.

He gave her a stern look. "Would it really make that much of a difference?"

Aria was silent. She and Troy gaped at the Sorcēarian. Just like that, Dovian reduced all their recent efforts to nothing. Even as top soldiers, they couldn't do much outside of getting in his way. Just as the recent attacks were beyond the militaries' comprehension, their complexity was similar for the species. The humans were of no use.

"I don't care what you say, Dovian," Aria snarled. "You are not going alone."

"I cannot risk your lives on top of the ones that have already been lost," he mumbled.

"We have the Hawk; you need it," she argued.

"I have a human-made frequency tuner, which would easily shred your body to pieces if you tried using it," he pointed out. "I'd already been in Ives by now."

She placed her hands on her hips. "You said it yourself last night; you were outnumbered when you came across Euclid's base."

"And how many can you take down?" Dovian questioned.

Troy stepped forward. "Does it really matter?" he asked with irritation. "Listen, you can fight the battle alone if you'd like, but don't count us out. It isn't your race that is in jeopardy; it's ours. As humans, we must fight. If we don't, then what's the point? What's the point in saving a race that doesn't value themselves?"

Dovian stared at his comrades, his stern expression softening. *That's an excellent point,'* he thought. Though, it wasn't quite in the context Troy meant. Did humanity value themselves? They made it a sport to kill one another with endless wars. All Euclid wanted was to speed up the process.

"We're not getting anywhere any faster by arguing," Aria said. She glared at Dovian. "Whether you like it or not, we're coming. Someday, you'll need us by your side, you'll see. We can save you, too." With a loud click, she loaded her weapon.

Dovian's cerulean eyes watched her green ones. A small smile threatened to turn up a corner of his lips as he felt more than he heard her thoughts. She was worried about him. Even though Troy refused to show it, he also felt camaraderie with the Sorcēarian. No matter how much Dovian argued, the two would not give up. And if it were the other way around, neither would he.

"Let's go," Dovian finally agreed.

The wait was only thirty minutes before the Hawk arrived in Roma, given special clearance by Dario Benvenuto to land in the center square. Aria couldn't help but notice the relief on the man's face at having her and her team gone from his city.

"Take your bad luck with you. I've had enough these past few days," Benvenuto said, covered in bandages from the battle that occurred in Saray after the treaty signing. "I was hoping for peace and quiet for a change, but it looks like that won't be coming any time soon."

"I'm sorry, sir, but this war involves everyone. We *will* need help if we want to succeed," Aria replied.

"Don't worry about that. I've already been in communication with Alijah Dizdarevic. He's willing to help us out now that our military has been diminished."

"Try calling Lebedev. Maybe he and Kovacevic can pull a few strings now that they have a new alliance," she suggested.

"I'll keep that in mind. Lebedev owes me one anyway," Benvenuto said, wiping his forehead. He looked slightly flushed despite the chilly air.

"Anything will help," Aria said.

"I wish you the best. Take care of yourselves out there. It's a far too dangerous war for only three people."

Aria feigned a smile, trying to stay optimistic over the whole ordeal. What she needed were more than three people. She required an entire army, but everyone else was busy rebuilding their militaries and cities, and the ones that were supposed to have her back currently hunted her team. They truly were on their own.

She turned to the Hawk 90, staring at the empty seats inside the cabin. Apprehensively, she and the two men boarded the vehicle. Setting her baggage in the back, she spun, instinctively looking for the pilot. How desperately she wished it were Gavin sitting in the cockpit, but it was a foolish thought.

"Class A-5, Commander of Special Tasking, Aria Ivanov?" The pilot asked, unbuckling from his seat. He took two massive strides toward the woman, offering her a hand. He was young, incredibly young. His slicked-back hair was a dark auburn streaked with hints of orange. His eyes were green with brown centering the pupils, shimmering with anticipation. He looked taller than he was with a thin physique, standing only a couple of centimeters higher than Aria. His voice was medium in tone, only giving him more of a rookie appeal. Aria forced a kind smile and shook his hand in return. "Hagar, Aren Hagar. C-5 pilot," he eagerly said.

Turning to Troy, the young man held out his hand again, feeding the soldier a big and toothy grin. Troy quickly followed up with one of his own. "Class A-4, Lieutenant Commander of Special Tasking, Troy Moreau?" he asked.

"That's me." Troy shook the boy's hand.

"Aren Hagar, sir. It's an honor to meet you two. I've heard a lot about your work during the False Syndicate war in Britainia," he chirped.

"Don't remind me," Troy scoffed.

"Just when I was forgetting all about that mission...." Aria rolled her eyes, remembering a specific chilly night in the middle of the bushes and Troy's constant antics, which had served as a more humorous memory than the gut-wrenching others from the mission.

"You saved many lives. I know that," Aren said, his voice lowering as he looked upon Dovian. "And you must be the, uh, sorcerer everyone's talking about."

"Sorcēarian," Dovian corrected.

"Right." Aren reluctantly held his hand out, shivering under Dovian's cold stare. "Delighted to meet you, sir."

Dovian stared at the waiting appendage, making the young pilot feel awkward for a few moments before finally grasping his hand and shaking it.

"I hope you know how to pilot this thing to its best potential," Dovian stated dryly.

"I'm the second-best there is, sir." Aren frowned then. "Well, *was*. I guess you can call me top of the Hawk pilots now." Aria took her seat, staring out the side window. Aren stammered a bit before adding, "I had the best teacher I could hope for, Mr. Sigo…." Aria's eyes lifted to the young man. "He taught me everything he knew."

"Gavin taught you?" Troy asked.

"Yes, sir. And I'm sorry he's gone now. I know you all were close." Aren cleared his throat. "Sorry to bring it up."

"It's all right. It's nice to know that he had a hand in your upbringing." Troy patted the pilot on the back, taking his seat beside Aria.

"Right. Well, how 'bout I get my ass to work, then?" Aren quickly turned, climbing into the cockpit. "Where we headin'?"

"Ives," Dovian replied, leaning against the wall as the doors to the cabin closed.

"Ives?" Aren sputtered. "You, you mean the place surrounded by hurricanes? The supposedly impassable place?"

"That's the place!" Troy winked. "Gavin got us in; let's see if he taught you well."

"Roger, sir!" Aren nodded quickly, slipping on his helmet. He diligently worked at lifting the copter off the ground. "We have takeoff. Destination: Ives. ETA: 08:45."

Troy, noticing Aria's fallen face, fed her a gentle smile.

"Cute kid," Troy said mentally to the woman.

"Don't get any ideas," she replied, finally looking more spirited. *"Wouldn't want to freak him out on his first day."*

"Damn, I like making the pilots blush," Troy chuckled.

"Have I misplaced your sexual orientation?" Dovian butted in, taking a poorly chosen social cue from Kovacevic's book.

Aria snickered.

"It's a joke, Dovian! I'm kidding!" Troy quickly countered, turning his head to the Sorcēarian.

"Actually, there was that one time, Troy," Aria interrupted, but he quickly silenced her.

"Hey, I'm not judging," Dovian replied. *"Besides, I think the young man was quite taken by you, based on his thoughts."*

"You're kidding, right? Is the kid a flamboyant?" Troy's face turned a bright shade of red. There was no reply. *"IS HE?"*

Dovian did not answer but chuckled, watching outside the small window beside him.

"Shut up." Troy folded his arms childishly. *"You're just jealous. You know I'm cute!"*

"Actually, more than once, now that I think about it," Aria mumbled.

"Shut your flaps, woman!" Troy hissed.

The woman sighed, turning her gaze out the window. It was going to be a long flight.

Wandering and padding against the rock with scaly feet, Hector sniffed the air with his tongue pointing outward. After searching for so long, he was finally close. Of course, it didn't help that he got lost a couple of times along the way, tempted by green pastures and nests full of fresh albatross eggs. What could he do? Dovian had spoiled him since birth, feeding him heaping piles of soup and jerky. Hunting wasn't Hector's forte; it was incredible he even made it this long out in the wild. Needless to say, his extra belly fat had diminished during the past week and a half; Dovian would be proud of him for persevering for so long.

Halting, he sniffed at the air again. Very close. So, awfully close.

He continued his scuttle, his talons clicking against the large boulder as he tried to scale down the side of the wall leading to the valley's cave system. Hector decided to take quick, broad steps. The stones were extra hot in the unusually bright and sunny weather. Looking to the sky, he poked the air with his tongue. As expected, the humidity was strangely low in this part of the island. Hector couldn't remember a single day of his reptilian life where it didn't rain, at least for a short while. Things sure were strange since Dovian left. It was like the island itself rebelled against the disappearance of its keeper.

A sound alerted the lizard. Hector stopped; his flaps expanded from his neck as he listened intently. No, that was not the sound he was looking for. In fact, that was a sound he did not want to be near at all. Hector paddled forward, quickly making his way down the side of the valley in the opposite direction from where the terrifying shriek came.

Another thing that changed since his master's disappearance was the overall *feeling* of Ives. There was something not right about the land. It wasn't peaceful. It felt…evil and dark. If that sound was any indication of what the valley held, Hector wanted nothing to do with the horrors that lay in the caves, but it also meant it was pertinent he followed through with his mission. He had to hurry.

Scurrying down the last couple of boulders, Hector slipped, the smooth surface sending the plump reptile onto his back at the foot of the hillside. Hissing, he flipped over, and sand got in his beady eyes. Blinking slowly, he stuck out his long pink tongue, trying to gather his bearings. The smell was somewhat worrisome, and so were the sudden vibrations that shook from beneath his scaly underside. As he raised his head, his flaps abruptly expanding, Hector scampered back into the rocky wall behind him as he saw a massive monster of a beast lurching toward him. It was a frilled monitor at least fifteen times the size of Hector. With each pounding step the creature took, charging at full speed, little Hector bounced slightly, his stomach slapping against the rocky ground. The beast slid to a halt, dust billowing in tan clouds around its body as it voraciously roared with neck flaps flopping out to the sides, making it appear even bigger.

It was the one-of-a-kind King Lizard, the very lizard Dovian had warned Hector about. Also, the same lizard he was searching for. Large tattoos lined the creature's skin, markings that were centuries old, given by the Sorcēarians. Down the side of its neck was another colorful stretched pattern that was hard to read from a lizard's point of view. 'Petey' it was called. It watched tiny Hector with golden eyes, and its head turned slightly to the side. The King Lizard called out again, the bellow echoing throughout the gorge. From the caves, hundreds of scurrying monitors neared the valley's center, surrounding Hector and the frightening Petey.

Hector flapped his frills again, honked the loudest he could manage, and gave Petey the meanest look possible. Then, he hunkered down, praying that the King Lizard wouldn't make him his afternoon snack.

"I didn't know you could play the piano," James said as he quietly walked over to the grand piano in the living area of his apartment. Pulling up a chair, he sat beside the small girl who softly played the instrument.

"Mommy taught me." She looked up at him, her fingers stopping.

James fell silent a moment, staring at the girl's hands. "Please, continue playing. It was a beautiful song," he said quietly.

The little girl with bright green eyes and long black hair looked back at the keys of ivory and obsidian. Carefully, she continued her song, her small fingers expertly pressing against the large keys. It was a sad melody but still beautiful all the same. James watched the girl as she kicked her dress-shoed feet back and forth, unable to touch the pedals of the large piano. The sun slowly set on the horizon, casting an aura of light around the girl's body as she played. He smiled as the scene made the man a tad-bit sentimental. This is what he fought for every day—a peaceful life full of sweetness and joy. Sadly, the reason the child lived in his apartment was the opposite of what he wished to achieve in his line of work.

As the song slowed to a lower octave, James' eyes dropped to the small plate in his hands. Chocolate chip cookies and a glass of milk. Would it even make a difference in this poor girl's life? Would she even want to be around him in the future once he mustered the strength to tell her the truth, tell her that he was the reason her parents were no longer alive? Wrong coordinates or not, it wouldn't bring her parents back. Nothing would. Lost in his thoughts, he didn't notice that the girl had stopped playing and watched him with sad eyes.

"James?" she asked timidly.

"Yes, Aria, my dear?" he replied, lifting his head and smiling.

"Why do you look so sad?" she asked, crawling on her knees on the black bench, her blue dress crinkling underneath her posture. "Do you not like cookies?" She pointed at the platter in his lap.

"Oh, I was just lost in my thoughts, sweetheart. In fact, I brought the cookies to cheer us both up." Setting the plate on the bench, he lifted a glass and handed it to the small girl. She grinned and giggled, sipping with both tiny hands holding either side of the glass.

"What is this?" she asked, setting the drink down.

"Milk. Have you had it?" he asked, sipping from his own.

"No, well, maybe once, but I can't really remember." She shook her head, her long hair falling over her shoulders behind her blue headband.

"Do you like it?" he asked.

Taking another gulp, she made a funny face. "I think so."

"Here, let me show you a trick," James said. Taking a fresh cookie, he dunked it into his glass.

"What are you doing? You're ruining it," the girl gasped.

"This is how you're supposed to eat the cookie." He chuckled, taking a bite out of the delicious dessert.

Aria watched, her tiny mouth hanging open as the man nibbled on his treat. Slowly, she took a giant cookie of her own and dunked it into her glass, the milk touching her fingertips. Giggling, she grabbed a second and repeated the actions. "One for each hand!" she exclaimed.

James laughed, watching the child bite from one cookie and then the other. "You certainly catch on quickly."

They sat for a while, slowly eating their cookies until they drank all the milk. Little Aria dumped the last drops of her drink onto the largest crumb she could find. They had eaten nearly a whole dozen between the two of them. It was not the healthiest of dinners, but it was the best James could do, and Aria didn't seem to mind.

"I drew a picture today," the girl said once they finished.

Hopping from the piano bench, she trotted to her school bag and pulled out a small digital book. With the item clenched between two hands, she ran up to the man and hopped unexpectedly into his lap. After poking the screen a couple of times and turning a few pages, she mentioned her homework for the day.

"Whatcha got there?" James asked.

His smile quickly fell as he saw the title of her assignment. On the screen was the label, 'family.' Below, Aria had drawn a picture of two small urns belonging to her mother and father. Then, off to the side was a tall man in a military uniform and another little boy.

"That's mommy, and that's daddy." She pointed at the urns. "And that's you." Giving a big grin, she looked up and over her shoulder at James, her finger pressed against the image of the militant.

"It's a lovely picture," James whispered, kissing her head. Looking at the small boy, he poked the screen. "Who's that?"

Aria hesitated, giving a slight shrug. "It's Troy."

"You consider him family?" James asked, chuckling.

"I don't know. Maybe he can be my brother someday. I always wanted a brother or a sister."

"Maybe, one day, you will be family." Grabbing the digital book, he lifted Aria off his lap and quickly strode into the kitchen area.

"What are you doing?" she asked.

James tapped on the side of the notebook and held it beside the refrigerator. Dragging his finger across the screen, he copied and pulled the image onto the cooler's door. Smiling, he handed the notebook back to Aria. "Now, I have a copy."

A blush spread over the girl's cheeks. She turned and quickly ran to her bag, placing the notebook inside again. The room was already dark; green and blue lights flickered from the advertisements outside. James quickly made his way into the room, waving on a side lamp.

"It's getting late. We should finish up your other homework," he said.

Aria frowned, wrinkling her nose.

"Don't make that face; it's important."

Unenthusiastically, she made her way to the dining room table, where an arsenal of weapons lay. Lifting one of the rifles, James ensured the magazine was out, the safety was on, and the chamber was empty.

"Now, what's this?" James asked, holding out the gun. With the other hand, he picked up a couple of ammunition shells.

Aria rolled her eyes. "That's easy. It's a bullpup Fernstal 300, tactical forward grip, red laser, and night vision sights, equipped with a SABO launcher and 30 cal. high-density, armor-piercing rounds." She thought a moment with a finger on her chin. "Oh! And an extended mag with trace planters."

"Very good," James said, smiling. "You're going to be top in your class for sure."

Hopping on the balls of her feet, Aria grinned, asking him to test her knowledge of another weapon.

'*Voom.*'

A rumble jerked Aria from her restful sleep. She hadn't even realized she had dozed off. She lifted her head, her stiff neck aching at the sudden movement, and rubbed her skin from between her armor and helmet, trying to soothe the tight muscles. She looked at Troy, the man stretching out his legs as he must've fallen asleep, too. He turned his head, looking from behind his helmet's lenses at the woman beside him.

"We've reached Ives. It seems the weather forecast is in our favor today." Aren's voice called from over the intercom.

"That is very odd," Dovian murmured, standing from his seat to look out the cabin window. The man was shocked to see that Ives appeared bright and sunny, not a single cloud in the sky. It was the first time in thousands of years that this had occurred. It made the Sorcēarian anxious.

"Looks like there's no need for a HALO jump," Aren said. "You want me to take her down?"

"Pull her down. There's a valley about 50 kilometers to the south. I take it this has stealth capabilities?" Dovian asked.

"Yes, sir," Aren affirmed.

"Good; use all that you've got. Land about 5 kilometers away. Euclid won't detect us if we're lucky, but I'm assuming he already knows we are here." Dovian pushed away from the window, readying his staff as Aren flipped numerous switches. The Hawk hummed, its outside walls deteriorating visually as it took in the reflections of the blue sky, making it undetectable by both human eyes and radar. "We'll walk the rest of the way."

Aria and Troy nodded, letting Dovian take the lead. It was his territory; he knew it best.

After a few minutes, Aren landed the Hawk effortlessly, the propellers smoothing the blades of tall grass to the ground. The cabin doors slid open. Aria, Troy, and Dovian quickly gathered their weapons and packs and hopped out of the Hawk 90.

Aren quickly darted into the back, hollering from inside, "I'm coming with you, right?"

Aria and the others looked back at the young man. He leaned out the Hawk, hand gripping the support bar. His posture was lax. In his other hand was an Air Force issued automatic pistol with auto-aim capabilities. Despite having a rookie appeal, his eyes were hardened and serious. He was ready to take the plunge.

"No," Aria and Troy quickly replied.

Aren's face fell, his brow wrinkling.

"Aren, we need you in the sky. If something happens to you, we're stuck," Aria said.

"…Okay," the pilot hesitantly replied.

"We're not dealing with humans out here. I'm sure the Air Force hasn't prepared you for anything like this. Not saying anything about your skills as a fighter, but we need you to be on the safe side, ready to pull us out at any moment," Troy said, trying to do damage control.

"What do you mean we're not dealing with humans?" Aren asked with genuine curiosity.

Aria and Troy exchanged equally confused looks.

"What do you know about this war we're fighting?" Aria asked.

"The President didn't say much. I was told it was a Black Book project. I assumed we were supposed to be sneaking into some secret Cherno military base. They've declared war since Mr. Walten took over Elixis," Aren explained. He noticed Aria and Troy's looks of disbelief. Dovian stood with arms folded, looking at the sky in annoyance. "And that's why they nuked Athenia…to get back at Mr. Walten."

"That goddamn bastard!" Troy kicked a rock on the ground. Aria shook her head. "He's lying to our people? Our own soldiers?!"

"I'm not surprised," Aria said. "He's trying hard to cover his tracks."

"Y-you mean, Mr. Walten's lying?" Aren asked with surprise.

Troy laughed. "That pompous, sadistic prick? When is he not lying? People always follow the dollar signs before they ever try to look at the truth."

"I'm afraid he's pulled the wool over your eyes, Aren," Aria said, eyeballing the irate Troy beside her.

"But what do we do?" Aren asked. "He's sending the army out to Cherno as we speak. They've announced war on Cherno."

"Shit!" Troy cursed.

"This would have been helpful to know before we left Roma," Aria agitatedly said.

Aren shrugged. "I assumed you knew!"

"Walten's been after our asses since we started this mission. He wants us dead. He's trying to cover up his tracks by eliminating us," she explained. "And now he wants to annihilate our allies as well."

"So…what exactly is it that we are fighting?" Aren asked nervously.

Aria sighed. "It's too complicated to explain. Here." She stepped toward the man, clicking on her DNAIS. "This is a report I've compiled since we started. It will be everything you'll need to know about our current situation. After reading, you'll understand why you'll need to stick to the skies." She pulled up the data and copied it into Aren's DNAIS. The man's eyes widened as the pages of documents flickered into his wrist, some revealing scary images of the creatures Aria had come across. "And it'll make a good backup if something happens to us."

"What was that?" he asked, staring at his wrist.

"Read it," Aria ordered before returning to Dovian and Troy's side. The pilot watched her with a frightened expression. "Get in the air, Aren. Mission starts now."

"R-roger!" Aren said, saluting the woman quickly before darting into the pilot's chair.

Dovian led the way through the tall grass. The Hawk 90 whirred as it lifted. The optics of the golden-brown grassy plain filtered into beautiful blues as it reached the sky. Quietly, as an invisible eye, Aren stayed in the air, watching his team travel toward the rocky valley a few kilometers away. It would be a long walk, but Aren could be at their destination in seconds if they needed an emergency evac.

As the pilot hovered in midair, hidden behind make-believe clouds, he reviewed the intel Aria had given him. He looked over the report in Cherno, images of the Brawlers and Brutes flickering on the screen.

"Holy shit!" Aren sputtered.

Apprehensively, he turned the page, looking over the report from Saray. A Spewer spun three-dimensionally from his wrist.

"Holy shit!!" he whimpered.

He continued turning pages, reading about the attack in Roma, the attack on the Underbelly, the conspiracy involving Walten and General Feyette, and the information on Euclid and Ivory. Finally, he came across the file on Gavin's death.

"Mr. Sigo…" Aren murmured. His teeth clenched as he read the report. "They told me it was anti-aircraft missiles from Cherno." Angrily, the young pilot punched the chair beside him. "Those damned bastards! After everything you've done for them over the years, this is how they repay you and your comrades? They are making a mockery of our lives!"

Calming his fury, Aren slowly released his breath. This is why he wanted to be in the Air Force—to make a difference. And be damned if he would let a conspiracy like this get swept under the rug. He owed it to his fallen comrades, Gavin, and, most importantly, his grandmother and girlfriend. They lived in the Underbelly and were killed during the attack the Saraian and Roman soldiers supposedly initiated— the new allies of the Cherno forces, thus enemies to Fountains. Walten tried to eradicate his competition through lies, which the citizens and military thoroughly believed. Walten wouldn't get away with it, at least not while Aren was alive. He would make sure of that.

A small beep pulled the pilot out of his daze. Looking out the window, three red circles appeared on the glass. They funneled in toward three dots on the horizon, pulling the image closer as it zoomed in. Aria, Troy, and Dovian were close to their destination. Aren sat forward, closing the documents in his DNAIS. He had to be at his best. Leaning toward the dash, he stared in the direction of the valley with wide eyes, not daring to blink. His hands rested on either side of the control stick, ready to speed forward when the others called for help.

Dovian crouched, hiding in a thicket. He sniffed and then wiped his nose.

"Sulfur," he murmured. "There's an entryway in one of these caves."

Looking over the tall man's shoulder, Troy noticed the dozens of holes that burrowed deep into the sides of the valley.

"Any idea which one?" he whispered.

"Not in the slightest," Dovian replied, looking over his shoulder at the man.

"Why are there so many of them?" Aria asked.

"Dragon Valley. It is home to the indigenous reptiles of Ives," Dovian said.

"Sounds lovely," the woman sarcastically stated. "Any reptiles we should be worried about?"

"Only one." Dovian, staying low, walked cautiously toward the cliffside. "And when you see him, you'll know why. I'd suggest running unless you want to become its mid-afternoon snack."

"So, not only do we have demons to worry about, but we have man-hungry lizards on the loose," Troy said, lacking enthusiasm.

Dovian abruptly held up a hand, coming to a halt. "Quiet," he mumbled.

Aria and Troy slowed to a stop, looking straight ahead into the deep valley.

From one of the massive caves came a single Roman robot. Its headdress bobbed with each step, the metallic feet stomping up dust clouds. It walked toward the valley's center and then paused, turning about-face. A loud siren rang, a call from the machine, and the rest of the army marched from the other tunnels, filling up the base of the gorge. After a few minutes, the machines halted with a click of their heels, their backs to Dovian and the others. One after another, they saluted and looked toward the left. From the center cave, the main artery of the system, a Brawler crawled on all fours toward the leading robot. It licked the machine, tasting the metal. Afterward, the monster stood upright, its large, clawed hands digging into the backside of the mechanical soldier. The robot fizzled and beeped as the demon tore off its back paneling. Frantically, the Brawler unplugged a series of wires and reconnected a few. After shooting out a couple of sparks, the robot went dead, its knees bending as its head drooped. The Brawler then shrieked and began to shake violently. After having what appeared to be a seizure, the creature dropped onto the rock floor. It did not move.

"What happened?" Aria asked quietly.

Dovian's eyes narrowed. He quickly pulled up his optical camera, zooming in on the beast's body. He watched a pale haze of vibrations quaking in the monster's place. The mist moved forward into the backside of the machine and disappeared. Giving a couple of mechanical beeps, the Roman soldier awoke once again and straightened in posture. Looking at its feet, it stomped with one foot forward and then another. Excitedly, the robot twitched and moved in a circle.

"It's inhabited the machine's body," Dovian said dryly.

"You mean that thing is now living inside that robot?" Troy gawked. "Is that possible?"

"Seems it is," the Sorcēarian grumbled.

"For what purpose? Why not just rewire them?" Aria asked.

"I'm uncertain. Perhaps they are interested in the technology. They could be running tests," Dovian said.

"What kind of tests?" Troy questioned, watching as the general of the Roman soldiers giddily stepped from side to side, testing out the machine's range of movement.

"Your guess is as good as mine. Perhaps they plan on using them as a sort of Trojan horse," the robed man suggested.

"Trojan horse?" The male soldier lifted an eyebrow from behind his helmet.

Dovian gawked at the man. "Something associated with the origins of your name, and you know nothing about it?"

Troy looked at Aria, who merely shrugged.

Dovian palmed his forehead. "Troy was the name of an ancient city in the country that was at one time called Turkey. A war between Troy and the Achaeans took place there called the Trojan War. Epic story told short, the Achaeans fooled the warriors of Troy by offering them a gift under the pretense of their packing up and sailing home. It was a giant wooden horse. Inside the horse were soldiers. Troy accepted the gift and pulled the giant horse into their walls, unknowingly allowing the enemy into their home. That night, while everyone was drunk and asleep, the enemy slipped out of the horse, opened the gates for the rest of the army, and attacked and burned Troy to the ground."

"Pretty epic," Troy muttered. "What were they fighting for?"

"A woman..." Dovian replied dryly, glancing at Aria. "Not the first time man ruined themselves because of temptation."

"Dad always did say that a woman would bring about the ruin of man," Troy said.

"You have no idea," Dovian chuckled.

"Will you two shut up? Or a woman will bring about the end of your days," Aria butted in.

Dovian and Troy, momentarily distracted, straightened their postures as they looked upon the robotic army before them. The robot general called out to the other robots, telling them to remain at attention. Then it turned to the left and returned to the cave system the beast had initially exited.

"I think I know which cave we should check out first," Dovian remarked.

Aria slipped to the side, her weapon in front of her. "Then let's move out."

"Moving," the Sorcēarian replied.

Together, the three slid carefully down the side of the valley behind the Roman army. Dovian shielded his form with his staff, his body disappearing. Troy and Aria did the same, messing with the configurations on their forearms. Their bodies swirled with rocky patterns and quickly vanished into the landscape. Slowly, with quiet steps, they entered the dark cave. The rocky cavern twisted and turned for a few hundred meters, lowering deeper underground. The darker it got, the more Aria and Troy's armor adjusted. Aria kept moving forward, staring straight ahead. A low, muffled grunt sounded from her as she ran into an invisible wall. A second later, another invisible force bumped into her from behind.

"Whoa! Who put on the brakes?" Troy mentally asked.

"Damn it, Dovian. Why'd you stop?" The woman glared ahead of her.

"We are close. I can feel him," Dovian whispered in her mind.

"Euclid?"

"Yes," he hesitated, *"and something is slightly amiss about his signature."*

"What?" Aria asked, staring straight ahead into the darkness.

"He seems to be in an awfully bad mood. Something very sinister is in this cave. In fact, I am unsure whether it is Euclid or not."

"What else could it be?"

"I don't know. Let's go find out. There's a light ahead."

Moving on, Aria stayed as close as she could to the Sorcēarian. She moved slowly, feeling Troy's hand on her shoulder as he made sure not to lose her in the dark. After traveling a small distance, they came to a makeshift staircase made of slick rocks and broken stalagmites. Climbing up the steps, the three entered a hollowed-out chamber. Giant torches cast an eerie pale glow within the cavity, lining the rounded walls. At the back center of the room was a sizeable makeshift throne. Flat black rocks lay on the ground, stacked by three. From the floor spiraled two giant stalagmites on either side of the chair. Another flat surface connected them, creating armrests that joined an enormous, rectangular back. It was an unnerving sight.

"Is this his throne room?" Aria asked quietly.

"Appears to be," Dovian replied in an equal volume.

A shuffling sound came from behind the throne, coupled with the tinkling of chains. Shooting out from behind the stone furniture appeared a head covered with curly blonde hair. Large blue eyes stared up fearfully in their direction. The woman looked from side to side anxiously.

"Ivory," Aria whispered. Uncloaking, the female soldier appeared in the middle of the room. Taking quick steps, she neared the throne. Dovian and Troy did the same and checked the sides of the room with their weapons at the ready as Aria looked over the imprisoned woman.

"N-no. No," Ivory whimpered. "You shouldn't have come. You should have stayed away."

"We had to come for you, Ivory. We couldn't just let Euclid take you." She looked at the massive metal ring clamped around the blonde's wrists. "Dovian, can you get this off of her?"

"No, no," Ivory said shakily. "You don't understand. You don't understand what's happening."

Dovian quickly neared Ivory, grasping the chains. He looked at the terrified woman with worried eyes.

"It's not just Euclid. It's far worse," Ivory whispered to Dovian. At any moment, it looked like she could have a nervous breakdown.

"What are you doing here?" A small voice invaded the conversation, echoing against the stone walls.

Troy and Aria spun, aiming their weapons at the intruder. Dovian locked eyes with Ivory. His hands trembled, slowly letting go of her binds. With trepidation, he cautiously turned toward the source of the little voice. It sounded sweet and innocent, but there was an underlying tone that left the Sorcēarian feeling the worst dread he had felt since the annihilation of his people.

"We can ask the same to you," Aria replied, rifle aimed at a small child. "Were you kidnapped, too?"

The ghostly little girl, with pale skin and ashen hair, giggled. Her blue-grey eyes shimmered in the firelight that decorated the chamber walls. She shook her head carelessly, her tiny fists gripping the sides of her white dress. Dovian clenched his staff tightly, looking at the child with a face that clearly expressed he was frightened of her.

"What's your name?" Troy gently asked the girl.

Giving another sweet giggle, she replied, "Sapphire."

"Losing Hope"

CHAPTER 22

Dovian, a giant statue frozen by his fear, watched the child in the chamber's center. His fingernails dug deep into his palm and drew blood, the crimson a lively contrast to his pale skin. A deep breath of the musty air flared his nostrils as he had momentarily forgotten how to breathe. He watched with his glowing eyes the amused little ones coming from the girl named Sapphire. The giggle that tore past the wretched girl's lips burned his ears. He couldn't move, couldn't process a single thought as he gaped dreadfully at the small intruder. Two hands clamped around one of his legs, tearing the Sorcēarian out of his trance. It was Ivory. Her hands were cold, and Dovian felt them through his robes.

"And how did you get here, Sapphire?" Aria asked. The name repeated from the woman's lips caused Dovian to cringe. Luckily, she never lowered her weapon, holding a more concerned pose.

"This is my home," Sapphire replied.

"Shoot her. Shoot her now!" Dovian shouted in the soldiers' minds.

Troy looked at Dovian, bewildered. Aria flinched but still hesitated.

It was too late. Sapphire's eyes tapered, her pupils enlarging to cover the irises in blackness. An invisible force exploded from the child's body, slamming into Aria and Troy. Their shields flickered and became obsolete from the blast as they collided with the rock wall, sending fractures up the sides. Loud grunts sounded from the two soldiers, and their limp bodies dropped to the floor.

"You invade my home and then think you can attack me?!" the child shouted. Her mouth didn't move as the voice erupted in a dual oscillating tone, with one pitch octaves lower than the other.

Dovian guarded the blast with his staff, a transparent shield sparing him and the frightened Ivory. Sapphire's dark eyes glared at him, slowly flickering between black and blue.

"Euclid!" Sapphire's monstrous voice called out for the estranged man.

A vibration distorted the air near one of the entrances with a quiet rumble, and a shimmer of azure emerged. "You called?" A smile lined Euclid's face as he looked at the fallen and broken soldiers on the opposite side of the room before bringing his attention to Dovian, who stood rigidly beside the throne. He chuckled. "You look like you've seen a ghost, Dovian."

"What is this that you've brought to this plane?" Dovian gruffly asked, eyes shooting daggers in Euclid's direction.

Euclid laughed heartily at this statement. "Dovian..." he shook his head, "Dovian, Dovian, Dovian." Euclid clasped his hands together, walking around Sapphire, keeping a safe distance from the child. "You mean to ask what this is that brought me back to this plane."

Dovian's face fell further. "Then it is as I feared." He returned his attention to the angry child, her appearance returning to normal.

Giving a small sigh, Sapphire shook her head. "Euclid, his weakness is overwhelming. Destroy him."

"My pleasure," Euclid quickly spat.

Before Dovian could even budge, Euclid rammed against him and crushed his body into the back wall. Ivory dropped to the side, her head slamming against the arm of the throne.

"Careful of the prisoner, you idiot!" Sapphire shrieked, staring at the now unconscious blonde. "We need her."

Euclid shuddered under the child's terrible tone but kept his menacing stare fixated upon Dovian, who sagged, his body pinned into the rocky surface. "Get up. At least try to accept your defeat with dignity," he snarled.

"You always pride yourself before the battle's even begun," Dovian growled back. His eyes glistened with double the intensity. He lunged forward from his resting place, his enormous, feathered wings pushing him outwards. He tackled Euclid, the two flying past Sapphire as she sidestepped out of the way with an indignant look on her small face.

The two Sorcēarians rolled to the side, guarding themselves as they slowly circled in the middle of the room. Noticing the struggling bodies of Aria and Troy, Euclid gave another cocky smile. "Can I kill the humans? Make him watch as I tear them limb from limb?" He sent multiple images into Dovian's mind of his disgusting plans for the two militants. Dovian gritted his teeth, taking a millisecond to look upon his comrades. Troy's shaking hand reached out for Aria, nudging her gently.

Sapphire watched the two armored humans with disinterest. "No. They are weak and insignificant. I want to watch the hope drain from their souls as they watch their Sorcēarian die a terrible death. Afterward, you can do what you like with them."

"Your quarrel is with me; leave them alone!" Dovian roared. "Besides, I've been the only one who's prevented you from carrying out your plans. Without me, they are no threat to you."

"You have no say in the matter," Sapphire monotonously replied.

Sending a blast at Euclid, Dovian rolled on the ground and twisted to the side, pulling his staff around. The winged tip dragged the azure man's legs out from underneath him. He grabbed Euclid's blue overcoat, lifted him off the ground, and smashed his fist into his nose. Dovian followed through with his foot against the other Sorcēarian's chest and sent him crashing into the wall.

The loud shouting and booming of the magical beings brought Aria out of her painful daze. She moaned, her hands trembling. Troy shook her shoulder again, sending waves of pain throughout her body.

"Are you all right?" Troy asked. It could have been the first time he asked or the tenth; she didn't know for sure.

"I feel like every bone in my body is broken." She grimaced.

"You too, huh?" Troy muttered. "Goddamn…."

"I feel like I'm going to throw up."

"Do these suits have morphine?"

Aria slowly tugged her arm up to her face. A sharp stabbing erupted through her shoulder, making her gasp. Quickly pressing a button labeled with a medic symbol, her suit hissed, and her body promptly numbed and tingled as injections traveled up her spine into her nervous system. A quiet moan passed her lips as she gave a small, relaxed smile. Her mind swirled with giddiness, and she patted Troy on the shoulder with a shaking hand and blurted out a giggle.

"P-push the button," she whispered.

Troy quickly complied with her request. His curved body immediately uncoiled. Rolling onto his backside, he smiled stupidly from behind his helmet, staring through the visor at the pointed rock ceiling.

"Much better," he sighed.

A scream alerted the two. With quick twitches, they looked to the source of the noise. Blurs of red and blue sped across the flickering orange light, shadows bouncing around the room. Troy's eyes darted anxiously from left to right, trying to make sense of the movements as Euclid and Dovian crashed into one another, the walls shaking with each tremendous impact.

Euclid's hair had fallen over his eyes as blood dripped from his nose. He glared at Dovian, cupping his face as he healed his broken features. "You know how redundant this is?”

“Very,” Dovian replied.

Euclid lifted his eyes to the ceiling in irritation. “Then why do you keep fighting? You know I will only heal myself in turn.”

“And I will do the same, so why are you fighting me?”

“Because you stand in my way.”

“And what is your way?” Dovian twirled his staff, the wings scraping against the cave floor as he walked to the side.

Euclid’s shoulders sagged. “You already know my way, Dovian! Stop wasting time!”

The azure man held both of his hands out to the side. Closing his eyes and breathing deeply, he pulled his palms together, elbows out like in prayer. Then he rotated his wrists, turning his hands upside-down. He watched Dovian from behind his long raven-black hair. A portal opened behind Euclid, and numerous Brawlers lunged out, surrounding Dovian, howling and snarling like dogs. It was a new power that Euclid had learned. No doubt something Sapphire had attributed him.

“You tread on the dangerous side, Euclid,” Dovian said.

“Likewise,” he replied.

“You’ve betrayed your purpose.”

“Purpose!” Euclid shouted, the sound reverberating loudly. “Like the tool that I am? Why? To live an enslaved life by a moral code that I disagree with? To let terrible things happen in a corrupt and disgusting world? And you think I’m the evil one?”

“You are blasphemous with every breath you breathe!” Euclid’s transgressions angered Dovian. “You are just as fallen as those before, yet you think you are somehow better and more deserving of His love.”

Seated at her throne, Sapphire lifted her gaze, sending a heated glare at Euclid, which he could feel without matching.

“No…not love. You don’t want His love. You want His power,” Dovian said accusingly.

“I want His control!” Euclid snapped.

“There is no control! Everything you have done and felt—every tear, pain, laugh, and cry—has been your own doing!”

“He threw us in this hellish world and left us, forsaken us, to live by His selfish design because He did not want to deal with it Himself! He didn’t want to admit He failed!”

Euclid lunged forward, sending a potent wall of power against Dovian’s body. The six monsters that Euclid called upon surrounded the fallen man. One clicked its nasty talons against the floor, anxiously waiting to taste Dovian’s blood. The scarlet Sorcēarian pushed up, kicking one of the creatures in the face. With a shriek, the others darted forward. Dovian twirled and cut across three and instantly sent them to ash.

"They are no match for me, Euclid," he muttered. "Just as you are no match for me, and you are no match for Him!"

Dovian ducked as one creature jumped for his head. Expertly, he sidestepped, avoiding a second, and shoved his staff behind him, planting the wings of his weapon around the creature's neck. The blue orb electrified its body as Dovian pulled up and over, throwing the demon directly at Euclid. Frowning, the black-haired man raised a palm, sending the nearing monster's body into ashes.

"It was never He who left! It was you who had forsaken His gift!" Dovian shouted as he continued his attack on Euclid. They tussled about, exchanging powerful blows that slowly deteriorated the cave walls. Dovian spun, his staff sending a horizontal wave toward Euclid, and then rolled his shoulders to bring the weapon downward, sending a vertical wave after. He had pinned Euclid against the wall as the man ducked beneath the first attack and tried to jump to the side. The second shot cut through Euclid's left leg, and he dropped to the ground. Dovian gripped Euclid's front, tugging him close to his face. "He didn't leave; you left Him."

"Says the one who destroyed everything He stood for," Euclid sneered. "Dovian, has it ever occurred to you that you followed through with the largest part of my plan?"

Dovian gaped at his enemy, looking shocked.

"You were always a little slow, weren't you?"

"It was for humanity's own good!" Dovian growled.

"Was it? Look at them, Dovian. You are only postponing their untimely demise!" Euclid gestured toward Aria and Troy. The two soldiers were sitting up, resting their heads against the wall. "He saw that the wickedness of man was great in the earth and that every intention of the thoughts of his heart was only evil continually. They always have and always will be of darkness!"

Dovian frowned, his mind flickering to the horrors of humanity. "It wasn't our job to judge."

"It should have been!" Euclid shouted.

Glowing eyes stared at shining eyes as the two argued back and forth. One of the creatures dared an attack. Dovian staffed it in the jaw, cracking its skull open. Only one remained in the shadows, watching curiously over the two.

"The darkness of the filthy creatures is overwhelming, overshadowing any minuscule amount of good that may still exist," Euclid scoffed.

"There can be no darkness without light," Dovian muttered. "Even amidst complete annihilation, they maintain their hope."

Euclid glared, his hand gripping at the large wound in his knee. Blood gushed freely onto the brown earth. Sweat beaded on his brow. His breaths were labored as he pulled energy to heal himself. "And there can be no light without darkness," Euclid said behind closed teeth. "Without enemies, there can be no heroes. Without heroes, there would be no enemies."

"This is your problem, finding the balance."

"The only way, Dovian, is for all of us to die."

"Not if we do as we are supposed to. It's our job to maintain the balance within ourselves."

In a flash, Euclid gripped Dovian's forearms. Lifting the other man off the ground, Dovian pushed away.

"And you've done such an excellent job at that, eh?" Euclid jeered. He limped, scowling in pain as he struggled to heal. "Without that back apparatus, you'd give in to your selfish, evil inhibitions just as easily as anyone else."

"At least I care enough to try to do what is right."

Euclid snarled and disappeared. Dovian tensed and awaited impact as Euclid reappeared behind him, wrapping his arms around Dovian's neck. Euclid kicked at the back of Dovian's legs, sending him to his knees.

"Your hypocrisies amaze me, fool!" he hissed in Dovian's ears.

With a gasp, Dovian's face turned red, matching his robes. "Yet, you are too ignorant to realize your own," he groaned.

"Enough! You will die now!" the madman shouted, his lips grazing Dovian's ear.

"This won't do it," he replied smugly to the dark man.

"I will incapacitate you. While your system regenerates, I will sever your head as you did to me all those years ago."

"Not very climatic, is it?" Dovian chuckled, coughing as he tried to get air.

Euclid faltered, momentarily loosening his grip. How badly he wanted to break Dovian's neck, snap every bone in the other man's body, rip out his hair, and skin him alive. And it all wouldn't do the trick. Dovian could simply heal himself. Euclid preferred torture, but he needed to eradicate Dovian quickly, not give him any chances to escape. He pondered his plans for a few seconds, catching Sapphire's boiling stare.

"Kill him already!" she screamed.

"Dovian…" Aria whispered. She lifted her weapon and aimed. The child that sat upon the throne glared at her, sending another shockwave in their direction. Troy pushed Aria out of the way, and they both crashed to the ground, narrowly escaping another atrocious blow.

"Don't interfere," Sapphire ordered.

Dovian's body fell limp in Euclid's arms. Pulling from his distracting thoughts, images of Dovian's gruesome end, Euclid quickly dropped the Sorcēarian. He snatched up Dovian's weapon and raised it over his head.

"It's over!" He hooted. "You may be able to regenerate yourself, heal better than any Sorcēarian before you, but you can't grow back limbs! You can't grow back a head!"

A bright flash temporarily blinded Euclid from Dovian's staff, filling the cave with intense light. It had lasted only a second before it dissipated. Dovian's body remained on the floor at Euclid's feet. Relaxing a bit, the evil Sorcēarian laughed manically once again. "I can feel the power course through my veins!"

The winged blades cut through Dovian's armor and body as he brought the weapon down. The silver-haired head bounced away and into the shadows. Euclid's frenzied scream echoed loudly within the chamber. Shakily, he released the staff. It rattled noisily in the silent room. A soft cry erupted from the corner, tearing the azure man's attention to the soldiers. A wry smile crossed his pale face as he looked at Aria, who Troy held back.

"Your turn," he hissed.

A soft crackling sounded from beside Euclid's feet. Frowning, he looked back down at Dovian's dead body. The headless form splintered with yellow light. The beams crackled over the body, and it crumbled to ash within seconds. Euclid's eyes widened. Sorcēarian bodies didn't do that, at least not from what he had ever seen. Turning his gaze toward Dovian's severed head in the corner, Euclid shouted. In its place was a detached Brawler head, its long tongue hanging out in the middle of its hot blood. It began to crackle and turned to ash as well.

"No!" Euclid cried.

A massive force shot from the shadows and collided with Euclid, smashing and embedding him into a wall.

"You forget one important thing, you bastard!" Dovian barked as his hands shoved into the other man's back. Gripping the cloth, he pulled the broken and battered Euclid from his shelf and tossed him carelessly onto the floor.

A loud, gasping breath erupted from Euclid as his frightened eyes gaped at the glowing silhouette of Dovian's body. Flickers of light emitted from the Sorcēarian's form, giving him a full halo effect as he glared down with white holes for eyes, an empty stare of judgment. His red and black robes were shimmering in gold and silver; giant white wings spread widely from his backside. The dark demonic wings twitched behind the others. His staff was clenched tightly in his fist as he looked down at the trembling Euclid.

"While you were dead, I was alive, mastering all the arts!" Dovian shouted, his voice booming and commanding. "I have reached Gold status."

"N-no," Euclid gasped as blood dripped from his nose and the corner of his mouth. He stared into Dovian's white eyes and felt a terrible burning in his chest.

"You're going to die now, Euclid." Dovian took a slow, deep breath and closed his eyes. "There isn't a grain's worth of forgiveness for you."

"You can't judge me, Dovian!" he choked. "It's not your place, remember?"

Dovian's pale orbs reopened, and he looked upon the wavering Sorcēarian at his feet. "No, but He has."

"Wait!" Euclid reached out, his head vaporizing into a trillion particles, misting in all directions.

Dovian stared at the body on the ground, Euclid's dark-blue robes soaking up the crimson blood. It was over; Euclid was dead. And he wasn't coming back.

Feeling uneasy within the room, Dovian turned his blank stare to the standing soldiers in one corner. They looked in his direction, weapons at ease. To them, he was the most menacing creation they had ever seen. They watched in awe with their expressions hidden behind their helmets. Neither dared make a move.

"Good show," Sapphire's tiny voice sounded within the chamber.

Dovian was abruptly knocked off his feet. Suddenly, one of his arms twisted, pulling out of the socket. He let out a shout of pain, reaching for the joint with his other hand.

"Nope." Sapphire sat on her chair. An elbow was propped on an armrest, her fist supporting her chin. She gave a small wave with her free hand, and Dovian's other arm pulled and twisted like the other, breaking out of place.

"Stop it!" another voice interrupted.

Sapphire turned her head, eyeing her prisoner. Ivory was awake, watching Dovian with angry eyes. Returning her attention to the gold Sorcēarian, the little girl pulled her fingers toward herself. Instantly, Dovian's fingers snapped in all directions as she broke his phalanges.

"I said to stop it!" Ivory screeched. The blonde-haired beauty tried running to Dovian's side, but the chains tugged against her arms, forcing her to her knees.

"No, you stop it." Sapphire glared at the disobedient woman. An invisible force violently slapped Ivory across the face, sending her crashing to the floor.

"We have to do something," Aria spoke to Troy.

"Like what? We do anything, we're dead."

Ivory's body twitched, the chains tinkling as she began violently convulsing. With each cry that erupted from Dovian, her form lifted higher. Soon, the strange woman levitated, her body making a bizarre vibrating noise. With jittering movements, her head turned to look at Sapphire, the child matching her stare.

"What are you doing?" the little girl asked.

With a violent tug, Ivory's arms wrenched free from the bindings around her wrists. Light ignited from her shoulder blades, forcing her body to go limp at the waist and fold. With an explosion of noise, two massive metallic constructions erupted from her dorsal side. They spread open, one blade after another, making the appearance of mechanized wings. Brilliant blue and yellow thrusters shot her body to the opposite side of the room, the woman raising her torso. Her face was void of emotion; her eyes had tiny dots for pupils in the center of baby blue. She pointed in Sapphire's direction. Her right arm twitched and bulged, tearing away her long satin glove. One by one, pieces of Ivory's arm broke and separated from her body. The sections molded and pulled apart. From around the appendage swirled a visual distortion. A portal opened, and the pieces snapped together. Within a second, Ivory had a giant gun for an arm.

"Target acquired," a hollow voice droned deep within the woman.

The thrusters from her wings blasted outward, the heat turning the rock wall behind her red-hot. A low rumble sounded as the cave's walls began to shake and crumble. At the force of the vibrant fire, her blonde hair blew wildly over her head. Tattooed on the woman's neck were the words 'Bio-Tech Military Corporation.'

"Oh, my God," Aria gasped. "She's one of Camery's biomechanical androids from the clone project."

"I thought they were all disposed of." Troy stared at the horrifying sight in front of him.

"Were they?" Aria turned her head, Troy doing the same, and they stared at one another.

Ivory lifted her normal arm and, with a spreading palm, sent an unseen shockwave that shoved Troy and Aria back into one of the cave's tunnels. The wave crashed into the entryway, causing it to collapse and barricade the soldiers out of the room.

With a deafening whine, Ivory's weapon—an Amasser Particle Beam—readied to fire. Brilliant light flickered from her thrusters through her mechanized arm, sucking in particles of matter and amassing them into a high-density beam. The solid ray shot out with a blinding flash and sped toward Sapphire. Every sound in the room turned to a deafening silence as the light moved and collided with its target.

Dovian rolled out of the way, instantly snapping his broken joints together, casting a healing light over himself as he pressed against the wall.

The amasser's light exploded against Sapphire's tiny body, instantly crystallizing and turning everything in its path to glass. The following sound was atrocious, a crunching rumble that vibrated the whole tunnel system. One after another, the walls caved in on themselves. Shouting in Legacy, Dovian lifted his staff, creating a force field for the room's interior. He held up the crumbling chamber, watching Ivory as she erupted in one continuous stream at her target. Any longer, and she'd annihilate everyone, including herself.

"Ivory!" Dovian shouted. His voice was unheard. "Ivory! Stop! You'll kill us all!"

The woman's body jerked, her arm dropping to the side as the light immediately diminished. Sputtering, the thrusters on her back fizzled out, and the woman collided with the floor like a ragdoll, her puffy masquerade gown splayed around her. She was a beautiful and broken creation.

Once the quaking halted, the room fell into an eerily displeasing silence. Dovian cautiously released his hold on the barrier. He looked over his shoulder, and his white eyes widened in shock. The entire chamber was encased in glass. With a shimmering sparkle, the oversized throne looked beautiful in the now glass-covered firelight. At least, it would have been stunning if it weren't for the horrible little girl who sat atop it completely unscathed. Beside her tilted head was a large, perfectly round hole that penetrated the throne and the whole system of tunnels, a small white dot of light shimmering through the very end.

"You know, I was indifferent about Euclid's survival." The girl vibrated from her throne, reappearing beside Euclid's now crystallized, decapitated body. She kneeled, reaching into his coat. With a rough tug, she pulled out Euclid's talisman, the source of his power. While giving it a hard squeeze, the amulet shattered into dust. "Didn't like him to begin with, but his stupidity had its usefulness. He at least lured you out."

Dovian, shaking slightly, watched the little girl. His body continued flickering like a flame in his golden attire. "You wanted me?"

"Of course. Why wouldn't I want the one Sorcēarian who can withstand anything? The supposedly invincible Dovian…the one who annihilated the entire Sorcēarian race, the one our Father personally denied death. Funny, some would think that a truly magnificent gift." She lifted her grey eyes to the tall man. "But we all know how much of a curse that really is."

"Who are you?" Dovian asked.

Sapphire giggled. "I think you know the answer to that."

"Then why are you doing this?"

The child's face distorted into a furious glare. "I'm tired of being denied what I rightfully deserve! I'm great! I'm wonderful! Why can't I have what was originally promised?! Clearly, He and I are equals, yet He still thinks I enjoy playing these games. I've had enough. I'll make my own if He doesn't allow me to return home. I'll create my own race! I'll create my own world, one that will worship me and love me!"

"You cannot rule and force people to love you based on fear."

"What would you know?" she growled again in her dual tones. She quickly regained composure. "We can create a new race, Dovian. Wouldn't that be nice? A whole new world just for us, just for you and Ivory."

Dovian looked upon the woman's thin body a couple of meters away. "How do you plan on going about this?" he asked.

"You see her? Isn't she a marvelous creation? Humans, always trying so hard to be their own gods, create such monstrosities! He hates them, so I embrace them. Soulless clones are used for war. They are the perfect vessels for the lost souls that wish to live again." Sapphire walked toward Ivory, her white shoes clicking against the glass floor.

"You're housing the clones and androids with demon souls." Dovian carefully observed her. She kneeled beside Ivory, petting her hair.

"But that's not all. You see, Ivory's special. She's the only biomechanical android that maintains some of her vital organs. Once, she was an ordinary human, and Camery stole her and countless other bodies from the crematories. Funny what money can get you. Such a sick experiment. I love it." Sapphire snickered.

Dovian neared the girl and unconscious woman. He stood on the opposite side, watching Ivory with unreadable eyes. "She still has her reproductive system," Sapphire said.

Dovian's mouth parted, stunned.

"She can house soulless children for me. And, once again, those damned will be able to walk on this world—the original Fallen. We came to this earth looking for our own monarchy. We wanted humans as slaves. Why not? They are cattle compared to us. Worthless, abominable creations. They are so much less than we are!" Sapphire spoke passionately, looking at Dovian with conviction. "Don't you agree?"

Dovian hesitated, feeling the pain and anger that the child exuded.

"You hesitate, Dovian, but you won't for long. Obviously, you know about I'Lanthe, correct?"

He began to feel dizzy. "What about her?"

"Euclid told you about her, right? About how he found her at the beginning of our mission, curled up in the bottomless pit of Hell. That's what *He* did for you. He threw her into the pit."

Dovian swallowed thickly, holding onto the glass wall beside him.

"Now, how fair is that? After everything she did, He damned her. Why?"

"I, I don't know," Dovian stuttered.

"See? There's no reason. There's no sense to the things that He does. He only wants to punish you, Dovian, for doing what you thought was right, what was right for those precious humans of His." Sapphire watched him menacingly.

"No, it can't be true," he mumbled.

Dovian stumbled when he felt the child touch his arm.

"But of course, it is, silly. If she wasn't in Hell, why does she occupy the vessel?"

Dovian lowered to his knees, staring at Ivory. His lower lip trembled as he thought about I'Lanthe being in Hell this entire time. How terrible it must've been.

"Somehow, while we were crossing into this plane, she inhabited one of the clones we had stolen from Camery's lab. How lucky for us that it was the one vessel that could reproduce! Sadly, the original woman who lived in that body died from a bullet wound to the head. Half of her brain is living, and the other half is mechanized with organic computerization. This causes a terrible amnesiac effect. I think that's why Ivory doesn't know who she is, doesn't know that she is I'Lanthe."

"This can't be happening," Dovian muttered.

Sapphire smiled widely and clapped her hands together. "Want to know the best part?"

The man looked at her with tired white eyes.

"Far down Ivory's human lineage is a Sorcēarian gene!" she exclaimed cheerfully.

"Impossible," he countered.

"Is it? You said it yourself. You can't die. Why can't a human being bear a Sorcēarian's child?"

"It's too powerful. If the pregnancy lasted that long, it would kill her and the fetus instantly during birth."

"Maybe the mother did die during birth. Maybe someone removed the child from the womb, raised it as a Sorcēarian, or raised it secretly. You all were *so* good at genetics. Possibly created your own Nephilim? My, my, how history repeats itself." Sapphire clasped her hands together, swaying back and forth on her toes.

"You think Ivory can give birth to hybrid children," Dovian said.

"Precisely. I want the closest thing to a Sorcēarian I can get."

Dovian loosened the clasp on his armor, feeling suffocated in the surreal situation. "And how do you plan on impregnating her?" He already knew the answer, and the thought made him intensely nervous.

"You, of course. You two will have at it and make me some beautiful babies!" Sapphire threw her hands into the air, giggling. "And then we can house them with the souls of those who have waited thousands upon thousands of years and create our superior race. The humans will serve us. If not, we'll destroy them all. Either way, I'll be much happier."

Dovian placed his hands on the ground, resting on his knees. He closed his eyes, feeling sick. Slowly, he sat up as Sapphire put her tiny hand on his. She was so damned eerie and beautiful.

She smiled. "You can be my father! And she will be my mother!"

"Why not house her vessel yourself?" Dovian asked.

Sapphire wrinkled her nose. "And go through the curse of endless childbirth?!" she scoffed. "I don't think so. I'll wait for you to make the perfect child, and then I will house it."

"I cannot let you do this."

Sapphire leaned down, cupping Dovian's face. Her platinum hair fell over her shoulders as her pale pink lips twisted into a sweet smile. "Why not? Admit it. You like the idea. You said it yourself…humans are weak and worthless. You are the only one who made a difference in this war. To what purpose have they served you in return for all you sacrificed? Was it worth watching I'Lanthe die? Was it worth watching every friend and family member you loved disintegrate into oblivion?"

Dovian frowned, his hands gripping his robes tightly.

"Say it, Dovian. Was it worth it?"

It was a question he had pondered a million times over. Was his decision the right one? If it was, then why was he damned? Why had he been cut off from Him? Was Dovian's endless devotion not enough? Was there something he had missed?

He scowled, lowered his head, and tightly clenched his eyes. All humanity did was proceed to kill and rape each other senselessly. Only a sliver of good was left in the world, quickly diminishing with each weaponized death.

At the speed of light, memories flooded into the Sorcēarian's mind—the first day he met I'Lanthe, the sound of the rain and the feel of her skin as they lay in bed, the horror on her face the night before she died while he sat imprisoned, her blank stare after the battle, the cold feel of her pallid flesh, and the terror of being alone forever. He thought of the hope he had for humanity that was so easily shattered during the rape and murder of a small girl, the many times he should have died but was denied such a release, the anger, the pain, the sadness, the hopelessness, and abandonment. He remembered meeting Aria and Troy, the fleeting hope of falling in love again, the warmth of Aria's body, and the sound of her voice. He thought of the church in the Underbelly destroyed along with the city, the endless wars, and the argument with Ivory that served as a painful reminder of all he had lost.

Did any of it bring any hope to the Sorcēarian? Was this the world he wanted? Was this what he considered when he disagreed with Euclid's plan?

"Say it, Dovian. Was any of it worth it?"

Dovian groaned, and his teeth clenched as he muttered, "No."

"Now is your chance to make things right. Make everything as you want it to be. We can be among others like us, given a second chance. You can be with I'Lanthe once again. You two can have children together. You can live happy lives without another fret for all eternity, as it was supposed to be. All we've got to do is destroy humanity—those who ruined our precious love, our divinity, cursed us just as they cursed themselves before and continue to do."

Sapphire watched as Dovian stood. He looked upon Ivory for a moment, staring at her serene face. She was gorgeous. He lifted his gaze and stared at nothing in particular as he listened to the child, absorbing her words.

"You can make all of your dreams come true. You can have a perfect life with the perfect wife. What do you say, Dovian? Will you join me?"

Dovian blinked once, replaying all his memories and thoughts. What else could he do?

Opening his mouth, he shamelessly uttered, "Yes."

"Gold Status"

EPILOGUE

An ominous rumble shook the entire channel. Chunks of shattering rock and dirt collided atop General Yoshitaka's helmet. He paid no mind to the tiny impacts as he looked over the tunnel system map, scratching out the entries and exits destroyed over the past few weeks by the nonstop battle. A flurry of heavily armored footsteps darted behind the attentive man, one man quickly scuffling to a stop beside him.

"Sir?" A lieutenant saluted quickly.

"Saito, you have good news for me?" Yoshitaka asked, his voice echoing from within his heavy armor.

It was the same question he asked daily, and the responding news was often contrary.

"Actually, I do."

They turned away from the map on the wall and quickly began following the rushing soldiers.

The lieutenant pulled up, from his DNAIS, a map of Dai-Ni-Tokyo. "It seems the frontline has finally made it through and has cracked into the enemy's underground channels. After a week, Hidaka and Watanabe found a source of their original locations."

The map spiraled to the side, quickly lowering beneath Dai-Ni-Tokyo's city into the underground tunnels. Down one path, the trail dug beneath the oceanic crust, following a deep trench that led to the middle of the Americas. Yoshitaka watched the image flicker in the center near the City of Fountains.

"Very interesting news," Yoshitaka muttered. "Have we been able to make any contact yet?"

"No, sir," the lieutenant said, shaking his head. "Nothing past our walls."

"Any news of our civilian count?"

Saito twisted the map, pulling it back to the upper side of the city. He highlighted two of the few surviving prefectures. "Osaka has been wiped out. Kyoto is currently unmanned; however, sixty percent of all civilians and soldiers have safely made it underground."

"That *is* good news," Yoshitaka said, his voice lifting in spirit.

"I think we are finally gaining the upper hand, sir."

"I hope you are correct."

"General Yoshitaka! General! Sir!" A workforce soldier slid to a halt, saluting roughly before tugging his arm back to his side.

"Can't you see I am busy?" Yoshitaka asked.

"It's very important, sir."

Yoshitaka turned toward the excitable soldier, watching through the dark eyes of his sculptured mask.

"While burrowing, we've come into contact with a trans-world, fiber-optic com line," the soldier sputtered.

"Yes, I know of this. Have you made use of it?"

"We've hacked it, sent out a distress signal, and have received a response."

"What kind of response?"

"Sir, we've made contact with a Mr. Grayson. He says he has valuable information for your eyes only; he has also countered with a distress query of his own."

"We send out a distress call, and they ask us for help in turn? Do they not understand our losses in the past two weeks?" Yoshitaka asked, turning to continue his trek down the channel. "Tell this Mr. Grayson that I am too busy saving my own people to bother helping him."

"Yoshitaka, sir. He told me to tell you that if you said that, I was to relay to you that Mr. Clarke is calling in a favor."

Yoshitaka froze mid-step. Slowly turning, he curiously asked, "Where did you say this call came from?"

"Sir, Bio-Tech Military Corporation."

Saito quickly added, "That's Fountain's main corporation."

Yoshitaka smiled. "Saito, gather as many troops as you can. Also, I want you to contact the Iga clan."

"I-Iga, sir?" Saito stuttered. The thought of the unruly clan made the lieutenant shiver.

"It is time we settled our differences and realized there's a bigger problem at hand," Yoshitaka said. He looked back to the other man beside them. "Soldier...."

"Yes, sir?" The worker saluted.

Standing at attention, Yoshitaka continued. "I'd like you to relay a message to Mr. James Clarke of Bio-Tech Military Corporation. Tell him reinforcements are on the way." Another explosion sounded from above ground, sending a flurry of debris over their heads. Yoshitaka slowly lifted his gaze. "And we are bringing some friends."

"The Sorcēarian's Home"

Aria's DNAIS

Caution!

The following content contains
- Character Bios
- Bestiary
- Weapons & Armor Listings
- And More

Spoilers may lurk within the DNAIS.
Please read with caution.

BIOGRAPHIES

Aria Ivanov

- Age: 52
- Height: 198cm, 6'6"
- Weight: 81.6kg, 180lbs
- Eye Color: Green
- Hair Color: Black
- Blood Type: 0-
- Old Nationality: Italian-American, Russian

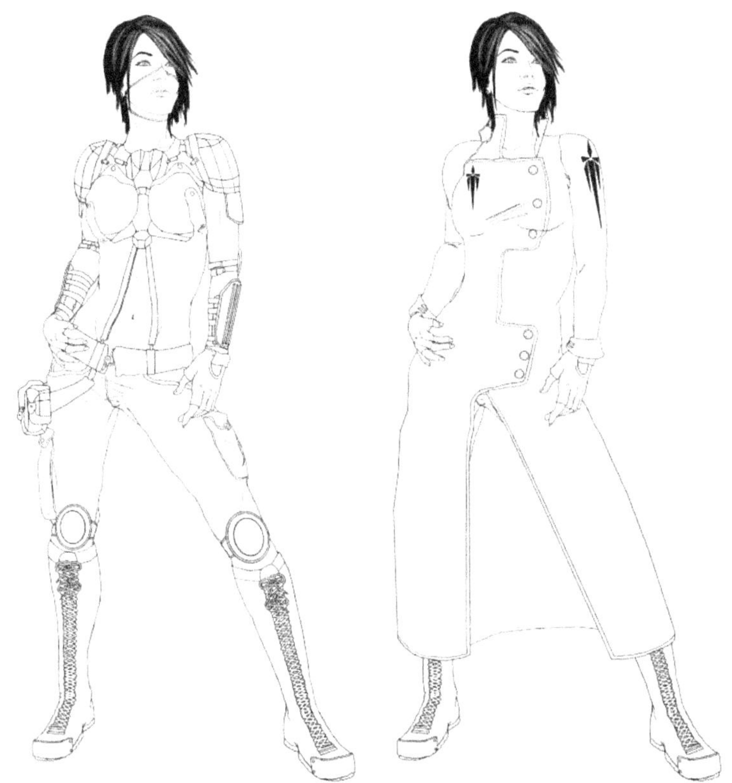

Aria was born in Cherno, Russite. Her father was a professor of literature and mythology, and her mother taught art and music. At the age of nine, Aria's upscale life turned upside-down when her parents were killed right before her eyes in a tragic accident that left her an orphan. Not long after the incident had taken place, Aria was rescued by a soldier named James Clarke. He comforted her during her loss and took her into his home at Bio-Tech Military Corporation in Fountains, where he taught her all there was to know about hand-to-hand combat and weaponry.

By the time she was a teenager, Aria was at the top of her class. Seeing her potential as an elite soldier, James paired Aria with Troy. After years of successful missions, both were upgraded to high-status in their twenties and put in charge of their own Delta crew—later dubbed Team Phoenix after the False Syndicate War. Currently, Aria and Troy are deployed on Bio-Tech's most top-secret missions. When not being used as a backup for the two soldiers, the rest of Team Phoenix is implemented for special ops and espionage worldwide.

Despite surviving countless battles and the suicidal False Syndicate War, Aria seems to have met her match in the latest enemies threatening not only hers but also the entire world's militaries. Fighting in a war against humans had become an easy task for Aria. The question is whether or not she can master the art of war against monsters.

Troy Moreau

- Age: 55
- Height: 218.5cm, 7'2"
- Weight: 140.6kg, 310lbs
- Eye Color: Green
- Hair Color: Brown
- Blood Type: 0+
- Old Nationality: French, American

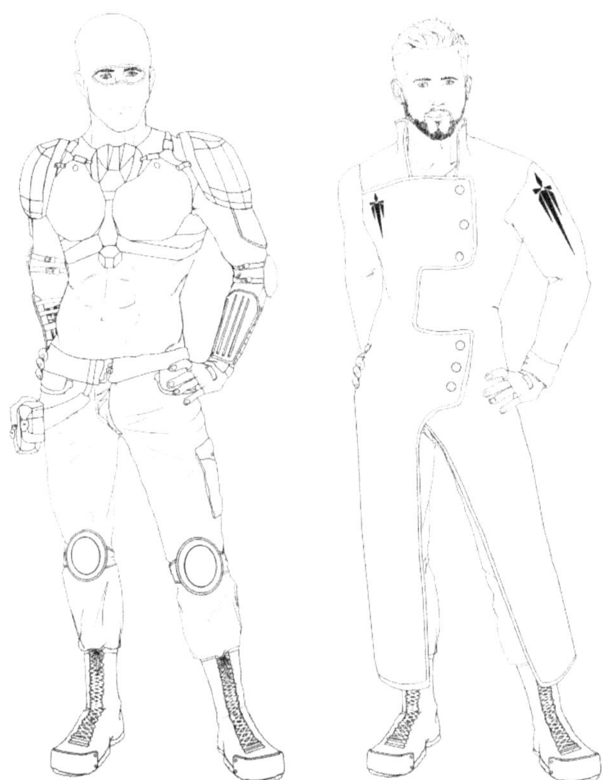

After losing his mother while still an infant, Troy was raised by his father within the military. However, the man was killed in action when Troy was only eleven. Since Bio-Tech Military Corporation owned his father, Troy's transition into the military was simple. Bio-Tech adopted him, allowed him to keep his father's apartment, and he began training the next day. Having been raised by a soldier, Troy was already skilled with weaponry and was named a prodigy in marksmanship. Not one to be good at giving orders, Troy did better at obeying them and adapting when necessary. He was the perfect soldier.

By his teens, Troy was second in his class behind Aria. Being complete opposites but equal in talent, the two were made partners. However, they often competed for dominance over the other. While in their twenties, Troy and Aria were allowed to train their own squadron, but there could only be one leader. During the final exams to determine who would lead the Delta team, Troy missed the opportunity by a few points when he was late to his last exercise due to a laxative placed in his morning coffee. Having questioned Aria about it, she never confessed but did proclaim that whoever had done it was a genius and that all was fair when it came to war.

Despite having their differences and sometimes butting heads, Aria and Troy have always proven to be the perfect team. In the current war, where Troy's understanding and beliefs about the world are repeatedly questioned, he must choose what to believe in and the adverse effects it could have on his relationship with Aria.

Dovian

- Age: 17,000+
- Height: 249cm, 8'2"
- Weight: 174.6kg, 385lbs
- Eye Color: Blue
- Hair Color: Silver/Gold
- Blood Type: Unknown
- Old Nationality: Sorcēarian

Dovian is the sole survivor of the Sorcēarian race. His great-grandfather, Elder Gaius, was one of the original angelic beings to come to Earth, forming Ives out of the Indian Ocean. Sorcēarians were given the task of preaching the word of God to the human populace. After a few thousand years, the Sorcēarian race became tainted by sin, and an immense war broke out between the human and angelic races. Details of the war remain unknown, but the results led to the extinction of the mythical race. Only Dovian knows the tale, and all he wishes to share are hints of the existence of his people, giving few facts about their demise and his supposed fault for it.

Being small in stature compared to other Sorcēarians, Dovian was somewhat of an outcast growing up. He felt immense pressure from the Gaius lineage—a formidable, leading heritage. Believed to be weak, Dovian proved his family wrong when his temper got the better of him as a child, and he nearly destroyed one of the cathedrals in his home. It was a turning point in his life as people no longer doubted his strength as much as they feared it, only making Dovian further estranged.

Elder Gaius was a prominent figure in Dovian's life, acting more in the fatherly role than Dovian's father, Gaius III. The Elder placed immense faith in Dovian and developed preventive measures to help control the young Sorcēarian's energies. In the end, Dovian's controlled actions caused more harm than good, and he feels he is to blame for the race's annihilation, leaving him depressed and full of regret. However, upon meeting Aria and Troy, he agreed to assist in their war, though his true motives remain unclear.

Ivory

- Age: Unknown
- Height: 213cm, 7'0"
- Weight: 88.5kg, 195lbs
- Eye Color: Blue
- Hair Color: Blonde
- Blood Type: Unknown
- Old Nationality: Unknown

Little is known about Ivory. Having been discovered unconscious on Ives by Aria and her team, Ivory has no recollection of her past or how she arrived on the theoretically impenetrable island. Not knowing her purpose or past life, Ivory joined the team in hopes of discovering her true identity and eventually finding her way home. However, due to Walten's interest in the mysterious woman, Ivory was placed in Aria's company for protection. As battles arose, Ivory began to develop lost time and seizures, which caused shifts in her personality. Originally thought to be a symptom of post-traumatic stress disorder, Ivory's alternate personality revealed a more bizarre connection to a past that did not belong to her, a history that belonged to Dovian.

Living in confusion and fear, Ivory keeps her thoughts primarily to herself, eventually creating a wedge between her and her teammates. Not only do her personality shifts bring about questions about her true identity, but her strange physical abilities are an anomaly that only places her in unwanted and traumatic situations. And though looking for answers, Ivory finds that the further she travels with her comrades, the more questions arise about her existence.

Gavin Sigo

- Age: 54
- Height: 208cm, 6'10"
- Weight: 127kg, 280lbs
- Eye Color: Brown
- Hair Color: Brown
- Blood Type: A+
- Old Nationality: Native American, American

Gavin is a spunky, light-hearted pilot for Bio-Tech Military Cooperation. He is one of the few in the military born and raised as a civilian who still has living parents. Expected to go to college and follow through with a pilot's license for commercial airlines, his parents were horrified when the young man decided to enter the military to pilot the Hawk 90. Many think it was due to Troy's persuasion that Gavin signed his rights away to Bio-Tech, but it was because of his desire to do more for the people of Fountains—and possibly a certain green-eyed beauty he had met through Troy—that he decided to become a pilot.

Having passed all tests with flying colors and mastering the Hawk 90 in half the time most recruits do, Gavin was quickly given a Class C-5 status in the Air Force and immediately assigned to Troy and Aria's unit. For nearly 30 years, Gavin has been Aria and Troy's eye in the sky. While his comrades are on the field, Gavin remains on the alert to come to the rescue. The wait is sometimes excruciating, but he never misses a beat regarding his comrades' safety and quick transportation to and from the battlefield.

When questioned about his reasons for becoming a pilot, Gavin always replies, "Everyone thinks a hero needs to have a gun. Nobody thinks of the heroes that take to the sky. Though the ones on the ground always have all the fun, I always preferred to fly."

Euclid

- Age: 2,159 (Before Death)
- Height: 267cm, 8'9"
- Weight: 220kg, 485lbs
- Eye Color: Blue
- Hair Color: Black
- Blood Type: Unknown
- Old Nationality: Sorcēarian

Euclid is the son of Rhondin and grandson to Jaleal, who was one of the first to come to the land of Ives by Gaius' side. Due to his mischievous behavior, Euclid was placed in Azure status, where he excelled at illusion and espionage and worked on a covert team with Dovian. Euclid struggled with authority, having difficulty accepting his role as a Sorcēarian. His initial disdain for humanity started with the death of his mother, who died while fighting to protect the other race. Euclid's experience with human society worsened over the years, further feeding his hatred. Rather than seeing humanity as having two sides, Euclid only saw evil.

Eventually, he rebelled against the Sorcēarian code and started a war between the two races to eradicate humanity. Euclid nearly achieved his goal after betraying his only friend, Dovian. However, Euclid's war ended when Dovian decapitated him.

Somehow alive, Euclid plagues the world with seemingly random attacks, taking dangerous resources from each city-state. To his dissatisfaction, Euclid finds that he once again has to face Dovian to fulfill his plans for the destruction of the human race. There are many questions as to how Euclid survived. Has he been alive all this time, waiting for the right time to strike? Or are there other forces at play?

Sapphire

- Age: 8
- Height: 129.5cm, 4'3"
- Weight: 23.5kg, 52lbs
- Eye Color: Blue
- Hair Color: Blonde
- Blood Type: Unknown
- Old Nationality: Unknown

Sapphire is an enigmatic child who has no known origins. Despite being beautiful and seeming innocent, there's a darkness within the child that seems to make the bravest of men cower. Her strange appearances near the recent demonic war-torn sites lead to questions about who the child is, where she came from, and how she could possibly be involved in any of the bizarre attacks. What are her connections to Euclid, and what influence does she hold?

James Clarke

- Age: 78
- Height: 206cm, 6'9"
- Weight: 120.2kg, 265lbs
- Eye Color: Brown
- Hair Color: Grey
- Blood Type: O-
- Old Nationality: English, American

James Clarke is the President of Bio-Tech Military Corporation. He organizes and overlooks all of the corporation's military operations. Given almost complete control, Clarke works beneath Walten, the CEO and financial owner of the company. However, anything Walten says overrides Clarke, which creates tension between the economic and military sides of Bio-Tech.

Born and raised in Fountains, James Clarke's father was a military genius who spent most of his life battling. He trained James to be one of the best, and by the time he was in his early twenties, James led his own squadron. James was a rare individual. Despite seeing the horrors of war, he was firmly devoted to civilian lifestyles. Wanting to maintain some normalcy, James met a woman named Courtney and quickly settled into a domestic relationship with her. It wasn't long before they were engaged, and she became pregnant. However, James' small amount of peace was destroyed when a commercial airliner was taken down by Cherno forces, killing Courtney and her unborn child only days before the scheduled wedding, which ignited a war with Cherno.

With his squadron, James went to Russite, where he could track down General Lebedev and end the war, but not without casualties. James accidentally gave the wrong coordinates to a mortar team, and a civilian district was hit. Upon investigating the site, James found a child pinned beneath her father and her dead mother a few meters away. The child became his bargaining chip with Lebedev as she was in the center of the gunfight. James decided to spare Lebedev's life and take full responsibility for the child if the man agreed to call off his war and assent to peaceful solutions between the two city-states. With no options, Lebedev approved, and James adopted the little girl named Aria and raised her as his own.

Dr. Camery

- Age: 61
- Height: 206cm, 6'9"
- Weight: 108.8kg, 240lbs
- Eye Color: Grey
- Hair Color: Brown, Grey
- Blood Type: A-
- Old Nationality: English, American

Dr. Camery has been a scientist for Bio-Tech Military Corporation for most of his adult life. Having multiple doctorates and master's degrees, Camery is one of the most renowned scientists in the world. He jump-started the Biomechanical Research and Development program, using cloned DNA and robotic technology to create biomechanical androids. Having been awarded for his genius development, it was a shock to Camery when Bio-Tech pulled the plug on the program, destroying all he had developed and taking away his life's work. Having no real purpose, Camery was crushed and desperate for his life to return to normal.

Due to the recent attacks world-wide and the curious evidence connecting Camery, it's no surprise that the doctor is a key suspect. Questions arise about his involve-ment in providing technology to the enemy. How far would he go to achieve his goals? For what purpose would he help the enemy? Whether he wants to be or not, he is involved in the grand design.

Mr. Walten

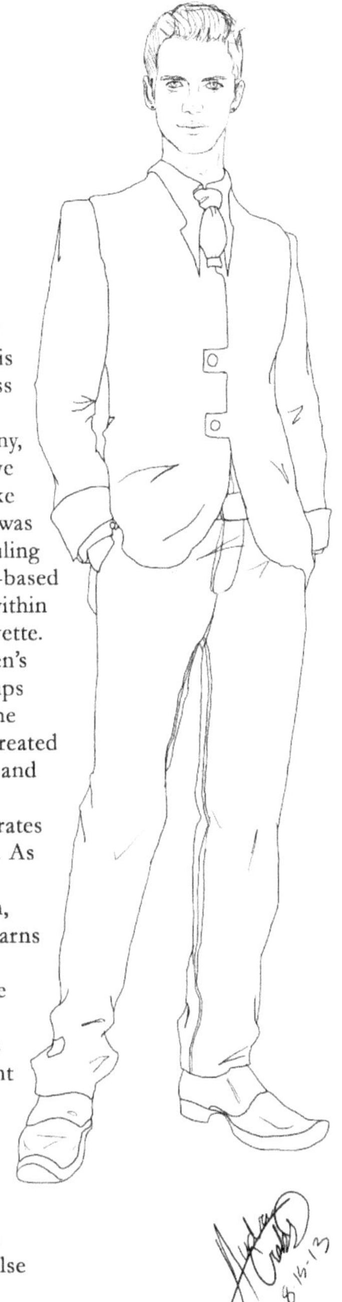

- Age: 38
- Height: 208cm, 6'10"
- Weight: 99.8kg, 220lbs
- Eye Color: Brown
- Hair Color: Brown
- Blood Type: A
- Old Nationality: German, American

Walten is the CEO of Bio-Tech Military Corporation. After the sudden death of his father, Walten inherited the family business at the age of thirteen. While the boy was considered too young to manage the company, Walten's father had stated in his will to give complete control to President James Clarke until Walten was of a mature age. Walten was nsulted, claiming that he was better off ruling on his own without the help of a military-based President. However, he still had his way within the company, thanks to General Jeron Feyette. Making sure James Clarke played by Walten's rules, Jeron managed certain military groups and actions behind Clarke's back due to the young CEO's demands. This eventually created a tense relationship between the financial and military sides of Bio-Tech.

Now a grown adult, Walten entirely operates Bio-Tech along with fifty other industries. As the days pass, his wealth and control over businesses and city-states increase. Walten, watching his father waste his potential, yearns to have mass control over all significant industries worldwide. Whether it is for the betterment or worsening of humanity is unknown, though Walten is not notorious for being compassionate. With the current events around the world disrupting the predictable flow of the consumer and military finances, many begin to wonder if Walten's strategic blows to the stocks have all been a coincidence or part of an elaborate plot. The question remains, is it Walten who is in control, or is someone else pulling the strings in this esoteric design?

Jeron Feyette

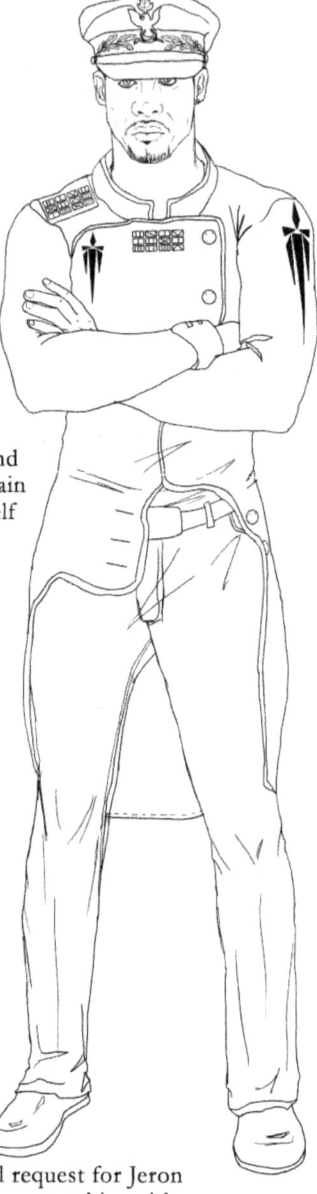

- Age: 65
- Height: 223.5cm, 7'4"
- Weight: 183.7kg, 405lbs
- Eye Color: Brown
- Hair Color: Black
- Blood Type: B+
- Old Nationality: African-American, French

General Jeron Feyette is a native of Fountains. Born with genetics deemed abnormal, Jeron was abandoned by his mother at an orphanage in the Underbelly. Growing up in the lower level of the city, Jeron often got into trouble due to theft and violence. Being different, Feyette had to train to be strong and capable of protecting himself and the other children in the orphanage. Jeron grew to be enormous in height and had phenomenal strength by his teens. Feyette was in the middle of a brawl with some criminals who attempted to steal money from the orphanage when the Bio-Tech recruiting squad showed up on his side of town. Impressed, a recruiting officer offered Feyette a job. With much hesitation, Feyette agreed to join the ranks of the military. The income was an overpowering temptation as it was more than enough to care for himself and much of the orphanage.

It wasn't long before Feyette became a general and the late President Walten's bodyguard. Feyette owed his life to the company. If it weren't for Bio-Tech, his orphanage would have been closed, and the children would have wound up on the streets or given to the front lines to serve in the wars. The President had guaranteed protection over Feyette's home, to which the general was eternally grateful. So, when the late President died and left a final request for Jeron to watch over his thirteen-year-old son and protect him with his life, General Feyette gratefully accepted. He became the young boy's shadow, taking him in as he had done for the children of the Underbelly.

Kovacevic

- Age: 70
- Height: 211cm, 6'11"
- Weight: 131.5kg, 290lbs
- Eye Color: Brown, Grey
- Hair Color: Bald
- Blood Type: A+
- Old Nationality: American, Bosnian

Kovacevic was born in America and raised by his single mother in the Columbia city-state. His father, a soldier from Saray, had been fighting within Columbia over natural resources. After being severely injured, the soldier was discovered by Kovacevic's mother. Being a nurse, she snuck him into her home for fear of the military finding him. While caring for the soldier, Kovacevic's mother developed feelings for him, and the two had a short-lived relationship. Once the man had healed, he disappeared, leaving Kovacevic's mother alone and pregnant in the war-torn city. After years of conflict, Kovacevic's mother died on the streets while gathering rations, leaving Kovacevic to fend for himself at an early age. Homeless, the boy joined the military at the soonest opportunity with one goal: to find and kill the man who caused his mother so much pain. His only clue was his last name—his father's name.

As an adult, Kovacevic became a renowned soldier. He fought for many years before being given a chance to infiltrate Saray for reconnaissance. Kovacevic went against orders and abandoned his team in search of his father, the general of Saray. After successfully chasing down and killing the man without effort, Kovacevic found himself captured, beaten, and taken as a prisoner of war. His city-state didn't dare rescue him due to his abandonment and going against orders, so Kovacevic stayed in Saray. Eventually, the man received the option to fight for the enemy, to which he gratefully accepted. Within a few short years, Kovacevic rose through the ranks, bettering all of Saray's soldiers, and eventually became general of the military he was once a prisoner for. Having killed his father didn't relieve any pain or anger he felt, for the man hadn't even remembered Kovacevic's mother in the sea of women he had past relations with. Now, Kovacevic fills his days with the one thing he knows best—fighting.

Fiona & Roy

The Underbelly, a separate city beneath Fountains, is dirty, poor, and full of the strange and outdated in society. Anything that didn't meet the middle ground of the majority is frowned upon, thus flourishing in the Underbelly. Designer genes are often used during pregnancy to prevent genetic differences such as pale or dark skin, too light or dark hair, or disease. However, sometimes the designer genes clash with the embryo's genetic code and create undesirable effects. When this occurs, a child is either aborted or moved to the Underbelly for a chance at survival in the orphanages or streets until the military eventually snatches them up.

The Underbelly thrives on genetic differences and old technology so much that the lower-level people often hold resentment toward those above. This creates animosity between the two districts despite being part of the same city-state. Though the Underbelly welcomes differences with open arms, violence is not a rarity. The streets of the Underbelly are dangerous due to criminals who dwell in the poor district and civilians of the upper plate who receive pleasure from abusing and murdering those who reside in the lower half.

BESTIARY

Brawler

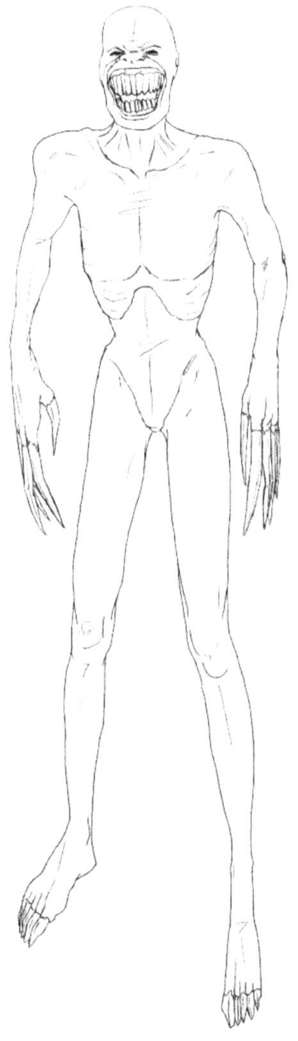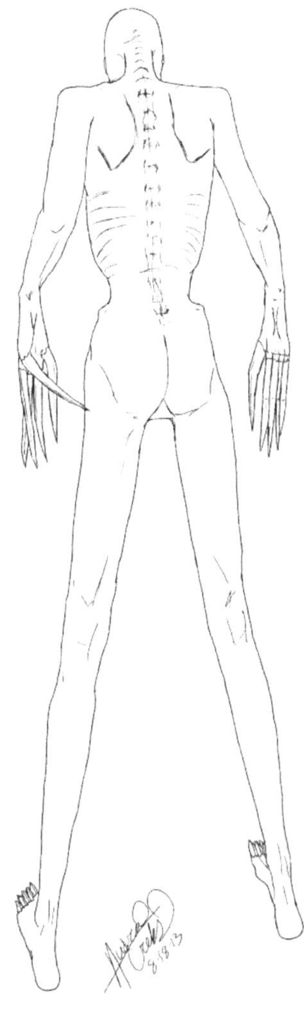

Brute

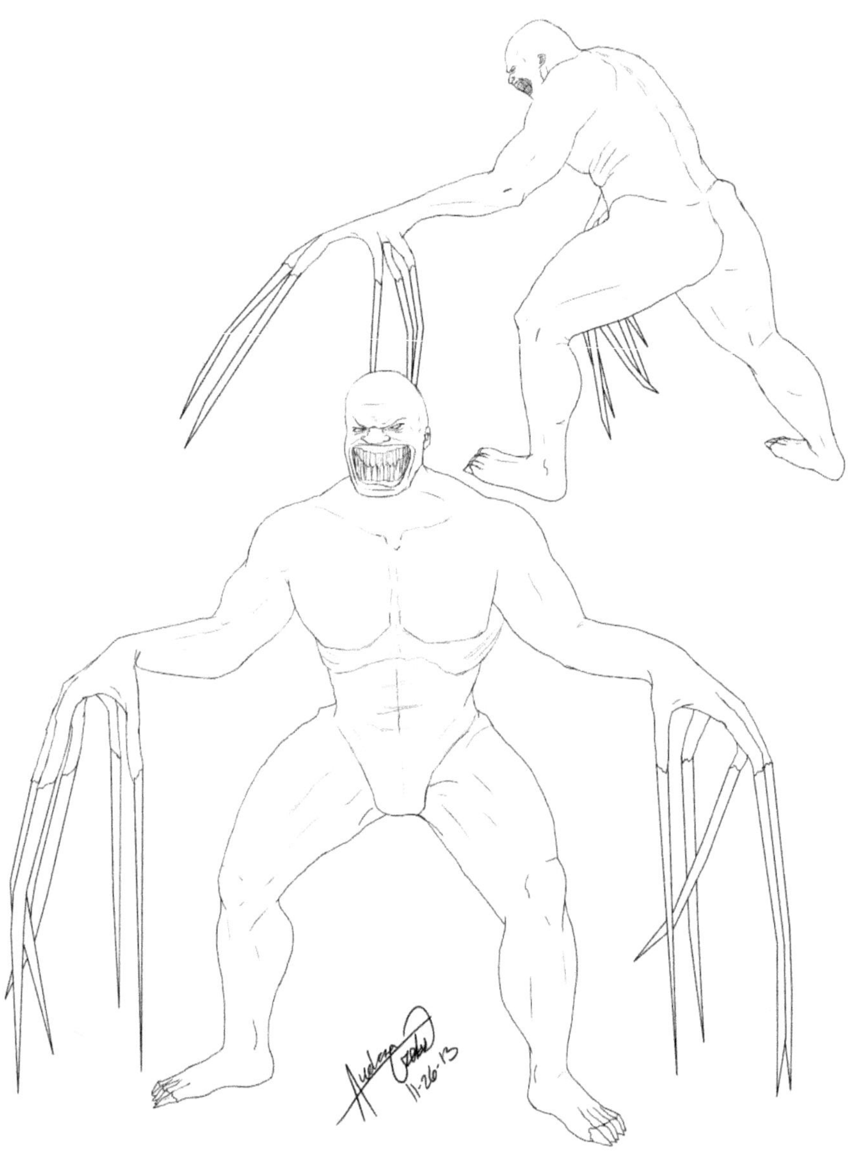

Spewer

Stilt-Man

Hector

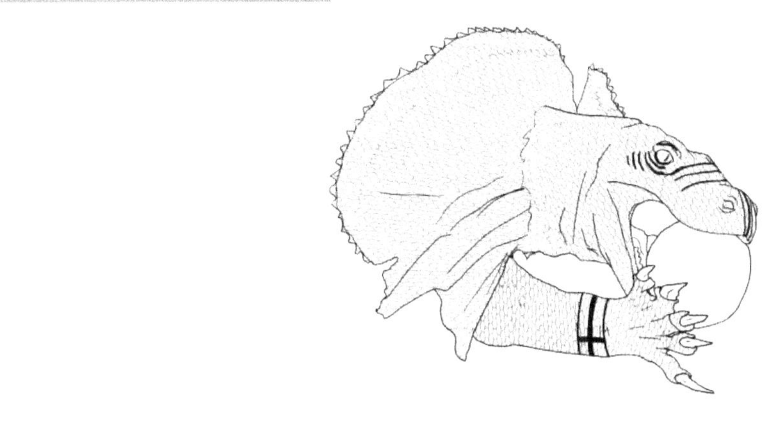

ARMOR

Cherno Armor

Fountain Armor

Soldier of God

WEAPONS

20mm EMFD Sniper Rifle

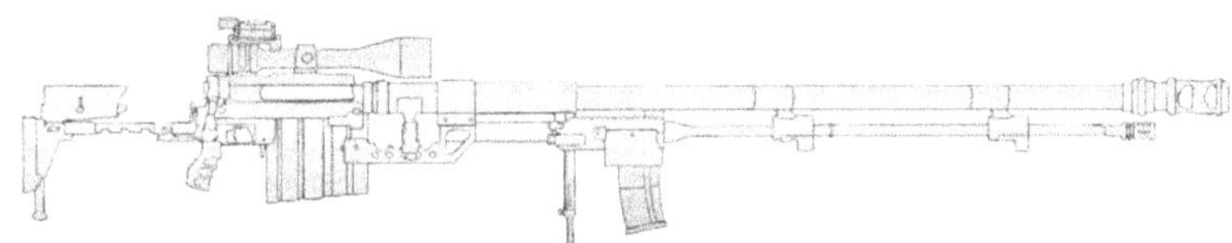

Auto-Aim Standard

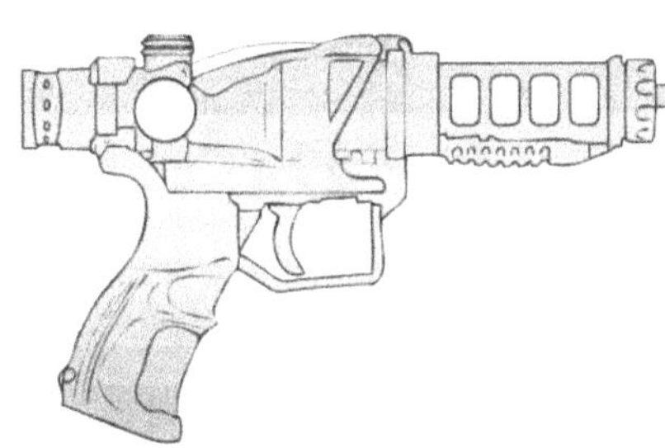

ECRG-15

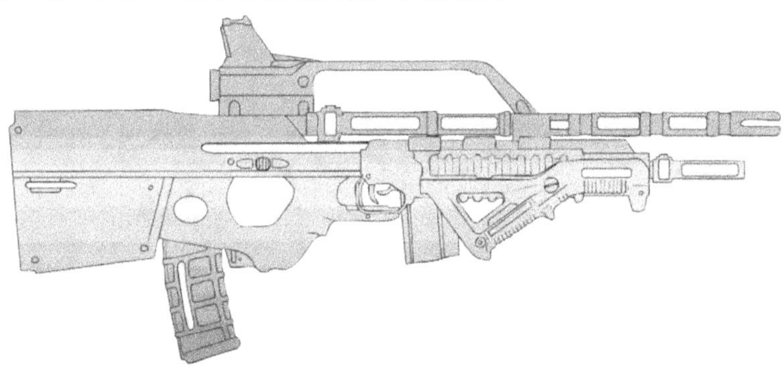

EM-M4

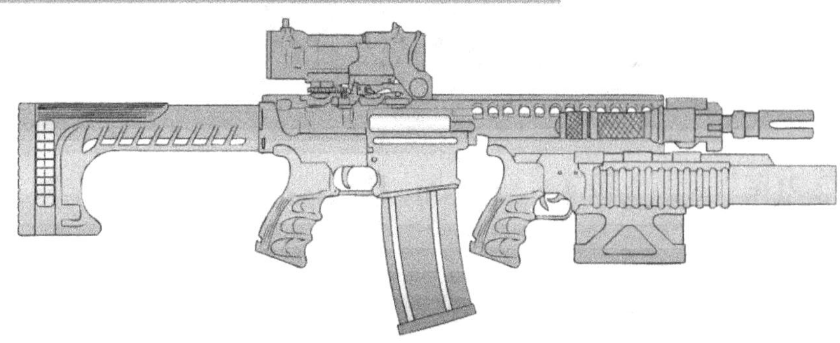

EM-36C

Ignition Rifle

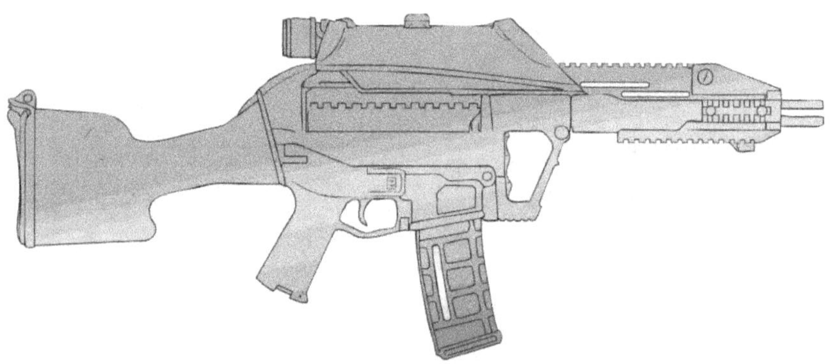

.50 Cal. Liberty Eagle

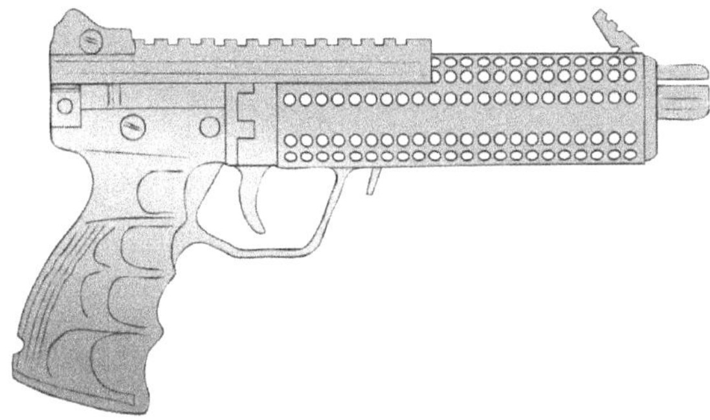

Mini Liberty Eagle

Amasser Particle Beam

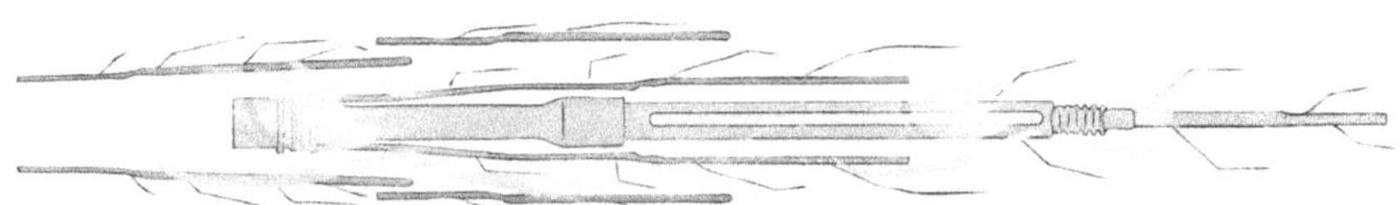

Dovian's Arm Band & Back Apparatus

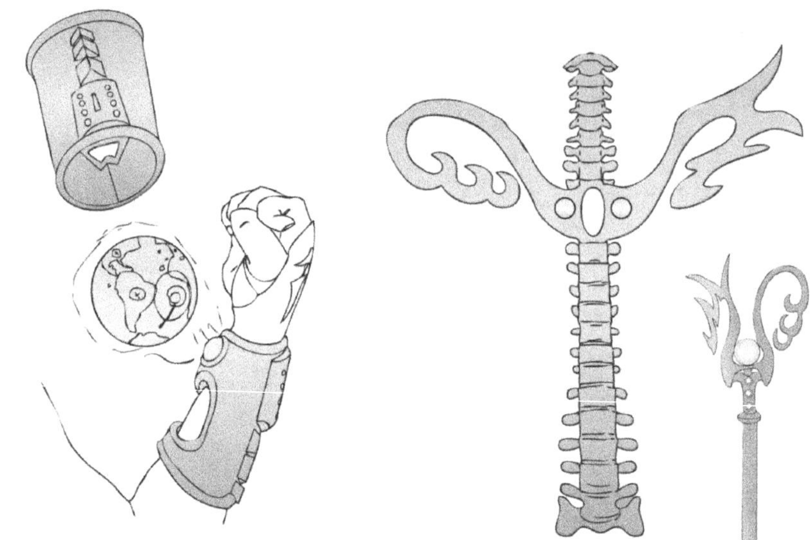

Dovian's Optical Camera & Staff

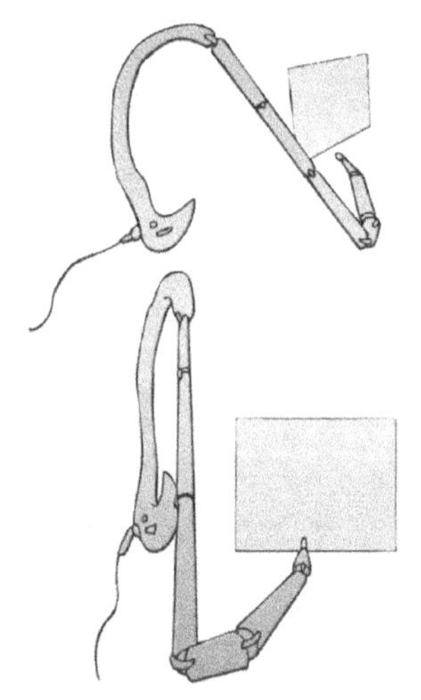

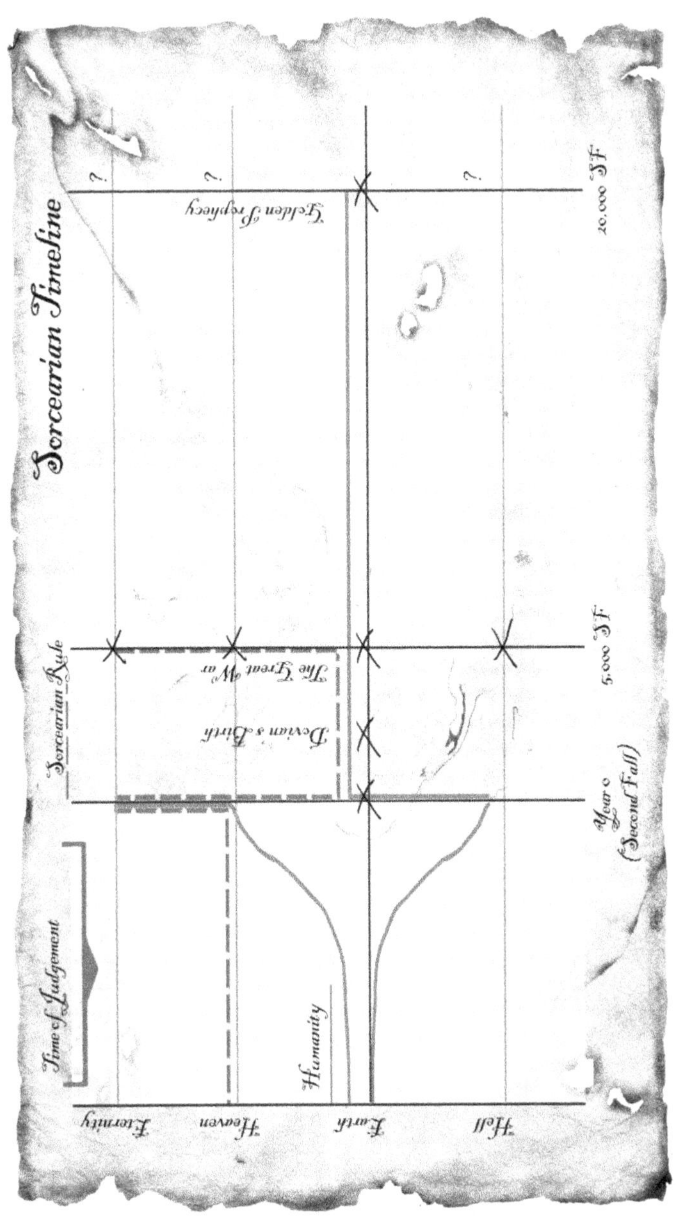

Sorcearian Timeline
Golden Prophecy
Sorcearian Rule
The Great War
Devian's Birth
Time of Judgement
Humanity
Eternity
Heaven
Earth
Hell
10,000 SF
5,000 SF
Year 0 (Second Fall)

A MAP OF EARTH, MILLE 19 S.F.

After thousands of years of nuclear war, Earth's plates have shifted. Ground-penetrating nukes used to hit fault lines and underground bases have created geological upheavals, causing some islands and coastlines to be submerged. Nuclear winter has produced permanent icecaps to form along the northern continents. The rest of Earth is a desert, void of organic life. Constant warfare has also damaged the ozone. The planet's water resources have dwindled massively due to pumping massive quantities into the upper atmosphere to reflect and absorb the sun's solar radiation. A high percentage of the remaining water is contaminated due to nuclear radiation. Fresh aquifers deep underground provide the last amounts of natural freshwater. Corporatism has formed a monopoly on the reserve, only causing more warfare over the final remains of Earth's resources.

Legacy Alphabet

Capital A: א	Lower g: г	Capital N: Њ	Lower t: ŧ
Lower a: א	Capital H: ה	Lower n: њ	Capital U: Ÿ
Capital B: Æ	Lower h: ה	Capital O: Ö	Lower u: ü
Lower b: æ	Capital I: €	Lower o: ö	Capital V: B
Capital C: Ç	Lower i: ℓ	Capital P: P	Lower v: в
Lower c: ç	Capital J: J	Lower p: p	Capital W: ı
Capital D: Δ	Lower j: j	Capital Q: ق	Lower w: ı
Lower d: δ	Capital K: K	Lower q: ﻗ	Capital X: Ξ
Capital E: Ē	Lower k: k	Capital R: R	Lower x: ξ
Lower e: ē	Capital L: Λ	Lower r: r	Capital Y: '
Capital F: Φ	Lower l: λ	Capital S: Ŝ	Lower y: '
Lower f: φ	Capital M: M	Lower s: ß	Capital Z: 3
Capital G: Γ	Lower m: μ	Capital T: Ŧ	Lower z: з

Legacy, the native language of the Sorcēarian race,
comprises letters from multiple languages around the
world. Thought to be a unique language used only by
the Holy, some speculate that Legacy was once the
dialect used by the world as a whole before the time of
Babel.

ABOUT THE AUTHOR

A. R. Redington is a number one Audible and Amazon best-selling author. Born and raised in Kansas, she thrived creatively at an early age, focusing on art and storytelling. Her passion for gaming and character design led her to pursue an artistic career. She attended the Rocky Mountain College of Art + Design, receiving a BFA in illustration/children's book specialization. With experience in graphic design, formatting, illustration, editing, publishing, and writing, Redington creates and designs everything for her novels while working freelance on the side.

She is the author and illustrator of the sci-fi/fantasy series The Esoteric Design, Masters of the Ellem (fantasy), Trouble with Mystery (romantic thriller), Whispers from Beyond: 30 Miniature Tales (horror), and "The Trophy" from Predator: Eyes of the Demon. You can learn more about A. R. Redington at her website: www.ARRedington.com.